Benjamin Rudall grew up and went to school in the West Country of England and had a passion for writing from a young age. Having studied History extensively it's only very recently that Benjamin merged story-telling with real historical events. Using inspiration from other acclaimed historical fictional writers, 'The Forgotten Rebellion' is the first of Benjamin's historical works to be published. Benjamin's lifelong love of Scottish history even took him as far as the rugby pitch, playing for London Scottish. As such he felt it was appropriate that his first published work should be about Scottish history.

THE
FORGOTTEN
REBELLION

By my Son

My Magic Box

I will put into my box,
A fashioned cloak with turquoise diamonds.
My third eye to see the past,
A swish of the wings from a peregrine falcon.
I will put into my box,
A flash of light from a rapid lightning bolt.
The purple paw prints of a prowling panther,
The sparkling, shimmering sun so that darkness never comes.

Inspired by *The Magic Box* by Kit Wright

BENJAMIN RUDALL

THE FORGOTTEN
REBELLION

AUSTIN & MACAULEY
PUBLISHERS LTD.

A CIP catalogue record for this title is
available from the British Library.

ISBN 978 1 84963 204 1

www.austinmacauley.com

First Published (2012)
Austin & Macauley Publishers Ltd.
25 Canada Square
Canary Wharf
London
E14 5LB

Printed & Bound in Great Britain

*"We look to Scotland for
all our ideas of civilisation..."*

Voltaire

Ellerslie, Scotland

1282

The child stood before his father, shivering, his shoulders slumped forward and long hair covering his ashen face. His father went to one knee and reached out to clasp the boy's small damp shoulder, then turned the lad to face him. He reached under his son's chin to lift his head, then looked hard into the boy's eyes.

"Get out of those wet clothes, boy." The man gestured to the back of the room where a small bed stood with a curtain hung around it to shield the light of the fire. "Your mother will have your supper ready soon enough." The boy turned dejectedly and walked to the bed, and his mother and father watched anxiously as he pulled off his wet clothes and dropped them to the floor. Just hours before, the man had pulled his young son from a pile of corpses.

That morning, Malcolm Wallace's inquisitive son had followed him deep into the Coyle Valley between the Glengillan Hills surrounding their home. Malcolm was to meet with other Clan leaders to discuss a treaty agreement offered by the English, and he had strictly forbidden his son to attend.

A spot of rain had hit the side of Malcolm's face, and he looked up at the dark clouds gathering overhead. The journey home would be wet, but all thoughts of a warm fire and the comfort of his house were far from his mind as he strode deeper into the valley. He had neared a bend in the heart of the valley where both sides were thick with ancient trees looming high in the gathering gloom of the approaching storm. He kept close to the tree line as he rounded the bend so he could stay out of sight of anyone who approached from the other direction until the last possible moment. As he rounded the bend, he could see the far side of the Coyle valley in front of him, but the contour of the hill upon which he crouched didn't allow him to see directly below his position to the valley floor. As the clouds parted slightly, the sun, which had been battling against the weather all day, appeared for a brief second, something reflected in the ray of light off to his left — a weapon perhaps or a piece of armour. Instinctively, he looked to the source of the reflection but it was gone before he could focus. He thought perhaps his eyes were playing tricks upon him in the shifting light.

He quickly reached the valley floor and walked to the brook that was wedged between two small hills in the valley centre, in dead ground and so unobservable from almost anywhere else in the valley. Thus he did not see the carnage strewn in every direction until he was amidst the dead, the bodies piled about where they'd been thrown by the dozen in an effort to disguise the ambush site. Some of the corpses were half naked, their worldly goods stripped from them, and others were riddled with arrows and held wounds too ghastly to warrant the theft of their possessions. Malcolm saw comrades among the dead, men he'd known since he was a boy. Rival clansmen were next to them, though he felt no joy at their demise. Emotionless, unbelieving, he had looked over the bodies, searching for a clue as to what had happened. These men who had fought in so many battles together wouldn't have been caught easily; they had to have been ambushed.

The Clans must have been betrayed from within, but by whom Malcolm would probably never know. He knew that the culprit's corpse was probably among those before him. Wallace had lamented that he didn't have time to bury the dead — there were probably soldiers patrolling in the area — as he walked further upstream to where the bank was climbable and started to scramble back to the valley floor. As he had neared the top, he froze. He'd distinctly heard a muffled moan coming from the piles of bodies.

Quickly he turned and slid back down the bank, cursing himself for not checking the bodies more thoroughly. He ran to each body in turn, but they had all been hacked upon even after they fell, their injuries so horrific that none could have survived. After he had checked a dozen bodies, he began to give up hope as he made his way towards the corpses lying further downstream. The bodies of the men further away were obviously trying to escape the ambush when they were cut down by a swarm of arrows. Wallace had gone a few metres when he heard the groan again, but this time louder and behind him. He turned and looked for a sign of life among a pile of bodies thrown down the bank at the edge of the river. A small hand suddenly emerged, pushing and clawing at the bodies surrounding it. Malcolm sprinted toward that small sign of life and pulled one crumpled body after another off the pile until he revealed the bloodied survivor underneath.

His boy was covered with dried mud and thick dark patches of blood. Malcolm said nothing as he checked his son for injuries, horrified that he might find that a wound was the source of the blood and not the piled dead. Apart from a few whimpers, William remained silent. Malcolm picked the boy up, and without a word, lifted him onto his shoulder. Making sure he had a firm grip on the boy, he then scrambled back up the bank.

The shortcut William had taken to catch up with his father had led him beside the Doon River that ran through the Coyle Valley where he knew the clansmen were meeting. He had crept along the bank, out of sight of the men who'd gathered just fifty yards from the river's edge. At least a hundred men were sitting or standing in small groups, talking and arguing about the meeting due to take place with the English lords. William couldn't see his father, and he presumed he hadn't arrived yet. He lay there for ten minutes, listening and watching the men with fascination. He'd been watching Duncan Campbell and his eldest son Thomas in heated discussion with the McBride's when a faint rumbling seemed to fill the morning air. Men suddenly stood up and shouted for quiet. The thunder seemed to grow louder, encompassing the whole valley. The clansmen had looked in all directions but couldn't see far because of the surrounding hills. Duncan Campbell drew his heavy broadsword and began to run up one side of a hill. When he reached the crest, he paused with a look of horror on his face, turned back, and began to shout something when an arrow flew quietly through the air and slammed into his chest, piercing his spine and throwing him backwards. The whole world seemed to explode. The boy had heard tiny whistling sounds piercing the air as more arrows flew from the far bank of the river and sought out targets among the group of Scotsmen, and soon after Duncan was thrown back, a hoard of horsemen burst over the edge of the hill. The thundering herd threw up clods of earth as the riders screamed war cries. Duncan's body had smashed into the nearest horse and went spinning down the hill towards his horrified comrades. William had seen the approach of the archers just before Duncan ran up the hill, but he had been afraid to alert the men. Ten clansmen fell in the first shower, some pierced with half a dozen or more arrows. Others tried to flee from the horses that rolled towards them like a storm, but these were run down or hit by the second wave of arrows. Some clansmen stood huddled in brave defence, their shields raised against the terrible volleys. All escape routes were blocked, except one. William could see that the only available path was the river, and their route to safety was directly through his hiding place.

The men fled the field with their backs to the enemy and became easy targets for the riders bearing down on them. William was terrified at the scene unfolding in front of him and hadn't moved from his position. When the Scots broke towards him, he lay as flat as he could, petrified he'd be seen. A number of men burst over the edge of the bank, their momentum taking them past William and down into the river. One man almost reached the other side, but William watched as three arrows, and then a fourth plunged into his back, throwing him into the river. William saw the man's arm rise from the water and grab at the grass on the far bank, and in death, the warrior's grip stopped him from floating away with the current. William looked for survivors among the others who had run for the river, but they lay at the water's edge, their blood seeping into the river and downstream in brown streaks.

The thunder of hooves sounded suddenly closer to the bank, and William turned his gaze towards the sound. A pair of mud-splattered legs appeared on the edge of the bank right in front of him. The figure turned with his back to the river and stood still, waiting for a horseman who was bearing down on him. The Scotsman readied himself, sword raised, and stabbed forward as the horseman rode past. The rider had parried the blow easily and sliced back with his own sword as he rode by, cutting deep into the man's neck. His horse leapt down the bank and into the stream, the force of the jump throwing showers of water and blood into the air. The blow hadn't toppled the Scotsman, but he now twisted around so he was facing the river. He stood clutching a hand to his neck, trying to stem the flow of blood pumping from the wound. William looked up at the dying man, whose tunic was now a deep crimson, his hands and face splattered with blood. The Scotsman looked down at the same time and noticed through blurring vision the tiny figure lying in the mud. Then straining desperately with the last of his strength, the warrior launched his sword towards the horseman in the water. The horse reared as the blade dug deep into its flank, almost throwing its rider. His enemy momentarily distracted, the Scotsman fell to his knees, and taking either side of his cloak in his hands, fell on top of the boy. The man took hold of William's hand hidden beneath him, and with his dying breath, told him not to utter a sound.

When the horseman steadied his steed, he walked the creature to where the man lay and looked at the corpse, wondering if indeed the man was dead or alive. He fumbled with the hilt of his sword, looking for any movement. He'd hunted this man out from amongst the crowd — the traitor hadn't been hard to find. The man had stood there when the others had run, thinking he alone would be spared from the slaughter, but the man had betrayed his friends and his family, and now, along with all the others, the rider had made sure the man paid the price for rebellion.

Satisfied, the Englishman rode up the bank and barked orders to his men to quickly bury their fallen. The task for the moment was complete. This had been a skirmish that never happened and would never be recorded, at least not by an Englishman.

The rebellion had, for the moment, been crushed; but fate decreed that the traitor's dying gesture keep a young boy alive. A future leader of Scotland was created that day, born of the memory of his people betrayed and slaughtered. His hatred would grow and make of him the greatest Scottish hero of all time.

St Andrews, Scotland

March 1 1815

The choir of St. Andrew's church was in full song. The morning rehearsal had been better than ever, and choir members were all enjoying themselves immensely. Their voices resounded around the ancient corridors of the magnificent church in perfect harmony. Father William Hardy had been overseeing the practise and he was satisfied they were more than ready for the evening service. Father Hardy had also taken the opportunity to supervise the repair of three of the old pews that had been damaged during years of devoted use.

Two workmen, already exhausted from a full day's work on other areas of the church, hammered away frantically, trying to get the job done between the choir's rehearsals. Hardy noticed the choir wanted to continue their practice, so he walked over to the two dust covered individuals and suggested they take the bench outside to work on it. Grateful to continue outside the cramped confines of the church, the men packed away their tools and, with some effort, picked up the old oak pew and began moving it towards the exit. The massive weight of the bench impeded their progress to a slow shuffle and the men had to keep stopping to get a better grip. As they neared the entrance to the church, they had to navigate around the enormous stone plinth, which had once held a sandstone statue of St. Andrew. The plinth hadn't been moved since the statue disappeared from the church centuries before. The craftsman nearest the plinth moved to the left of the stone, and his partner at the other end of the pew followed his lead. As he swung the enormous bench quickly to the right, the workman at the front of the pew caught his tired partner at the back completely by surprise. The man at the rear lost his grip and swore loudly as the bench slipped from his grasp and crashed to the marble floor and toppled onto its side.

The noise sent birds flapping from their perches in the belfry, errant feathers and dust rising into the air, and the noise reverberated through the church with such force that dust was shaken from the wooden beams above. Father Hardy almost collapsed with fright. The pew had fallen to the left of the entranceway near a supporting wall of the church that was covered with plaques commemorating the deaths of noblemen and senior members of the community for the last 500 years. Both workmen looked with apologetic faces at the shaken priest, who stood nearby spluttering and coughing from the dust. Father Hardy was about to chastise the workmen when a large cracks suddenly appeared in the wall to the left of the door. Plaster began to fall, and the three men stared as the crack widened and moved upwards, racing towards an ornate marble plaque of a nobleman of the fourteenth century. The fissure seemed to stop as it reached the old marble tablet as if it blocked the crack's path to the ceiling. The men stood staring with their eyes open wide as if the entire wall was going to fall down.

The workman who dropped the bench let out a deep sigh of relief when the crack stopped, and he bent down to pick up the fallen pew. As he did so, masonry above his head exploded outwards and the plaque came away from the wall and crashed to the floor, smashing the ancient work of art into a hundred pieces. Plaster and concrete came down with the artwork, covering the three men with white dust and shards of stone. When the dust eventually settled, the workmen turned expecting to see a furious priest bearing down on them, but instead Father Hardy was staring through the haze at the ruined wall with a curious frown on his face. The two workmen walked backwards to where Hardy stood, to see what had drawn his attention, expecting to see nothing more than a gaping wound in the wall. What they now saw was a neat manmade hole, about a foot square, deliberately carved into the wall. The hole had been covered by the marble plaque, which now lay shattered and forgotten on the rubble-strewn floor. Standing upright in the hole was a leather-bound book with beautiful gold encrusted facings that glowed yellow through the dust. The book seemed to look imperiously down on them, as if offended at its rude awakening. As the dust cleared, the majesty of the book was clearly visible and held all three men as if in a trance. It was a chance discovery in the most revered of Scottish sanctuaries, one that would change the course of Scottish history forever.

CHAPTER 1

March 25, 1815

A bright orange sun rose high over the rolling hills surrounding the magnificently grey Scottish city of Edinburgh. Although the light attracted a variety of natural colours that adorned the landscape, the dark brooding city seemed like a fortress against it. A few weary heads turned to admire the sight, but most people went about their daily business, the beauty of the scene lost to familiarity. Such were the times in the great capital of the north. Everyone was busy trying to be productive, whether supporting the war in Europe and America or trying to scrape out a living from what meagre pickings were left over. Times were hard for most people in the New Britain, and times had never been harder in the Scottish capital.

The centre of the city was especially crowded on the warm hazy morning of March 1815, the crowds mainly concentrated around George Street and outside the building that housed Edinburgh's major newspaper, *The Scottish Times*. Rumours had spread throughout the city the previous day that Napoleon was once again on the run and the wars in Europe would soon be over. The word flying around the crowded streets this day was that Russian and Prussian armies had entered Paris and were knocking on the Emperor's own front door, but the war had been going on for so long that few dared to believe the rumours. Many people thought this war would never really end at all.

Maggie Burns hadn't timed her morning journey to work well and had to fight her way down through crowded streets. People and horse-drawn carriages were jostling for space, slowing her progress and making her not only late but irritable. She'd also heard the rumours the day before, and in fact she had tried to leave home early, hoping to miss the chaos; but by nine-o clock, every main street in the city was clogged. It was another hour of noise and panicky horses before she eventually reached the steps to the building where she worked. Exhausted and her feathers severely ruffled, she brushed off the dirt and tried to make herself presentable. She made a mental note not to ignore her father the next time he suggested taking their private carriage instead of walking.

Maggie worked at *The Scottish Times,* and over the past few months, a crowd of people seemed to have taken up permanent residence in front of the building. The paper had prospered through its years of coverage of the war and had grown to become the most popular in Scotland, its profits and popularity built on its young industrious reporters going to war-torn Europe to gather firsthand information about events as they happened — and telling these stories with little or no censorship. These young reporters were on the front line and sometimes right in the thick of battle, which had inevitably resulted in the deaths of some of the more adventurous among them, but the proven danger never seemed to stop another reporter from stepping in. The paper had also been dragged deep into the dangerous arena of Scottish politics, for to its readers, the newspaper had become a more reliable source of information than the government itself. Armed local militia were now positioned outside the building to keep troublemakers out, but Maggie was immediately let through when one burly officer recognised her face among the crushing crowd of people.

As she climbed the great marble staircase that dominated the building's entrance, a familiar figure descended the steps to greet her. "Morning Maggie. It's a little chaotic this morning, don't you think?"

"I've never seen it quite as bad as this before, Father." She watched the old man pass her and head towards the crowd, and when he reached the street, he raised his arms into the air and the entire crowd, having spotted the small grey man, slowly fell silent. Once he had their attention, he spoke to them through a deep powerful voice far stronger and louder than his size and frailty would suggest possible.

"We've all heard the rumours," he boomed, his voice reaching the ears of all onlookers. Even the horses seemed to prick up their ears in anticipation. "And I know you're all keen to get information," he continued. "We will of course tell you all the news that we've gathered, but not until we're sure the information has proved to be correct." He paused for a moment to let his message sink in. "Will everyone please go about their business and we can all read about it once the new governor has finally accepted one of my very reasonable bribes." Most of the crowd smiled or laughed at his comment, and many immediately began to move away, back to their daily routines. The old man turned and walked back up the stairs where Maggie could see he was visibly relieved that the crowd hadn't pushed him for more information.

Sir Henry Burns, Maggie's father and the owner of *The Scottish Times*, was sixty-three, a small man but gifted with an infectious personality and a political brain that had made him one of the most influential men in Scotland. Not afraid to confront the mob, or to take criticism for doing so, he'd made himself a father figure to the people of Edinburgh, and they loved him like a national treasure.

Maggie was waiting for him at the top of the stairs, and she smiled as he approached. "One of your shorter speeches Father," she said, smirking.

"Yes, well certain people have been putting me under a great deal of pressure, my dear, to disperse the crowds as quickly as possible. Bit of a shame really," he continued as they walked side by side into the building. "That was the largest crowd of my career to date; should have been the town crier you know," he said, looking sincerely at his daughter, but she just laughed and hugged him fondly.

Father and daughter walked through the marbled and pillared hallways of one of the grandest buildings in Edinburgh, the structure mirroring the success of the paper, but Sir Henry would be happy to remind everyone the foundations were built on heartache and frustration. In fact, Sir Henry and Maggie Burns were the only members of their illustrious family left alive. The war in Europe had claimed the lives of Henry's two sons, who'd given up their jobs at the paper seven years previously and paid for commissions into the army; the life of a dashing British officer fighting abroad preferable to that of a newspaperman in Edinburgh. The Burns boys' first major battle was the bloody siege of Badajoz in 1809. Eli, an Infantry captain in the 64th and a volunteer of the "Forlorn Hope," had been one of the first through a breach in the great city walls. He had been seeking instant notoriety but had died in the attempt. His second son, Hamish, was a cavalry officer whose troops had harried and harassed the enemy as they retreated in defeat from the captured city. But his men were caught between retreating French infantry and French cavalry that had advanced to aid the infantry's retreat. Hamish was presumed captured or killed by the French, his body never found.

Maggie was the youngest of the three, and apart from her father, was suddenly left all alone. Their mother had died of influenza when Maggie was very young, and so, together, the three men in the family had brought her up. She'd grown up to be fearlessly independent, and she defied many of the conventions placed upon Scottish women in a strongly male dominated society. Sir Henry had never re-married, and he and his daughter now lived together, sharing the burdens of the times.

From a very young age, Maggie had wanted to be a part of the paper, from the day an Arab Sheikh, whose name she spent three days trying to pronounce, visited her father's home — the reason he'd been there she'd never actually learned. The majesty and mystique of the strange foreign man had forever been burned in her mind and soul. The Sheikh and so many other people of various colours and origins were much a part of her father's life. After hearing many stories and meeting so many people from exotic places or with exotic lives, it was inevitable that her interests would take a similar path as her father's, his life being the single major influence in her tiny existence.

Maggie and Sir Henry entered the heart of the building where dozens of people were scribbling away with pencils and quills. Machinery was being made ready for the arduous task of printing hundreds of copies of the newspaper to be finished that evening. Paper flapped and rustled, and the smell of fresh ink touched their noses as they moved silently through the room. On one side of the room, a staircase climbed up to a balcony high above the workroom floor. Sir Henry led his daughter up the stairs, and once at the top, they turned to survey the scene below. Burns had built the balcony 10 years before to observe his employees at work. He hadn't built it to keep an eye on them, but rather, he'd installed the balcony purely to relax by watching the routine movements of his staff. An enormous pair of polished oak doors lay open at the end of the terrace, and twenty or so figures were waiting patiently beyond. As the couple approached the room, the conversations quieted, and when the Burns entered the great doors, the room went silent. The doors were closed behind them by two servants, and Maggie moved across the room to join the waiting crowd. The room was highly decorated, paintings lined the walls, and finely woven carpets adorned the floors. Against one wall was Sir Henry's most treasured possession, an original bust of Julius Caesar that he'd purchased in Milan some years earlier, before Napoleon had become Emperor. It was rumoured that Napoleon had coveted the bust himself but Sir Henry had refused all offers for the masterpiece. The story of Napoleon's offer, whether it was true or not, had only served to push the bust into the realm of the priceless.

Sir Henry liked to keep his meetings informal, and so leather sofas and chairs were scattered about the office. He sat in a luxurious brown leather chair strategically facing all the others in the room and took a sip of tea from a cup a servant had placed on a mahogany table next to the chair. Then he sat back and looked up at his staff.

"Please sit down, gentlemen...and lady," he said, smiling at his daughter. "We have a serious problem that I'd like to share with you all. The people gathered outside this building and others around the city want news of the war, but we don't have any information to give to them." He took another sip of tea. "The news is coming from Europe in bits and pieces, and the government is holding out on us until they're completely sure of the situation. Even I can't get any information out of them, so there must be something wrong." Most of those gathered laughed and he cast a wry smile towards his daughter, who was smiling approvingly at him. "For the moment I want you all to remain focused on the war and the job at hand. I know you've all heard about the unrest in the city, and this is extremely significant, but there are frightened and suffering people outside these walls who need us now more than ever." He paused for a moment and studied each of their faces in turn, giving them all an intense look that none of them had seen before. "We can't be sure the war is close to its end, and we must assume it will continue until the government gives us their firm assurance, but the crucial point is that the people of this country no longer have faith in our government's policies. We can't deny the feeling in the city anymore. What we need is good news, and so I want all of you to work harder than ever to find some and to report to me directly." He looked at each of them again as he spoke. Finally, he lifted his cup of tea and finished the last drop. Then he stood up and dismissed them. "You may all go; but Maggie, please see me in my study," he said before she turned to leave.

"Yes, of course, Father." She excused herself from the group and followed him into his study.

"Close the door behind you, would you my dear?" he said in a tired voice. "Maggie, I have something very important for you to do for me." She sat down and waited for him to continue. "I'm coming under increasing pressure from the government to put notices in the paper denouncing any people in the city who might be inciting rebellion." He took his glasses off and rubbed the lenses with a cloth. "I haven't mentioned it to you before, but I have been made aware of some unknown sources deliberately inciting rebellion. However, I'm not going to be a party to prosecuting the entire Scottish people before I have all the facts to hand." He put the glasses back on and looked up at her. "I'm not going to let the government walk over us on this, Maggie — the newspaper won't be subject to any English propaganda. I just thought I should let you know in case we encounter any trouble."

"Yes Father," she said almost unable to contain her compassion. Her heart felt as if it would burst from her chest for the love and adoration that she felt for him. Even at his tender old age, she could see the fire in his eyes and hear the steel in his voice.

"I'll be away for the next few days in London, so you will be on your own for the time being. If you run into any difficulties, which I'm sure you won't, I've instructed a number of my associates close to the governor to keep you informed of any developments," he said with a sly look on his face. "There was one other thing. This letter," he passed it to her. "This letter arrived for you this morning. William the porter said it was delivered by a monk." Maggie looked at the letter and frowned. There was nothing unusual about the letter, but delivered by a monk? "William was rather shaken up actually," her father continued.

"Why was that?" she said, suddenly intrigued.

"Well, William said the monk was probably the biggest man he'd ever seen, so tall in fact that he couldn't see the man's face behind his hood, and he delivered the letter without uttering a single word." Maggie looked at the front of the envelope, which was completely devoid of any writing.

"How did he know the letter was for me?"

"When the man began to leave the building, William apparently called after him, asking to whom he should deliver it. All the monk did in response was raise his arm and point to the portrait of you that hangs just inside the entrance to the building. A very strange episode indeed, wouldn't you think?"

"Yes, very strange." Maggie chuckled at the thought of William being scared half to death by a huge shrouded monk. She walked to the other side of the desk and gave her father a tender kiss on his old wrinkled cheek. "I will see you in a few days then."

"Yes, I shouldn't be gone too long," he replied. She looked affectionately into his eyes, and he lovingly returned her gaze.

"Be careful, Father. You're getting far too brave in your old age." He smiled and gave her an obedient nod in confirmation.

"I'll see you soon," he said. She put the letter in her pocket and left him to continue his day's work.

Maggie immediately went down into the vaults of the building, eager to continue the work she'd been doing over the last few weeks, a profile of one of the indigenous people recently encountered by the British in America. Sinking herself into the work, she hoped, would also take her mind off other things, such as the obvious stress the war was beginning to place on her father.

After two hours of reading old brown papers and scanning travel-worn documents, her eyes began to tire and she leaned back in her chair, stretching her limbs sensuously like a sleepy cat. She flexed her muscles until the ache went out of her back and arms, and then she scrunched up her nose, suddenly realising the air in the room had become very dry and stifling. Reaching into her purse, she pulled out a small cosmetic mirror, and quickly glancing around the room to make sure she was alone, she studied her tired face. She pressed at the lines around her eyes, the result of restless nights worrying about her father and wondering if he was under too much stress. When the blotches returned looking more enflamed, she sighed and put the mirror away. Reaching across the table she closed all the books and rolled up parchments scattered across the desk. She then leant back against the chair, looked up at the ceiling, and then closed her eyes.

Amid the dull, leather-bound books and tatty brown scrolls, Maggie's pale creamy skin glowed in the light emanating from the lanterns that were scattered along the walls of the room. Maggie's father was a Scot but her mother had been Irish, and it was her Irish blood that made Maggie's features so striking. She'd inherited her mother's jet-black hair that never seemed to dull whatever the condition, and she had it cut to her shoulders and rarely tied it up, which went against the tradition followed by most other well-to-do women in the city. Her eyes were emerald green, and her dark hair accentuated the creamy pearl colour of her skin, making her face look almost fragile, like delicately fired porcelain. Affluent men had tried to court her in the past, mostly the rich and privileged young aristocrats with whom a woman of her class and status usually socialised. Her beauty attracted these men but they were also motivated by the power her family wielded. Maggie generally drove them away deliberately, or they ran away shocked and confounded by her overwhelming confidence and lack of inhibition. She cast men aside with the strength of a woman in control of her own destiny. Where most young women of her age and status were happy in the home with their husbands and children, she was very much a lonely figure working in a man's world, seeking something more out of life, something most women only asked for in their dreams.

As she dozed in the chair, a thought suddenly leapt into her mind. Opening her eyes, she reached down into her pocket and drew out the envelope her father had given her that morning. She pulled apart the seal, noticing a strange ornate crest punched into the dry red wax depicting two claymores, one crossed over the other. The letter was an anonymous invitation from an order of monks asking her to view some historical literature the letter writer deemed of great political interest. She read the final line of the invitation in fascination: *It will be of value to you but also to the rest of Scotland forever.* The address to attend the viewing was a monastery near Linlithgow, an area she knew quite well. The page wasn't signed, but the same crest pressed into the wax on the envelope had been stamped at the bottom of the page, and there was a Latin inscription underneath. She folded the letter away as quickly as she could, snatched up her cloak, and rushed out of the room.

She felt the same twinge of excitement she always experienced when she read something different and interesting, the same twinge she felt when she heard the stories of adventure brought back from lands far away as a child after dinner by the fire. The vagueness of the letter had the scent of adventure about it.

She'd finished all her other work for the day and relished the chance to go riding on one of her horses. The address was near Linlithgow, and so it wasn't far away. It was midday now, and she could be in Linlithgow by dusk, stay the night in an inn she knew, and visit the monastery early the next day. Running down the steps of the building, she hailed a carriage and ordered the man to drive to her home, which was outside the city, as quickly as he could.

Standing in shadow on the other side of the street was a tall figure in long dark robes. He watched Maggie leave the building and climb into the carriage, ignoring the strange looks passersby were giving him. None could see the face behind the shadow of his hood, let alone the smile that etched his solid dark features. He walked slowly into the street and raised his arm at an approaching carriage.

Climbing into the back, he beckoned the driver in the direction Maggie had taken. As the carriage pulled away, the sun suddenly broke through the cloud cover, and for an instant, the day was bathed in glorious sunshine.

Thousands of people throughout the city looked up from their work, thankful for the warmth of the sun on their faces. A dark robed head protruded from a carriage speeding through the city streets, and now passersby saw the look of pleasure on the man's face. He looked as if he hadn't seen the sun for a long time. The light shone off the olive skin of a man born far away under its warm tanning rays. For two very different travellers, the day would bring many such instances of pleasure, for spring had at last come to Scotland.

CHAPTER 2

It was wonderful to be free of the city and away from the stifling environment that Maggie's life had become. She went out riding whenever she could, relishing the time alone, away from the bustle and worries of Edinburgh. She adored the sounds and smells of the open spaces, the luscious fragrance of the wind in her face as her horse pounded out the miles beneath her. The aroma of grass and heather, of ploughed fields and newly cut crops was the taste of freedom she loved so much, a chance to make her own decisions and mistakes. She tested herself, avoiding the direct routes by jumping hedges and fences or crossing streams and rivers, and adoring the excitement.

Horse and rider reached Linlithgow as the sun was setting, bathing the landscape in a crimson blanket infused with touches of yellow and orange. She headed towards a small inn in sight of the old ruins of Linlithgow Palace, pausing briefly to look at the magnificent building, destroyed in 1746 by an unattended fire in a bedroom that had gone out of control and spread to leave the building a roofless shell. The inn was in the centre of the village about five hundred yards from the loch. She remembered it from a previous visit to the town a year before.

As Maggie was dismounting, two horsemen suddenly appeared at the crest of the valley surrounding the town. If she'd turned at that moment she would have seen their figures silhouetted against the red sky, but she was too preoccupied with her horse to notice. A stable hand came out to meet her, and she handed the reins to him and a small coin so the animal would be watered and fed. The boy led the tired mount away as she entered the small thatched building. The innkeeper was stoking the dying fire when Maggie walked through the door, and he managed to disguise his surprise at a woman entering unaccompanied at that time of night. Maggie met his glance and smiled confidently back in greeting.

"Good evening," she said immediately.

"Good evening back to you, lass. Travelling alone, are we?" he said, replacing the steel poker back onto its rack. The man couldn't remember a time when he had seen a lovelier woman enter his inn.

"Come on in! Come on in!" he said, with more enthusiasm. He pulled out a wooden chair from under one of the tables and offered it to her. "Come and sit down. It looks like you've travelled some way. I don't recall seeing you around these parts before." Maggie sat down as he moved to the other side of the room, to a shelf containing numerous bottles of liquid. "Could I offer you a drink, lass?"

"Wine would be fine, thank you." The inn wasn't quite as nice as she remembered. It was in need of repair, and the stale odour of alcohol and old sweat hung in the air. She guessed by the state of the place that business probably hadn't been good for the innkeeper lately. The man returned with a small glass of wine and stooped to place it in front of her. Maggie took a sip and found it pleasantly refreshing. The man stood hovering at the table, waiting expectantly.

"Will there be anything else, Miss?" Maggie noticed the more polite tone to the man's voice and the respectful form of address.

Sipping the wine again, she looked up at him. "Yes, actually. Would you by any chance have a room available for the night? I've ridden a long way today, and I'd hoped to stay here before moving on."

"Why, of course we do, Miss," he said quickly, but realising he'd been a little overzealous, he quickly composed himself. "I'm sure we do. Just let me check though. There may have been some late bookings I wasn't aware of." As he casually walked into the next room, Maggie couldn't help smiling; but secretly she wished she didn't have to stay at the Inn. She tried to reassure herself that the bedroom would be fine, but looking down at the greasy table and dirty floor, she wasn't hopeful. She decided she'd slept in worse places, and besides, it was either a room here or her travelling blanket on the hard ground in a field in the surrounding countryside — and she was positive it was going to rain.

After she'd eaten a pleasant meal of cold meats and stewed vegetables, and washed in a piping hot bath with water fetched by the innkeeper's daughter, she settled into her room for the night. First, however, she went down to the stable to make sure her horse had been properly cared for. A shoe had come loose on the journey and she wanted to make sure it'd been re-shod properly.

While Maggie was checking her horse, the innkeeper began closing up for the night but was interrupted. He couldn't believe his luck when two more travellers entered the building. Both men were very heavily robed, which surprised the innkeeper, as it seemed far too warm in the evenings now for thick woollen clothes. The men walked across the room and sat at a table already shrouded in semidarkness, and one ordered the innkeeper to fetch them some wine. When the innkeeper returned, one of the men had disappeared, he presumed to tend to their horses, and the other sat silently looking at the door. When the innkeeper asked if they were to stay overnight, the man remained silent and kept staring straight ahead as if he hadn't heard. When Maggie eventually returned, the second man had reappeared. She saw both of them sitting silently at the table as she went upstairs to her room but didn't give the men a second thought.

The room was clean but sparsely furnished. It contained a small bed, a desk and chair, and a bowl and jug for washing. So it wasn't surprising that the first thing she saw upon entering the room was something that hadn't been there a half hour before, a small leather-bound book on her pillow with a note attached that was addressed to her. The note had the same seal as the letter her father had given her that morning. She remembered the men sitting in the inn downstairs and realised they fit the same description as the monk who frightened William. They were the only two other people she'd seen all day, apart from the innkeeper, and it seemed obvious they put the letter in her room. She felt a slight twinge of irritation that they'd come into her private room while she was outside, but she also felt a strange foreboding — and a little fear. She knew that she must have been followed, or at the very least, seen entering the village. She leapt out of bed and locked the door, and then she pulled one of her pistols out of her bag, loaded the weapon, and cocked it for good measure. She then climbed back into bed and pulled open the seal on the letter. She soon forgot about her fear and unconsciously made the pistol safe by taking the tension out of the lock spring.

The note read: *Maggie Burns, the path has been laid out for you. We desperately need your help. We appeal to your sense of national pride and curiosity.* The note wasn't signed, but the same ornate crest was printed at the bottom. Maggie breathed a little easier, for there didn't seem to be any threat implied in the letter, and she reminded herself that, if the men downstairs had wanted to harm her, they could have done so by now. She was a little bemused though. Did the letter mean the men would show her the path to the monastery? That wasn't necessary, as she already knew where it was, but why not just include the directions in the letter? At least they could have given the note to her in person. The circumstances were very odd and confusing, but this fact only added to her curiosity.

She looked down at the small leather-bound book beside her on the bed. On the first page, written in big black bold letters, was the title of the book: *The Wallas of Blin Harry.* She flipped through the pages and realised it was a book of poetry. She moved the lamp closer to her bedside and began to study the book in more detail. The writing seemed to be in an old form of English. She'd studied Chaucer as a child, and this writing was very similar, but a few of the words had a Celtic structure and a sound she had never come across before. There was a date at the front of the book: 1350. Presumably the year the first copy was issued, or maybe this indicated a year in the life of the author. As she flipped further, she noticed the names of some people had been underlined but couldn't immediately see any relevance to them. She presumed this was a duplicate of one of the books she'd been invited to see in the monastery, and suddenly felt very disappointed. Even if this was one of the books she'd ridden all the way to the monastery to see, she couldn't fathom what was so special about it or why it would be of value to her and the rest of Scotland "forever." She shut the book and turned off the oil lamp. Lying awake in the dark, she became aware of every noise in the night, and for a fleeting moment, she felt like getting up and riding straight back to Edinburgh and forgetting the whole thing. She fell asleep before coming to a decision.

Maggie was up and on her way before sunrise. She had bid the innkeeper goodbye, climbed onto her horse, and pushed the animal straight into a canter. She wanted to reach the convent by midmorning so she'd have sufficient daylight to get back to the city. There was no sign of the two robed men, either in the inn or out in the semidarkness, and she hadn't thought to ask the innkeeper about them.

She reached the monastery quicker than she had expected. Except for the labourers in the fields, she didn't pass another soul on the way. She had stopped on several occasions and waited to see if she was being pursued, but nobody appeared behind her. The walls of the monastery were high and intimidating, and they contained numerous deep dark windows from which an enemy could watch her every move. Inside the walls, the main keep was massive. It looked like a single huge square block of granite hewn from the earth and seemingly impenetrable. Towers rose from each corner, rising protectively into the sky. Even Maggie, with her untrained eye, understood the strength cleverly disguised in those walls. Flowers and vines adorned the front of the building, breaking up the shape of the massive structure into a maelstrom of colour and distracting the casual observer from the castle's impregnability. Thousands of birds were nesting in the foliage and in the crumbling brick, a farmer was using the empty moat and surrounding fields to feed his livestock, and Maggie could see evidence that children had once used a tree that had since fallen for a rope swing. But with all this evidence of neglect, there was an air of malevolence and force to the place. The tree line had been cut back so that open ground stretched three hundred yards in front of the walls, and an enemy attacking the castle would face uninterrupted fire without cover for minutes only to be faced, those who survived, with the grim prospect of scaling the fifty-foot walls. The walls were also dotted with hundreds of windows and arrows slits, and the thick oak gates were still very much intact.

Maggie entered through the main arched gateway. The huge oak doors lay open as if inviting her in, and there were no guards to stop her. Vines crept along inside the walls and up onto the ceiling, and looking up as she passed through, she caught sight of the sharp steel barbs of the portcullis pointing toward the ground and dark murder holes through which untold horrors could be dropped onto an enemy. The entrance opened into a small cobbled courtyard surrounded on all sides by high walls. She noted that it was suddenly much colder as the sun wasn't yet high enough to penetrate the palisade, and she shivered involuntarily. The only route forward was a small gateway across the other side of the courtyard, so she nudged her horse towards it.

She wondered why the monks had chosen to live in such a grim place, assuming that the monks had simply moved in after the previous owners had abandoned the castle. It seemed inconceivable that the monks had rebuilt and strengthened the fortification themselves.

She passed through the second entrance into what must have once been the main courtyard. In front of her was the main building, and another oak panelled door opened into the courtyard and she could see a faint glow of light beyond. Above the doorway, shining bright in the early morning sunlight, a huge burnished shield had been attached to the wall. Embellishing the front of the shield were two shining golden claymores crossed one over the other, the same crest as on both the letters she'd received. She leapt from her horse and tied him to an iron rung jutting from one of the walls. As she walked across the courtyard, she distinctly felt that eyes were boring into the back of her head. She glanced up at a sudden movement to her left in one of the cross-shaped windows, but when she stopped to look again, the movement had gone. She felt fear slowly rising from the pit of her stomach until it reached the back of her throat. She kept walking and tried to convince herself that the people who lived in the castle were only a few tired old monks who were probably restricted from talking to her. Still, she was afraid for it seemed odd that they knew she was coming and would have seen her arrive but no one had been at the gates to meet her.

She peered inside the doorway and could see lanterns burning along the inside walls. A corridor stretched out in front of her, but she couldn't see further than a few metres because of the bad light. She couldn't resist taking a quick look behind her to see if anyone might have appeared, and then she stepped over the threshold and began to walk down the corridor into the heart of the castle.

It occurred to her that she might have arrived while all the monks were at prayer. After all, they hadn't specified a time for her to turn up. She knew that the logical thing to do would be to call out and attract someone's attention, but something was stopping her. It was almost as if she was deliberately hoping to stumble into somebody. If the monks hadn't realised she'd arrived, as she assumed previously, perhaps she might see something she wouldn't normally be allowed to view. Her eyes were slowly becoming accustomed to the dim light when she caught sight of something glistening above her. The light barely reached up more than a few metres, but through the haze, she spotted what seemed to be rows upon rows of metal shields lining the walls, positioned in semidarkness just above the glow of the lanterns so they weren't easy to spot. Each shield seemed to represent a different coat of arms, but she couldn't make out any of them clearly. The line of shields stretched right to the end of the corridor. Another relic of a forgotten era, she assumed. Another open door, this one much smaller, greeted her when she came to the end of the corridor, and she could see a brighter glow emanating from beyond. Her breath caught in her throat as she entered. The room on the other side of the doors was immense, and she realised that this one room probably took up almost the entire structure of the main keep. Row upon row of huge polished oak pews lined the floor like a regiment of soldiers on parade, and massive granite pillars, ornately carved into the shape of Lotus plants, lined the walls, reaching a hundred feet to hold up the ceiling. The roof itself was an intricate weave of wooden beams, each hewn from an entire tree. The whole room was like a cathedral but on a smaller scale, and the design and engineering was just as impressive as any she'd seen.

At the far side of the cathedral was the altar, an enormous slab of granite standing silently, ominously watching like a sergeant over his oak clad troops. The only other decoration in the huge expanse was a silver cross mounted on the altar and surrounded by a bouquet of fresh flowers. There wasn't a single window in the room, only small cross-shaped vents to circulate the air. If this was their single place of worship, she thought to herself, then it was by far the largest but least grand she had ever seen. There wasn't a single statue, image, or religious depiction in the entire room, and the place was bereft of any colour except for the flowers on the altar. A thousand souls could easily fit into the room, and their thousand voices would be magnified ten times over if they were to all sing at once.

A flicker of movement caught her eye and brought her back to reality. Behind the altar was another small door she hadn't noticed. In the opening stood a figure robed in black and facing her. A hood totally covered his face, but she could sense that he was looking at her. She stood still for a moment and shivered involuntarily as the chill of fear shot down her spine. Her body wouldn't move. Her legs seemed to be rooted to the ground. Slowly she forced herself to take a step forward despite her fear. As soon as she moved, the monk retreated through the door and out of sight, his dark robes fluttering behind him. Her fear disappeared instantly.

She ran forward and cried out after the fleeing monk. "Wait!" Her voice resounded loudly around the room, reverberating off the walls, and the shock of the sudden noise made her reel sideways. Cursing her outburst under her breath, she reached the open door and stopped, listening. Beyond the opening was utter darkness. She hesitated. Then it occurred to her that she'd been deliberately led to this place, indeed to this particular door, and what had happened thus far had been orchestrated. She knew she had to continue, that she had to see this through. A part of her wanted to turn around and run away, but not out of fear, rather to see if the monks would try to stop her. The invitation to enter into the darkness was just too strong, and steeling herself, she stepped through the doorway. Her eyes quickly became adjusted to the lack of light. Small candles had been scattered randomly, dimly lighting a small antechamber. The room was almost perfectly round, and there were exits leading to other parts of the castle. In the gloom, she could see the walls were adorned with more warlike regalia: suits of armour, more shields, and hundreds of weapons — trophies and honours of battles fought long ago. Distracted, she almost walked into a wooden lectern standing in the centre of the room. She caught herself before knocking it over and peered down at what she assumed was probably the reason for her strange journey.

A large, leather-bound book lay open, the pages handwritten in ancient black ink and withered with age, on top of the lectern. The book was obviously worth a great deal, as she could see the glint of gold on the paper and gold leaf around the edges of the pages. The fact that the book had been placed in such a prominent position in a room filled with hundreds of other priceless artefacts suggested the monks valued the book very highly. The book was open to the front page, and she mouthed the now familiar title and marvelled at the workmanship of the script. She very carefully turned the page and bent closer to read the lines in the little light available. The entire book was written in Latin, and even in the gloom, she could see the words were still clear and full of colour, as if the writing hadn't aged at all. She checked for the date of the manuscript, but to her disappointment, she couldn't find the date for the year the book had been written or the name of the author. The only visible mark of ownership was a Latin inscription at the very bottom of the page: *Tutis per Amicitia.*

"Who is this Wallas of Blin Harry," she whispered to the walls. When they failed to answer, she pulled her copy of the book out of her pocket, remembering the names that had been underlined, presumably by the mysterious monks from the previous evening. She slowly turned the pages of the older book to where she guessed the names would be. After fifteen minutes of searching, she had almost given up, but then, from her basic knowledge of Latin, she recognised the paragraph she was looking for. Comparing the two texts, she realised why the paragraph had taken so long to find. The names in the older text were completely different from the names in her modern version. Quickly she took out a pencil and wrote down the new names in the margin, then put her book and pencil back in her riding coat and carefully closed the old manuscript.

She looked down again at the ancient book, and for some reason, felt a sudden compulsion to leave the monastery as if she'd seen everything she was meant to. But stronger than this feeling was the premonition that, having seen this book, her life would never be the same again; she'd now put herself in mortal danger. She took one final look around the room as she walked away from the lectern. Then she almost jogged through the enormous chapel, and when she reached the corridor, she could see the doorway to the courtyard ahead. Risking a look back, she saw the same figure as before standing by the altar. He was watching her leave. She immediately turned and fled, not daring to look back to see if he'd followed. Running down the corridor and out into the courtyard, she was instantly blinded by the sun that had now climbed high enough to reach over the castle walls. She stumbled on the cobbles and fell to the ground, and anger automatically replaced her fear. Gritting her teeth, she got to her feet and gingerly brushed the dirt from her knees. She marched across the courtyard to her waiting horse, more humiliated now than afraid, and mounted up. She rode quickly from the courtyard and the monastery, not stopping until she reached a rise of ground some distance from the gates. Pulling up angrily, she hesitated before turning around, but she couldn't resist a look back at the building. She was shocked to see the entire rampart lined with dark robed figures, hundreds of tiny figures on top of the massive walls staring in her direction; and on one of the towers, a single tall dark figure raised his arm in a gesture of farewell. Impulsively, almost against her will, Maggie waved in response, then turned and rode away, unsure whether she was thrilled or simply terrified.

Maggie had plenty of time to get back to Edinburgh before dark, and after the morning's excitement, she was eager to get home. The day's events had aroused a strange passion in her. The fear so evident while she was in the castle had disappeared, and instead, her mind was filled with a torrent of unanswered questions. The experience had been by far the most bizarre event she'd ever encountered in her entire life, but upon reflection, the whole day had really amounted to very little. She'd discovered some strange names in a strange book, but there were many unanswered riddles. Although the book had obviously been very old, it could easily have been brought to Edinburgh and shown to her there. Instead, she'd travelled dozens of miles to a monastery in the middle of nowhere, and after being scared half out of her mind, she had nothing really to show for it. Someone, she thought, and for whatever reason, had gone to a great deal of trouble to entice her to go through this ordeal and had somehow known how she would react. She almost laughed out loud at the foolishness of it all, but deep down, she was extremely concerned that someone was capable of determining her every emotion and every move.

She decided to rest her horse and rode to a small brook, dismounting in a grove of trees out of the heat of the noonday sun. She tethered the animal by the stream to drink, then sat down under the shade of a willow tree to think. Watching the horse grazing a short distance away, her thoughts drifted back again to the events of the day. Leaning back against the rough trunk, she dreamily watched the motions of her mare tugging at the long grass. Then she noticed something different about her saddle, something that hadn't been there before. She walked to the horse and plucked an envelope from one of her saddlebags, the corner of which had been protruding slightly out of the pocket. Full of anticipation, she sat down again under the tree and opened the letter, which read: *Maggie, we can tell you very little, as the more information you know the less safe you become. We need your help. We will contact you soon to see if you are willing to help us. Beware. Trust no one. Find out about the four names. They are the key to the mystery! The destiny of Scotland may lie in your hands.*

She inexplicably felt the need to look around to make sure she was alone, and then, not really understanding why, she tore up the letter and buried it in the soft ground. Dumbstruck, she sat staring at the patch of ground where the letter was buried. It was looking more and more like she'd got herself involved in affairs that were a thousand leagues over her head. Certain words from the letter were hammering away against the inside of her skull, like "Danger...trust no one..." She felt like digging up the letter to double check it had been addressed to her and not someone else, but she didn't. She glanced around nervously, fearful of watching eyes, and after a while, she stood up and looked into her horse's gaze.

"I've been taken this far. I suppose we should find out how far they want us to go," she said quietly to her mount, and the mare nickered quietly in response. Quickly she gathered herself together and climbed into the saddle. She guided the animal from the copse then looked back the way she had come as she brought the horse to a halt. The land was deathly quiet and she could see for miles around. There wasn't a soul to be seen. There were a hundred and one questions she wanted answered. She patted the horse's neck and nudged her into a trot. The note was definitely wrong in one respect — she did have someone to turn to, to trust. She would go back to the city and speak with her father. If there was one man in Scotland who could understand what this was about, it was he.

CHAPTER 3

Day was turning to dusk by the time Maggie returned to Edinburgh, and her father's house was quiet. She'd deliberately bypassed the city and gone to her home in the country about a mile to the west. After handing the reins of her tired mount to the stable boy, she went straight inside and headed upstairs to her room. The thought of snuggling up in her bed next to a roaring fire had her almost asleep on her feet. Her home, situated just outside the city on 70 acres of rugged countryside, was splendid even by Georgian standards. It was built in 1789, but the Burns family had lived there for a relatively short time. In twenty years, her father had turned some of the property into farmland and built stables for his horses. Fires were always kept burning in all the main rooms of the house, under the strict orders of Sir Henry. Neither he nor Maggie had a routine regarding his houses in the city or the country, so when they arrived, both wanted the house warm and homely as if they'd never left.

Maggie washed as quickly as she could and changed into her nightgown. She devoured a stew, lovingly prepared and brought to her room by Mrs. Mullen, the Irish housekeeper. Then she wearily but happily climbed into bed. As soon as her head hit the soft pillow, she was fast asleep. She woke in the morning to another roaring fire and a hot breakfast, the strangeness of the previous day all but forgotten for the moment.

A light knock on the door disrupted her meal, and Mrs. Mullen came quietly in to the room. "Morning, Mrs. Mullen. How are you this lovely morning?" she said, looking up affectionately at her housekeeper. The woman placed some clothes in a drawer and turned to face her mistress with her hands on her hips. She was a plump old lady of around sixty years of age. Maggie didn't know exactly how old she was, and she'd never asked, but the woman had the look of eternal Irish youth in spite of her snow-white hair. Her wrinkle-free face always shone red in the cheek and she had a twinkle in her eye.

"I looked in on you last night, and you were tossing and turning, crying out in your sleep, even talking to yourself. In all my years here I have never heard you mutter a word in your sleep, but last night I was a little shocked. It was like listening to a Shakespearian tragedy. What have you been up to, young lassie."

Maggie sat up against the dressing down completely lost for words. Even more perplexing was that Mrs. Mullen, a self-proclaimed revolutionary against the written word, should even know who William Shakespeare was let alone compare something to his work. When Maggie's mother died giving birth twenty years ago, Mrs. Mullen had looked after Maggie and the family, and although she still called her Mrs. Mullen, Maggie looked to her as a mother to replace the one she'd never known.

"I'm fine," Maggie replied. "It was probably just a bad dream." Mrs. Mullen's face softened a little as she walked forward, took Maggie's face in her hands, and gave her an affectionate kiss on the cheek.

"I just don't like you going out all day and night on your own, is all," the older woman said as she looked into Maggie's eyes. "I was worried. It's dangerous for a wee thing like you to be out in the countryside with no one for protection." She turned away suddenly and started making the bed.

"I've done it hundreds of times before," Maggie pleaded with a smile. She watched the old woman with affection. It was reassuring to know she had someone to look to for the kind of comfort that only a woman seemed to be able to give.

"Yes, well it's done now, and you're safe, so that's the main thing." Looking up from the newly made bed, she stared at the girl still in her nightwear and now hovering by the fire. The old woman noted with a regretful eye how her little girl had turned into a young woman. Through the thin cotton nightdress Maggie's naked body could be seen silhouetted by the light emitted by the fire. Mrs. Mullen recognised the strong muscled limbs of a woman nearing her prime, the supple curves of a young vibrant body. Her breasts were round, her firm hips flared with a delicate line, and her waist was narrow as a teenage boy's. "I hope you're not going to church dressed like that." She stared disapprovingly at the girl, but before she got an answer, she had to beat a hasty retreat as a cushion that had been within easy reach on a chair by the fire came hurtling in her direction.

Maggie had forgotten it was a Sunday. The Burns household generally went to mass on Sunday morning at the Church of St. Catherine of Alexandria in town. Her father still hadn't returned from London, and so only Maggie and Mrs. Mullen attended the service. The old priest at St. Catherine's had heard the confessions of the Burns family for as long as she could remember, but the old man had been struck down by a strange illness a month ago and had passed away unexpectedly. He'd only very recently been replaced, in fact in the last couple of days. This was the first time Maggie had been back to church since Father Jacob's death, and she watched the new priest, Father Clifford, from her usual seat near the front of the church. The man must have been in his late thirties, but he seemed much older. His hair was thinning, but unlike most priests, he wore it long. He looked awkward in his cumbersome crisp white robes, and the incense smoke from the burner on the altar kept making him cough. His eyes looked red and swollen as from lack of sleep or excess drink, and she could see his teeth were black and rotting as he spoke to the congregation from the pulpit. His tone was harsh, bitter sounding even, as he read a verse from the book of Kings. Maggie took an instant dislike to the man, then immediately felt guilty for, whatever he looked like or sounded like, she should never have such thoughts about a man of God — but it was hard to ignore her feelings.

After the service, she made her way to the confessional, intent on talking to the new priest, even though she was worried about speaking openly to a complete stranger let alone a man she disliked, even if it were without some firmer merit than her first impression of him. In her father's absence, she desperately needed advice from someone in authority. She decided not to tell him everything, but the full story would probably sound so ludicrous to him anyway that he'd throw her out of the church and tell her never to come back. She sat down in the confessional and the shutter separating them opened slowly.

"Bless me Father for I have sinned. It's been a month since my last confession."

"Do you not remember when you last spoke to a priest, my child," he replied. His voice seemed to Maggie to have a mocking tone as if he might be relishing hearing her confession. She paused for a moment, still wondering whether or not to confide in him. "Speak, child. Do not be afraid to confess. Remember, confession is the Lord's bidding." His tone was now softer and more encouraging.

"I've been sent a number of letters Father, and I am worried about their content."

Clifford paused briefly before answering. "Who sent you the letters?" he then replied casually. Maggie was biting her lip — she felt more than unwilling to tell him anything.

"The letters were given to me by...a monk," she said slowly. Again there was a pause and Maggie felt awkward. How could she explain any of this to him? The letters and her visit to the monastery were bazaar even to her.

"Perhaps we should meet at another time," he suggested, "so I can look at the letters and discuss them fully with you once I have read their content. I'm sure this would be of far greater use to you." His voice was compelling, but Maggie had no intention of relinquishing any of the letters.

"I have destroyed the letters, Father," she lied.

"Then we shall have to discuss them without my having read them. Come to me in two days. I have a few things to attend to before then, but I promise to give you my full attention in two days' time."

"Very well, Father." No matter how hard she tried, Maggie couldn't throw the negative feelings about the priest from of her mind. Suddenly the confined space of the confessional felt like a tomb and it felt like she'd made a dreadful mistake in talking to this man, though she was uncertain why she felt this way.

"Have you anything else to tell me, child?" The sarcastic tone had returned to Clifford's voice. He sounded bored, and Maggie wished she'd never even decided to go to Mass.

"No, that was all, Father." Without waiting for her penance, she exited the confessional.

Rebecca Mullen was waiting for her at the front of the building. Most of the congregation had left the church by now, but as she walked away, Maggie noticed a couple of robed figures kneeling in prayer in one of the sectioned off chapels. One of the figures turned to look in her direction as she walked down the aisle. A hood covered the man's face so she couldn't see his eyes, but she knew he watched her intently.

Father Clifford, the last confessions of the day over, opened the confessional door and noticed the look of fear on Maggie's face as she left the building. He followed her gaze and saw the kneeling figures in the shadows. As quickly as he dared, he stepped to the left of the altar and into his private vestry. He turned and locked the solid oak door behind him and leaned against it, breathless. His mind was working fast. Then he saw a small movement out of the corner of his eye, and he moved his head slowly towards it. His throat went dry and seemed to tighten, and the muscles in his legs turned to jelly as he peered at the towering figure standing not ten feet away. The monk was in half darkness, but Clifford could feel the man's eyes boring into him. There was little difference to his appearance from the monks waiting in the chapel, but Clifford knew that underneath those robes beat a far darker, a far more dangerous heart than any he had encountered before.

"I had no idea the men outside were yours, my Lord," Clifford whispered through cracked dry lips, half inclining his head as he spoke. The monk remained silent, obviously revelling in the fear he inflicted on the sweating priest.

"The girl?" The monk's deep voice boomed across the room, seemingly to pluck at Clifford's ear and making the priest flinch.

"She mentioned your letters my Lord, but refused to comment on her plans. I'm afraid we may have to use other methods to get her father to do what you want. I could take her at any time, my lord. Henry Burns would be forced to bow to your every command when he knows you have his daughter." Clifford half smiled at the thought of Maggie's firm young flesh in his hands.

"You will continue with the plan as I have ordered," the monk declared. "Sir Henry will do my bidding soon enough, and you will be free to do as you will with his daughter once I have what I want from her. I will deal with the girl personally from now on. Without another word, the monk exited through the side door he'd originally entered, and Clifford was released from his terror.

The next day, Maggie found herself completely tied down with newspaper work, stories about the war, the government, and politics. Not surprisingly, her mind wasn't on any of it, however. The Burns family business had grown into a small empire, and she was very much a part of it. Although she had no significant title of her own within the business, the newspaper certainly could not run properly without her. The Burns family had influence in hundreds of enterprises, from small local businesses to foreign investments, but none more significant than the newspaper. The personal opinions of Sir Henry Burns were respected more highly in Edinburgh than any other local authority, and his newspaper had grown into the most widely read source of information in Scotland. Copies were even sent to Spain and France, where Scots made up a large proportion of Wellington's hard pressed and politically fragile army. Political and military careers had flourished or been toppled by the influence of the articles printed in the newspaper, or by the political clout of Burns himself. He'd worked under the wing of British politics for nearly half a century and was one of the great survivors. Any man who hoped to gain a prominent position in politics and Scottish society at large found it crucial to win the backing of Sir Henry or the tide of public opinion could be turned against him in an instant.

Not for the first time since the war in Europe had begun more than twenty years previously, the people of Scotland were rebelling, but this was the first time since Wellington marched his tiny British force onto the continent to fight the French that Scotland had come so close to civil war. In the last decade, Scotland had become a drain on the political and economic resources of the British Empire. The people were poverty stricken, and London had been increasingly called upon to prop up the flagging Scottish economy. The war in Europe was almost over, but the Empire could not sustain, and those who ran her did not want to sustain, the burden that was Scotland. Some politicians in England believed that giving Scotland greater control over their affairs, or even going so far as to let the country set up its own system of administration, would ease the pressure on England's resources. Burns did not believe this. Sir Henry was certain that, if England were to let Scotland govern itself, the land would be plunged into political crisis and economic collapse. Burns knew that Scotland was far from ready for this kind of responsibility, but from bitter experience, he also knew that, if the Scottish people rebelled again, the government would be forced to inflict more severe penalties than ever before.

Somewhere in the building a clock struck five o'clock. Maggie's head felt heavy. Her eyes were tired and she was still very anxious about her run-in with Father Clifford. For most of the day, she'd worked in her father's office, away from prying eyes so she could get some privacy. She turned away from the desk and stared out the window, peering at the city in which she'd spent her whole life. The setting sun cast an orange glow over the dark stone clad buildings that dominated the centre of the city, and Maggie glanced up at the castle, majestic and brooding on its hill, a stoic symbol of Scotland's pride. The castle's walls had never been breached, and it stood watch over the city, its imposing shadow embracing the buildings below it as the sun slowly disappeared.

The light was waning quickly, so she decided to go down to the archives and hunt for some clues about *The Wallas of Blin Harry* before going home. Grabbing a couple of candles on her way out, she headed down the stairs to the depths of the building. She had to find something in the archives relevant to the events of the last couple of days or she knew she'd never sleep properly again. Thankfully, she caught Hector the night watchman before he locked up the archive room. He helped her light the candles and promised to bring her a cup of tea in an hour. A twinge of excitement filled Maggie's entire body when she was finally left alone in front of shelves filled with thousands of books and parchments, any one of which might hold a relevant clue or piece of information.

"Let's see what we can find," she whispered to herself, but with so little to go on, she didn't really know where to start. The information she already had was less than helpful; indeed it was completely meaningless. She didn't even understand the title of the book let alone its content, and what was the history of the monastery and who were the monks who resided there? Most importantly, what was the significance of the four names underlined in her book?

She decided looking up the name of the book would be a good starting point. Finding out the identity of the monks was a priority, but the need to understand more about the book was too strong not to start with that. Within ten minutes she'd found some interesting information. *The Wallas of Blin Harry* had a number of references in the archive, but the information was sketchy. The original text was attributed to a fourteenth century Cardinal named David Beeton, the last bishop of St. Andrews. The archive was not substantial enough to offer any other information, so she resigned herself to look in the main city archives later. Blin Harry, on the other hand, was referenced in more detail or Blind Harry as he would be called if he'd been alive during the nineteenth century. His name was mentioned in a document relating to a group of blind people in the fourteenth century who travelled around Europe reciting poetry and stories. She also noted it was the local clergy who taught many of these blind people the stories they would eventually tell. These people memorised and then recited what they'd heard so they could earn money and wouldn't be a burden on society.

She folded up the parchments she'd been studying and put them away in a safe place. It was getting late, and Hector had brought her three cups of tea already. She sat back pondering her discoveries. Harry was one of the blind nomads scraping a living from telling his stories, but why was he so special? Cardinal Beeton had written the contents of the book — she understood that — but why would a Bishop, a man at the pinnacle of the church hierarchy, teach a blind beggar these stories? The four names in the book seemed to be insignificant, and perhaps the names were mixed up in translation over the centuries. Beeton's book had been written in Latin and the version she had was in the almost alien language of the fourteenth century. She needed to find a more modern translation, if it existed, because at the moment she still had no idea what the stories were about.

She suddenly felt very tired. The candles had burned down to stubs and the poor light was straining her eyes. The identity of the monks would wait until tomorrow. Their religious connection to Beeton seemed circumstantial, but their true significance in all of this she couldn't fathom. Maggie lit her last candle and walked back upstairs, bid Hector goodnight, and went to her father's private bedroom on the top floor.

Maggie slept late the next morning. Without Mrs. Mullen there to wake her, she found it almost impossible to get out of bed. She was finally enticed out of bed when she heard more noise than usual coming from the street. A crowd had gathered outside the front of the building, which wasn't unusual, but there seemed to be some sort of disturbance further up the street. She walked towards Hector, who was standing at the front door looking distressed. He turned at the sound of her approach and raised a hand to stop her from going any further.

"You don't want to go out there, Miss Burns." He genuinely looked concerned. "There's trouble goin' on and I don't like it." She looked beyond him at the crowd gathering in the street below,

"Why? What's going on, Hector?" she said as she moved past him. Other employees of the newspaper had gathered at the top of the steps but moved aside when they saw her approach. A number of the men suggested she should stay inside, but she was curious and continued on. A large crowd had gathered in the street but seemed to be mainly onlookers. The point of interest was the score of people marching slowly toward the newspaper building from the far end of the street towards. The marchers carried banners and were shouting an as yet inaudible chant of protest. Protests like these were quite common in the city, usually organised by the hungry, homeless, and out of work. The crowd of protestors was normally quite small and almost never caused any serious trouble. This protest was far more organised than usual, and Maggie suddenly felt fear and dread well up in the pit of her stomach.

She could see a small group of the city's yeomanry moving towards the newspaper building, but they were too far away to be able to cut the crowd off. There was always a dozen or so armed yeomanry near the building as a precaution because, over the last few years, the newspaper offices had become the focal point for the many people who wanted to vent their frustrations at the way the country was being run. In most circumstances, Sir Henry would comment about any demonstrations in the newspaper, and as a consequence, the protests had become more frequent. Returning her gaze to the approaching mob, Maggie noticed a large man peel off from the main group. She wouldn't have picked him out if it weren't for the fact the man was significantly larger than anyone else around him, and he was wearing long dark robes. He stopped by a doorway and started talking to someone who was partially hidden from view. She drew in her breath sharply as she realised who the figures were.

"Are you alright, Miss Burns?" She looked to her left. Thomas, one of the printers, was watching her.

"Yes, I'm fine," she said, returning her gaze to the doorway. Thomas shrugged and looked back to the commotion.

Just visible, his hooded head protruding from beside the doorway was another tall robed figure in deep conversation with the man who had left the mob. Maggie had no doubt these were some of the monks who had pursued her, and she thought perhaps they were part of the protest now drawing very close to where she stood. She suddenly lost sight of the two figures as the mob's banners obscured her vision. The yeomanry were now almost in front of the crowd, but they were thoroughly outnumbered. Maggie noticed another robed figure in the crowd, and he seemed to be pointing and issuing an order to a colleague. Immediately, a burly, rough looking protestor was brought forward carrying an enormous lance with a single flag of St. George attached to one end. Another followed with a flaming torch, and the rest of the crowd came to a halt. The lance was tipped forward and the flag was lit, bursting into flames in front of the spectators, who cheered and started shouting anti-English slogans. The Yeomanry ran towards the crowd priming their muskets. The flames must have indicated to them that the situation was far more serious than a standard peaceful protest.

Maggie watched in horror as another man, bare-chested and covered in blue painted tattoos, walked from the mob. Casually, he snatched the burning lance from his comrade, walked towards the steps of the building, and hefted the lance into a throwing position. The flag smouldered on the end as the lance wavered in the air. The crowd went silent and Maggie could hear the sound of the flag burning away through black wisps of smoke. The yeomanry were almost on top of the blue painted man, but he ignored them and instead seemed to search the area for a target. He looked up at the small huddle of people crammed at the top of stairs where Maggie stood. When he saw his quarry, he jerked back his arm in one fluid motion. Maggie froze as she realized the painted man was looking directly at her and the lance was aimed at her heart. Some of the staff next to her began to move away when they saw where the man was looking, almost falling over one another in panic. Maggie couldn't move, her own eyes now locked on his and her feet rooted to the spot in terror. Forcing herself to tear her eyes away from the man's face, she looked to her left and saw the soldiers reaching out to stop him. Despite the danger, the man remained unwavering, his muscles taught, ready to unleash the weapon with the flag now almost burned away. She looked back into his unblinking eyes and he smiled cruelly back at her. With what seemed to be inhuman power, and just before Maggie unleashed the scream that had been building up inside her chest, he launched the missile through the air, not once taking his eyes off Maggie. The smile never left his face.

Only Thomas had remained by her side. He could not believe what was happening. When he saw the lance level out and aimed to his right, he glanced sidelong at Maggie and saw the terror in her face. He tackled her at chest height and they both fell heavily to the ground. A second later, they heard the sickening thud as the lance struck its target. Maggie was devoid of any emotion, her body numb with shock as she looked up from the floor. The huge man who'd thrown the lance was throwing off two of the yeomanry. The first soldier had tried to club the attacker to the ground with the butt of his musket, but his intended target had moved out of the way with astonishing speed. The soldier was put completely off balance as the musket hit thin air. The attacker then crashed a huge fist into the side of the soldier's head with bone crushing ferocity. The soldier hit the floor and was not moving. Maggie's attacker then proceeded to grab a second soldier in a vice like grip around the throat while a third soldier decided to keep well clear and instead raised his musket ready to fire. Before he could aim the weapon, the attacker lifted his helpless victim from the floor and launched him through the air at the third man so that both soldiers were sent sprawling to the floor. The remaining yeomanry could only gawp in amazement. The attacker's final move was enough for him to escape back into the crowd, which opened up and swallowed him as he plunged into it. The episode had all happened in a matter of seconds, but Maggie would remember the moment for the rest of her life.

"Are you alright Maggie," Thomas asked, holding her hand. "Maggie..." She couldn't hear him. Her eyes were focused on the robed figure she'd seen earlier standing in the shop doorway across the street. She was in deep shock and suddenly very afraid that the world had dragged her into affairs far more dangerous than she could possibly comprehend. A soldier came up the steps towards the two prostrate figures still lying on the cold stone floor.

"Is she well?" he asked Thomas.

"I'm not sure," Thomas said looking at her.

"You did a brave thing my lad, but I don't think he was aiming at her." Thomas looked up at him, puzzled. The man turned and pointed up and behind them. Both Maggie and Thomas stared upwards in bewilderment. "A strong man, that one." The soldier walked back down the steps to the crowd that had looked so dangerous five minutes earlier but had now started to disperse. High above them hung the blue and white flag of Scotland fluttering in the breeze, and next to the flag, protruding from the building, was the lance. The lance had pierced the intended target straight through its centre. No longer flying but rather pinned to the stone face of the building was the red, white, and blue of the union flag of Britain. Maggie looked away from the flag, her mouth wide in silent exclamation, but the figure by the shop window had gone.

CHAPTER 4

Sir Arthur Cheltenham sat quietly in his office at Whitehall studying a letter he had received an hour ago. The news was not totally unexpected, but the details of the confirmation so excited him that he'd read the letter more than a dozen times. Cheltenham had only recently risen to the rank of Lord Lieutenant of His Majesty's forces stationed in Britain. Although each county had its own Lord Lieutenant, Cheltenham was the commander in chief reporting directly to the Duke of York. The position had been awarded to him after powerful members of his family in government had somehow influenced the Prince Regent, who had given Cheltenham the job instead of more suitable and experienced candidates, causing an outcry at Horse Guards. Horse Guards, unable to refuse the request of the Prince Regent, had reluctantly given Cheltenham the post, but in order to keep Cheltenham out of trouble, they put in so many layers of administration in place that the job was almost redundant. In fact, the job had been turned into a military dead end and Sir Arthur knew it, as did his family and the whole of London society.

The real soldiers were abroad and had been for ten years, and where those soldiers went, the glory went. Cheltenham would see none of it. The militia he commanded was ill-trained and inexpertly officered by country gentlemen. The militia was exclusively for home defence and could not be called upon to fight outside the country. Sir Arthur was a bitter man who believed his skills and vision deserved far more than what was now a simple desk job. A quiet tap on the door dragged him away from his thoughts and sent a slight twinge of irritation through his body.

"Come," he bellowed after putting the letter down on his desk. The door opened slowly and a fearful looking young man came into the room. "Yes, Peters. What is it?" Cheltenham snapped as he glared at him from behind the desk.

"The...the man you asked f...for is outside, Sir Arthur," Peters stuttered, obviously petrified of Sir Arthur. Cheltenham couldn't resist a patronising smile.

"What a good chap you are, eh Peters? Send him in, would you?" A moment later a well presented young cavalry officer walked in behind Peters and stood to attention in front of Cheltenham's desk. Peters then left, closing the door behind him. Cheltenham looked the man up and down and smiled with approval. He wanted a special kind of man for the task he had in mind, but most of the good men were abroad fighting in France. Cheltenham needed spies he could trust, and the next best thing was standing in front of him. He looked at the young face and noticed hardened lines of age, premature for a man seemingly so young. Cheltenham had asked for the best officers remaining at Horse Guards to be sent to him, but specifically, only the most debt-ridden officers available. In Cheltenham's opinion, a man in debt, however loyal to his employer, would be far more willing to work well, if the price was right.

"What's your name then, man?" Cheltenham asked casually.

"Captain Richard Stone, sir," the officer, still at attention, replied.

Cheltenham paused for a moment in thought. "I thought you were a pauper," he remarked testily. "How come you've got yourself the rank of captain, and so young with it?"

Stone stared straight ahead. He'd heard about Sir Arthur Cheltenham and knew he had to tread carefully. By all accounts Cheltenham was a bitter, jealous man full of contempt for all others who had in any way succeeded in life. Some said he was mad, or about as close to madness as you can get, anyway. It was well known throughout London that, as a young officer, Cheltenham had been accused of murdering two prostitutes in a drunken rampage after they had refused his debauched advances. Having ruined his career, he had been saved from court martial and a hanging by the intervention of his family, who concocted an alibi for his whereabouts during the incident. Even so, his name was in tatters and he was for the time being condemned to a life as a military administrator in the dusty back offices of Horse Guards.

"People have said the same thing before about my age sir, but in fact, I'm far older than I look."

"Well, all that's not very interesting anyway, is it? Sit down." The officer relaxed a little and sat in front of Cheltenham in the only other available chair in the room. "What I'm about to tell you may have a detrimental effect on the security of this nation. Therefore, you will not discuss this conversation with anyone outside this room. Are we understood?"

"Yes, sir."

"You will be paid a sum of money above and beyond your normal army pay for your help in this matter." Stone managed to hide any reaction to this statement, but his curiosity was definitely piqued. Cheltenham continued in a matter-of-fact tone. "There seems to be some trouble brewing in the North," Sir Arthur continued. "An associate of mine has informed me of an organisation that is trying to cause trouble by stirring up anti-English feeling among the local people." He spoke to Stone while reading a document on the table. "This has all occurred due to certain things that you don't need to concern yourself with at the moment." He looked up at Stone. "The bottom line is this, Captain: we could have a serious rebellion on our hands in the next couple of months if we don't do something about it immediately. If we've got to put up with the Scots, we might as well keep them to heel, eh lad? What do you think?"

"Yes sir, I totally agree with you. A rebellion in the north now could be disastrous for our war effort against Napoleon." Stone decided he was going to be as amenable as possible, at least until he was out of earshot.

"Anyway, for want of a better reason, we need them on our side for the war effort if for nothing else, cannon fodder and all that." He chuckled at his own distasteful humour. Stone forced a smile, which seemed to please Cheltenham. "It looks like we are of the same opinion, Captain."

"Yes sir, it seems so." Cheltenham looked back down at the document on the table and the smile on his face turned to a lascivious sneer.

"My informant also tells me that a young woman of some influence is becoming increasingly involved in these affairs." He looked back at Stone, "Have you heard of *The Scottish Times,* Captain?"

"Yes, sir. I've read it many times."

"Good. At the moment, I'm unsure what threat this woman poses to the stability of the nation, but one of my men in Edinburgh suggests some pressure is being placed on her to act against her will." He stood up and walked over to stand in front of a picture on the far wall. He turned back to Stone, his hands clutched behind him. "You see Captain, it's not so much the woman we are worried about, but those who want to influence her. Her family owns *The Scottish Times,* Mr. Stone. If the single most significant source of propaganda in Scotland falls under the influence of our enemies, we would be in a most dire situation. Is this all clear to you, Captain?"

"Very clear, sir."

"I see we're going to get along just fine." Cheltenham returned to his seat and produced a piece of paper.

"There was a disturbance in Edinburgh yesterday. Miss Burns, the woman's name by the way, was threatened in public, we think by the same men who are trying to influence her." He slammed the paper down on the desk and fell back in his chair in a fit of raucous laughter. "Do you know what they did to her Stone? Do you?" He was going red faced as he tried to force words out through his breathless laughter. "They threw..." Unable to continue, he let his laughter subside, then sat quietly with a smirk on his face. "Unfortunately," he continued in a more serious tone, "they burned the flag of St. George in the middle of the street in full view of the general public; an act we both know is a capital offence." Stone saw that the knuckles clenching the document whitened. "No one has done that for a long time Captain, and never as so blatant a gesture of defiance. Horse Guards don't like it and neither do I, and so here's what we're going to do about it." Walking to the edge of his desk, he peered down at Stone. "We know where the problem lies." Stone involuntarily leaned forward in his chair because the situation was becoming more intriguing by the minute. "It seems a group of monks have been the instigators of the problems thus far."

"Monks, sir?"

"Yes, monks, Captain. An interesting prospect I agree, and I'm sure there is more to them than just robes and prayers. So I want you to go to Edinburgh and find some information for me. I want you to follow this Maggie Burns and try to find out what she's up to. You will meet with an associate of mine already in the city, and he'll give you the rest of the details."

"Might I be permitted to know his name, sir?"

"Of course, but you realise his identity is to remain known to only you and I."

"I understand, sir."

"Good. His name is Clifford, and that is all you shall know about him." He tapped his fingers on the edge of the desk and studied Stone's face carefully. "There is one other detail I wish you to know before you leave." Stone sat stony faced, certain of what was going to be said. Cheltenham walked to the window and stood with his back to the room. "You may have ascertained that the job I require of you goes beyond the call of normal duty." He didn't wait for a reply. "Let it be known Captain, that if you succeed in doing what I ask, then I'll make certain any debt you have outstanding in this city will disappear." He turned back around and looked Stone straight in the eye. "Do I make myself clear?"

"As water sir," Stone replied with only a small twinge of uncertainty in his voice.

"Let us hope it's not water from the Thames then, eh Captain." Cheltenham's voice had a threatening edge, which made Stone realise his life was in the balance even as he sat in the chair.

Clifford will tell you everything you need to know," he said in a matter-of-fact tone. "Go now. You have your orders." He turned away again and looked out of the window.

"Yes, sir." Stone hesitated for a moment and then got up to leave. He opened the door and left quickly. Peters was almost cowering on the other side of the door. Stone looked at the dishevelled individual and suddenly realised that he'd gotten himself into an awful mess without even trying.

CHAPTER 5

Sir Arthur returned to his chair, leaned back in the seat, and stared across the room at an old painting hanging on one of the office walls. Mustering a small smile of satisfaction, he looked away from the canvas and opened another letter from the pile gathered on his desk. While he was studying the message, a side door to the study silently opened and a shrouded figure strode wordlessly into the room.

"It went well?" the man asked in a whisper from the shadows of one corner of the room. Cheltenham had been expecting the man but still found it hard not to flinch at the sound of his voice.

"It went very well, your holiness," he replied, trying to sound utterly confident, only a small amount of the actual fear he felt for the man evident in his voice. "The newspaper and the girl will soon be ours to do with as we please. I'm having her monitored twenty-four hours a day by my men. If I've chosen my man correctly, and I believe I have, that young officer who was with me a moment ago should have considerable influence on her. As you wanted, I've ordered Clifford to make sure Captain Stone and the girl disappear off on a little adventure. When Sir Henry realises we have his daughter, he should bow to our every wish. If you're sure you and your men can control the Scottish mob and with the newspaper soon to be under our control, we should have a rebellion in the north before the month is out."

Cheltenham tried not to wriggle in his seat as the huge figure moved out of the shadows and walked slowly towards his desk. The man placed two massive hands on Cheltenham's desk and leant his enormous frame towards Sir Arthur, now a pathetic quivering figure.

"Be assured," he whispered with such force that Cheltenham felt the man's breath on his face. "My men are already in position and ready to aid in this rebellion." He stood up, and in a whirlwind of robes, turned away. "But these people are weak!" he bellowed, and Sir Arthur nearly jumped out of his chair as the walls reverberated from the sound of that mighty voice. He turned back to face Cheltenham again and his voice returned to a whisper. "The people will not rise unless we can get this newspaper to print the propaganda we need to back this rebellion up. We need Henry Burns' voice in order to give the rebellion substance or it will die before it's started. Bloodletting is the easy part. Making the people trust the rebellion, as a nation, will be far more difficult. Without these ingredients Sir Arthur, you will not have your great victory. To crush a mob is nothing, but to conquer a people is to make history." He stood for a moment in silence, studying Sir Arthur's pale complexion. "We must take the newspaper by any means possible, and you must make sure your forces are ready to do my bidding. In all other matters, my men and I will succeed. Once this officer of yours has the confidence of the girl, then we will push forward with the plan. Already she follows the trail I have left for her in the book discovered from the church in St. Andrews." He paused. "Do not fail me…" Without another word he swept silently from the room.

Cheltenham sat unmoving at his desk for a while afterwards. He looked again at the painting he'd recently purchased as a reminder of what he wanted to achieve. As always, the man in the painting stood silently, as if mocking him, as if challenging him. The figure's cold blue eyes scorned Cheltenham during the day, but by night, in his nightmares, the eyes were brighter, alive and unforgiving, testing his mind and his sanity. Cheltenham had taken up the challenge laid down by the man in the painting. The English army as portrayed in the painting had been laid waste before the figure in the picture, thousands of lives taken by the mighty sword in his hand. Cheltenham was standing by to crush a new Scottish rebellion with his own English army, a rebellion created by his own hand. He would exact revenge on this historical figure as well the people who had come to epitomise Cheltenham's failures in life, the people who were now the target of his lust for power, which had tipped him into the abyss of madness.

Maggie had remained in her rooms for two days following the protest. The incident in the street had shocked her deeply, and she had taken very few visitors and had rarely left her bed. Her father had been informed of the attack and was on his way back to the city. Maggie was now torn between impeding isolation when he returned or plucking up the courage to sneak out of the building to the library to satisfy her growing curiosity about Cardinal Beeton's *Wallas of Blin Harry*. Despite her fears, she felt compelled to do some fact finding, which was obviously impossible while sitting in her apartments doing nothing.

She made her way out of the building at 7:45 in the morning, when the streets were busiest, wrapped in a travelling coat to disguise herself. She went straight to the library in Parliament Square. The building was quiet, and only a handful of people, mainly local magistrates and accountants, were inside. The books in this library belonged to the university and were the pride of the city, but the public was allowed to use them as long as they were registered members. Maggie was a regular visitor and gained immediate access. She found herself a secluded spot away from unwelcome eyes and began her search in earnest. She quickly found two books of interest and took them back to her table. She allowed herself a smile as she fumbled through the parchment of the first volume entitled *The Bard Blind Harry*. There was very little written about Blind Harry, however. The information was focused more on translations and descriptions of the poems he'd read to the people on his travels. According to the book, the man had been well known all over Scotland in the 14th century. He had not only recited verse, but with the aid of the church, he had also written his own poetry and stories. Crowds would flock to see him when they heard he was performing, and each performance was renowned to be as good as the last. His favourite performance had been "The Wallas of Blin Harry," named after him because he recited it so much. Maggie read through the first few lines of the story quoted on the page she was reading:

> *We rede of ane rycht famouss*
> *of renowne,*
> *of worthi blude that ryngis in*
> *this regioune,*
> *And hensfurth I will my process*
> *Hald,*
> *Of Wilyham Wallas yhe haf hard*
> *Beyne tald*

She couldn't find any other references connecting Blind Harry and Cardinal Beeton. So she went back to the small piece of text and tried to repeat the first few lines out loud to see if she could say them properly. The words seemed to make more sense when she read them out loud, and after a number of attempts, the script began to flow and became more understandable. She stopped suddenly in mid-recital, mouthing the same words she had just read over and over again. She put a hand over her mouth to stifle a laugh as the realisation of what the book was all about came to her.

"Wilyham Wallas. Wilyham Wallas." She said it twice out loud. She blew a random strand of hair from her face and picked up her copy of Blind Harry's book from the table.

"The Wallas of Blin Harry." She said it slowly. The story of a Scottish hero. She suddenly realised she had uncovered her first clue. *His name alone could inspire a people.* She remembered the phrase from one of the letters she'd been sent by the monks. She had also seen William Wallace's name two days ago, scattered among the banners of the protesters — but that wasn't unusual. The name William Wallace was used all the time in stories, festivals, and as a symbol of bravery and honour, a symbol for Scottish pride and independence. She had a sudden clear feeling of inevitability, the same feeling she'd felt on her way to the monastery. Events were pulling her along, and no matter what she did, she was going be dragged along with them.

It was long past noon when she gave up her search in the library. She hadn't found anything else of interest, and she was beginning to get hungry. She made her way upstairs to one of the galleries to put a book back into its shelf, then leant against the rail and looked down on the floor below her. A gust of cold air brushed her face as she stood there, and instinctively she glanced at the main entrance. Two people tried to enter the library but moved politely aside as a lady walked through the door at the same time. As she passed these men, the lady seemed unconcerned that they were both very tall and dressed in long dark robes. Maggie moved slowly away from the edge of the balcony. She remained just out of sight of the monks but just close enough to the railing so she could see what they were doing. One of the men stood by the door as if guarding the entrance as the other moved into the room, and Maggie watched, frozen to the spot, as the man removed his hood. He walked slowly over to where Maggie had been sitting. She grimaced, realising she had left her cloak on the chair. He was much younger than she expected, probably in his twenties, no older than Maggie. He had fiery, long red hair tied back with a piece of cord. He looked like any other large red headed Scotsman she'd ever seen. She leaned forward slightly so she could get a better look at him, and as she did so, she glanced over at the monk standing guard by the door. Her heart leapt into her throat and she only just stifled a scream. The other monk was looking straight at her, his face dark under the hood but his eyes clear in the candlelight. He made no move to alert his comrade, but she still found it impossible to move. She had nowhere to run anyway, and there was certainly no one here who could protect her. The other monk had now moved below the balcony and was also looking up at her with deep blue eyes, his face flushed red from the cold outside. To Maggie's utter surprise, the man beamed, sending a warm smile up at her. The smile was irresistible, and she couldn't help but slowly, tentatively, return the gesture as life seemed to return to her body. The man then immediately turned away, and with his companion, hurriedly left the building. Maggie was now completely puzzled as she leant on the rail of the balcony, wondering if she had just imagined the whole episode. She then gingerly walked back down to her desk, keeping half an eye on the entrance, expecting a hoard of monks to suddenly crash through the door and attack her. But nothing happened, and lying on the table next to the rest of her books was another letter addressed to her. Dreading what was inside, she opened the letter and quickly read the contents. The letter claimed she had put herself and her father in great danger by talking to her priest, and it informed her that they wanted to meet with her immediately. How could they have known she had confided in Father Clifford, she wondered?

The letter went on to explain that they hadn't spoken to her directly yet because they'd wanted to see for themselves how committed she was to helping them. The message ended by asking her to go back to the monastery, where they would explain their intentions in full.

Maggie snatched up her coat and almost ran out of the room, leaving the rest of the books on the desk. With no clear understanding of what dangers she might face if she went back to the monastery, she decided she had to go for her peace of mind. If her father had been put in danger as the letter informed her, then she had to find out how to make sure he would remain safe. There had been monks at the protest, but as far as she was aware, they hadn't threatened her directly in any way. She was now beyond caution, and the doors she'd already opened to this mystery were drawing her inside. At the very least, some of her questions would be answered, and besides, the monks seemed to know her every move and could hurt her if she went or not. She pulled on her coat and walked out of the building and into the cold.

Richard Stone watched Maggie leave from his vantage outside a bakery across the street from the library, where he had stood since he'd followed her there earlier. She was wearing a cloak with a hood, and so he couldn't see her face properly, which was frustrating because he still didn't have a firm idea of what she looked like. He'd watched the two monks enter the building and then leave again within a few minutes. He'd been told they would be going into the library, but he had no idea what for. As Cheltenham had promised, Clifford had given him his orders and only as much additional information as he needed. He was to make contact with Maggie — the meeting place had already been arranged — and he was to gain her confidence by any means possible. After that, he and the woman were to disappear together, but that was all he'd been allowed to know of the plan. Clifford had then thrust a bag of gold sovereigns into his hand, and off Stone had gone to find Maggie.

Moments after he made his way to her apartments, she appeared, but he didn't follow her. Clifford, although seemingly more than a little unhinged in Stone's opinion, was very well informed and had told Stone what her movements would be, so all he had to do was wait and watch. Stone knew what Maggie's destination would be now, as well, and so he merely walked in that direction rather than trying to keep her in sight.

Sir Henry had been delayed on his return trip to Edinburgh due to bad weather, and Maggie was slightly concerned for his safety. A letter had arrived at their home while she'd been at the library stating he was stuck on the border after a river had burst its banks and flooded the whole area. In a way, she knew the delay was a small stroke of luck because he would have eventually found out about her encounters with the monks and forbidden contact with them immediately. She knew she was putting herself in danger by going to the monastery once again by herself. She had few friends she could trust, but getting any of them involved could put them in jeopardy as well and she didn't want that on her conscience. By lunchtime, she was ready to leave, and her only other travelling companion, apart from her mare, came loping up to her wagging his tail madly, his big red tongue hanging out of the side of his mouth.

"Rufus, you old devil. I was just about to come looking for you." Delighted to see the old creature, she ran up and put her arms around his shaggy neck. He was an Irish wolfhound, and definitely the pick of the litter, a big dog by any standards, head and shoulders bigger than the average size for his breed. The beast was completely devoted to the family, but Maggie was his favourite. She often took him out hunting on her own, and they'd spend hours on walks together. "We're going on a little trip." She stroked the animal's head. "How would you like that?" The dog wagged his tail and sat down beside her.

She left the hound where he was and went into the stable to retrieve her horse. Her mare was a little unhappy that she had to go out in the cold, but with a few encouraging barks from Rufus, the trio were soon ready to leave. Maggie climbed into the saddle and the horse snorted irritably at the big hound that was running around her legs. "Come on, girl," Maggie hollered, and the beast trotted off with Rufus in hot pursuit.

Reaching to her side, Maggie felt the reassuring presence of the pistol in her belt. She was one of the few people she knew, let alone a lady, who was skilled with a pistol. Having grown up around men, she'd learned how to hunt and shoot and had practised until she was as good as any of her brothers. If something threatening were to happen, she would at least be prepared to fight back.

Apart from the odd farmer waving a greeting from a field or occasionally when Rufus disturbed game from the undergrowth, the journey passed without incident. Her only stop was at the brook where she'd watered and rested a few days earlier, and she reached the hill that looked down on the monastery just as the last of the light was fading. It was only as she watched the sun going down that she wondered where she was going to sleep that evening, but as with every other sensible thought she might have had on this adventure, it was soon forgotten. From where she sat she could see no sign of life within the castle. No lights or sounds penetrated the dusk as it closed in on them. She rode slowly towards the building, passing near a small copse of trees to her right fifty yards from the path.

As they passed the trees the mare grew a little jittery, and Maggie reined her in and patted her reassuringly on the neck. "What's the matter, girl?" The horse suddenly pinned its ears back and reared slightly after Rufus emitted a ferocious snarl at the darkness beyond the trees. The hound was staring at the trees and was inching menacingly towards them. Maggie squinted in the gloom and noticed a figure standing just beyond the tree line. Instinctively, she put her hand to the pistol at her belt and held her breath. The figure moved out of the trees into the remaining light and was immediately greeted by another snarl from the big wolfhound. Maggie relaxed slightly when she saw the figure was wearing dark robes of a monk, but she refrained from calling the hound to heel. The man removed his hood and Maggie recognised him as the monk who had left the letter in the library. He beckoned her to him then disappeared back into the trees. Not wanting to lose sight of him in the fading light, she kicked the nervous horse forward towards to copse.

Maggie leapt down, tied the mare to the nearest branch, and ran after the retreating monk. As she entered the trees, a path opened up in front of her and she caught sight of the monk a few metres ahead and leading the way forward. She followed with Rufus obediently trotting silently, but warily, by her side. The path gradually began to climb, and after some minutes, became quite steep. A clearing appeared in front of her on the summit of the hill, and she stepped out of the gloom into a large open area surrounded on all sides by tall oak trees that rose into the darkening sky. In the centre of the clearing stood twenty or thirty robed figures, some carrying flaming torches. Other monks were crouched around small fires, either cooking or just trying to keep warm. All of the men were completely silent and staring straight at her and Rufus as they appeared through the trees.

Stone followed Maggie to the castle all the way from Edinburgh, and he had so far remained undetected. He'd stayed further behind her than he'd wanted when he realised the hound travelling with her would easily catch his scent if he got too close and alert Maggie to his presence. He almost lost her when Maggie suddenly got the urge to go galloping over fields and hedges. So he stayed as close as he dared even though he knew her destination. He had been just close enough to see her disappear into the trees, so he tied his horse out of site further down the tree line and followed her up the path. He realised this must be where the monks had decided to meet her. Good of Clifford to let him know about the meeting place, he thought. He had to double his efforts to remain quiet and undetected as he walked up the path, and as he reached the clearing, he moved off the path and into the trees.

He got down on his belly and crawled to the edge of the clearing so he could see what was going on. As he peered out into the light, he spotted Maggie in conversation with a group of robed men. Clifford had failed to inform him of one or two important facts on this mission already. There had been no mention of an evening rendezvous or robed men in the wilderness, and so there was obviously a great deal more going on with this girl than a simple observation exercise. He listened intently. There was something going on and this was the perfect opportunity to find out what it was. If he was already over his head, and it was a distinct possibility that he was, then he needed some cards to play for himself, just in case things started to get nasty.

Both parties stared at each other for a moment before one of the larger monks made a move towards her. Rufus immediately emitted a dangerous growl, but this time Maggie hushed him into silence.

"We wish you no harm, Maggie." To Maggie's surprise, the voice was a woman's. She spoke in English but with a slight but very noticeable foreign accent. We've led you to this place so that we can ask for your help, so we can explain why we desperately need you. The woman beckoned her to come closer. "Come, Maggie. Time is short and there are enemies close by."

As Maggie walked towards the fire, the robed figure pulled back her hood. Maggie noticed she had the same deep blue eyes as the man from the library, but instead of red hair, she had bright blond curls that shone in the light of the fire. The woman was middle-aged, but Maggie could see she had once been very beautiful. She had a particularly Roman look about her, a long strong nose and square jaw that was almost masculine but softened by her creamy white skin and intense olive-shaped eyes. Maggie had seen statues of such women in the classics sections of the museum in Edinburgh, and she wondered if this woman was a descendant of those ancient people.

The woman seemed to be in charge of this small group of monks, and as Maggie approached she raised her hand in greeting. Maggie smiled and accepted the rather manly gesture warmly. The robed woman was a good three or four inches taller than Maggie, but her grip was gentle and her hands were soft. Even though the woman seemed harmless, Maggie felt slightly intimidated by the power and presence she commanded. She looked around and saw all the other members of the group had lowered their hoods as well. The men around her were a mixture of ages, but only a few were older than the woman. The majority seemed to about Maggie's age. All of them were staring at her in fascination; as if she was rumour they'd heard about but thought they'd never get to see. Maggie noticed that all them were six feet tall at least and stood tall and straight, more like warriors than monks. The woman escorted her to the large fire in the centre of the glade and issued commands to the nearest men in what Maggie realised, to her astonishment, was perfect Latin. Immediately, a number of the men moved to the edge of the clearing to stand guard around the perimeter and didn't move for the rest of the evening.

"Are you hungry, my dear?" Maggie hadn't really thought about food until that moment, but the nervous feeling in her stomach now made her feel a little nauseous.

"No, not really," she replied, unsure if she should oblige or get the meeting over with as quickly as possible.

"Good. It's straight down to business then." The woman smiled and sat down opposite Maggie with her back to the trees. She sat quietly for a moment, studying Maggie's face, and then looked away briefly to check on the status of the camp.

"Why are we sitting out here and not in the monastery?" It had taken Maggie some time to pluck up the courage to ask the question, but it felt good to speak first. Returning her gaze to Maggie, the woman then closed her eyes very slightly for a split second in what may have been a hint of annoyance, but the look disappeared as quickly as it had come.

"Before we discuss anything, let me introduce myself," the woman said softly, her smile now returned. Maggie visibly relaxed, her question, for the time being, forgotten. "My name is Ruth. I am a member of a religious order that presides in the monastery at the bottom of this hill." She pointed in the direction of the castle Maggie had already visited. "The other people around you are members of the same order but are also its guardians and protectors." Maggie glanced around at those men near enough to listen to the conversation, and they nodded their heads in greeting. "In answer to your question, we are sitting outside because the home in which we live, and have lived for many years, is no longer safe for us to stay in. We're sitting outside so that we can have a conversation without our enemies hearing what we say."

She paused for a moment, and then smiled again at Maggie. "We have no intention of causing you any harm, Maggie. We know you're an intelligent woman, which is the reason we asked you to help us in the first place. I will be straight with you, Maggie, if you promise to be straight with me." She didn't wait for Maggie to reply. "There are people in this country who would like to see Scotland plunged into a conflict with itself and with its neighbours." Ruth saw the fear appear in Maggie's eyes but continued speaking despite the uncertainty she knew Maggie must be feeling. Ruth forced another smile, happy that she had the girl's attention. Leaning closer to Maggie, her voice lowered almost to a whisper, she said, "It is time for you to know some of the truth, my dear. Let me tell you the tale from the very beginning."

CHAPTER 6

"You have already read and heard of Cardinal Beeton?" Maggie's heart seemed to miss a beat. The question hung in the air for a moment.

"Yes I have," she replied. "I read about him a couple of days ago."

"Good, then our faith in your initiative wasn't unfounded. Beeton was the last Bishop of St. Andrews, as you probably already know, and by all accounts, a good and devout man. He spoke out against the treatment of the Scottish people when others like him in the church kept silent. He was also still alive when William Wallace was executed, when his body was torn apart and sent to the four corners of the country." She paused again briefly and moved even closer to Maggie, who was now completely entranced by the story. "What I'm about to tell you has been kept a secret for over four hundred years."

Leaning back again, she drew in a deep breath and blew softly out in Maggie's direction. The cold night air turned her breath into mist, and then it disappeared. Maggie smelled Ruth's fragrance of flowers and musk, and she seemed to fall further under the woman's hypnotic spell. "A young Lord in the English army at the time of the Wallace rebellion was also secretly a Scottish sympathiser. He was asked by his cousin to collect the pieces of Wallace's body after the remains had been scattered. The Lord, with the help of some of Wallace's former allies, removed the pieces and took them to a secret location and buried the body. It was no coincidence that the young Lord's name happened to be Beeton. Soon afterwards, the man left the army, but we know very little about him after that."

Maggie sat astounded and almost speechless. She managed to ask, "What has all this got to do with your order — and with me."

"A number of months ago, a wall in a church in St. Andrews suffered some damage and partially collapsed. Behind the wall, hidden away for four hundred years, was a secret compartment wherein were found a book and a letter from Cardinal Beeton himself, both intact and completely legible." Ruth watched Maggie's puzzled expression in amusement. "Beeton had been the bishop of the church at the time, and he probably made the compartment himself after he'd written the original book," she said answering Maggie's bemused expression. The fire crackled with burning sap, making Maggie jump. Ruth prodded the fire, then tossed on a couple of logs, making the flames sizzle greedily. "The book from St. Andrews was the one you saw in the monastery, and that book is almost a direct translation of the copy we left for you in your room the day before.

"There's no explanation of what the four names represent in the letter Beeton wrote. We've spent weeks trying to discover the significance of the names, but as of yet, we've nothing to go on. Beeton left some mysterious information in the letter, which I can only assume he did deliberately because he wanted whoever found the letter to uncover its secrets. He spoke about himself in the letter, about his life and what he thought about the world he lived in. It seems he began a strange and interesting game when William Wallace died, a game we're now playing five hundred years later."

She prodded at the hot coals again to keep the fire alive. Ruth reached into one of her pockets and drew out a small book and held it up to the firelight so Maggie could see it. "Beeton believed the story of Wallace's life should be told wherever anyone would listen. So he translated the story for a blind man, who was one of the most gifted storytellers he could find, Blind Harry."

Maggie stared at the book in Ruth's hand. The front cover was blank, but she knew it was the same book she had in her own pocket. "What we didn't know, and could never have learned without Beeton's letter, were the secrets hidden in this book. Beeton wrote in his letter how ironic and justified it was that a seemingly pathetic, defenceless blind man was free to roam the land reciting the tales of William Wallace. But at the same time, the listeners, Englishman and Scotsman alike, unwittingly, through the stories themselves, were being told the actual location of Wallace's body. Beeton must have seen this as a personal private victory against his people for not trying to save Wallace and against the English for his death. Have you been able to read any of the pages Maggie?"

"Not very easily," Maggie replied, slightly embarrassed.

"We think the location of the body is somehow hidden in the text, and the only clues we've got to work with are the four names in the original that differ from names in these modern copies." Ruth paused again so Maggie had a chance for these details to soak in.

"Near the end of the book, Beeton states that Wallace will return one day to wreak bloody vengeance on the English."

"That doesn't really justify starting a revolt or a civil war," Maggie blurted out. She wasn't sure why she said it.

Ruth looked at her with a stony expression on her face. "Let me explain why I agree with you, Maggie," she continued slowly. We don't want to cause trouble with the English, nor do we want the country to revolt. You and your father have very similar opinions to our own in this regard, which is one of the reasons we came to you. You both hold great influence, something we will need to use if we are to stop this country from plunging into civil war.

"Why did you choose to bring me here then? Why not my father?" Maggie interrupted.

"Your father is a good man Maggie, and if he knew about our cause, I'm sure he would aid us. What we need from you, however, your father would not be able to provide; and secondly, he might not approve of your involvement as there will be a great amount of danger involved.

"But I saw one of your people at the demonstration in Edinburgh the other day. Whoever the person was seemed to be in control of the whole thing. There was a man there who threatened to kill me." Her voice was suddenly filled with anger, but Ruth raised her hand to stop her.

"It's true that a number of our order was present at the disturbance, and in all probability, they organised it." Ruth's face took on a pained expression. "But the order has broken into two factions. When we discovered the truth about the book, some decided to break away from the order and take matters into their own hands." She stood up over the fire and looked into the flames. "I tried to explain to them that now was not the time to be starting a rebellion. One day soon Scotland will be more of a country in its own right, with our own government and our own rulers. But that time is not yet. Not now."

Maggie watched her and finally began to understand. "They want to use the body," Maggie said more to herself than to Ruth. They want to use Wallace as the figurehead for their revolt." Ruth smiled inwardly at how easily she'd taken Maggie into her confidence. At the same time, she felt more than a little respect for how quickly the girl had judged the situation and grasped its importance.

"The name of their leader is William Campbell," Ruth said as she looked down at her. She'd made the name up on the spot, looking to carry the story further and take advantage of Maggie's gullibility. "He's a good man, and I don't believe he is capable of the things he's been accused of doing."

"What things?"

"Last night, Cardinal Beeton's book, the original you saw in the castle that we found at St. Andrews, was stolen from the monastery." Maggie looked up startled. "We had guards at every entrance and exit no one could have gotten past them."

"Someone who was already inside the monastery?" Maggie asked.

"We've suspected for some time that not all of Campbell's supporters left the castle."

"Do you know now?"

The pained expression returned to Ruth's face. "We found the body of the monk we suspected in his room. His throat had been cut, we can only assume to silence him." She spoke with an awful bitterness. "I'm sure Campbell wouldn't have ordered anyone to be killed, even his worst enemy."

Maggie could see how hard it had been for Ruth to talk about the murder. "I will do everything I can to help you," Maggie said softly. Ruth nodded her head in appreciation; realising Maggie had now been totally taken in by her lies.

"We will have to move fast. We must stop Campbell before he gets out of control. We must find the body of William Wallace before he does, and that is where we need your help." She put her hands on Maggie's shoulders and looked into her eyes. "Times will be hard Maggie, but we will end all this, you can be sure of it.

Stone had settled himself onto a small patch of ground just within earshot of the two women. He hadn't dared to move throughout the whole conversation because a guard had positioned himself at the tree line only ten paces away. Stone's muscles were beginning to stiffen up in the cold night air and a tree root was jabbing painfully into his ribs. He had lain on the ground totally transfixed by the tale, wondering how much of it was true and how much more manufactured lies. At the end of their conversation, he saw Maggie stand up and turn towards the trees where he was lying. He squinted through the trees and edged forward so he could get a better look at her in the firelight. Even through the darkness and the shadows he could see she was a stunningly beautiful woman. Her coal-black hair shone in the firelight, and it was so rich and dark that it had a blue hue to it. The shadows accentuated her elegant features and enhanced the seemingly perfect lines of her face. He was suddenly transfixed by her, and for a moment, completely unable to look away.

As the small party in the clearing began preparations to bed down for the night, Stone quietly slipped away, crawling through the trees to where Ruth had set up her billet. Stone watched as the woman went through the usual preparations for sleep. Then he heard a very low whistle emanating from the trees to his right. Rufus pricked his ears up and looked around but then went back to his nap. Ruth immediately stopped what she was doing, and as silently as the night, disappeared into the trees. Stone's heart was racing — he had to follow her to see who she was meeting. As quickly as possible without making too much noise, he crawled towards the trees where Ruth had disappeared and strained to hear. As he moved deeper into the wood, he heard the murmur of voices nearby. The voices became louder as he approached another smaller clearing in the wood, and he stopped a few feet from the tree line. Alarmingly, he was suddenly aware that the entire wood around him was swarming with men. He'd managed to crawl into the midst of what seemed like a small army gathered in the woods and there were monks standing not three feet away from him on all sides. He tried not to panic and instead he focused on the two figures talking to each other in hushed voices in the centre of the glade. Ruth suddenly became more animated and both her voice and the voice of the man she was talking to reached Stone's ears as he lay shaking in the trees.

"*Etes vous prenant a un grand risqué, mon seigneur.*" Stone cursed his luck again. He hadn't spoken French in months, and his grasp of the language was shaky at the best of times. He knew she was asking the man if what he was doing was risky, and she was addressing the man as "my lord." So the man was obviously important. Stone concentrated his mind and translated their words as quickly as he could to make sure he didn't miss a thing.

"I will not kill the girl until she has served her purpose," the man replied.

"But we can find the body of Wallace ourselves, if that's what you want my Lord," Ruth replied.

"I can't spare the men, and besides, I've watched the girl — she is intelligent and resourceful and will find the location of the body as quickly as any of us could."

"What if she doesn't help us?" Ruth responded, still trying to press her point.

"Then we will kill her," he replied in a calm voice. "And we will find the body ourselves."

"Very well, my Lord," she said, seemingly satisfied with his answer.

"Do not worry," he continued. "I was listening to your conversation with the woman and you were very convincing. I would have believed your story myself. You have her total confidence and that is enough."

"May I ask another question, my Lord?"

"Of course, but be quick — my time here is short."

"Why do we need the body of this William Wallace so urgently? What purpose will it serve with the rebellion already in its final stage?"

The man paused for a moment, and Stone listened to the silence. Then the man answered with clenched fists. "After we have helped that fool Cheltenham raise this rebellion, and later, when we crush him and his English army with the very Scottish rebels he has raised by his own hand, when order has been restored and we have control in this country, we will need a powerful symbol to win the loyalty of these people. The body of William Wallace is a potent image of power and respect for them, and with the body in our hands, our task will be made easier a hundred fold. The Scottish people, with our help, will have a great victory against the English, and they will need strong leaders for the future. We will use the body to consolidate our position and take over this land." The monk paused again, and Stone wondered what he said next could possibly be any more amazing than had already been said.

"The British army will be forced to return home, to retreat from France once our rebellion has been victorious," the man continued. "And when they do, Napoleon Bonaparte will once again be the master over Europe, and with the imperial soldiers he has promised to send, we will crush the remaining English sent against us and then govern the entire country from the north." Stone couldn't quite believe what he was hearing.

"The land in Malta that was taken from us by the English so many years ago will be returned to us tenfold, and we will take our revenge by cleansing this country of English greed." The monk's voice returned to a whisper as he hissed a warning at Ruth. "You will find that body for me at any cost, and God forbid you should fail me." He snapped his fingers and the hundreds of men that surrounded the pair suddenly marched away in unison through the trees and down the hill. Ruth was left standing on her own in the middle of the glade. Her head remained bowed, and Stone watched her in silence. Eventually she walked back to the camp and Stone followed close behind, nursing fingers that had been trampled and bruised by a heavy military boot.

Stone decided he'd seen and heard enough and quietly made his exit back down the hill to his waiting horse. He stood next to the animal and looked out into the darkness, towards the castle that was now hidden by the night. After the evening's encounter, he felt different in some way, but he couldn't put his finger on it. He had no loyalty towards Cheltenham, and he realised just this night, to his own country either. After everything he'd just witnessed, he should have been galloping to the nearest garrison to send a message of warning to Horse Guards. He would be a hero of the nation, and if he did nothing, he would be deemed a traitor that deserved to be executed — but none of that mattered. All he could think about was that beautiful face in the firelight. If his whole existence meant anything, it was to see to it that he protected Maggie whatever the cost. In his soul he knew the right thing to do was to blow this plot wide open, but he was such a small player in a big game that had almost run its course that he doubted he could stop the plot anyway. His own career was already in tatters, and so he cared little about himself — it was only Maggie's safety that counted. He had to make sure she went through with the monk's wishes, or her life would be in great danger. He decided to carry on working for Cheltenham but only if that meant he was close enough to Maggie to protect her. If Cheltenham's army was defeated and the land was plunged into war, then he would take Maggie away until the world was again put to rights. He climbed onto his horse and trotted quickly away. As he rode into the night, he felt like singing to the stars, and with a stab of uncertainty, he realised he was in love.

The activity in the camp grew louder as the evening meal for the camp was being prepared, waking Rufus. The dog rose from his position by the warm fire, took a long deep stretch, and then looked around, surveying the situation. Ruth, having returned from her liaison in the woods, noticed the animal and walked over to him. She called to Maggie who was untying her bedding. "He looks like a fine companion."

Maggie looked at the animal and smiled at him. "I must admit, I do feel safer when he is nearby."

Ruth looked down at the dog, and then offered her hand. He stretched out his head, gave her a quick sniff, then wagged his tail in acceptance. She knelt down in front of him and took his head in her hands. "Maggie will need your protection over the coming weeks, my friend." She looked over at Maggie, who was busily sorting out her bed for the night, and she almost felt sorry for the girl. Rufus followed Ruth's gaze, then trotted over to her and lay down at the foot of the bed.

The next morning, Ruth instructed Maggie to go back to the city and assured her that they would contact her immediately about what they wanted her to do. She also warned Maggie to be on her guard as Campbell would know she'd been to the monastery. In the meantime, while she was waiting to be contacted, Ruth asked her to find out how much information her father knew about the movements of potential troublemakers in the city and what he'd heard about any rebellious activity in the region but keeping all they had said and agreed secret from her father. Maggie agreed to do as she asked, and as Ruth had hoped; in return Maggie wanted to do more to help find William Wallace's body by doing as much research with Cardinal Beeton's book as possible.

Maggie regretted having to go back to the city, not because of the newfound safety she felt around Ruth and her monks, but because there was more excitement and adventure to be found with them and she wanted to know so much more. All she could hope to do was to make an impression on Ruth and assist her where possible. Their goal was to make sure their country wasn't plunged into civil war and that the traitors Ruth had mentioned were brought to a swift justice. Maggie suddenly felt like there was a mission to her life. She had the opportunity to make a difference, and although it included a huge amount of danger, that seemed irrelevant compared to the fun she could have.

The city seemed strangely quiet when she returned. She rode down the old streets and paths she knew so well towards her home and looking down on people from her mare as she passed, she felt a huge responsibility on her shoulders. She suddenly had a part to play in all their lives, whether they liked it or not. Doubt began to creep into her mind as to whether she was doing the right thing or if this mission was purely a selfish desire to live out her own dreams of adventure. Then she began rehearsing what she would say to her father when she got home. As she passed the newspaper building, she looked up at the spot where the spear had pierced the flag. A new flag had already replaced the torn one and was fluttering silently in the breeze. Her father would be upset at her absence that was certain. Thomas greeted her at the doorway to the building, a grim smile on his face. On the lookout for her on her father's orders, she assumed. He must have been waiting there all day, she thought. She tied up her horse and climbed the steps towards him.

He greeted her. "Miss Burns, it's good to see you." He didn't sound enthusiastic. "Your father asked me to look out for your return. He wanted to see you as soon as you got back. If you don't mind me saying, Miss Burns, I think he's been very worried about you."

"I've been fine, Thomas. I'm a big girl now, you know." She noted that he seemed nervous. "What's the matter, Thomas? Is my father alright?"

"Yes, he's fine...I think. We haven't really seen much of him since he got back." He frowned slightly. "This morning someone brought a letter to the door addressed to him. I happened to be standing here, so I took it up. And then...

"What did the person look like?" Maggie interrupted.

"Sorry?"

"What did the person who delivered the letter look like?" she repeated anxiously.

"Well, he was an Englishman, young looking — nothing more to say than that really.

"Did my father say anything about it?"

"Well that's what made me a little nervous. Before I gave him the letter, he was quite angry with you for going off on your own. We haven't really heard or seen him since."

"Thank you, Thomas. I think I'll go up and see my father now."

She made her way to her father's study, tapped on the door, and waited for a moment.

"Come."

Gingerly she pushed the door open and closed it behind her. Her father was seated behind his desk with his back to her. She walked over and stood in front of the desk in silence. Her father stood up slowly and walked around the desk and stood in front of her. He looked at her with tired eyes, and then gently embraced her. After a moment, he pushed her away and took both her hands.

"I was very, very worried about you, Maggie. What you did was stupid and dangerous, especially when people are threatening your life." He let go of her and took two pieces of paper off his desk.

"Read these." He handed her the papers and watched her face as she read. Without another word, he turned and went into his bedroom and shut the door. Maggie stared at the door with a twinge of guilt. He probably hadn't slept since hearing she had gone. Quietly she sat at his desk and read through the letters again.

It was near dusk when Sir Henry woke, only a few hours after he had left Maggie in the study. Maggie had organised supper to be brought to their rooms and had laid it out ready for them. He walked out in his evening gown, the tiredness gone from his face and his eyes bright and alert.

"Looks good," he said, glancing at the food and rubbing his hands together in anticipation. He took one of the plates and piled it high with cold meats, cheeses, and bread. Maggie poured him a glass of wine and put it in front of him as he sat at the desk. They ate in silence for a moment, savouring the food.

"By the way, I have hired someone on to help me with the work I'm doing at the moment; more as my private secretary than anything else." He grinned.

"Who is it?" she asked calmly.

"A young man from London who came highly recommended by a friend of mine at *The London Times*." He smiled and put an oversized pickled onion in his mouth. Maggie winced as he bit down on the sour vegetable.

"I didn't realise you knew Sir Arthur Cheltenham personally. He must think the situation in Edinburgh is bad indeed to write to tell you he is coming to Scotland." She referred to the recently delivered letter. Wiping his mouth, he put the napkin on the table and stared at his daughter.

"Obviously, I have read the letter from Sir Arthur and pondered his words at great length, and I now truly believe we have some serious trouble ahead of us," he said quietly.

"When Thomas told me you had received a letter, I somehow knew it would be something significant," she replied.

"If Cheltenham thinks a full-blown rebellion is around the corner, and he obviously thinks there is, then it is definitely a cause for concern," her father continued. "I don't know where he got his information, but I certainly can't see where a rebellion is going to come from or who is leading it."

"What about the demonstration the other day and the man who attacked the building?"

"Yes. That incident was certainly strange, but a rebellion of any size needs more than just men. Ammunition and guns, horses and supplies are required. We don't fight with just swords any more, and a war is no longer won with a single battle. An uprising from this city could be stopped with a single blast from the cannon up at the castle. No, there is something far more sinister at work here, and Cheltenham must know about it to come all the way up here from his comfortable office." He paused in thought for a moment. "I'll grant him a meeting, but I certainly will not put any of his English propaganda into the newspaper. More soldiers flooding into the city will cause enough trouble, and denouncing all traitors to the crown would only exacerbate the situation." He popped another pickle into his mouth and spoke to his daughter while chewing. "No, my dear, we must remain as neutral as we can to make sure everyone in this country has a voice. It's at times like these that the world needs to read the truth so that people can make their own judgements, and we must stand by this principle no matter what happens." His took a sip of wine to wash down the pickle. "And nothing will deter me from this belief."

Maggie flushed with guilt at her father's words particularly as she had first-hand knowledge about the rebellion. Cheltenham was a very powerful man and she couldn't help thinking that only trouble would come from her father's resistance to the English if a rebellion actually started.

CHAPTER 7

Cheltenham paced up and down his office reading a letter he'd just received: "...target triggered, no problems...monks in position." The letter was signed with a C. His face creased into a smile as he crushed the letter and tossed it into the fire. Reaching up onto the mantelpiece above the fire, he took a splint and lit it from the flames. Shielding it with his hand, he carried it across the room. On the other side of the office, he touched one of the wooden panels on the wall. Immediately, a secret door popped open, and pulling the door open, he walked through the opening and closed the door behind him. He lit an oil lamp on the wall and a small room was slowly illuminated. He walked to a shelf on the opposite wall and took down a copy of Cardinal Beeton's *Wallace of Blin Harry*. He'd studied the text in minute detail every day since the discovery of the original book in St. Andrew's church. Every evening he'd work himself into a frenzy trying to find a clue to the existence of Wallace's tomb, but the book refused to give up its secrets.

He carried the book to a small table in the centre of the room, lit two partially burned out candles, opened the book, and began to read. Sometimes he read for a minute, and other times for hours at a time. He would often go into a rage, breaking the furniture and pounding the walls until exhausted. He wasn't an intelligent man and only had a small capacity for learning, but what he did have was a firm belief in his greatness. After buying a commission into the army, he sought out war wherever it could be found. Although full of enthusiasm, he wasn't by nature a good soldier, and was in reality a coward looking for acceptance. After numerous failed commands, his reputation was finally shattered when he was accused of the murder of two prostitutes. Forced to carry out the rest of his career in Britain, he decided to look down other avenues to achieve the success he craved, and by chance, he stumbled onto the opportunity he needed to immortalize himself. A trusted employee by the name of Clifford — he had never learned his real first name — a man he had rescued from the gallows for rape and murder five years earlier and kept him on as his hired assassin, his wages paid for by the government, provided this opportunity. Clifford had served as a sergeant in a battalion Cheltenham had commanded in India during the war with the Maharajas, and he had remained loyal to his master ever since. Clifford was as evil and devious as Cheltenham, but he was also an extremely efficient killer.

Clifford found out about the discovery of Cardinal Beeton's book and the letter it contained while disguised as a Catholic priest in Edinburgh. Clifford made contact with the monks immediately after he realised the book had fallen into their hands, and everything had slotted nicely into place after that. The monks were an ancient order of knights in hiding after being banished from Malta when the island was seized by the English in the last century. They'd taken up residence in Scotland after a nobleman had heard about their plight, giving them land and a castle to live in temporarily. Although reduced in numbers, the knights were still a formidable force, man for man as good as any fighting unit in Europe. In Malta they had been known as the Knights Hospitaler, and their Grand Master was a man called Raymond Du Puy.

Clifford, realising the financial potential of playing on both sides of the fence, secretly told Du Puy of Cheltenham's ambitions for power. Clifford, who had been working for Cheltenham in the north for a number of years, explained to Du Puy how close Scotland already was to rebellion. He also explained how a symbol as powerful as the body of William Wallace would be extremely potent in the right hands, and Cardinal Beeton's legacy had given them the means to find where he was buried. Du Puy and Cheltenham met together and formulated a plan. With a deal secured and with the assistance of the knights, Britain would be plunged into civil war, giving Cheltenham the chance for the victory he craved and the knights the opportunity to return home to Malta. In reality, however, The Grand Master had a far more sinister plan in mind, and Cheltenham's blind, reckless ambition was the perfect platform upon which to bring his own plot together.

Du Puy had easily convinced Cheltenham that the plan would work, and from that moment, Cheltenham had fallen under the Grand Master's spell. Cheltenham understood exactly what the knights wanted, and he was willing to promise them anything for their help in starting a rebellion that would ultimately end in complete victory for his English army — and his everlasting fame. Cheltenham had no intention of trying to get their homeland back for the knights, however. Cheltenham had neither the power nor the will, and once he had defeated the rebellion, he intended to cover his tracks by rounding up all the knights and imprisoning them, quietly executing them all for treason. Until that time came, Cheltenham and Du Puy were allies with common unscrupulous goals.

Over the last few months, Clifford and Raymond Du Puy had gathered a horde of French mercenaries to help them organize the rebellion, hired thugs to fill the ranks of existing rebel groups giving the Scots confidence that their numbers were swelling. Most of the Frenchmen were in fact prisoners of war that Cheltenham had secretly freed from Scottish POW camps and put under the command of Du Puy and his knights.

The overall success of the plan depended on a number of key factors. Fortunately for the conspirators, the motivation for the rebellion had been in existence for more than a decade — starvation, disease, high unemployment. To gain further support, however, the rebellion needed a potent symbol that would give the people reason to fight. Recovering the body of William Wallace would provide the perfect national symbol, but finding it would be the problem. All Cheltenham really needed to do was make the Scottish people think the body could be discovered and returned to them, and the evidence for this was written in Cardinal Beeton's letter, but he wanted to see if he could find the body without revealing the source of his knowledge. Naming the actual location of the body was far more convincing than a five hundred year old letter that simply declared the body had been recovered and hidden.

Cheltenham knew he couldn't count on ordinary people to pick up weapons. The average people of Scotland had lost their stomach for a fight over the years, when up against overwhelming odds in the form of the English army. So the French mercenaries had spent the last few months organising rallies for young Scottish men. Cheltenham's own men thus infiltrated every club and society where young men gathered, and these men were recruited surreptitiously. At the same time, Du Puy fed the members of these groups with anti-English propaganda and flooded the towns and cities with weapons and supplies. Slowly, Cheltenham and Du Puy's rebellious army had grown, until without actually having been brought together, their forces on paper numbered more than twenty thousand men.

The other key factor in making their plan work was propaganda. Cheltenham had done his homework on Sir Henry Burns and his newspaper. Cheltenham understood the impact of propaganda for he'd seen it at work many times before, particularly in war. Sir Henry Burns had this power at his disposal in Scotland — the people read his words and they believed what he said. Cheltenham realised that he could use *The Scottish Times* to subtly channel anti-English propaganda, and the people would flock to the rebel flag in the thousands. He also knew that there was no way he could influence Burns easily. The Scotsman's moral code was incorruptible, and so control of the newspaper had to be gained by blackmail or by force. Cheltenham and Du Puy had targeted Maggie as the simplest means to gain control of Sir Henry. They laid a trail for Maggie to follow and used her well documented passion for adventure to make sure she took the bait. Once she'd fallen under their influence, they could manipulate her to do what they wanted. Burns would be told his daughter had been taken hostage, and Cheltenham could then demand full access to the paper. Maggie would assume she was working with the monks to stop a war from breaking out, and would be duped into working for Cheltenham to find Wallace's body while at the same time unwittingly being a hostage to manipulate her father into giving Cheltenham control of the newspaper.

Stone was to be the inside man for Cheltenham. He would get close to Maggie and make sure she did as she was instructed. He was to get romantically involved with her if necessary. Once Maggie and her father had served their purpose, they would be disposed of quickly and quietly. Cheltenham had paid Stone more than enough money to be confident he would carry out his orders, but Du Puy would always have men close by in case Stone decided to take matters into his own hands and disobey orders.

Clifford had recently intercepted a message from Sir Henry to an old colleague in London asking if the friend could recommend anyone as a personal assistant. Cheltenham had responded, pretending to be the friend, and told Sir Henry he was personally sending a highly regarded assistant to help Sir Henry with his affairs. Stone was to be the assistant, and that was how he could get close to Maggie without raising suspicion. Their plans were starting to fall into place.

It was late into the night before he gave up reading through the book. Exhausted, he placed the book back on its shelf, lifted the candle and walked to the hidden door. Pausing before the door, he held the flame up to another portrait he'd recently hung on the wall. He had picked up the painting months ago, this painting and the one in his office. He looked at both paintings regularly to remind him of the challenge he had set for himself. This painting was of a burning city, its inhabitants laid to waste. A rebel army was leaving the smouldering ruins of the city behind, and their leader, a blue faced man with a mighty sword, marched at the front of the army. The light flickered, casting the shadows eerily around the room. Cheltenham smiled at the image. Each day brought him closer to success. Soon his mercenaries and rebel followers would be strong enough to recreate this man's dream in the 19th century, and then Cheltenham would crush the dream as his own ancestors had done centuries before.

A light tap on the door broke Maggie's concentration. She had stayed up most of the night with her father — who was now at his club — composing an article to publish in the morning's paper. The document was basically a direct plea from Sir Henry himself to the citizens of Edinburgh, a passionate message asking the people for restraint in this time of crisis, famine, and uncertainty. He was asking all the influential people in the city to follow his lead and look towards caution before inciting any rebellious activity, and he warned them that, otherwise, they might all pay a heavy price in the future. She was reading through the article when the messenger arrived.

The previous week, her father had secretly met with friends and colleagues in London, some of the most powerful businessmen in the country, to discuss the worsening problems in Scotland. Their discussions had mainly been about the good times before the war in Europe, about Scotland as a feudalist state in which the lower classes accepted their place in society because the upper classes had always looked after them. Now, in a new era of industrialisation and urbanisation, communities were breaking down, tenants being thrown off the land they'd lived on for centuries, and people bled dry for profit. Combined with higher taxes for the war effort, the people of Scotland had now begun to starve. Sir Henry and the others discussed the issue for days but had not achieved a viable solution. All they could hope to do was to patch up some of the existing problems and continue to hold society together until life improved.

One reason Cheltenham was so keen to get Sir Henry out of the way was the Scotsman's influence over the people, in fact, all the people — the wealthy elite and desperately poor. Cheltenham had eyes and ears everywhere, and he was fully aware of the meetings Sir

Henry was hosting. He knew that, if he didn't move quickly, Burns could seriously damage his plans for rebellion.

The messenger at the door had a letter for her from her father. She was to meet him for lunch so she could meet with the man he'd employed from London as his personal assistant. She caught a carriage outside and rode to her father's club, Grosvener House, in the shadow of Edinburgh Castle. Her father was seated at his usual table, in a corner away from prying ears and eyes, with a young gentleman who had his back to her. As she approached the table, her father rose and walked around the table to greet her.

"Ah, there you are, my dear, and you are looking lovely as usual — better to be late than never to arrive." He leaned over and kissed her, avoiding her evil glare. The other gentleman also rose and waited patiently next to them. "Maggie, I'd like you to meet a new friend of mine." She turned and offered her hand to the man, who seemed to pause for a moment as if he was just coming to his senses.

"Madam, the pleasure is all mine, and if I might say, it is an honour to meet you at last. Richard Stone, at your service." He offered her the vacant chair and they all sat. "I've been looking forward to making your acquaintance for many days now. Unfortunately, my journey from London was delayed or I would have been here far sooner."

"The journey from London can be quite treacherous, especially in these troubled times."

"You speak more truth than you know, Miss Burns. The journey was indeed...eventful." Stone smiled ruefully as he took a sip of his wine. They'd already ordered lunch, and their food arrived quickly as most of the other diners had already headed to the sitting rooms. Burns and Stone continued their previous conversation, and Maggie listened closely while studying the men intently. Stone seemed, on first impression, to be younger than his physical years suggested. He couldn't have been any older than she was, and yet, she was unable to put an age to him. He was a big man, and it seemed to Maggie of far sturdier build than other young men of her acquaintance. He towered over her father and the others in the room, and she guessed him to be at least six feet tall. He was broad as an ox but held himself like a thoroughbred racing horse. The cutlery looked like matchsticks in his hands, but he used them with grace, and his whole demeanour was dignified. He would occasionally look at her and smile and she noticed he had the confidence of speech that most English gentleman seemed to possess. But his charm wasn't forced and her father seemed to be enjoying his company enormously.

As they were ordering dessert, a messenger arrived with a note for Sir Henry. Burns read the note quickly and there was a concerned look in his eyes when he raised his gaze from the page.

"Is something the matter, Sir Henry?" Stone asked quietly, as some people in the room were looking in their direction. Burns got slowly to his feet and asked for waiter his coat.

"I sincerely hope not," he replied. "But I'm afraid I must leave you two to finish lunch without me. There's been another disturbance at the newspaper, and I must make sure that no one has been hurt." The waiter came back to the table with Sir Henry's coat and the man helped him on with it. "I'll see you young people when you've finished up here."

"Are you sure you wouldn't like us to accompany you, Sir Henry?" Stone said with a worried look on his face. The old man contemplated the possibility for a moment but shook his head.

"Perhaps you would stay with my daughter, Richard, and finish lunch. After all, you will be working closely together and it seems appropriate for you to get to know each other a little better. It seemed to Maggie he had a wicked twinkle in his eye aimed at her.

"It would be an honour sir — if it is acceptable to Miss Burns of course."

"Maggie?" Burns asked with an amused expression on his face. He knew Maggie hated to be put on the spot. She looked at both of them, obviously trying to keep her face expressionless.

"I would be delighted, Mr. Stone. It would be a shame to let all this food and wine go to waste, after all."

"Good. I shall see you both later. Mr. Stone. Maggie."

"Be careful, Father." He gave her a quick kiss then left with the messenger who'd been waiting close by. She watched the empty space where he had been for a moment, then turned back to her new colleague at the table. Stone had been watching her face intently.

"I'm sure your father will be fine," he said reassuringly. He called the waiter over and ordered some more wine. His words hadn't eased her mind. She deliberately started up a new conversation to take her mind off her father, but she couldn't really concentrate on what Stone was saying in response.

"So Mr. Stone, you've come all the way from London to help us with the newspaper," she said, deliberately leading the conversation.

"Yes, that's true. But please, if we are to work together, do me the honour of calling me Richard."

"Of course," she replied. She felt a sudden urge to tease him a little, not only to bring her out of her gloom but also to see how he would respond. "Richard, it is…" She paused to take a sip from her newly charged glass. "You were going to say, about the newspaper," she continued. She had to take another sip of wine to stem the smile forcing its way to the surface. Stone looked uncertain for a fleeting moment, but he quickly realised he was being tested and composed himself. She was sure she caught a slight twinge of disappointment on his face after she failed to return the compliment.

"I'm here to help your father as his assistant. It seems your father is an extremely busy man and he needs someone to make sure his affairs are kept in order."

Maggie suddenly felt slightly guilty at being so rude to Stone as he seemed pleasant and quite sincere. She looked carefully at the other people seated around the room as Stone talked to her about what he used to do in London. She realised people watching had become a bit of a habit after her recent adventures.

"Richard," she interrupted him in mid-sentence. "I should apologise to you for being so rude, and for being so distant," she said, looking into his eyes. "The last couple of days have been a little…strange, and I haven't really been myself. Perhaps we could dine again tomorrow, if we have the time and if I'm not being too forward."

"I would like that very much," he said, smiling warmly at her. It was in fact the first time a woman had asked him to dine, and although not noticeably, he was quite taken aback. He was glad Maggie couldn't hear the beating of his heart because, to his ears, the roar was deafening, like a great bass drum.

After discussing the newspaper further and how they could work together in reducing Sir Henry's workload, Maggie felt they should return to the office to see what had dragged her father so urgently away. She started to rise, and Stone helped her with her chair and then helped her into her coat. Maggie called the waiter over and asked him to add the meal to her father's account. They decided to walk back to the office as it wasn't too far and the sun was shining. Stone had commented to her that he'd never visited

Edinburgh before, and so she felt it was her duty to show him some of the sites. Their conversation drifted to talk of the city, then to talk of London and other places they'd both visited. Maggie described the significance of the places of interest and landmarks as they passed, and as they neared their destination, Maggie felt suddenly sorry that the time had passed so quickly as she had been enjoying Richards's company immensely.

"I think it'll be very interesting working with you, Miss Burns," Stone said sincerely as they came in sight of the newspaper building.

"Please, Richard. It's only right that I offer you the same courtesy as you've shown me — please call me Maggie. After all, we will be working closely together." She said the last sentence mimicking his English accent. This time she was positive she saw him blush, and couldn't resist a triumphant smile. He looked down at her with a thoughtful expression on his face, and then he responded in the most absurd accent she'd ever heard.

"It would be a pleasure me wee bonny lassie to cal ye be the name ye wa burn wit," he said, scrunching his face in an effort to get the words out. The bizarre attempt at a Scottish accent sent Maggie into a fit of laughter, and when she'd pulled herself together Stone offered her his handkerchief to dab away the tears. As they continued up the street, Stone kept Maggie amused with his refusal to say anything until she had apologised for laughing at him. Neither of them took any notice as a young man hurried towards them carrying a bundle of papers. As he passed, he pulled out two pieces of paper from the pile and thrust them into Stone's hand. The couple stared at the paper bemused as the man ran by. They watched as he accosted another couple on the opposite side of the street to give them some paper as well. Stone looked at the crumpled sheets in his hand.

"Does it say anything?" Maggie asked.

"I think you should take a look at this," he said after a moment. Stone handed the paper to her. The writing was in bold black print:

COUNTRYMEN

ROUSED FROM THE TORPID STATE IN WHICH WE HAVE SUNK FOR SO MANY YEARS, WE ARE AT LENGTH COMPELLED FROM THE EXTREMITY OF OUR SUFFERINGS AND THE CONTEMPT HEAPED UPON OUR PETITIONS, REDUCED TO TAKE UP ARMS FOR THE

REDRESS OF OUR COMMON GRIEVANCES. OUR PRINCIPLES ARE FEW AND FOUNDED ON THE BASIS OF OUR CONSTITUTION, WHICH WAS PURCHASED WITH THE DEAREST BLOOD OF OUR ANCESTORS. WE HEREBY GIVE NOTICE OF OUR INTENT TO RESTORE OUR COUNTRY'S INHABITANTS TO THEIR NATIVE DIGNITY. LIBERTY OR DEATH!

Maggie paled as she read and her legs seemed to turn to jelly under her. Stone noticed groups gathering on street corners reading the pamphlets. Clifford had told him the campaign for rebellion was organised, but this was astounding. He shuddered at how far the plans might already have gone and what the consequences would be. He looked at Maggie and his stomach muscles suddenly tensed. He couldn't let her come to any harm. Without a word, he grabbed her hand and ushered her forward. They approached the newspaper building and could see Burns standing in front of a crowd.

"Father, what's happening?" Maggie cried out to him. Burns turned and spotted the couple coming towards him.

"Maggie, Richard, thank God you're both safe. There's no time to talk now. Get inside quickly."

"But Father..."

"There's no time, Maggie. Richard, take her inside, will you? I'll be along soon." He smiled at her, then turned back to the crowd. Richard took her gently by the arm and led her up the steps. When she looked back she saw her father addressing the crowd. More people were arriving quickly, swelling their numbers. Stone followed her stare and realised how dangerous the situation could become.

"Maggie, we must go inside. Don't worry. He'll be fine. The people won't hurt your father. He's the only man in Scotland who tells them the truth." As he said the words, he realised that was the single reason Cheltenham wanted Burns out of the way. He ushered her inside and turned back to survey the scene himself. The groups that had gathered were turning into a mob, taunting any wealthy looking people or soldiers in the street.

"Why is your father talking to them?"

Maggie took a moment to answer as she watched through the window. "It probably has something to do with the article we printed in today's issue." She turned and looked at him. "Have you read it?"

"Yes I have," he replied quietly. "Turn your backs on the troublemakers, things will get better, that sort of thing." He watched his new employer gesturing to the growing crowd.

"Usually a crowd gathers and protests about the lack of food or something like that," Maggie said. "They're generally very peaceful, and after a while, most get bored and go home. The police let them blow off a little steam, stomp around a bit and make a lot of noise. They feel they've made their point and go away. If no one makes any trouble, the police allow them to demonstrate and don't get involved." The strategy made sense to Stone, but he had an awful feeling that this crowd was going to turn into something far more than an easily assuaged and disorganized crowd.

They both noticed the rising commotion outside. A large group of people, a hundred or more, were marching down the street towards the centre of town waving flags and banners. Stone strained to read the slogans.

"Maggie, stay here. I'm going to fetch your father." He pushed open the door and leapt down the stairs two at a time. The crowd was chanting, their words becoming more audible as they came closer. Some of the banners the crowd carried had messages, others had images. Maggie read a sign written in bright scarlet letters as if in blood: ALL WHO WANT LIBERTY, RALLY TO OUR STANDARDS.

Maggie suddenly felt the world lurch around her feet, and she had to reach out to the wall for support. What they'd all feared most was finally happening, and she couldn't think of a single way to stop it.

CHAPTER 8

The banners read: LIBERTY OR DEATH. The same message had been written on the pamphlets distributed around the capital and probably in every other town in Scotland. One banner had the portrait of William Wallace and a message against tyranny and oppression scrawled underneath, but Maggie sensed something wasn't right about the crowd. People were joining the growing mass by the dozens and working themselves into frenzy, but the men in the centre of the mob, those who were carrying most of the banners, seemed unconcerned by the madness around them as if oblivious to the whole thing. From her vantage point she could see the group clearly. They were moving in time with each other as if they were marching, pushing the crowd along in front of them, almost forcing the people forward. She looked down the steps and saw Richard nearly dragging her father away. Stone pushed the door open and held it for her father to walk through.

"Thank you Richard," Burns said, a little sheepishly.

"Mr. Burns, it was better that you came inside. I can assure you there's going to be far more trouble in the city tonight than you've ever seen before."

"You may be right, my boy," Burns said bitterly. "But someone needs to try to calm them down." Stone turned and looked at them both. After a moment he smiled.

"Believe me sir when I tell you that there is no way you will be able to stop what is going to happen today." Sir Arthur and Maggie stared at him.

"What are you saying, Richard?" Burns replied. Stone looked form one to the other for a moment.

"We'll have time to discuss that later." He turned away from them and locked the door. "First we need to secure this building. Shut all the doors and windows and close the shutters. Mr. Burns, we don't have much time. Tell your staff to do the same. Stay well away from any windows that don't have shutters." He took the old man's arm. "Get your men to fill whatever they can with water — just in case." Burns paused for a moment to consider what Stone was saying, then he turned away and started issuing commands to his waiting staff. Stone watched with a grim expression as they carried out his orders. He grabbed one of the plants in the lobby and pulled it from its clay pot. He realised he had some serious explaining to do — he handed the empty pot to one of the staff to fill with water — but he knew it would be a while before he had the chance.

Shortly, the small demonstration turned into a carefully orchestrated full-scale riot throughout the entire city. Stone had taken up a position in the highest room in the building. With a telescope he borrowed from Mr. Burns, he studied the developing situation in detail. After a couple of hours of continually watching the crowds, he'd managed to pick out a number of men from among the rioters whom he believed were some of the ringleaders, probably mercenaries, he thought. They were obviously, well trained, disciplined, and very well organised. He guessed Cheltenham had hired them and given them instructions to be as destructive as possible. So it didn't seem all that odd to him when he spotted a bunch of men who were heavily robed and causing huge amounts of damage to shops and houses.

The rioting had spread so quickly and was so well organized that neither the local militia nor the army had a chance to mobilize in any kind of force. As Stone scoured the main contingent of the mob for men he might recognise again, a group of militia walked out of a side alley near some of the protesters. One of the militiamen stepped out and tried to seize one of the banners. Unfortunately for the young soldier, the man who held the banner was one of those Stone had identified as one of the ringleaders. The mercenary punched the militiaman in the face and chest and knocked him to the ground. As the other officers rushed in, another mercenary barked a command and a number of men rushed from both sides of the crowd. The militiamen were quickly overpowered and beaten to the ground. Once the crowd committed themselves to first blood, the situation deteriorated completely. The men who had attacked the militiamen raced around smashing windows and doors as they encouraged others to do the same. Then burning torches were thrown into some of the buildings without a thought to who might be inside. One group tore metal railings from building facades and armed themselves. Stone heard the first sounds of gunfire in the distance.

When the sun disappeared, the streets were bathed in darkness — no one would be lighting the street lamps tonight. Some of the rioters had lit torches, however, and flecks of light raced through the night like enormous fireflies. In some places, Stone could see a greater glow from his position, which he assumed were buildings on fire. Stone shut the windows and the shutters and folded the telescope away. Leaning back against the wooden shutters, his thoughts switched to Cheltenham and the strange monk he'd seen in the woods only a few days earlier. He told himself yet one more time that he was horribly out of his depth. He almost dreaded what tomorrow would bring.

The destruction could be heard throughout the night and into the early morning — gunfire, shouting, screaming — and Maggie slept restlessly, fearful that the mob would break into the building at any moment. She still couldn't quite believe let alone understand what was happening. She woke up once in the middle of the night to complete silence, climbed out of bed, and opened her window. Her room was far too high up in the building for any missiles to be accurate if thrown at her, but even so, she looked out the window with caution. She heard the scuffling feet of people running down the street far below her. Except for a few lights emanating from random buildings, the city was dark. She looked for a few minutes then closed the window and went back to bed. She lay there for a while unable to sleep, and as she finally drifted to sleep, her thoughts were of Richard Stone.

At 6:30 in the morning, Maggie climbed out of bed, put on a set of outdoor clothes just in case she had to leave in a hurry, and then went to the dining room. She was greeted by the fresh smell of Jasmine tea and warm newly baked bread. Her father was seated at the head of the table reading over some reports from around the city. Stone was sitting next to him also reading through some of the information. As she entered, both stopped what they were doing and stood to greet her.

"How are you, my dear?" Burns said immediately.

"I'm fine, Father." She looked at their tired eyes. "Have you two slept at all?" The two men looked at each other.

"A little," Burns said, pouring her some tea. He gestured to the food in front of him. "If there's one thing we can rely on come rain or storm, its Mr. Drummond keeping his bakery up and running." Maggie forced a smile.

"Is the riot over, Father?" She clenched the teacup in both hands for the warmth as he passed some of the reports to her.

"I'm afraid not, my dear. Richard went outside this morning to confirm what we'd already read in these reports."

"The mob is back on the streets this morning," Stone told her. "The groups aren't as well organised as they were last night, which in some respects makes the situation more dangerous." She sat down opposite them.

"Was anyone hurt...or killed?" The thought made her slightly nauseous.

"We haven't heard of any deaths as yet, but there were some people hurt, mainly the local militia, we think," Stone said. "Damage to shops and homes has been the main focus of the rioters. I think we need to assume the situation will get worse before it gets any better." Burns stood up before Stone had finished and walked to the door.

"Richard and I have been discussing the situation," he said. "And he's divulged some interesting information to me." Burns whistled and Rufus came bounding into the dining room. Burns then closed the door and looked sympathetically at Stone. "Don't be too hard on him, my dear." He smiled wanly at Maggie. "Try to let Richard explain before you react." Maggie looked hard at Stone from across the table, which prompted him to take a sip of his tea to wet his already dry throat.

"I'm afraid I haven't been totally truthful with you or your father, Maggie," Stone said quietly as he looked into Maggie's eyes. Maggie peered back at him in silence. "I was sent from London by Horse Guards to watch you and your father." He was hoping she wouldn't ask any questions before he'd finished. His story was shaky in his own head without Maggie confusing him even more. He'd spent most of the night getting his story straight, and his ultimate goal was to convince both Maggie and Sir Henry that he could be trusted so he could get Maggie out of the city and to safety as soon as possible. Stone was happy to betray Cheltenham, but he'd grown fond of Sir Henry and he wanted to escape with Maggie as painlessly as possible. That meant Stone needed Maggie's consent to leave, and if possible, Sir Henry's blessing, but the latter was not ultimately necessary.

"I'm a British officer Maggie," he said. "As I've already explained to your father, I was ordered to watch you by people in the highest authority. However, from what I've learned over the last few days, I believe that order was not only ill advised but unlawful. Therefore, I have taken it upon myself to disregard this direct order and to tell you why I was sent here." Maggie continued to sit in silence as Stone continued. "I was ordered to send the authority in Horse Guards any information that might suggest your newspaper was either challenging the crown or unwilling to help silence the critics of the British government by allowing insurgents to issue statements in the newspaper." Stone paused and deliberately tried to look awkward as if he was embarrassed by his revelations. "If I found any such information, then Horse Guards would use it to find you and your father guilty of treason and the government would then take control of your newspaper." For some reason he didn't think Maggie was convinced.

"Maggie, Richard has been following us both for some time now, and he is slightly concerned about what you've been up to for the past few days. Do you have something you wish to tell me, my dear?" The question hung in the air for a moment while Maggie blushed with embarrassment.

"Maggie, I followed you to your meeting with the monks yesterday and overheard every word," Stone confessed. In fact he'd learned far more in the woods than he was ever going to let anyone know, for their very lives depended on not hearing the whole story. Maggie's eyes flashed with anger and Stone realised he should have let her confess before prematurely confirming her guilt.

"I was going to tell you eventually father, but I wasn't sure how much of the monks' story was true. I wanted to confirm the story before bothering you with it because I know you're so busy at the moment." She looked at her father with tears in her eyes and an apology in her expression. Burns lifted a piece of leftover bacon off a plate and threw it for Rufus, who was lying obediently at his feet.

"I think last night was confirmation of the monk's involvement, don't you agree?" he replied grimly. "It's not your fault, Maggie. The situation was outside your understanding, and the monks had no right to involve you without contacting me first." He stood in thought for a moment, watching Rufus chew on the bacon. "Richard has been watching the city all night," he continued, "and he has confirmed that the monks are involved and are possibly in a position of great authority with the ringleaders. Now Maggie, you need to tell me everything you know about these monks so I can formulate a plan to stop this country from plunging into civil war. I'm not convinced they have been telling you the entire truth and they seem to have far more resources than one would expect from a group of monks."

Stone sat back and watched Maggie as she told of her interaction with the monks over the last few days. Both Sir Henry and Maggie were obviously convinced of the truth of his story, but from what Burns had said, Stone couldn't afford for the old man to delve too deeply into the monks' affairs. It looked like he had to make plans to get Maggie out of the city sooner rather than later, before Burns found out too much about what was going on. His only option was to get Maggie to contact Ruth, so she could persuade Maggie to leave without her father knowing. The difficulty was not lost on him: the only way he could see Maggie escaping the city unharmed was by getting their enemies, who ultimately wanted to destroy Cheltenham, to help them. As Stone sat sipping his tea, he realised he would do anything in his power to protect Maggie, even if it meant betraying everything he had come to believe in.

CHAPTER 9

By midmorning, the effects of the previous day's rioting could be seen across the whole of southwest Scotland. Radicals in every town had risen in conjunction with the riots in Edinburgh in a well-organised and well-funded campaign. The regular garrisons in Glasgow and Edinburgh were standing to arms, and a thousand-strong Regiment of the 1st Battalion Rifle Brigade waited in their barracks, as yet not unleashed through the city. A small number of artillery pieces had been rolled out and stationed at vantage points around the most troubled areas, but as Burns had previously hoped, they were ordered to hold their fire until the situation became critical.

The majority of citizens in Edinburgh awoke to a tense and confused atmosphere, the like of which hadn't been felt since the uprising of 1745. Proclamations could be seen everywhere, on the walls and windows of houses and littering the streets of the city, and as the morning drew on, the streets began to fill with people again. It seemed that all inhabitants of the city had hurried out to read the proclamations and inspect the devastation of the day before. Those who couldn't read listened with rapt attention as the posters were read aloud to the crowds of onlookers.

Two abreast, a column of sixty Hussars cantered purposefully along the weather beaten road towards Edinburgh. Despite their flamboyant blue, crimson, and gold uniforms being coated with dust from a hard ride, the soldiers held themselves upright and alert in their saddles. They rode in impeccable order as if they were back on the parade ground even though they were alone on the road and tired to the bone. The sun had long since risen behind them and the road was bathed in early morning light, but the clear brightness of the sunshine did little to ease the nerves of the men in the column. Anxious glances were cast continually at the wayside, bushes, and trees from under their black fur shakos. Major James Peters, Deputy Quartermaster General of his Majesty King George IV's army in Scotland, also shared the men's fear of ambush, but he kept his eyes resolutely on the road in front.

Major Peters considered this journey to be unnecessarily dangerous, and the fact that he had been ordered to undertake it was almost as incredible as the news brought to his garrison earlier yesterday evening. A despatch rider from Lt. Colonel North's 1st Battalion of Rifles stationed in Edinburgh Castle had arrived with the astonishing news that all southwest Scotland had risen in open rebellion and a ten thousand strong rebel army was besieging Edinburgh itself. Colonel North's force needed immediate assistance.

There had been rumblings of a general uprising for the last few years, but no one, as Peters recalled, had ever taken the matter very seriously. On hearing the news from the dispatch rider, the Commander in Chief of the army in Scotland, Major General Sir Thomas Bradley, had radiated great calm, or so it appeared to Peters. He immediately ordered a squadron of the 10th Hussars to escort the entire General Staff to Edinburgh, and he left orders at his headquarters to make preparations to secure the country from any attack in his absence.

To rush through to Edinburgh, before ascertaining the exact extent of the uprising, was to Peters an enterprise lacking in any wisdom. After Sir Thomas had relayed orders to his staff, Peters took the unfortunate messenger aside, out of the General's sight, and gave the man a good dressing down in order to get as much information as possible. Peters accosted the messenger more out of frustration at the General's orders than anything else, but all the same, Peters couldn't help feeling that something was amiss with the messenger. The man was clearly unshaven, and his uniform was old and tatty and didn't fit him properly. The messenger also had a look about him that reeked of insolence and disrespect. If Peters had taken more time to question the rider, the fact that the messenger had never worn a British uniform before or ever served in a British Regiment would have been quickly exposed, but there hadn't been time and now the Hussars, with the General at the head of the column, were riding under false pretences against an unknown, fabricated enemy and a very well laid trap.

In the villages and towns along their route to the capital, crowds of people had rushed onto the streets to jeer at the soldiers as they passed. In Airdrie, people had even thrown stones and rotten vegetables that struck men and horses alike. The Hussars hadn't broken formation or even acknowledged the crowd's existence, and with eyes front, had ridden stoically through the barrage of missiles until the people were out of sight. Apart from these minor interruptions, the countryside beyond the garrison had revealed no other sign of insurgent activity. Just the same, Peters reasoned that any rebels in their right mind would take any opportunity to assassinate the Commander in Chief if they had half a chance. His instincts told him that the most likely place for an attack would be in the suburbs of Edinburgh. Attackers could appear then melt away without a trace into the protection of the houses.

Apprehensively, Peters peered through the haze at the General's short, thickset figure, shrouded in a greatcoat to keep out the chill of the morning, riding immediately ahead of him. At the age of fifty-two, Sir Thomas had managed the military affairs of Scotland for less than one year. He was a blunt, outspoken Yorkshire man and a hardworking and a proficient Commander, whose real talents lay away from the battlefield and behind an administrator's desk. Unfortunately, he was a man brought up in the old school of military occupation — crushing any and all radical agitators to "teach them a damned fine lesson" — and now he had the perfect opportunity to do so.

The men noticeably braced themselves as the first buildings on the outskirts of the city appeared in the distance. Sabres rattled in their scabbards as the men tested their looseness in preparation for an attack, and the cloths protecting powder from the rain were taken off the firing pans of their carbines. They neared a blind corner in the road ahead, surrounded on both sides by tall hedges, the first perfect place for an ambush. Peters felt the nervous tension in his stomach move up to his throat. Instinctively he moved his hand to the cold hilt of his sword. He felt more secure in its presence but it didn't stop the beads of sweat appearing on his brow.

The horse carrying the General suddenly came to a halt and Peters suspected Sir Thomas was going to send a scouting party ahead. Sir Thomas then raised his hand slowly into the air signalling the column to a halt. All eyes remained transfixed on their Commander, who sat silent and unmoving. The only movement came from his greatcoat as it was tugged and blown by the wind. Suddenly, out of the silence, the sound of hooves on cobbles came from around the corner. They grew steadily louder as three riders appeared from out of the haze in front of them. As the three riders squared up to the column, they reined in their mounts and stopped twenty feet from the General. Peters flinched as one of the horses behind him in the ranks skittered and shifted. The General suddenly urged his horse forward at a trot and rode towards the three strangers. Peters couldn't believe his eyes as his Commanding Officer moved away from the protection of the column, putting his life at unnecessary risk.

"Sir," Peters called out to get his attention.

"Remain here, damn it!" Sir Thomas barked back, not even turning or slowing his horse's step. As the General approached the strange horsemen, the rider in the centre lowered the hood of his travelling coat.

"A pleasure to meet you again General," he called out in a raspy voice through a toothy grin.

"So, he's sent you to me, has he?" Sir Thomas replied as he reined in his horse. "Can't say you're the best thing I've seen on this journey so far Clifford, but then it hasn't started raining yet, has it?" he said vehemently. The General knew Clifford's reputation because he'd used the man's services often enough. He detested being in the assassin's presence, and deemed it an insult to have to even speak to him in person for Clifford had no honour, no country, and no respect for anyone or anything. He was, in Sir Thomas's opinion, the worst type person any man could be without being the devil himself. "I see your little rebellion has begun to take root already," Sir Thomas continued, obviously having to force his conversation.

"Yes. Actually, it's been hard work, now that you mention it," Clifford replied with a sickly grin. "But at the same time, rather enjoyable...and profitable, eh General," he said with a wink.

Peters was unable to hear what they were saying. He studied the two other men who had remained silent. The man to the right seemed normal enough, but the rider to the left was massively built. The man's horse was far bigger than the other two and he was stooped in the saddle, so the first impression that he was no larger than his companions was deceptive. But Peters could now see that the man would be easily six and a half feet tall.

"Your men look in good form General," Clifford said, surveying the long column of Hussars. The General gritted his teeth — Clifford was clearly already getting under his skin.

"They're good men," Bradley answered with a growl. "And when this country really comes apart, it's these men and not your French mercenaries who'll gain all the glory, so don't you forget it."

Clifford raised his hands in defence. "Of course, of course, they will General," he said with a smirk. "I would never deny you the glory of dying in battle." The smirk had now gone from

Clifford's face. "Fortunately, our mutual leaders have decreed that your name will indeed go down in history as a major contributor to our little war, but the uprising has been slow in starting. So, unfortunately for you, the first chapter of this war will be written by me right here on this path." The rider to Clifford's left gave a muffled laugh.

Peters heard the laugh from where he was sitting and the breath caught in his throat as a sudden dreadful fear pierced his heart. Then, without warning, the huge man to the right turned his horse and trotted back around the corner.

Clifford seemed surprised for a moment as he watched the man go, but with a shrug, he turned back and drew a pistol from his belt. Aiming at the General's head, he pulled back the trigger and fired. Sir Thomas couldn't have been more than two feet away and the force of the shot blasted the back of his head wide open and threw him from his horse into the muddy path, the puddles of water filling with dark red blood. Peters froze in terror, his eyes locked on the crumpled form of the General lying sprawled in the mud. He seemed to hear the General's murderer shouting orders, but he couldn't hear the man clearly through his stunned senses. Then he realised why he hadn't been able to focus on what the man was shouting. The words were unmistakable now he could hear him shouting his orders in French.

In seconds the front rank of Hussars, all seasoned campaigners, realising their second in command was too stunned to issue orders, were already drawing their swords and charging forward. As they rushed past their incapacitated officer, the hedges on either side of the road seemed to come alive, and ranks of men appeared from behind them with rifles raised. A terrible volley of gunfire rang out as a score or more men fired into the charging ranks of Hussars. The first wave of riders was annihilated in an instant, horses and men falling under a shower of lead and smoke. The breeze blew the smoke and noise into the faces of the second rank of charging riders that were spurring their mounts into the onslaught. The next volley thundered out a heartbeat after the first, and as Peters watched the world in slow motion, he seemed to see every bullet hit home, the lead, flesh and blood mingling into one nightmare. The second barrage bit deep into the confused ranks of Hussars and downed another dozen men. Thankfully, the smoke from the rifles began to obscure the aim of their attackers as they'd fired their next volley. Peter's senses suddenly came back to him as he realised his men weren't being attacked by a group of disorganised rebels but by very well disciplined and well trained soldiers, possibly foreign mercenaries.

The gunfire started to come sporadically now that the order to fire at will having been given by Sir Thomas's killer. Peters could see the man through the smoke. He was sitting calmly on his horse issuing orders and directing the battle. Peter's realised the only option open to them now was to retreat. If anything, he had to escape to make sure Horse Guards knew what had happened. This was no chance ambush and must have been planned well in advance. In a few more minutes, these men, Peters' men, would all be completely annihilated. Taking one last look at his fallen General, Peters spurred his horse and galloped back down the track barking the order to retreat as he passed his remaining men. He felt bullets whizzing about his head and body as he galloped away. The air remained filled with the noise of gunfire, screaming men and horses lying together on the ground, their blood gathering in dark pools like from a rainstorm. Peter's miraculously rode by the carnage without being struck by the hail of lead still spitting from the trees and bushes. He felt the presence of riders around him as his remaining men regained control of their mounts and spurred away in retreat on his command.

The noise of gunfire began to fade as their mounts galloped back down the road in the direction they had come. Peters dared not slow down their escape as their attackers would certainly be in pursuit. It was obvious to Peter's that their enemy, whoever it was, clearly didn't want anyone to tell the tale of this ambush.

He led the men back down the path at full gallop for a few more miles hoping to put as much distance from the enemy as possible before taking a rest. Peters was formulating the report in his head that he would give when he got back to headquarters when he spotted the fields off the road that he had hoped to reach and the comfort of open ground. Peter's hit the first gap in the hedge at full speed in the knowledge that safety was only a few seconds away, but as the riders plunged into the field, they spotted the mass of crouching figures in the field only twenty paces ahead, fifty muskets levelled to the firing position and aimed at the dozen remaining horsemen. With a muffled curse against his dead General, Peters bellowed a final order to charge with all the hatred he could muster. The cry died in his throat as smoke and noise filled the air once again and Peter's was plucked from his horse by a dozen bullets. His body was shredded to pieces and fell motionless into the newly ploughed field. A single volley was enough to fell the remaining riders, and any dying men were butchered mercilessly with bayonets to make sure none were left alive to tell the tale.

The rebels had won a famous victory, and within a day, the news of the slaughter had been broadcast across the country. The massacre had sealed the start of the rebellion and a war that neither the Scottish nor English people ever really found out how it all began.

CHAPTER 10

Throughout the rioting in the city, the newspaper building remained untouched by violence. Cheltenham had sent express orders to Du Puy that the building and the people remaining inside were to be unharmed. Cheltenham saw the building as a perfect headquarters when he eventually arrived in the capital, but it was also one of the finest properties in the city and he wanted to own it for himself.

On the same morning that the column of Hussars was destroyed by Du Puy and Cheltenham's men, a dozen monks marched up to the newspaper building and requested immediate entry. Cheltenham had sent orders to Du Puy to make sure the occupants of the building, especially Sir Henry, were put under house arrest so they couldn't cause any trouble. For the moment, the monks were present in the newspaper building under the guise of protection for Henry Burns, his family and workers, a false measure that had been proposed to Sir Henry by Ruth.

So when the residents of the newspaper building awoke that morning, they found every entrance and exit guarded by tough looking men in robes who barely spoke, and restricted access to and from the building. The Captain of the Guard presented a very distraught Sir Henry Burns with a letter from Ruth stating she had been given word that his family and staff had been targeted by insurgents and that her men were there for his protection. Burns was less than convinced by the letter, sceptical that anyone in the city would want to harm him or his daughter, but the Captain was adamant about his orders and Burns realised he had very little choice in the matter as every monk was armed to the teeth and he and his staff were defenceless. He feigned thanks to the Captain for his service, but Burns realised he was being manipulated — by whom he couldn't yet guess. Burns spent the rest of the morning composing a letter to Major General Sir Thomas Bradley, the commander in chief of the army in Scotland, about his predicament and the situation in the city. Burns was sure the General must already be aware of the rebellion and was probably taking measures, but he doubted the General was aware of the part the monks were playing in the revolt and knew he would appreciate the information.

Burns intended to sneak the letter out of the building later and send it to the General's headquarters south of Edinburgh. Little did Burns know that the crumpled and bloody body of the General was lying in a military morgue, the army had been left in complete disarray, and Cheltenham, his plans running like clockwork, had assumed command of the army and was already on his way north to pick a well-planned fight with the entire Scottish people.

When Burns dismissed the Captain of the monks guarding the building, the Captain sought out Stone and presented him with another letter this time from Clifford. The letter was straightforward and to the point and Stone read it almost with relief — it was time for Maggie to disappear and Stone supposed begin her search for the body of William Wallace and fulfil her promise to the monks. Stone had been sitting in the library contemplating his next move when the Captain again found him for his answer. The arrival of the monks in the building had prompted Stone to rethink his escape plans for Maggie, and this letter from Clifford confirmed how in control the monks really were. The letter was not so much a request but an order, and as he read it he could feel the eyes of the Captain boring into him. Stone sensed any refusal could meet with serious consequences, and he gave thanks again for the information he'd heard in the woods after following Ruth. Stone looked up at the Captain and nodded his acceptance, and the Captain saluted, turned on his heel, and marched out of the room. Stone scrunched the letter into a ball, threw it into the fire, and watched it burn. He realised in that instant, as the paper disintegrated before him, how much he loved Maggie and how much he feared for her safety. The monks and Cheltenham now had total control, and the only way for Maggie to survive was for her to abandon her father and leave Edinburgh as soon as possible. Stone had to follow his orders until the opportunity to escape presented itself. But before they could leave he had the infinitely more difficult task of persuading Maggie to leave without telling her father what she was doing. For Stone that meant living with the fact that Maggie would leave and might never see her father alive again.

The doors to the library suddenly burst open and one of Sir Henry's aides stumbled through, almost falling over the monk guards standing inside the room. In a split second, the two monks leapt in front of him, blocking the path to the room with swords pressed to the poor man's throat. With a petrified squeal, he asked one of the huge guards if he could relay a message to his master, Sir Henry. One of the guards looked over his shoulder at Stone, who gestured for the messenger to be sent over.

"I'll give the message to Sir Henry."

"Thank you, sir," the young man whispered, not taking his eyes off the huge men, who had returned to their posts on either side of the library doors as if nothing had happened. The messenger passed the note to Stone. "The letter came two minutes ago by government courier, sir," he declared, a little sheepishly. "I was told to bring it straight to Sir Henry. I didn't mean to interrupt sir," he said, with his head bowed.

"No, you did the right thing lad," Stone assured him, patting him on the back. Stone quickly read through the letter while the messenger stood there. "Thank you er...Patrick isn't it?"

"Yes sir," the boy replied, a little more confidently, pleased that Stone had remembered who he was.

"That will be all. Thank you, Patrick. Please wait outside just in case I have other tasks for you." He smiled at the lad, who flushed with pride at Stone's praise. Stone re-read the letter as the messenger left the room, taking a moment to commit it to memory, and being careful not to show any emotion to the guards at the door. The letter was plain and to the point, like all military and government correspondences: *Column of sixty Hussars ambushed and massacred by radicals outside Edinburgh. The whole military power of the district will be employed in the most decisive manner to prevent the laws of the land from being violated by the disloyal. The consequences must be on the heads of those that have seduced and misled the inhabitants. These consequences will be fatal to ALL who resist the overwhelming power at our disposal. GOD SAVE THE KING.*

The letter was signed by Sir Arthur Cheltenham. Stone folded the letter and looked up at the two monks by the doors, who in turn were watching his every move. "So the war has begun," he thought. "God save us all."

At six o clock in the evening of the same day, the Riot Act was read to the city by Cheltenham's forces. Later, when the streets had still not cleared of the mob, the cavalry was ordered into action. Rallies headed by radical leaders and attended by large crowds of local people were charged at indiscriminately, the cavalry advancing on the crowds with their swords drawn, their orders to arrest the ringleaders. They managed to trample several people to death, including women and children, without capturing a single ringleader. Many hundreds more were injured in the onslaught. Later troops of the 9th Hussars galloped into town to reinforce their comrades, but they were also looking for revenge for their slaughtered comrades. By early morning, an uneasy quiet had descended on the town, and hundreds of bodies littered the streets, the people too scared to remove them. Cheltenham was systematically causing murder and mayhem in a deliberate attempt to provoke more common people to the insurgent's banner.

The mood in the Burns household was low. Messages were passed backwards and forwards all the next day between Burns and Government House. The Governor insisted his sources were telling him the majority of people still did not want rebellion, and he couldn't account for all the violence that was happening throughout the city.

By late morning on the fourth day, the crowds were once more out on the streets, but in far greater numbers than before. The cavalry managed to contain most of the crowds in designated areas until three companies of the 79th regiment arrived. As these reinforcements marched down Princes Street towards a depleted line of their cavalry, an enormous crowd suddenly charged them from the left, seemingly from out of nowhere. The soldiers were met with a shower of stones, and sharp shooters dressed in robes began to fire at them from high positions. Men in the front rank received fatal head wounds in the barrage and the hail of lead. Instead of firing a volley into the air, which might have scared the attackers into flight, the commanding officer, realising the potential for slaughter, ordered his men to fire directly into the crowd, decimating the rioters. He then ordered the cavalry to charge and disperse the remaining rioters, and wounded men were trampled to death in the process. The initial charge broke up the bulk of the crowd but could not be followed up. Planks had been laid on the street to impede the cavalry's progress, and any ringleaders who had been targeted escaped into the mass of fleeing townspeople and went into hiding.

Five more monks arrived at the newspaper building that evening with another fake message stating it was time for Maggie to go out and find the location of the tomb of William Wallace on the premise that Ruth's men could find it before the rebels. Sir Henry was still in his study, so Stone ushered Maggie into the library. Taking her aside to a corner of the library, so he could talk to her in private, he explained to her that the monks in the building had volunteered to be at her side and each one was committed to going on the journey to assist her in finding the body of William Wallace. Stone took her hand as Maggie sat listening in silence.

"Each one of Ruth's men has pledged their lives to you, Maggie, and would die before seeing you come to any harm." Stone understood how powerful guilt could be as a weapon. He knew Maggie would never be able to refuse doing what Ruth wanted because Maggie believed so much had been done to protect her already.

"I understand," Maggie replied quietly. She already put so much trust in what Ruth wanted that she was quite willing to do anything that was asked of her.

"Do you need anything before we leave, Maggie?" Stone asked.

"I'll need to go to the city library before going anywhere," Maggie replied. "There's a piece of information about Cardinal Beeton that I must have to be able begin my search."

"Maggie," Stone said softly, and he felt his heart miss a beat as Maggie's green eyes locked onto his. Stone prayed that, coursing through her veins, Maggie might have some of the feelings for him he felt for her; otherwise his plans and his love would be shattered in an instant. "There's one thing I need to ask you to do, otherwise our mission will fail before it has begun." He took her hand and could feel it trembling, but if it was through fear, he couldn't tell. He prayed it was because he had just touched her. He didn't hesitate or draw out the moment. "Maggie, I'm certain your father will not let you leave Edinburgh because of the danger outside these walls, but we are going to have to leave tonight — and you will not be able to say goodbye to your father. He loves you too much to see you come to any harm." He moved closer and enclosed both her hands within his. He was so close now he could smell her sweet perfume, and it was intoxicating. He felt his love for her flooding out of his body and hoped it would soak into her skin so she would love him in return.

"You cannot tell your father you are leaving, Maggie," he whispered. He felt her shoulders shudder and her hands begin to shake harder as if she was trying desperately to keep her emotions inside. "It's best that we all leave tonight without your father knowing where you've gone. That way we can save him the pain of saying goodbye. He must let you go, Maggie. You know that, and this way, we save you both from anger and emotion." He paused for a moment to let Maggie think about what he was saying. "You know in your heart it's what you must do, and I know how difficult it will be to leave without saying goodbye, but you must do it." Maggie slowly broke free of his grip, stood up, and walked over to the window so Stone couldn't see her face. Maggie stood at the window in silence for five minutes, even though it was boarded up and she couldn't see outside. Then she slowly turned back to face the room with only a hint of emotion on her eyes.

"Very well," she said in a strong solid voice, "but on two conditions."

"What are your conditions?" Stone asked.

"I leave my father a note explaining why I've left without saying goodbye and Rufus comes along with us as well." Stone had to fight hard to keep from smiling, so he simply nodded in acceptance.

Maggie wandered over to a table where she'd left a pile of books. The only way to control the mix of emotions cascading through her body was to focus her mind on something completely different. She picked up one of the books and read through the paragraph she'd found earlier in the day. The book revealed a small piece of information about Cardinal Beeton and where his family estate was situated. The estate had apparently fallen into the hands of another Catholic family, who kept the house relatively unchanged across generations and over the centuries. The author referenced another book that had more detail about the estate, which Maggie needed to retrieve from the library before they left the city. She put the book back on the table and then looked at Stone, who was busily writing a list of supplies they would need to take on the journey. There were some emotions in her body that she didn't want to push aside because they felt wonderful even though she also felt so wretched about leaving her father. As she watched Stone, she felt her pulse quicken, and suddenly the room felt very warm. She wanted to feel him close to her again so he could ease her pain, but she realised his touch would be to satisfy something more physical than that, she suddenly wanted to smile and the thought of leaving wasn't as terrible as before.

The group of travellers were to leave Edinburgh under the cover of darkness and travel as far as they could from the city before morning, and then continue throughout the following day. The small company gathered in the courtyard of the newspaper building where

Stone and the monks checked all their equipment. Sir Henry had retired for the evening, and Stone had posted a guard at the door to the bedroom to make sure their departure wasn't discovered.

Stone watched Maggie check her gear and wondered if she was up to the long journey they had ahead of them. He was unsure if she could survive the many months, even years they might have to spend on the run if they wanted to escape Cheltenham's grasp. On reflection, he decided she was probably made of sturdier stuff than he gave her credit for and that she would probably fare better than most men in the same position. Stone quietly walked over to her, almost hating having to take her away from her old way of life, but time was of the essence. He cleared his throat.

"Maggie, it's time we were moving." Maggie looked up at him and nodded her head in silence. He offered her his hand, and she put her foot in the stirrup, took his hand, and climbed into the saddle. The monks who were left to guard the building watched as Stone mounted his grey stallion, a beast he'd handpicked from Sir Henry's stable. "We'll send word back in a few days to let Ruth know where we are," Stone said from the saddle to the nearest monk. With a parting salute, he then turned and led the party through the gates. Rufus plodded silently behind, sniffing at the horses' legs, then pausing briefly to look back at his old home.

CHAPTER 11

The small group of travellers rode cautiously through the darkened city. Stone led them to the rear of the city's library, making sure they stayed to the back streets so they could remain hidden from prying eyes. When they reached the library, Stone made everyone dismount and then walked over to Maggie and whispered in her ear.

"Are you sure we need to be here?" She looked at him for a moment, and then nodded her head. "Very well," he replied, "but let's be quick." He posted a guard at the end of the lane and at the rear door of the library, and when he was satisfied their position was well covered, he let Maggie make her way to the building.

Maggie led the party into the library using a key the librarian had given her so she could use the facility "out of hours." In the darkness, she could sense the galleries of books around her as she headed to the clerks room where she knew the candles were kept. In a gallery to her left, Maggie sensed movement and immediately thought one of the monks had circled around beside her. Looking behind, she counted the dark shapes of Stone and the monks coming into the room behind her — they were all there. Her legs froze to the floorboards as she realised they weren't alone in the building. She was about to alert Stone when she saw a bright flash in the corner of her eye, and instinctively she dove for cover as the air erupted with the sound of gunfire. A ball of hot lead struck a wooden beam inches from her head. The sound was deafening, echoing around the cavernous spaces in the roof of the building. Another bullet smashed into the wooden panelling in front of Stone's face, sending splinters into his eyes and making him flinch violently to the left. The flashes of light were accentuated in the darkness and temporarily blinded Maggie as she lay on the floor. Acrid smoke filled the air as the library was turned into a battleground. In the second that the gun was fired, Stone had shouted for everyone to get down on the floor, and then his voice became lost as the air was filled with the noise of two more gunshots.

Stone was momentarily stunned by the shock of the ferocious onslaught, but as his senses came back, he ordered the monks to fan out on either side of him. He told them to keep their heads down but not to return fire. If their attackers were in any way connected to Cheltenham, then Stone didn't want to complicate matters by leaving the library scattered with corpses. He could hear men reloading across the room, which confirmed there were probably only three attackers, but he couldn't be sure. Besides, he reminded himself, each man could have any number of weapons with him. Listening intently in the silence, he realised there were only four men at the most. Stone looked to his left and right and saw his own men now guarded the entrance and the exit to the building. Whoever their attackers were, they would have to fight to get out of the building alive.

The smoke cleared slightly and he could faintly see three men through the haze. They were standing behind some shelves with a fourth man behind them and frantically looking for something among the shelves. Stone could see Maggie crouching on the floor in front of him, and he made an attempt to move towards her. Immediately, two guns responded to the movement. The bullets crashed around their ears, sending wood and paper flying about the room. Stone signalled the monks to his right, who had the best angle, to fire back but to aim high. As they fired, sending more smoke into the air, Stone rushed forward and dropped down beside the shaking woman. Quickly checking she was alright, he then weighed his options in the remaining seconds before their attackers could see through the smoke that was temporarily hiding them from view. He quickly made a decision and said a silent prayer to any God that might be listening. Raising himself slightly from the floor, he called out to the attackers.

Du Puy, Grandmaster of the Knights Hospitaler, had watched the small party of travellers from behind a bookcase as they entered the library. Du Puy had set out with three French mercenaries as soon as he received word from his knights that Stone and Maggie had left the newspaper building, managing to arrive at the library just before them. He'd had little time to prepare an ambush but all his other plans were falling nicely into place. The rebellion had begun as planned, and Cheltenham was marching on Scotland with his English army and Du Puy's own army was being readied to crush Cheltenham as soon as the opportunity presented itself.

All that remained to make Du Puy's destiny complete was to find the one symbol that would consolidate his position of power in

Scotland, but his keen instincts had told him that Maggie Burns could jeopardize that plan. Du Puy had received word some weeks previously that Clifford unsurprisingly had betrayed him by taking a king's ransom in gold from Cheltenham to assassinate him when Du Puy was of no more use. Therefore, considering any number of assassins could be lying in wait, the safest place for Du Puy to be until his army met Cheltenham's on the battlefield was anonymity. Du Puy had decided to become part of the mission to find the body of Wallace and he had the perfect plan to make it happen. Not only could he remain safe under an assumed name as part of the group, but he could directly manipulate Maggie to make sure she didn't veer away from her task. If he was lucky, he might be able to dispose of Clifford at the same time. As he stood waiting in the fog of gunpowder he hoped his men, assigned to protect Burns, had received their new orders.

"Gentlemen!" Stone shouted across the room. "You may have observed that you are outnumbered and surrounded. We've blocked the exits and there are reinforcements outside." He thought a little lie might go a long way in this situation. Stone didn't get a response and he couldn't see any movement from behind the bookcases, and so he raised his voice a little more. "We have no wish to cause you harm. Damn it! We haven't even fired on you." A volley from all three hidden enemies crashed into the desk in front of Maggie and Stone. Splinters and dust landed on the couple as they huddled underneath. Maggie flashed a venomous look up at Stone, who shrugged his shoulders ruefully as if he knew that was going to happen. He looked up from under the desk and could see movement beyond. All four of their attackers seemed to be shuffling slowly towards the exit. They'd obviously found what they wanted among the shelves and were going to make a break for the door. Stone's only desire was to get Maggie and his men out of the library alive, and if that meant letting their attackers escape, then so be it. Stone had no intention of being a hero, and whatever these mercenaries had been up to it was none of his business anyway.

Stone's men at the entrance were standing firm but were now coming under heavy fire, the strangers were firing and reloading with mechanical precision like well-drilled infantry. Surely they must have realised that Stone's men had been ordered not to fire back at them, so it seemed strange to Stone that they were still using force. It was almost as if they were trying to provoke an attack. Stone guessed he only had a couple of seconds before he would start to take serious casualties — he was very surprised that had not happened already. He looked at the door and caught the eye of the monk closest to him. He held up two fingers and made a throat-cutting signal. He saw the monk speak to the other men and prayed they didn't miss.

Two shots, almost simultaneously, came from the door and the front two mercenaries were thrown backwards to the floor. Through the smoke, Stone could just see the men both sprawled out on the floor, their chests a bloody mess. Obviously realising they had underestimated their opposition; the remaining attackers backed off and began to look for another way out. Stone watched as one man levelled his musket at the exit and fired blindly into the smoke. Then rushing backwards, he pushed one of the tables up against the wall, picked up a chair, and threw it at one of the windows. The heavy oak chair smashed into the wood and glass, sending debris across the room. He picked up the discarded muskets of his dead comrades, then shouted something to his remaining companion.

Stone was in a direct line to the new escape route created by the mercenary, and he stood so he could bring his rifle to aim. The other mercenary saw the movement, turned one of his muskets towards Stone, and fired in his direction. The bullet whizzed past Stone's left ear and smashed into the wall behind him. Stone ducked back down beside Maggie, swearing loudly as he checked his ear to make sure it was still in one piece.

"You men at the door bring the bastard down, would you?" He'd just about had enough now and that last shot was too close for comfort. The monks at the door fired again, but the smoke from the previous shot obscured their target and the bullets went wide. For an instant, both attackers disappeared behind one of the bookshelves shielded from Stone's view. A second later, they rushed out from behind the bookshelf, running half crouched towards the shattered window. One of the men jumped onto the table and out through the open window, and the other man guarded the window for a moment then made a move to escape.

Stone heard activity outside the window and guessed reinforcements were waiting in the street. The last man emptied his rifle in Stone's direction, and then leapt up onto the table. Stone saw the man, who was now all but clear, seemingly slip as he stepped through the window. He teetered on the windowsill for a moment, then started to fall backwards. The man tried to grab the frame of the window but it was too late. The man gave a startled cry as he fell backwards, crashing onto the table and then rolling to the floor. In a second, Stone was on his feet and moving towards the prostrate figure.

The man saw Stone approaching and immediately reached for one of his pistols at his belt. The instant his hand touched the butt off the pistol, a menacing growl, deep and powerful, sounded from behind one of the tables. Rufus sprinted forward from the shadows, his teeth bared in a terrible display of power. The man was trying to pull the pistol but Rufus moved far too quickly and clamped his huge maw around the man's neck. The man panicked briefly as he realised he was about to die, but he stopped struggling when Rufus didn't follow through with the killing bite. Rufus held him by the throat and continued to growl until Stone reached them. After Stone had taken the man's remaining guns, the massive dog let go of the man's throat and sat down close by, watching his prisoner intently through glittering eyes.

"Well done, boy," Stone said sounding surprised while admiring the shocked expression on the face of their new captive. "I think you're very lucky to be alive, monsieur," he said, looking down at the man. Du Puy looked up at Stone and was almost of the same opinion even though he'd set up most of the entire episode.

Stone posted a guard at the front and back doors, while another man watched their new captive. Du Puy was now sitting opposite Stone and the rest of the party silently contemplating his fate. Stone walked over to his prisoner and pulled apart the rough leather tunic the man was wearing, revealing another jacket underneath. Maggie walked over to take a closer look at the jacket, then exchanged a puzzled glance with Stone. "What is it, Richard?" she said looking at the jacket. "Is it a uniform of some kind?"

"Yes Maggie. That jacket is the standard uniform of a French Grenadier, if I'm not mistaken." He pulled the jacket open further to look at the badge of rank. "And a French Grenadier Colonel at that. *N'est pas, monsieur.*" The man remained silent and his expression remained blank. Du Puy had at the last moment decided to embellish his plan by creating a disguise that would give his story some credibility. Stone then went to the two bodies on the floor and pulled their jackets open. Although a little bloody from the gunshot wounds, he revealed similar uniforms. Both men were regular French infantrymen. "No wonder they were so damn well trained," he said to himself as he looked down on the broken corpses. Stone turned and looked back at their prisoner. The Frenchman held Stone in a silent, calm gaze.

Black marks stained the Frenchman's face from firing a musket, and Stone guessed the man's mouth would be dry and bitter from the taste of gunpowder. All four Frenchmen had been using infantry muskets, and the weapons had to be loaded and charged by a small cartridge filled with gunpowder and ball. To open the cartridge, a soldier had to rip it open with his teeth, and it was impossible to stop a little of the powder entering your mouth. Then the ball had to be spat down into the barrel of the musket. The dead men on the floor were plain infantrymen, and Stone could see the deeply ingrained scars full of dirt where the powder burns would have constantly hit their faces. Stone remembered what the bitter tasting powder was like from his own battles. Looking at this French officer's face he could see the man didn't have the same scaring, as a gentleman didn't fight with a musket. Stone guessed this man was indeed an officer and had probably seen action many times before. Stone suddenly realised he couldn't interrogate the man in front of Maggie as the prisoner might reveal things about Cheltenham and the rebellion that Stone didn't want her to hear.

"Maggie, would you mind going over to the shelves where our friend was hiding and see if you can find what he was looking for. This might also be a good opportunity for you to find what we came here for." Maggie looked uncertain for a moment, but she moved obediently away when she realised Stone was ordering rather than asking her. When she was out of earshot, Stone turned back to the Frenchman.

"*Bonjour mon amis*," Stone said in a friendly tone. "*Parlez vous Anglais?*" The Frenchman looked at his captives, especially at the heavily armed monks guarding the exits. He stood slowly and bowed gracefully to Stone.

"Yes, monsieur. I do indeed speak English." He straightened his clothes as best he could and made some effort at brushing off some of the dust. Obviously mustering what remained of his dignity, he smiled and sat back down again. "I must congratulate you on my capture, monsieur. My name is Jacques Lacroix, Colonel in his Imperial Majesty's personal bodyguard. These men…" He gestured to the dead men on the floor. "These men were Corporal Jean-Pierre Blanc and Sergeant Henry Menel, also of the Imperial French Army." Stone was taken totally by surprise by the Frenchman's honesty. Stone had met many French officers before, but to come face to face with one of Napoleon's Immortals, one of his personal body guards, who were perhaps the most skilled fighting force in Europe, was something altogether different. The French boasted to the rest of the world that the Immortals were undefeated in battle and the only rightful guardians of their beloved Emperor. It was an arrogant statement and therefore to be expected of the French, but one Stone knew the rest of Europe ignored at their peril.

The French Colonel, unlike his men, was clean shaven except for a small moustache and a pointed goatee. He held himself like an aristocrat while the dead men lying around them were unkempt and their clothes were nothing more than rags. He had a proud hawk-like face and shining black hair that fell thick and straight to his shoulders. He stood almost as tall as Stone and had an impressive physique, and his piercing green eyes took everything in around him like a leopard stalking its prey. Stone sensed the Colonel was an extremely skilful and dangerous man and not to be trusted.

Stone pulled out a chair from under a nearby desk and sat down opposite the Frenchman. "Why are you here, Colonel Lacroix?" Stone decided his interrogation should be straight to the point as he wanted to be away from the city as soon as possible and without attracting any more attention.

"Firstly, monsieur," Lacroix replied. "Please offer me the same courtesy as I have shown you and introduce yourself. A defeated man likes to know who has vanquished him."

"Captain Richard Stone of His Britannic Majesty's army." The Frenchman bowed his head in salute, and Stone was sure in that instant he saw a look of surprise in Lacroix's face that disappeared immediately.

"I ask you again sir: why are you in Edinburgh?" Stone felt his patience being tested by the mild mannered Frenchman, and he couldn't help thinking the Colonel was doing it deliberately.

"It is a strange and interesting story, monsieur." Lacroix smiled wolfishly at Stone, holding him briefly in that predatory glare. "I would not want to bore you with the details." He took a water bottle from his jacket and drank deeply.

"Very well," Stone said, now failing to hide his impatience. "Why not just tell me those boring details and I'll be the judge of how interesting they are." The Frenchman seemed amused at having provoked Stone.

"Captain Stone," Lacroix said, more formally. "I would first like to put on the record in front all these witnesses that I am not a spy of France and would not like to be treated as such in captivity." He gestured towards the monks around the room. "I am a soldier, not a mercenary, and I have not been paid for what I've done during the last few months." He paused for a moment in thought. "I still retain my honour, Captain," he said quietly, looking into Stone's eyes. "I assure you I am not proud of what has happened or what I've done. The only evidence and assurance I have for my innocence are these tattered uniforms and my word as a French officer." Du Puy could see he already had the Englishman completely hooked on his story — it would only be a matter of moments before Du Puy had complete control over the situation.

Stone sat silently for a moment and considered the mood change in the Frenchman. "Very well, monsieur. I will take you at your word, and I promise to do all I can to protect your honour. So now tell me what you know." Lacroix took another swig of water and settled back on the chair.

"My comrades and I were captured some eighteen months ago near Toulouse while defending the rear of the Emperor's baggage train as it retreated from Spain. The three of us and many others were placed in one of your castles here in Scotland to serve out the rest of the war as prisoners."

"Why weren't you exchanged for a captured British officer as is the usual custom?" Stone said, interrupting.

A tired look came over Lacroix's face. "I had tried to escape several times monsieur, thus breaking my parole and making me ineligible for exchange. I was sent to Scotland with the other French prisoners, and we were held in a cold, terrible place called Threave Castle. But we were only there for a month before we were released."

"Released?" Stone said, his surprise evident in his tone.

"Yes monsieur, released. Soon after we arrived at Threave, a new commander of the garrison was appointed to guard the prisoners. The new commander paraded all the prisoners and told us we had been chosen to be kept captive in the castle for a specific reason. He said the British army had recorded exactly who we were and where our families lived in France." Stone watched him expectantly, not quite understanding where the story was going.

"Months passed before we were called upon to do anything," Du Puy continued. "The new commanding officer of the prison camp continually threatened the lives of our families back home in France if we didn't do what he commanded, and there was no way to know if what he said was true. So we had no choice but do what he wanted. Every so often, some of us were taken from the castle to carry out tasks for him."

"What kind of tasks?" Stone interrupted. Lacroix peered at him with a look of resignation on his face.

"We participated in protests all across Scotland. We stole arms and ammunition and hid them in designated places, and we were ordered to kill anyone who got in our way. We never really needed to kill anyone, as we were given access to most military installations from which we stole arms. These thefts were all very well organised, and we carried them out in military style — nothing was left to chance." Du Puy then sat quietly back with his head bowed, waiting for a response.

"The column of cavalry destroyed outside Edinburgh?" Stone knew the truth already. Lacroix looked up and nodded slowly.

"Christ," Stone swore silently. "Cheltenham is using bloody prisoners of war to do his dirty work for him." He looked at the Frenchman again. "You know that camp commander of yours has probably been ordered to kill you all when this is over." The Frenchman nodded again. "And you're not getting anything out of this?"

Lacroix looked up at Stone, his face contorted in anger. "If you knew me monsieur, you would understand that I would rather die than let my family discover what I have done. If I've saved them from danger, that's all that matters." Du Puy was careful not to raise his voice too loud. He understood exactly what game Stone was trying to play. It was obvious when the Englishman sent Maggie away to search for her books. The girl obviously knew nothing of the situation outside of what Ruth had already told her, and it was clear Stone was somehow privy to far more information than he was letting on. Stone had probably fallen for the girl and was trying to manipulate her to get her out of the city and away from danger. His plan was probably to slip away from the monks in the night when the time was right and wait out the war with Maggie abroad. Du Puy had been correct in his judgement not to trust Maggie, however it was Stone he now needed to keep his eyes on. As Du Puy studied the Englishman through his feigned expression of anger, he thought about dispatching Stone immediately to maintain control. But he quickly changed his mind when considering that Maggie probably bore similar feelings and that bond between them might work in Du Puys favour.

Stone looked sympathetically back at the Frenchman. "Unfortunately Colonel, the British government, if they ever manage to get control of the situation in Scotland, will probably turn deaf ears on your predicament and string you up anyway." Stone then sat silently, reflecting on what Lacroix had said. Suddenly a thought occurred to him. "You don't happen to remember the name of the commander at Threave, do you?" Stone asked.

"His name will remain with me, monsieur, until the end of my days, and I look forward to the day when I might be able to take my revenge against him. His name was Colonel Clifford, a most intensely evil man, one of the most ruthless I have ever seen." One of Du Puy's objectives was to quickly convince Stone to go to Threave. Although he had never been there himself, Du Puy knew Threave was Clifford's base of operations, and therefore, that is exactly where Clifford would be keeping Cardinal Beeton's original manuscript, which Clifford had stolen on Cheltenham's orders. Du Puy was sure Beeton's book was one of the keys to finding the body of William Wallace, and this was the only opportunity he had to get the book back.

Du Puy raised his voice slightly as Maggie came into earshot. She was still walking among the book shelves. "A couple of days ago, I overheard Colonel Clifford talking about an ancient book he had stolen from a monastery. Could this in some way be relevant to what you are looking for here?" Du Puy sensed Maggie had overheard what he'd said as she had gone very still. Maggie started to turn around slowly as it dawned on her what Du Puy had just said. "I can get you into the castle if you think the book would be of some value to you," Du Puy continued. Maggie was about to respond when Stone suddenly woke up to the situation.

"No Maggie," he said before she had a chance to speak. "It's out of the question. Even if we could get into the castle, I'm not exposing you to that kind of danger."

"But it's Cardinal Beeton's book, Richard, and it could be the key to finding Wallace's body." Maggie looked nervously at Lacroix, unsure whether she should be talking about their mission in front of a complete stranger.

"Maggie, I refuse to take you into a situation where I may not be able to protect you." Maggie looked as though she was about to argue with him, but then she seemed to remember something and simply smiled at Stone instead. She held up a piece of parchment she'd been holding and waved it in his face.

"I've found what we came here to get, and the information is better than I expected. I know the location of Cardinal Beeton's old family estate, and according to these records, the estate has been left almost totally unchanged over the last few centuries. If there are any clues to be found, I think we'll find them in his old estate."

"So what are you saying?" Stone said uncertainly.

"You go to Threave with the French Colonel and try to retrieve the book, and I'll take a few men and go down to Troon, where the estate is located. Once you've got the book, you can meet me there." She smiled at him as if it was the simplest plan in the world. Du Puy had to admire her resolve, and he could see why it would be easy for a man like Stone to fall in love with her. Stone could see by the look in her eye that Maggie had made her decision, and trying to budge her would be impossible. He comforted himself with the thought that the passage to Troon would be fairly safe, and the journey would take her a long way from any of the fighting. Also, by going to Threave, the opportunity to kill Clifford might present itself and take at least one of the key impediments to Maggie's safety out of the equation. Stone looked at Lacroix, who simply shrugged his shoulders and smiled.

"The young lady has a sturdy heart, has she not, monsieur?" Du Puy said in French. Stone smiled grimly back at the Frenchman.

"Looks like we're off to visit your castle then, Colonel." Without another word, Stone picked up one of the spare muskets from the floor and handed it to Lacroix. "You're going to need this, but you only get ammunition if it starts to get nasty."

"Thank you, monsieur. What will you do with me once you have the book?" Stone slung his own rifle over his shoulder and motioned for his men to leave the library.

"That depends on two things, Colonel. First, whether or not we make it out of Threave castle alive." He checked to see if his weapon was loaded. "And second, whether or not the good guys or the bad guys win this rebellion." He looked pointedly at Lacroix. "But to be honest, I'm still unsure who's good and who's bad, and so we'll just leave it in God's hands for now. Shall we go?" Stone offered Lacroix the door while throwing a reproachful glance back at Maggie, who in turn lifted her pistols off the table, spun imperiously on her heel, and walked through the door to the waiting horses outside.

"This is going to be a long trip," Stone thought, as he followed his new French comrade out into the night.

CHAPTER 12

Thomas Blaird sat in the grass taking a well-earned rest. He and fifty other insurgents from the city had been hiding in the moors outside Edinburgh for two days. He had been the last of the four Blaird brothers to join the group. His loyalty to Sir Henry Burns and the newspaper he worked for had initially held him back, but the propaganda that had turned his brothers to violence and rebellion, spread so effectively by Clifford and the monks throughout the city, had finally convinced him to join the rebels.

The group of young men had become separated from a larger more organized group of rebels, and since then, they'd taken some serious casualties. A troop of cavalry had stumbled onto their hideout the previous afternoon and killed two of their number, one by sabre and one trampled under the hooves of the cavalry's mounts. Another older member had died from his wounds because of the cold wet days camped out on the moors. Thomas, sitting on the side of a damp hill with nothing but the cold to comfort him, felt leaderless — and now he had no real idea what they were fighting for.

Thomas and his comrades had been resting for only a few minutes when one of the lookouts at the top of the hill shouted down that he'd spotted a column of cavalry in the distance, and the horsemen were closing in on their position. Thomas could see the light shining off the soldier's burnished breastplates about three miles away. His stomach suddenly leapt up into his throat as he realised the column was coming straight for where they were sitting and the small band of rebels were caught out in the open. The soldiers obviously hadn't spotted them yet, but in a few minutes this ragtag group of rebels' brief resistance would be over. With half a mile to the nearest cover, the group would be overrun easily if they tried to flee. Once they were spotted, the group would have barely a minute to organise a suitable defence, and if they put up a fight in open ground, then there would be only one outcome. Thomas, even with his limited experience of battle, understood a man on foot was no match for a man charging on horseback. He also knew that to surrender would mean imprisonment or the hangman's noose. He watched as the self-appointed leaders of the band argued about what to do. One or two members of the group had more than anxious looks on their faces. A cry went up from some of the men as they saw the cavalry move into a canter. The insurgents had been spotted and the soldiers were now less than half a mile away.

Thomas watched helplessly as the drama unfolded, but then one of the few strangers in the group stood up and shouted at every one of them to be silent. Most of the men were either family or friends, but this man had joined on his own and refused to tell anyone where he was from. He'd hardly uttered a word in the week he'd been with them, and when he did speak, his voice was guttural and he had a slight European accent. None of the other men trusted him and all were afraid of him.

He was a big man and carried the only decent rifle in the entire group. He stood glaring at them all for a moment, then turned and stared at the approaching riders in the distance. He turned back to the terrified group of men and immediately started barking orders. The force of the man's presence and the fact that he'd drawn a vicious looking sabre from its scabbard and was waving it around at them urged most of the group into action, but they were already moving far too late. Thomas grabbed the musket he had been given when he'd joined the rebels and followed his brothers into action. The adrenaline was building inside him as he moved into position, and he was shaking so much he almost dropped the musket. He couldn't believe they were going to attack a group of heavily armed men on horseback. They all listened intently to their new commander, but more out of fear than any sense he might have been making. Indeed, Thomas noted that the man seemed to know what he was doing. The stranger looked at each of the men in turn and they stared back intently. Suddenly he grinned at them, raised his huge battered cavalry sabre into the air, and then turned to face the approaching soldiers. The rebels were on a small hillock and had the advantage of the high ground, but they would not last long, even Thomas knew that.

The stranger bellowed his challenge to the approaching soldiers, who had been ordered to slow to a trot. "Liberty or Death!" he screamed in challenge, then ran down the hill directly at the column. The whole band, suddenly totally enthused by the man's fierce bravery, roared their own challenge and raced after him. Thomas, caught in the ferocity of the moment, ran with them not even bothering to load his weapon. He glanced across at his brothers and saw them shouting a challenge, their faces contorted with hatred. He looked back down at the cavalry, who had stopped their advance at the bottom of the hill. Their commanding officer had brought the troop to a halt and he sat there with a bemused expression on his face as he watched the ragged line of men charge down the hill towards him.

Thomas suddenly couldn't help smiling and he almost laughed out loud. The enemy were just standing, seemingly struck senseless by their attack, and he felt delirious, the adrenaline and madness of the moment making him completely fearless. At that moment, he was immortal. The foolishness of the attack and the uneven odds didn't matter. Their bravery and courage would win the day. How could God let such heroism be defeated?

He saw the stranger who had led the attack drop to one knee ten yards in front of them and put his rifle to his shoulder. The noise of the rifle firing stunned Thomas back into reality. One of the nearest horsemen was snatched from his saddle and his blood splattered the rider next to him. Other men knelt down by their tough looking leader and aimed their weapons down the hill.

A small volley spluttered down at the horsemen, but most of the rebels fired too high and did little damage to the column. A ditch halfway down the hill gave the rebels a perfect firing step, and those men without muskets buried their homemade pikes into the ground, angled up and out towards the advancing cavalry.

The cavalry officer, finally realising the attackers were unsupported and completely exposed, signalled the advance. Twenty sabres left their scabbards simultaneously and the horsemen galloped forward to meet the attack. A burst of fire from the trench unhorsed a couple of riders as they approached, but the charge was too swift and the insurgents couldn't reload quickly enough. The Hussars reached the gap in seconds, and their horses leapt over while their riders cut down with their swords on the defenceless Scotsmen. One horse went down, pierced by the point of a pike. Both horse and rider crashed down into the trench, crushing the pike men and several others. The animal, in its death throes, kicked out and thrashed around with its legs, caving in a man's skull and scattering the nearest defenders.

The lead riders of the column, having negotiated the first line of defence, now attacked those insurgents who hadn't yet reached the trench, turning the small battle into a blood bath. Thomas had managed to reach the trench and was caught in the middle of the fighting, the Hussars now in front and behind their position. The cavalry attacking the front of the trench stopped short and fired a murderous volley down onto the defenders as their comrades who'd ridden past were slicing up the insurgents caught in the open as easily as if they were on the practice field.

Thomas watched in horror as his friends and brothers were cut to pieces. The sounds of metal slicing through flesh and bone mixed with the screams of terror from men and horse alike made the bile rise to his throat. Thomas discarded his musket without having fired a shot. The gunpowder had turned to sludge anyway so the weapon would only have been useful as a club. He saw the stranger who had led the charge smash the butt of his rifle into the face of a horse, making the animal rear away in pain and throw the rider to the ground. In the same moment the stranger turned and ran. Thomas stood dumbstruck as their only leader leapt on the back of the horse and made his escape. It only took a moment for the remaining insurgents to realise what had happened, and as if awakening from a spell, they fled.

Cavalrymen can only dream of the day when infantry retreat from battle and become no more dangerous than a moving target. Whoops of joy came from some of the horsemen as they saw their enemy run away. The Hussars, incensed by their losses, attacked without mercy and offered no quarter to their terrified quarry. The horsemen trampled the wounded deliberately as they passed, and unarmed men were cut down from behind and left to bleed to death in the grass.

Thomas had managed to head for a small clump of trees to the left of the trench in an area of dead ground away from the battle. He was within thirty feet of safety when a Hussar suddenly galloped past him. Instead of cutting Thomas down straight away, the Hussar arrogantly slapped the flat side of his blade across Thomas's back. The horseman then expertly turned his mount, blocking Thomas's retreat to the trees. Thomas stood still, breathing heavily, while the Hussar waited twenty feet in front of him. The men looked into each other's eyes, and Thomas saw very little mercy to be found there. He realised he was standing in the spot where he was going to die, but then something snapped within Thomas as the Hussar sat there smiling imperiously down him. He felt courage and anger pulse through his veins as his brain conceded that death was a reality, making his body react automatically to the inevitable.

Thomas had a pistol in his belt, and without thinking, he grabbed the weapon and aimed it at the horseman, even though the weapon was as damp and wet as his musket had been. The Hussar, not expecting any resistance, now looked in horror as he suddenly stared death in the face. It was an eternity before Thomas pulled the trigger. He made the Hussar suffer the expectation of death, the only punishment he could inflict on the man before his own destruction. The click of the hammer hitting an empty firing pan seemed to resonate across the hills, and the sigh of relief from the Hussar was louder still. The Hussar raised his sword in challenge and then kicked back hard with his spurs. Thomas stood terrified, rooted to the spot, as the world seemed to go into slow motion. He could see with the horse blowing a cloud of warm breath into the cold afternoon air while spittle and sweat droplets on its muzzle glistened in the twilight. The horseman stared intently at Thomas, his face flushed with pleasure or anger. The point of the rider's sword was gleaming wet with another man's blood, and it was aimed straight at his heart. Thomas tried to move to the left at the last minute, but his legs were like jelly. It was enough to make the sword go off target and enter instead through the top of his chest. The sabre pierced his shoulder blade, cutting through bone and muscle as the horseman passed, tearing off a portion of Thomas's upper arm.

Thomas was thrown to the ground by the impact, and he lay on his back, his body immediately numb from the blow. The Hussar arrogantly rode away searching for another victim. It wasn't a killing wound, but there would be no one to tend him before Thomas bled to death in the grass.

Thomas could see the tops of the trees he had almost reached just at the edge of his vision. He could hear their leaves rustling in the wind, the sound enhanced by his confused senses. The sky was blue but became hazy as his life force flowed out into the earth. He tried to think of something that he could have been doing rather than dying in an unknown field. He couldn't. His eyes filled with tears as his vision slowly darkened. "Liberty or Death!" he whispered, even as he realised they were one in the same, and with a sigh, he understood he'd wanted neither.

CHAPTER 13

Another night passed without incident, and the travellers made good progress. The weather had stayed fair, and even the normally solemn and quiet monks were talking amongst themselves. However they kept their conversation in Latin, which infuriated Maggie as she couldn't really understand what they were saying. They'd been riding for two days and hadn't met any trouble, but they continued to travel at night just in case.

They arrived at Cardinal Beeton's old country house just before dawn on the third day, and Maggie was full of anticipation. The buildings had obviously been redesigned and rebuilt several times, but the estate still had a pious and devout feel to it. The house was now the home of the local Laird, whose family had added a beautiful chapel, stables, and other buildings to the estate. The previous day, Maggie had sent one of the monks ahead to give word to the Laird that they were coming. She had learned that the current Laird was a devout Catholic and an amiable man and didn't feel it was appropriate to turn up unannounced. Fortunately, however, the Laird and his family were away visiting relatives, so when the party of travellers arrived, the housekeeper told them that the Laird had insisted on opening his house to them and that they were welcome to stay as long as they desired.

One of the stable hands came out to meet them as they arrived and ushered them into a barn that had room for all their horses. The monk's baggage was taken to the servants' quarters and Maggie's to the main house. The monks immediately set up a guard around the perimeter of the estate and left Maggie to begin her search of the house and grounds, although there was always a monk watching her every move.

Maggie entered the house through the main entrance, so she could take in the full view of the old building, which was more quaint than grand, and the later additions of pillars and statues served only to add baggage to a simple, almost delicate building. She imagined the original building from the thirteenth century had been changed so much it probably no longer really existed.

She asked a maid where to find the library and was informed that it wasn't actually a room in the house. The maid pointed upwards, and Maggie noticed the front atrium of the building was square and designed as an inner courtyard. The second floor was visible from the ground floor courtyard and all the walls were lined with hundreds of leather bound books.

She made her way to the second floor and spent a couple of hours scanning the shelves, but found nothing of significance. It seemed the Laird loved his books but had no real system for referencing them. One of the maids brought her a lunch of cold meat sandwiches and cider, and she took a break and sat with Rufus in the Laird's study, contemplating where to look next. Looking around the room, she noticed the Laird had a passion for collecting old, even ancient, artefacts. On the desk in front of her was a bust of the Roman Emperor Nero, and across the room was a twelfth century suit of armour. She studied the room carefully but couldn't see anything obvious that came from Cardinal Beeton's period let alone anything relating to the Cardinal himself.

She decided to clear the top of the Laird's desk and then laid out all the papers and books relating to Cardinal Beeton that she'd had brought with her from the city. The information amounted to very little, but she knew that somewhere amongst all the ancient manuscripts there must be a clue to point her in the right direction.

She decided to put four names of men described as the friends and supporters of William Wallace from her modern copy of *The Wallas of Blin Harry* next to the four names from exactly the same passage of text from the Latin version she had viewed in the monastery to study them in more detail. These names had been the first clue given to her by the monks, but neither the monks nor Maggie had yet been able to decipher their significance. For all she knew, the difference in the names might be a simple mistake.

> *Edward Little*
> *Patrick Anchinleck of Gilbank*
> *Tom Haliday*
> *William De Cranford*

Maggie looked at the names of all Wallace's closest allies as she had done a dozen times before, but the names really meant nothing to her. She compared them to the names in the original Latin version written for Blind Harry by Cardinal Beeton five hundred years earlier.

Edward Plummet
Patrick De Gustumo
Tom Tartsuns
William Maar

The only regularity between the two lists of names was the first name of each man. She'd searched for both sets of names in history books but hadn't found a single useful reference for any of them. The four names from the modern translation were well known historical characters, but they didn't appear anywhere in Beeton's original Latin version. Why had Cardinal Beeton deliberately changed the second names of these men in his original text while history related to the men with their correct names? The obvious conclusion was that the men in the original text never existed and were made up for some reason. She had to find out who these men were and why Beeton had changed their names. Whether she would find a clue in this house or on the estate, she had the feeling that, if she left without knowing why the names had been changed, the whole expedition would be a failure.

The other tantalizing clue was the Latin inscription written under the coat of arms in the original Latin text: *TUTIS PER AMICA.* Translated in her pigeon Latin meant the term meant *PROTECTED BY FRIENDS.* Maggie assumed the inscription referred to Wallace's friends and therefore had a direct relation to the names in the book. But the inscription meant nothing without understanding what these friends were protecting.

She leant back and let her head rest on the back of the Laird's leather chair. Her eyes flicked around the room again, looking for something to give her inspiration. It dawned on her that something was missing from the room. Among the entire collection of ancient treasures, books, and artefacts there wasn't a single religious object. The Laird was supposed to be an extremely religious man and professed to possess a magnificent collection of Catholic artefacts. Maggie realised she hadn't actually seen a single one in the entire house. She leapt out of the chair and called the startled Rufus to her side. She ran out of the front door and into the courtyard. She caught sight of the small spire behind a crop of trees and walked quickly towards it. She'd wasted an entire day looking for clues that were all probably located in the one place she'd completely forgotten about, the Laird's family chapel.

Maggie gently pushed the old oak doors to the chapel open so she could see inside. The doors swung wide on well-oiled hinges, dragging leaves and other debris in their wake. The inside of the building was oval shaped, with just enough seating for the Laird and his family. The domed roof had a beautifully detailed painting of the Temptations of Christ, and in its centre was a round stained glass window with a depiction of the crucifixion. The black marble floor had been polished to a brilliant sheen, and the whitewashed walls seemed to glow in the light streaming through the other windows. Maggie sat down in one of the pews in one of the most beautiful chapels she'd ever seen.

The building wasn't adorned with treasures, but those her eyes stopped to admire might well have been priceless. Angels and saints in brightly coloured clothes, their expressions sombre but majestic, adorned the walls. She studied the plaques of long dead ancestors, their names immortalised on the fabulous chapel walls. The Beeton name was everywhere. She felt strangely drawn to the place as if everything had been placed there for her to witness at this single moment in time.

Maggie stood and walked to the altar, and she noticed a small shrine in an alcove in the wall behind it. The alcove had a couple of chairs facing a small marble frieze partially hidden by a wooden screen. Brushes and paints were scattered on the floor where someone had obviously been doing some restoration work. She slowly pulled the screen aside to reveal the marble frieze, which was in bad condition, severely weather beaten as if it had been outside in the elements for a very long time. Looking closely, she could make out the figure of a man surrounded by what looked like four small animals. She guessed the man might have been Cardinal Beeton, as the figure seemed to be wearing a Cardinal's hat and a robe. An inscription was carved at the bottom but was still partially covered in dirt and mildew. She picked up one of the brushes and rubbed at the grooves, cleaning away some of the grime. When she'd cleaned off the worst of it, she stepped back to get a better look at the inscription. Each of the four animals seemed to have a name, and underneath the names was a single sentence. She drew in a sharp breath as she suddenly realised the significance of what she'd found. She had to sit down on the marble floor to regain her composure.

The depiction was not of the Cardinal but a king, and the hat was in fact a great crown. The animals were dogs, huge dogs, probably wolfhounds like Rufus. Their names were Edward, Patrick, Tom and William. Each of the animals was facing towards her with their great mouths open in a snarl. When the frieze was new, they would have been quite terrifying to all who saw them. The man was a king and he had his loyal subjects surrounding him. The single sentence was in Latin and Maggie could only stare wide-eyed as she mouthed the inscription to herself: *Tutis per amica – protected by friends.*

CHAPTER 14

It took the small company of men two days of hard riding to reach Threave. The castle was situated near Loch Ken in Dumfries on the coast of the Solway Firth, close enough to England and in such an uninhabited area to make it a perfect stronghold for Sir Arthur Cheltenham's henchmen.

The castle was situated on an island in the middle of the River Dee, and just getting to it would be a task let alone trying to assault the walls. Stone observed the structure through his telescope from down river to the north of the island. He lowered his glass and snapped it shut after having a long look. The surrounding landscape, he noticed, was boggy marsh and water, difficult terrain at the best of times. The castle itself was on the island with three hundred yards of flat open ground for the defenders to observe an attacker approach. This didn't include the fifty yards of deep cold water to get past before reaching the walls.

He surmised a small company of soldiers could hold the fort for a month against an entire army if they had enough ammunition. That was of course if the attacking force wanted to keep the fort intact. He couldn't see any artillery gun barrels poking out from the embrasures, so at least that was one thing with which he would not have to contend. He looked at Lacroix and hoped he had a good plan to share with them. This fort could not be taken by force through a direct assault with the small numbers of men they'd brought.

Not including himself and Lacroix, they had thirty men, all monks and all dressed for battle. He'd been surprised when the monks had arrived at the newspaper building two days ago. Most of the men looked young, in their late twenties perhaps, but all were grim faced and rugged. Their humble demeanour and robes did little to disguise the fact that each man was a fighter and probably had more experience with death than their years suggested. Each man was armed with rifles and pistols, and some of them with swords. But the sheer size of a few of them intrigued Stone. A regiment of these fighting men, he surmised, could make the bravest of Napoleon's personal body guard shake in their boots. But, Stone mused, he had yet to see them fight, and if any test was sufficient to prove their capabilities, then it was an attack on a well-defended enemy position where the odds were utterly against them. In the back of Stone's mind was the lingering thought that an opportunity might present itself to escape from the monks, collect Maggie and vanish. Plus, he thought to himself, escaping seemed a far less risky option than attacking a heavily fortified castle.

Once night had fallen, they approached the castle following the bank of the river and the cover of the trees, the flowing water disguising the noise of their advance. Lacroix had formulated the plan of attack, as he knew the layout of the building and the best form of assault. He told Stone that, once on the island, they had only to take the compound just inside the gates of the castle and the castle would fall. The castle itself was almost derelict apart from one room that housed the camp commander, so they could ignore the building totally. Once through the gates of the compound, they would spread out left and right along the walls, then advance forward to the centre. Lacroix assured him that only a company of redcoats and a small number of foreign mercenaries guarded the castle. The French prisoners of war were kept in the dungeons under the castle and in outdoor pens situated all over the island. The burning question was: how did they get over the water? Then the next question was: how did they get inside the gates?

The normal route over the water was from a small jetty on the near bank. Visitors rang the bell and a boatman would come from the island and take them over the water to the castle. Lacroix had other ideas. On the far side of the island, to the north of the castle, the Laird of Threave had laid an underwater stone bridge in 1640 as an escape route. The bridge could only be seen if you were literally standing on the first stone, the water being too murky to see the bridge from a distance, and the wind from the Solway Firth always rippling the surface and obscuring any other sign of it.

Lacroix told Stone that the mercenaries knew about the bridge but only used it on secret missions. It was agreed that the party fool the guards at the gates by pretending to be mercenaries returning to the castle at night. To add to the ruse, Stone suggested they should carry a wounded man, which might get the guards to open the gates quicker. It was a risk, letting the guards get them in their sites, and being in open ground right in front of the gates was bordering on insanity, but it was a risk Stone was willing to take.

The monks built a makeshift stretcher out of tree branches and their travelling cloaks, and Lacroix butchered a rabbit he had caught earlier in the day. Stone then lay upon the stretcher and Lacroix covered the front of his shirt in the rabbit's blood. He smeared it over Stone's face and hands, then instructed him to hold his stomach as if it was the location of the wound. Stone whispered a comment in Lacroix's ear about acting not being one of his strong points, and he asked, "Where the hell did you learn this bit of trickery?"

Lacroix smiled down at him. "Not all Napoleon's men go into battle in a suicidal column shouting *vive l'Emperor!*"

They crossed the water-bridge without incident, and it looked as if the only guards were those inside the perimeter of the castle compound. As they neared the compound, Stone whispered a warning to Lacroix, concerned that Clifford might be in the castle and would recognise them before they got through the gates. Lacroix just shrugged and suggested that, if Clifford were in the castle, he would probably be drunk and wrapped around a whore by now.

Just before they reached the walls and the gates of the perimeter ramparts, a voice shouted down in an English accent from the walkway above. "Who the bloody hell is that down there?" Two lamps were lit and the area in front of the gate was immediately soaked in bright lamplight. The attackers had to shield their eyes as they were momentarily blinded by the sudden light. Stone closed his eyes and started moaning as if in pain from his wounds.

"Quickly! Open the gates!" Lacroix shouted back in French. "I have a wounded man down here." He ran forward and pounded on the wooded doors.

"Who the hell are you?" the same voice replied.

"Sounds like another dopey bloody Frenchman to me," said another Englishman, whose comment created a chorus of laughter from the battlements.

"Well, are you one of our French bitches, or do I have to blow your bloody head off?" The voice sounded a little more menacing, and Stone distinctly heard the sound of a dozen muskets being cocked. He began to moan louder and cried out in French for extra effect.

"I am Major Dubois." Lacroix gave the name of one of the French mercenaries he knew was under Cheltenham's command and prayed he was still in Edinburgh. "I've come back with some men wounded in a mission a few days ago." He looked up into the light and gestured to Stone lying in a bloody mess on the stretcher. Stone said a silent prayer and hoped none of the soldiers on the wall knew Major Dubois by sight.

Thankfully the light in the front of the gates only exposed five of Stone's men. Lacroix had remembered the defenders would put on the oil lamps, but the light only reached about ten feet into the darkness beyond the gates. The men on the ramparts would only be able to see anyone within a few meters of the gates, but further out they would see nothing but blackness. The rest of the monks were lying in the grass a few yards out of the light, ready to charge forward once the gates had been opened.

Apart from the occasional theatrical moan from Stone, the monks waited in silence as the defenders deliberated about what to do. It was obvious they'd been caught off guard and were unsure how to proceed. Getting into trouble with the camp commander was their main concern. The camp commander would be very upset to hear that a party of men had reached the gates without being challenged, and if they let the men inside, the commander would want to know why he hadn't been informed of the mercenaries return as soon as they were spotted on the water-bridge. It was obvious to Stone that there should have been men guarding the perimeter outside the walls, but the men inside these walls had become lax in their security.

They seemed to come to a decision and the voice that had called down first shouted down again. "Right, drop all your weapons and put your hands on you heads. We'll open the gates, but if any of you buggers moves a muscle, we'll blow you back to France. Corporal Jefferies, open the gates. Stevens tell the Colonel some of his Frenchies have come home."

The huge wooden doors clanked and moaned as the locks were opened. The group of five men stood with their hands on their heads, their weapons strewn on the ground around them.

Each man knew what they had to do once the doors were open, and they trusted their comrades in the darkness to cover them. They would grab their weapons and hold the doors until the main body of monks were inside. All they needed were a few seconds and the fort would be open to attack. Stone tensed and drew himself up, ready to leap out of the stretcher and attack the gate. He prayed that the men in the ramparts above were in range of the waiting marksmen lying in the darkness — otherwise it would be a long and bloody night.

The gates slowly opened, and when they were wide enough for a man to get through, Lacroix gave a signal for the hidden attackers to fire. Two redcoats were instantly picked from the ramparts by precision rifle fire and thrown back into the courtyard. Stone leapt from the stretcher, gun in hand, and fired point blank into the shocked face of Corporal Jefferies. The man disappeared into a cloud of smoke and blood as Stone rammed his shoulder into the open gate, thrusting it forward.

The other men had reclaimed their weapons and were attacking the breach in the wall. Some of the defending redcoats had recovered their wits and were firing down on the attackers, but as soon as they showed themselves on the rampart, they came under a hail of bullets from the darkness outside.

In seconds, the rest of the attacking force managed to charge through the now wide-open gates. The monks who had penetrated the compound levelled their rifles and unleashed a volley at the scattered redcoats, before advancing around the perimeter of the compound. The Commander of the garrison had come out of the castle and was shouting at his men to form line. Redcoats were rushing from all directions, confused at being attacked in their own compound.

Most of the defenders along the walls dropped their weapons and surrendered as soon as they saw the grim-faced monks charge towards them. But more and more redcoats were gathering around their Commander near the entrance to the castle. Stone could see the assault wasn't going to be over as quickly as he'd hoped.

He ran to a group of monks lending support fire to some of their comrades on the ramparts. He'd noticed the monks were all carrying Baker rifles, a far more accurate weapon than the standard musket the regular British infantryman carried. The Baker rifle had grooves in the barrel, so the lead ball spun when it was fired, giving it far more accuracy and range than the smooth barrelled musket. He ordered five of the monks to turn their fire on the gathering redcoats, specifically targeting the English Commander.

He watched as the monks took careful aim at the mass of red uniforms, then they fired their lethal volley. The British Colonel, a final order on his lips, was thrown aside like a rag doll by a hail of bullets, and the men he had gathered hastily in defence looked at each other with doubt already in their minds. Stone saw the look on their faces and moved to seize the initiative before it was lost. He leapt forward, sword in hand, roaring a battle cry to spur on his men, charging headlong at the centre of the redcoat line. The monks followed suit and their shouts filled the air behind him as they charged forward.

Some of the redcoats threw down their arms and ran away, but others stood their ground, mostly out of pure shock at the ferocity of the charge and an instinctive need to protect themselves. Stone felt bullets whip past his face and others clutch at his clothes as he ran forward. He saw a redcoat levelling his musket at Stone's chest for a shot that couldn't fail to miss. Stone veered to the left at the last possible moment as the man fired. The bullet went wide and cracked harmlessly into the rampart wall behind him. Stone then, with the kind of utter calm that only comes in battle, charged the man who'd fired the shot, ramming the hilt of his sword into his face while punching the wind out of him. The redcoat fell to the ground holding his nose, which was crushed in a mess of blood and shattered bone. Another redcoat stabbed forward with his bayonet, but Stone parried the half-hearted thrust and swept his sword back to cut the man open in the midriff.

The rest of the monks joined the attack. Stone felt the force of their arrival at his back. The huge men charged into the red ranks, cutting and thrusting, their battle cries continuing through the charge as they moved forward. The monks moved like killing machines, every movement clinical and powerful. At close quarters the recoats didn't stand a chance. Most of the defenders had failed to attach a bayonet to their musket rendering the weapons practically useless after being fired. The monks were far too quick for the garrison's soldiers, even when wielding their muskets like a club. Red-coated bodies lay everywhere. Even those who'd thrown their weapons down were shown little mercy as the monks cut them down almost in frenzy.

Stone, in an act of self-preservation, backed away against a wall and watched the monks advance until every redcoat had been killed or had run away. The ground was littered with dead and dying men, and steam rose from spilled blood on the cold stone floor, rising into the cool night air. Even as the monks stopped their killing and looked around, they seemed physically unchanged by the short battle. Their breathing was steady and they laughed and congratulated each other as they cleaned their weapons on dead men's clothes. For the first time Stone understood what a deadly force these men were, and how defenceless he would be against them.

Stone wiped his own sword clean, then looked around to assess the situation. The attack had been a great success — the castle had fallen within fifteen minutes of their initial assault. The surviving redcoats were ushered together, stripped of their jackets, and herded into an empty horse paddock. He was surprised to see his small force had not suffered a single loss, just a few vicious cuts and bruises. Stone glanced down at his blood soaked shirt. He was the only one who looked like he'd really been in a battle.

Across the compound, he could see Lacroix opening one of the wooden pens the French prisoners of war were kept in during the day. Stone jogged over to meet him, wondering why Lacroix was letting the French prisoners free.

"Lacroix!" he shouted. "What's going on? Why are you letting these prisoners out of their pens? We're not here to free these men." Lacroix turned and saw Stone running towards him.

Du Puy realised his disguise as Colonel Lacroix would only last as long as the first time someone who wasn't aware of his plan recognised him. In Threave, there was one man who knew his identity, one of the French prisoners who was in fact one of his own men. Du Puy had planted him there to gather information on the movements of Cheltenham's mercenaries. Going to Threave was perfect for Du Puy, as he had another task for the spy trapped there. Lacroix pushed open the door to the pen, and one of the prisoners walked out and shook the Frenchman's hand.

Stone rushed up and stood in front of the men, his rifle half raised in their direction. The prisoner looked Stone up and down.

"Are you hurt, monsieur?" The prisoner looked tired and malnourished but held his head high, and Stone recognised the authority in his voice.

"No...I don't believe so...sir." Stone still didn't trust Lacroix, and he certainly wasn't going to let any of these men out of their confinement.

"Richard," Lacroix interrupted, "let me introduce Colonel Justin Lebeoff, a good friend and a senior officer in the French Imperial Guard."

"A pleasure sir," Stone said, raising his hand, but the Colonel just stared at him aghast.

"Another man's blood then?" the Colonel said. Lacroix smiled and gestured at Stone's bloody shirt.

"Just a ruse Colonel," Lacroix said, "an old partisan trick designed to cloud the judgement of a compassionate enemy." Lebeoff looked at Lacroix and seemed to come back to his senses.

"What do you intend to do with the fort now that you have captured it, Captain Stone?" Lebeoff continued.

"I hadn't realised I'd been introduced, Colonel," Stone said. The Colonel flashed a quick glance at Lacroix, who seemed unconcerned at Stone's comment.

"I merely mentioned to the Colonel before you came over, Richard, that you were the one who'd led the attack on the compound so that the Colonel would have the chance to congratulate you." The Colonel smiled at Stone as if the question had been answered, and Stone couldn't think of a reason not to believe him.

"Colonel Lacroix, could I have a word with you for a moment?" Stone asked.

"Yes, of course, Richard." The pair moved away from the door of the pen and out of earshot of the French prisoners.

"I don't want to be the cause of any problems, but I can't be responsible for letting these French prisoners out of the castle," Stone said quietly. Lacroix stood in silence for a moment, then put a hand on Stone's shoulder.

"But Richard, you have just killed dozens of your king's men. I don't think the disappearance of a few French prisoners is going to make much difference, do you? From what you have told me, the only man who knows these prisoners are here is Sir Arthur Cheltenham, and I'm sure he has far more to worry about at the moment." Lacroix smiled while Stone stewed over his words.

"I suppose you're right. Let the Colonel know he is free to leave at his leisure, and he can take whatever rations are in the castle as long as he and his men leave enough for us for a few days." Stone shouldered his rifle and walked back to the main building to see if he could find a clean shirt. Lacroix watched him leave, then turned back to Lebeoff.

"Prepare your men to leave, and head for the rendezvous point outside Edinburgh," Du Puy said to the Colonel. "I want you to be ready to meet with the French emissaries once they disembark. I need you to let Napoleon know we are ready, and prepare for his army to attack the British coastline once I have defeated Cheltenham...now go."

"Yes, Grandmaster." Lebeoff scurried away to prepare for his journey.

CHAPTER 15

By the time Stone got back to the compound, the monks had stripped most of the dead and piled the bodies against the compound wall ready for burial. The area in front of the castle's keep was smeared with blood, and a pair of dogs was fighting over some pale blue intestines.

Stone guided some of his men around the bloody mess and into the main castle building. They walked hesitantly through to the old quarters where the dead English Commander had made his home. Stone cocked his rifle just in case, but the rooms seemed to be empty.

A young woman, no more than a teenager, sat quivering on a bed in the corner of one of the rooms. Apart from a skimpy sheet covering her shoulders, she was naked. Stone nodded to one of the monks who offered the woman a blanket. It looked as if two or three people had been living in the room at one time. The Commander and his whore were two, but there was another bed in the corner, and surrounding it were scraps of food and an empty glass.

As he searched the room, one of the monks called out to him from the door. The monk was pointing to a table near the only window where some thick brown leather books rested a pile of papers. He was walking to the table when a shot was fired outside.

He looked out of the window, which faced the courtyard, and saw one of the monks on the ramparts aiming his rifle towards the secret water-bridge. Stone pulled his telescope out of his belt and focused on the figure running towards the river. He immediately recognised the man and suddenly realised who the third person living in the castle had been.

He shouted out of the window down to the monks gathered on the ramparts below. "I want everyone with a rifle on that wall at the double — that man must be brought down before he escapes." The monks already on the wall fired at will, but Stone saw the shots go wide, splashing harmlessly into the water. The man was on the bridge now and would be out of range once he reached the other side. Ten other monks had reached the rampart and were levelling their rifles, and as Stone watched the figure, he kept losing sight of him in the smoke. Then the man appeared through the haze. He was on the other side of the river. The man turned slightly and Stone tensed as he saw the man sneer and then laugh in contempt.

Stone considered sending a party after him, but Stone could see a farm in the distance, and less than a few hundred yards away were horses grazing in the fields. Their own horses were on the other side of the river, and the man would have escaped by the time they reached them. He closed the telescope and put it back in his belt. He glanced down at the thick brown books on the table, then looked back out the window. He watched the figure get smaller and smaller, the one man he'd hoped to kill from the beginning, and now Clifford was on the way back to his Master.

Stone sent a small party of monks to Troon to meet with Maggie and escort her to Threave. It took two days of travelling, but Maggie finally arrived at the castle looking tired, dishevelled, and not altogether happy. Stone greeted her at the main gate and helped her off her horse. She glared at him as he lowered her to the ground, and without saying a word, she walked towards the castle where she'd seen smoke from a fire billowing from a chimney. Warming her cold, tired bones was the only thing on her mind.

Pulling off her gloves when she reached the keep, she put her hands near the flames. Stone walked into the room behind her. He looked at Lacroix, who was sitting in the corner of the room smoking a pipe with a big grin on his face. The Frenchman just shrugged his shoulders and went back to the book he was reading.

"Is everything alright, Maggie?" Stone asked a little sheepishly. "How was your journey from Troon?" She whipped around and glared at him with steel in her eyes.

"Well," she said quietly through clenched teeth, "apart from having to travel the length of the country through the worst weather imaginable..." Her face started to go red. "Apart from being attacked on the way by every beggar and brigand in Scotland..." She began to undo her wet coat. "Apart from having no idea why I had to travel all the way down here in the first place... Apart from all that, everything..." She threw her coat on the floor. "Apart from all that, everything is fine." Lacroix chuckled from behind his book. Stone picked up her coat and hung it on a chair to dry.

"You'd better get those shoes off as well. We can't have you ill or we might miss your heart-warming smile and pulchritudinous face," Stone said, smiling apologetically at her and radiating outrageous levels of charm. He got down on his knees and started pulling off her riding boots. From the corner of his eye he saw the beginnings of a smile in the corner of her mouth.

After she'd changed her clothes and warmed up a bit, Stone told her about the assault on the castle and how he'd let the French prisoners go free. She seemed happy at that news, and she brightened up even more when Stone presented the papers and the big leather books that Clifford had left behind. Stone was careful not to give Maggie any hint about Clifford and his escape. If Maggie knew how much danger they were both in, there would be no stopping her from returning to Edinburgh.

The papers were copies of Cardinal Beeton's last will and testament, naming the family members the Cardinal had entrusted his treasured possessions to on his death. The rest of the papers were the accumulated life histories of each of those families. Stone guessed that Clifford had been ordered by Cheltenham to collect all this information, to find out who had any knowledge of Cardinal Beeton or the location of William Wallace's body. Beeton's book itself, now back in their possession, added nothing to their existing information for the moment, but one of the other documents in the pile proved very interesting.

Clifford had managed to discover one family mentioned in Cardinal Beeton's will, which over the last 500 years had retained its ancestral roots and family tree. All the other families had either disappeared over the centuries or had been fragmented sufficiently that the original family line no longer existed. Stone presumed Clifford had intended to contact the family to see if they could shed any light on Cardinal Beeton's book about Wallace.

They all agreed that talking to the family could be an option but might be a dead end as the trail was over 500 years old. The family now lived in England and Stone didn't fancy taking a trip all the way to London — the danger was too great. He would rather abandon the whole search and take Maggie away to the continent, away from danger, but he could see from her face that escaping to Europe wasn't an option.

Maggie asked Stone to close the door so the two of them could study the papers away from prying eyes. Even Lacroix had put his book down and was suddenly interested in what Maggie had found at Troon. There was suddenly anticipation in the air, and Maggie wondered if this was what it had felt like for Blind Harry when he had told his stories all those years ago. The fire continued to roar, and the room immediately became warm with the door closed.

Maggie grabbed Beeton's book and held it up to the men, who were now her audience. She pointed to the Latin inscription written under the coat of arms. *"Tutis per Amica – Protected by Friends,"* she read and translated it aloud.

"But protected by whom?" she said to them. Both men shrugged their shoulders. Stone had a big grin on his face. He could tell Maggie was enjoying herself, and he realised she had obviously discovered something significant at Troon. She turned to the page where the names of William Wallace's friends could be seen clearly underlined. She read each name in turn, and then she read the other names in the translated modern version.

"Which of these men were his friends?" she said dramatically. "Did they protect him?" She slammed Beeton's book shut and dropped it on the table. "I think not." She crouched down and picked up a piece of orange roof tile from the floor. The wall behind was black with smoke from the fire, and she began to write the names from Beeton's original book on it with the roof tile:

> *Edward Plummet*
> *Patrick de Gustumo*
> *Tom Tartsuns*
> *William Maar.*

"Who were these men? There is no written record that they ever existed, and yet each of them are mentioned in Beeton's text — an obvious starting point wouldn't you agree?" Lacroix and Stone nodded their heads. "Yet we've found nothing. We've spent weeks on research and we've come up with nothing…until now." She glanced at Stone, a big grin of approval on his face. She smiled quickly in return and then turned back to her notes.

"What I needed to do was find a connection between the names and the Cardinal himself." She wrote his name on the wall next to the other names.

> *Edward Plummet*
> *Patrick de GustumoCardinal Beeton*
> *Tom Tartsuns*
> *William Maar.*

"That's exactly what I've found." She picked up a roll of parchment from the desk and unravelled it in front of them. "This is a rubbing of a stone frieze I found in a chapel at Troon. You can clearly see a depiction of William Wallace dressed in the robes of a priest. In this case, it's not a disguise to escape captivity from the English, but an illustration of how close the relationship was between Wallace and the church." She pointed to the images at the bottom of the rubbing.

"At the bottom are four animals." Both men leant forward to take a closer look. "The rubbing isn't clear because the stone was eroded near the bottom, but I could see the outline of these animals and recognized what they were." She tapped on her leg and whistled softly. Rufus trotted across the room and nuzzled up to Maggie, then sat obediently beside her. Even sitting down he was almost big enough to reach Maggie's shoulder. Maggie patted him on the head and smiled at the two men.

"Monsieur Lacroix," she said quietly. "Would you be good enough to draw your sword out of its scabbard, but do it slowly?" Lacroix looked at her with a puzzled expression, shrugged his shoulders and grabbed the hilt of the sword. Before he had taken it out an inch, Rufus had drawn back his lips, revealing his massive white teeth and emitting a deep growl. The growl turned into a savage snarl as Lacroix drew the sword another inch, where the sword stopped as the Frenchman stared wide eyed and pale. Memories of those ferocious teeth clamped around his throat came flooding back.

"Thank you," Maggie said. "You can put your sword away now." She pointed at the parchment again as Lacroix replaced the weapon. "As you can see," she continued, "the animals at the bottom of the frieze are very similar to Rufus, massive wolfhounds all snarling as if they were protecting their master." She turned back to them.

"The connection between Cardinal Beeton and William Wallace is these animals." She opened another book. "It was pure luck that I found this frieze, but there are other clues left for us if we know where to find them." She opened the book at a page that had a depiction of the Cardinal in St. Andrews. "This book is full of images of the Cardinal, but this particular drawing is the most significant." She brought the book forward so the men could see. The Cardinal was walking near the old town of St. Andrews. The church was in the background and people were waving at him as he passed. Bounding around in a field nearby, chasing rabbits, were the four pets the Cardinal kept. The inscription at the bottom of the page simply read *The Cardinal and his faithful hounds*. "Four dogs," she said, reading their minds. She shut the book and pointed at the wall. "Four dogs called Ed, Pat, Tom and Will. The Cardinal kept wolfhounds."

She sat down at the table and watched Stone and Lacroix as they stared at the wall in silence. She could read exactly what they were thinking.

"What's the secret?" she asked them. There was silence for a moment, and then Lacroix looked at her with respect in his eyes.

"Their names mean something, their second names I mean," replied Lacroix.

"Thank you, monsieur. Yes, you're correct." She stood up again with her piece of tile and crossed out all the first names. "The secret is obvious when you know what to look for particularly when four of William Wallace's closest friends all had the same first name." She began to write on the wall again. "The translation was hard to work out and took me two days to put together." She had written a sentence on the wall in Latin: *Templum Gestum Duo Transitus Arma*.

Stone was busy translating when she turned back to them, but Lacroix knew exactly what it said.

"The book was written in Latin. Cardinal Beeton wrote everything in Latin," Maggie said. "It was simple really, a mere Latin anagram of his dogs' second names. I have to admit though that the Latin took some working out. Each name represented a Latin word — it was just a question of changing the letters around." She put her tile to the wall again. "Translation please," she said like a schoolmistress.

In unison Lacroix and Stone replied, *"The Church bearing two crossing swords."*

Maggie wrote the sentence on the wall and then dropped the tile to the floor. She looked at both their blank expressions and tried to imagine what they were thinking. "It's simple," she said. She walked to the door and called for one of the monks to come into the room. A monk walked entered and stood in front of the three of them, not quite sure what was expected of him.

"Look," Maggie said as she walked over and prodded the large man in the chest. "Excuse me," she apologised to the monk. "You wouldn't mind opening your robe would you?" The monk looked bemused for a moment but then undid his robes and pulled them apart to reveal his leather tunic underneath. After spending some days alone with the monks, Maggie had noticed that they all wore a separate set of clothes underneath their robes. Each man had an insignia on their tunic that she assumed denoted their particular order. In the case of the monks, their insignia was uncannily close to what she imagined they were looking for. She pointed at the insignia emblazoned in the middle of the monks chest, two crossed swords.

"The answers have probably been under our noses for five hundred years, and this clue has been staring the monks in the face. It's my opinion that we need to find a church with this symbol on it, and there we'll find the body and the hidden location of William Wallace."

Stone had a greater concern than where the body of William Wallace might lie: the escape of Cheltenham's key henchman, Clifford. Whatever the relationship was between the monks and Cheltenham, and whoever was controlling who, the English General wasn't going to be happy that Threave could no longer be used as an outpost. Stone knew Cheltenham was being betrayed by the monks, but he had no idea to what extent the monks had control. While he and Maggie stayed at Threave, they were obviously in danger.

Du Puy, on the other hand, through his disguise as Colonel Lacroix, was feeling much better about the situation. Even though Clifford had escaped, Du Puy was certain the assassin had fled without recognising him. By capturing Threave, Du Puy could not only send more loyal followers to his army but he could send a trusted man with a message to his French allies. Cheltenham was walking into a well-orchestrated trap and would soon be destroyed by Du Puy's larger, more experienced force — and Europe would be plunged into war once again.

Du Puy had also given his spies the order to release one final phase of propaganda into every major city in Scotland, pamphlets promising the Scottish people the return of their greatest hero. Du Puy would walk off the battlefield triumphant and march into Edinburgh at the head of his victorious rebel army with the body of William Wallace. The people of Scotland would flood to his banner, and they would support Napoleon Bonaparte, Emperor of France, also an enemy to the English. Du Puy watched Maggie clearing her papers away and had total confidence that the woman could find the body of Wallace in time for the final battle.

After a heated discussion, which Maggie was always going to win, she finally persuaded Stone that going to London was the only option open to them. They had to find the family outlined in the papers that Clifford had left behind. If the family had any information about a "church bearing two crossing swords," then their journey to London would be invaluable to the mission, and if that failed, then the libraries of Edinburgh would be their final hope.

Lacroix volunteered to go south with them. He told them that his family lived in Normandy, so travelling to France from a southern port would make his journey far easier. Although Stone wasn't entirely sure the story was the whole truth, he was glad to have Lacroix's experience at hand. Du Puy could afford to continue on the journey because it would be at least two weeks before his rebel army met the English in battle. If Maggie discovered the location of the tomb in good time then Du Puy could quickly ride back north to be at the front of his army. Cheltenham and Du Puy had even agreed on a date for the final encounter to avoid any confusion.

The band of adventurers headed east, following the north bank of the Solway Firth, but the weather began to worsen and it took them another day to reach the border. The group, including, Stone, and Lacroix, numbered twelve men, and they had two extra horses loaded with supplies. Stone decided to break the group up for security and to attract less attention. Four monks rode the path a mile in front, scouting for trouble, while four remained behind watching their rear. The remaining five members of the group rode in close formation, always alert and ready for trouble.

The following day, they rested in a small valley just outside Dumfries at midday. They decided go around the town and the nearby castle of Caerlaverock as the local garrisons were Borderers loyal to England. Cheltenham would almost definitely be using their support. Stone pulled his telescope from his belt and surveyed the surrounding countryside. He wanted to get a good look at the border before attempting a crossing. The town of Dumfries was just visible to their north over the crest of the valley. He could see smoke rising from numerous houses. To the south of the valley lay the massive castle at Caerlaverock. Even from two or three miles away the building loomed large in the spy glass. He wondered which regiment was garrisoned there, probably the King's Scottish Borderers, he thought. He clearly remembered the monstrous building from a previous visit; it was surrounded by a double moat and hundreds of acres of flat marshy willow woods. Caerlaverock was built to control the southwest entrance to Scotland, and if his history was right it had only been taken once, by Edward I, ironically during the war against William Wallace.

Suddenly his other eye caught a flash of movement to the left of the castle. He moved the glass around to focus on a hill in front of Dumfries a mile to the east. The four monks who were his scouting party were galloping down the hill towards him. As he focused on the monks, he saw them looking and pointing to the south towards the castle. One of them drew his rifle and aimed it towards Caelaverock. Stone pulled the glass from his eye and looked south. He couldn't see what they were pointing at. The scouts were on higher ground and could see over the lip of the valley. Stone passed the glass to Lacroix to have a look.

Lacroix saw a puff of smoke appear on the walls of the castle, which was followed almost instantly by two more. The popping sound of cannon fire followed, startling the horses and making them all jump at the sudden noise. Stone immediately assumed the gunners in the castle were taking target practice.

The scouts were closer now and they could almost hear their shouts. The other monks had mounted up and one was helping Maggie onto her horse. Stone and Lacroix still stood watching the castle as two more bursts of cannon fire exploded from the walls. Stone saw movement in front of the walls and lifted the telescope again. The gates had opened and a whole troop of cavalry charged out of the castle. Then, almost in the same instant, he heard the thunder of hooves and men running, which sounded too close for comfort. Then he realised to his horror exactly what was happening. The monks rode into the camp at a gallop and shouted at them all to retreat towards the town.

Stone stood frozen for a moment, but after a rough nudge from the Frenchman, he ran to his horse and leapt into the saddle. The day had suddenly turned into a nightmare. Someone had tried to attack the castle at Caelaverock, and the party had arrived just as the attacking force had been routed by the defenders. A force at least the size of a regiment was in full retreat from the castle pursued by hundreds of eager cavalrymen, and attacking and defending troops were all heading in their direction.

Stone led the party as they galloped back the way they had come. Stone glanced behind and saw a hoard of men appear at the lip of the valley. The beaten attackers seemed to be mostly peasants with meagre weapons, but he also spotted the distinct red uniforms and kilts of a Highlander regiment, which was now hastily forming to face the advancing cavalry. Stone led the group to the left, angling back towards the castle and a dense crop of trees at the edge of the valley. They pulled up, dismounted, and led the horses into the safety of the trees.

Stone and Lacroix crawled back to the tree line on their hands and knees, and Stone drew out his telescope again to see what was going on. The retreating army hadn't been big enough to stretch the length of the valley, so the travellers' flight hadn't been noticed. Stone watched as the cavalry gave the Highlander regiment a wide berth and instead mercilessly attacked the retreating ranks of Scottish peasants. The Highlanders fired off a volley, but only one side could aim at the passing riders and they did very little damage. The men in the square formation could only watch helplessly as their countrymen were slaughtered and the valley was left strewn with corpses. Stone saw some of the cavalrymen whooping with pleasure as they hacked away at the backs of the retreating Scots. Blades came down, hooves trampled — hundreds died as he watched. Some bravely turned and raised their weapons, but they were all beaten aside.

Stone realised the defeated army was heading straight for Dumfries. A line of men had sensibly formed on the far ridge of the valley and was firing down on the advancing cavalry, and riders fell from their saddles as the charge began to falter. The force of the charge had been lost as the cavalrymen sought out their own victims. Groups of riders in ones and twos charged at the thin line of men at the top of the valley but were beaten back in a hail of bullets.

The Highlanders, seeing the disarray among the enemy cavalry, began to move their square formation slowly towards the valley, and as they moved, they rained volley after volley on the horsemen. Sensing that their advantage was lost, the cavalry broke off the attack, but instead of riding back to the castle, they took up position on the edge of the valley between the castle and the trees where Stone and the others were hiding.

Stone cursed his timing, which couldn't have been any worse. Not only was the whole valley teeming with the battered remnants of a peasant Scottish army, now the Highlander troops had stopped dead in the centre of the valley, unable to retreat or advance because the contours of the valley would break up their square formation and they were wary of the watchful cavalry. Stone's group couldn't leave the valley in any direction without being seen by one side or the other, so they would have to wait until evening to make a move.

Stone trained his glass on the waiting Highlanders. One of the men within the square seemed to wave a flag in the direction of the castle. A bugle behind the walls sounded, calling the cavalry to retreat back inside. A strange move, Stone thought, because the horsemen obviously had the upper hand. As he focused the telescope on Highlander soldiers, he saw a dishevelled face in the centre of the square formation, one of the few men not in uniform. Clifford, who had escaped from Threave not two days earlier, was talking to a burly man in a kilt who seemed to be the commanding officer.

Suddenly the sun came out directly in front of Stone. He lowered the glass quickly, but it was too late. He swore out loud as one of the soldiers amongst the ranks of redcoats shouted to his Colonel. Immediately, a group of men broke free from the square in pursuit of what they thought were enemy scouts. Stone had only seconds to act. The Highlanders were only a hundred yards away, and with Clifford among their ranks, they couldn't afford to get captured. A group of cavalry, who had remained behind to keep an eye on the enemy, charged to head off the Highlanders, but they would be too late to cut them off before they got to the copse and the travellers cowering within. Stone had only one choice — to seek refuge in the castle.

He ordered the others to mount up again, and Stone led the party from the copse, away from the rebel soldiers and towards the advancing English cavalry. The group galloped off just as the chasing Highlanders came into range and fired off a volley. The shots fell short, but Clifford watched Stone's retreat eagerly through a telescope. He watched as the English cavalry escorted Stone's party back to the castle. As the gates to the castle closed, the battery of artillery opened fire again and the Highlanders beat a hasty retreat. Maggie and Stone had been recognised, and Clifford already aware of Stone's treachery from the attack at Threave had a few scores to settle.

CHAPTER 16

They cantered through the gates of the castle, escort cavalry surrounding them on both sides. Maggie had to crane her neck to see the tops of the walls, and there she saw cannon blasting their shot towards the enemy in huge spouts of noise and smoke. She also noticed the odd shape of the fortification, a triangle with only three walls and a tower at each corner. It was the strangest and most impregnable looking castle she'd ever seen. She couldn't fathom why such a small inexperienced force had tried to attack it.

As the gates shut with a thud behind them, soldiers ran up to help them dismount. The courtyard of the castle was in chaos. Hundreds of men were milling around doing nothing while others were tending to horses and the wounded or helping to take shot up to the walls. Stone noticed the rebel attack had inflicted some real damage. Numerous corpses were piled under the wall awaiting burial, and black scorch marks could be seen along some of the walls.

An officer came out of the gatehouse and walked up to Stone. He saluted smartly and offered his hand. "Lieutenant Hardy, at your service, duty officer of the watch." Stone shook his hand. The lieutenant looked over the party, not batting an eyelid at the mixed company of travellers. Then he looked back at Stone and smiled. "All of you look like you've had a bit of a fright. It's not very often you stumble onto a battlefield in the middle of nowhere."

Stone forced a laugh, not quite sure where the Lieutenant was leading the conversation. "Are you going anywhere in particular Mr...?"

"Stone, Captain Stone at your service. Yes I'm..." He took some papers from his saddlebag. "I'm escorting these religious gentlemen," he said, as he gestured to the monks who were sitting inconspicuously in the shadows under the wall, "to the border."

Hardy didn't even look at the monks, but instead took out his timepiece and studied it for a second. He handed back the papers to Stone without even looking at them, then gestured to one of the waiting orderlies.

"My man will help you deal with your mounts and show you to a billet for the night. I'm afraid you could be here until we have rid ourselves of this pitiful force at our gates." He waved towards the valley.

"Who are those people?" Maggie spoke for the first time. Hardy seemed shocked for a moment, then looked at her for a couple of seconds.

"Madam, please excuse my rudeness." He bowed slightly. "I didn't see you there and thus hadn't realised we were in such good company." She blushed slightly at the complement. "I'm afraid we have no idea where that army came from. This morning the valley and the land roundabout were quiet and we were readying ourselves to march to Edinburgh."

"You were leaving the fort?" Stone interrupted.

"Yes, sir. We have half the new northern army stationed here and we were going to join with the rest of the army at Glasgow." He paused as if to remember where he was. "Then suddenly this hoard appeared from nowhere and took us completely by surprise. If it hadn't been for the foresight of our commanding officer, Sir Arthur Cheltenham, we would have surely sustained far worse losses." Stone paled visibly at the mention of Cheltenham's name. "Are you alright, sir?" Hardy was looking at him with a worried expression on his face.

"I've an old wound that plays up occasionally," Stone replied.

What a day this was turning out to be, Stone thought. He'd almost led the party straight onto a battlefield and into an army that had appeared out of thin air. Now they were stuck in an impregnable castle with the one man responsible for the biggest uprising since Bonny Prince Charlie, and just outside the walls was a man who could implicate them in the attack on Threave. What Clifford was doing among the enemy when his master was inside the castle, Stone couldn't quite comprehend. And why hadn't Cheltenham followed up on his initial victory and crushed the attack before the enemy could regroup? Cheltenham had at least five thousand men crammed into the castle plus cavalry and could have destroyed the attackers easily.

Stone focused his attention on the officer, hoping for some answers. "Did you say Sir Arthur Cheltenham was your commanding officer?"

"Yes, sir. His Lordship has taken command of the army personally, and we're expected to march as soon as we've defeated the rabble outside."

"That rabble," Stone replied, "has got a whole regiment of Highlanders in their ranks. They won't be beaten by a simple cavalry charge."

Hardy looked at him with a calm gaze. "I'm sure His Lordship has everything in hand, Captain. Now, if you'll excuse me, I have a watch to change. Madam." With a salute, Lieutenant Hardy turned, issued an order to a servant, and walked back to the tower.

Stone gestured to Maggie to join him with the others near the wall. "Cheltenham's here," he said to everyone. "By the look of it, he's either planning to leave the fort immediately or wait until the rebels outside have been completely dispersed, which means we could be here for a while." Maggie watched as Stone's hand went subconsciously to the hilt of his sword.

"Maggie, would you mind if I have a quick word with Lacroix in private?"

Maggie had become accustomed to Stone's chauvinistic methods of managing the group. It was the only thing she didn't like about the Englishman, the fact that he obviously didn't think she could add anything to their travel plans. Accustomed or not, she felt slightly aggrieved because if it wasn't for her they wouldn't have gotten anywhere on the mission at all. Even so, this time the situation seemed more serious and so she put her strong female instincts for equality to one side for the moment.

"No, of course, Richard. You boys go and talk strategy amongst yourselves." Stone looked at her quizzically for a moment, not sure about the tone in her voice, but he could worry about Maggie's issues later. They were in a dire situation and he didn't fancy explaining the dangers of their predicament to Maggie.

"I think Cheltenham's up to something," Stone said to Lacroix away from the rest of the party. "Before we got picked up, I saw that bastard Clifford in the middle of that square. I'm positive he was signalling to the castle, because unless Cheltenham is a complete idiot, there's no way he would have broken off the attack." Stone pulled his watch out and studied it for a moment. "I'd say we're safe for now. It'll take that army a few hours to gather their men for another attack, if indeed that's what they're planning. But if Clifford saw us, then we're going to have to leave here in a hurry. We can't discount the fact that he is in direct contact with Cheltenham."

"You despise this man, Clifford, eh?" Lacroix asked.

"Let's just say things will get a whole lot easier for us when that man's dead," Stone replied. Du Puy couldn't have agreed more, but he wasn't going to tell Stone that, especially as he needed Stone to confide in him as much as possible.

Stone beckoned to a couple of the monks. "William, I want you to find a way out of here in case we have to make a quick exit." The monk nodded. "Lacroix, you stay here. We can't have your accent blowing our cover. Angus, you and I are going to locate Cheltenham — let's see what we can find out." Maggie walked over and took his arm before Stone could move away.

"Richard, are you sure it's wise to go snooping around. I don't want you to get separated from us." Stone looked into her eyes and took her hands in his.

"Don't worry," he whispered. "We're just going to do a little eavesdropping. I'm not ready to get myself into trouble just yet." He lifted her hand and kissed it gently. "You just make sure you're ready to leave if we have to." He turned back to the group. "The rest of you stay out of sight and don't talk to anyone. We'll be back as soon as we can."

"But why would we have to leave in a hurry, Richard?" Maggie called after him, but he was already lost in the crowd. "Surely this is the safest place to be," she whispered to herself, completely bemused as to what was going on.

Sir Arthur Cheltenham wasn't planning a strategy for the defence of the fort, but instead was having lunch, and he was already far drunker than any of his guests seated around the table. He and his senior officers were in a large wooden building situated near the rear of the castle compound. It didn't take Stone and Angus very long to find Cheltenham's headquarters, as it was very heavily guarded and the noise of cheering and laughter could be heard yards away.

As Stone watched, he realised there was no way to get inside and no way to get even close enough to listen to any conversations. He was about to give up, when a bugle sounded in the courtyard for the men of the fort to gather on parade for inspection. The inspections took place morning and night on the orders of Cheltenham himself, who felt the need to remind everyone of his power and importance. He inspected the men personally to remind them who was in charge, and the English commander was liberal with punishments when the men didn't come up to his high standards.

The castle erupted into chaos as hundreds of men ran to join their companies, slinging on jackets and shouldering arms. The door to Cheltenham's headquarters burst open and the man himself with his half-drunk officers strode out into the courtyard. Stone nudged Angus, and they walked towards the hut. All the guards had followed Cheltenham and were now standing behind him protectively as he watched his men assemble. Stone glanced around and saw they were completely alone. He told Angus to stay at the door and whistle twice if anyone approached. Stone then walked in as Cheltenham began addressing the troops.

"Men." A long dramatic pause followed. "Great days are ahead of us…" Stone lost the rest as he focused on the rooms.

The dining room was a mess of half-eaten food and spilled wine. He could hear the clatter of plates in the back room as servants cleared the kitchen. He went straight into Cheltenham's temporary office just off the dining room. A bed lay in the corner and a desk stood at the back in the centre. Two flags hung behind the desk next to the flag of the United Kingdom. Stone now caught snippets from the speech Cheltenham was giving to his men through an open window.

"Victory through strength…glory and power returned…"

Dozens of papers lay on the desk. Stone looked them over quickly and found nothing of interest. He rifled through the draws and cupboards, but again nothing. He stood still and looked around for a moment. His eyes stopped on a picture on the wall. Frowning, he walked over to take a closer look. It seemed to be a battle scene. William Wallace was portrayed as the conqueror. A bit strange, he thought, for someone who obviously hated the man.

Suddenly Stone realised he couldn't hear Cheltenham talking anymore. He froze as he heard a shrill whistle from outside. He listened as Angus ran away for cover and then heard feet on the wooden floor of the hut. Bloody hell, he thought — Angus could have given him more warning. Cheltenham walked through the door to his office, then turned back and shouted down the hallway.

"Colonel Winterbourne, to my office on the double." Stone had just enough time to duck behind one of the massive flags at the back of the room before Cheltenham walked into the room. Colonel Winterbourne hurriedly followed Cheltenham and closed the door behind him. Cheltenham sat down heavily behind his desk, inches from where Stone was standing.

"A fine body of troops, eh Charles," Cheltenham said, gazing out the window.

"Very fine, my Lord," replied the colonel, who stood to attention in front of the desk.

"What news then, Charles?" Cheltenham said, waving a hand at Winterbourne to stand at ease.

"Well, my Lord, it seems Clifford has managed to gather most of the rebels back together and is ready for another assault."

"Good, good. Excellent news," Cheltenham interrupted, slurring his words slightly.

"However, it does seem, according to Clifford, that the rebels are reluctant to continue fighting because of the odds against them. They lost hundreds in the first attack, my Lord."

"Damn it all!" Cheltenham slammed his hand down on the desk. "The bloody Scottish cowards will run away before we even give them a decent bloody fight." He pointed a finger at Winterbourne. "I thought we were giving them too much help as it is, but it seems we're going to have to give them another little victory just to pep their morale up a bit." He stood up and paced. "What will it take to get this scum to stand up and fight me properly?" he said to no one in particular. He sat back down and drew his pen from an inkwell. He wrote for a second, then handed the piece of paper to Winterbourne.

"At eighteen hundred hours, I want one of your men to open the gate as if we're going on the offensive, and Clifford is to attack at that moment."

"My Lord, is that wise?" Winterbourne interrupted.

"Don't worry, Colonel. We'll be waiting for them. Just make sure their attack lasts a little longer this time. Have your men hold their fire until the last second. I need these recruits trained in real combat, and they're not going to get the practice they need unless they are put under pressure." He wrote on another piece of paper. "Then dispatch this note to my contact in Edinburgh. He is to print an article about a great slaughter of rebels in the south by the barbaric English. Also make sure Horseguards gets a dispatch about a first English victory in the north. We need this first small victory, Charles, to keep the London bureaucrats off our back. The history of the campaign begins here, Colonel, and I don't want anything to stand in my way. Do you understand?"

"Yes, sir. Completely," Winterbourne replied.

"We'll see if this stirs the rebels up a bit. Oh, and Colonel, make sure my Highlanders don't front the rebel attack. I don't want any casualties from my own side, particularly from the one regiment I have that knows how to fight. Lord knows I'm paying them enough to be part of these fun and games".

The Colonel turned to leave, but then he turned around to face Cheltenham again. "My Lord, there was one other thing. According to Clifford's last messages, a group of people entered the castle an hour ago under guard. We can't be sure if Clifford is correct, but the message suggested the people were spies and should be captured immediately."

Cheltenham looked at him and frowned. "How on earth did anyone manage to get inside the castle with a bloody battle going on?" Cheltenham asked with a bemused expression on his face. Stone couldn't help squirming slightly from behind the flag as he realised the game was nearly up.

"I have no idea my Lord, but I will ask the duty officer immediately." Winterbourne turned to leave again. As he opened the door, Cheltenham called out to him.

"No prisoners, please Charles. You know the routine." Winterbourne paused for a second then closed the door. Stone cringed behind the flag. He had to get out of here. Otherwise, the whole lot of them were going to get caught and strung up.

Angus watched as an officer left the building and marched over to the gatehouse. A few minutes later, through the window, he saw Cheltenham go back into the dining room to a cheer from his waiting guests. A minute later Stone walked out of the exit, stumbling as if he'd had too much to drink. He made his way past the guards boldly, as if he'd sat down with Cheltenham himself. The guards glanced at him but paid little attention. Strangers going inside were suspicious, not strangers coming out.

Angus joined him and they walked back to the billet where the others were staying. They had an hour before the scheduled attack at six, and Stone wanted to be out of the castle long before then. When they rejoined the group, Stone turned to William with a hopeful expression on his face, hoping for an easy escape route out of the castle. The big man grinned back at him.

"We won't be able to take the horses, and we're going to get wet and dirty, but apart from that, I've found a way out of here," William said happily.

They quickly climbed the steps of the wall that led to the rear ramparts of the castle. Stone prayed all eyes were on the approaching enemy, who were probably already moving into position. The adventurers were the only people at the rear of the castle, which made their escape easier. Stone looked back and could see the advancing rebels moving into position for another frontal assault on the castle. Stone estimated there were about a thousand rebels, not including the Highlanders, who weren't to be committed to the attack on Cheltenham's order. The pitiful rebel force wasn't nearly big enough to assault a castle the size of Caerlaverlock. Stone was amazed that Clifford had managed to persuade the rebels to attack even after having suffered a heavy defeat. However Clifford had done it, the rebels were going to be slaughtered and Cheltenham couldn't have cared less. The rebels might as well have been cattle. Stone resisted the urge to turn around and put an end to the rebellion by sticking a knife between Cheltenham's ribs, but Stone now had a greater consideration, Maggie, and he had to get her out of the castle safely.

William led them to a section of the wall used as the garbage disposal area. Stone looked down a long chute cut through the stone leading down to the ditch thirty feet below. A miniature port cutlass usually blocked the exit, but it had been left open by a careless servant. At the bottom of the chute was a deep, black pool of water. Its edges were strewn with rubbish and rotten food, and the smell that rose up to their noses was totally repellent. Stone looked at William with a raised eyebrow, then patted him on the shoulder.

"Are you volunteering to go first then, William?" Without another word, and to Stone's surprise, the monk climbed into the chute and slid halfway down. When he reached the open metal gate, he grabbed hold of it to slow down his momentum. The metal gate was only ten feet from the ground, so the monk was able to heave himself out of the chute and jump to the ground, avoiding the horrible mess underneath. He immediately drew his sword and ran to the wall calling for them all to lower their rifles to him. The other monks had started to file through and drop to the ground when all hell suddenly broke loose.

Winterbourne had spoken to Lieutenant Hardy, the duty officer, and both had been frantically hunting around the compound for the missing travellers, whom they now assumed were rebel spies. Hardy was the first to notice the group of people gathered on the rear ramparts, and Winterbourne immediately ordered a company of infantry to open fire on them. As the bullets whipped around the remaining men on the rear rampart, the clock struck six and the doors to the castle opened, letting hundreds of screaming rebels burst through.

The first noises of battle momentarily distracted the infantry, and the rest of Stone's party managed to leap through the chute to the murky waters below. Stone paused briefly on the rampart to watch the mayhem erupt in the yard below. Crazed by the thought of victory, hundreds of rebels rushed into the compound but had no one to fight. Only at the last minute did they see their impending doom stretched out in front of them. Five hundred muskets were ordered to five hundred shoulders as the first two ranks of redcoats lined up at the back of the courtyard taking aim. Even though the two lines of red-coated men looked solid enough, the men were in fact as green as the rebels that faced them. Not a single man lined up in the English ranks had ever fired a weapon at a live target before, and they were more boys than men. Cheltenham's new northern army was made up of old scraps and young terrified boys. The best English soldiers were in France fighting Napoleon and none could be spared to put down a few "insurgents" in the north. Cheltenham was mad, but he was not insane enough to send these raw troops into a proper battle, at least not until they'd had some practice. The whole battle was stage-managed. The rebels had been enticed by the idea of an easy victory, and Clifford had told their leaders that Cheltenham's army was in chaos and the English were on the brink of mutiny. The rebels were informed that soldiers sympathetic to their cause would open the gates to the castle at an allotted time, but Cheltenham had set a trap and the Highlanders were in fact very firmly on the side of the English. But Cheltenham had severely underestimated the rebels resolve, and his young troops were far from ready to fight in a close quarter battle.

When the order was given to fire, the entire front rank fired far too high, missing their targets completely, and the rear rank hardly made a dent in the charging mass of Scotsmen. When the smoke cleared, the English realised their mistake and hurriedly moved to reload, but the rebels were quick to take advantage. There were enough rebels already through the gates to charge the petrified front rank of redcoats, who were reloading painfully slowly. Sergeants were screaming at their men to reload even as the first rebels hit the line in a sickening thud of metal and flesh, and more were pouring through the gate as the Scots suddenly sensed victory. The redcoats began to break rank, the ones and twos brave enough to disobey their sergeants who were still shouting for control but they had nowhere to run. The recruits were surrounded on all sides by the castle walls, and the compound was thick with men already fighting Stone smirked as he remembered Cheltenham's words describing how easy victory would be. This would be a hard-fought battle if won at all.

He was just about to leap down the chute, when he saw Cheltenham's reserve forces charging from a hidden part of the compound. Cheltenham had deliberately placed his weaker, younger troops in the front line to make the battle last longer and thereby get his men used to battle. It seemed Stone had underestimated Cheltenham's abilities as a commander. He watched as the rebels in the compound were surrounded and the battle began in earnest. The castle compound had become a seething mass of men, smoke and death as both sides engaged in old fashioned bloody hand to hand combat. There was no longer room to keep ranks and volley fire so bayonet met bayonet and any other weapon the rebels had managed to get hold of. As Stone slid down the chute, he realised the real slaughter was beginning, and he knew Cheltenham wouldn't take any prisoners.

The travellers could hear the noise of battle raging in the castle compound. Without horses they were exposed and had no choice but to run from the castle, away from the danger of battle. Because all the fighting was happening on the opposite side of the castle, they ran south, towards the Solway Firth. They would follow the estuary to the border. Then, if they could, they would buy some more horses and ride south to England.

CHAPTER 17

Sir Henry Burns was sitting in his study, reading one of the many reports that came flooding into his office every day about the rebellion. The monks had remained to guard the newspaper building ever since Maggie had left with Stone, and Burns had little means of discovering what had happened to them. Sir Henry, on hearing that his daughter had gone on an adventure, had been furious but had no one to vent his anger, so now he just sat in his office each day in a state of worried acceptance. It soon dawned on the old man that the monks were somehow in league with Sir Arthur Cheltenham, and by giving the pretence of cooperation with them, he had already learned a great deal.

Sir Henry had managed to secretly send out a few messages to see if he could discover where his daughter may have gone. Unknown to him, however, every message had been intercepted and destroyed. The monks now rarely left his side, and all Burns could do was sit in quiet contemplation about what Cheltenham and the monks were up to.

As Burns sat reading another letter, he jumped slightly as a loud bang filled the corridor outside his office. There was a scuffle and some more banging as the door to the study flew open and a man was thrown backwards into the room. Smoke began to filter through from the corridor and the acrid smell of gunpowder stifled the air.

The monk guarding Burns stared unsympathetically at the body on the floor. It was one of the newspaper employees, his chest a mess of blood and his eyes open wide in a deathly stare. Through the smoke at the door a shrouded figure appeared holding a smouldering pistol, and he had a big grin on his face. Behind the man, Burns could see at least two or three others struggling to hold another prisoner. The man who walked through the door looked at Burns, and then put the pistol in his belt.

"Ugly bugger," he said to Burns. "A shame to have wasted two bullets on him." He moved aside so the other men could bring the prisoner inside. Burns looked at the man on the floor and realised it was one of the printing press technicians.

"Apparently, you've been a naughty boy, Mr. Burns," he said, drawing the pistol again. "You've not been doin' what the nice Mr. Cheltenham has asked you to do." He started to reload the weapon. "Mr. Cheltenham says the only way to persuade you to do what he wants is to kill some people. Then kill some more people until you've done what he's asked." He levelled the gun at the prisoner's head that Burns realised was another member of his printing press staff and pulled back the cocking mechanism. He stared into Burn's eyes until the old man nodded his head in agreement. The man smiled again, then lowered his weapon.

"Well, that was perfectly easy, now wasn't it, Mr. Burns?" The man held out his hand and one of the monks passed him a large envelope.

"Mr. Cheltenham wants you to do it tomorrow at noon. See to it that there's a big crowd he says." He gestured to the other men to release the prisoner and to leave the room. He stood there alone, watching the young printing press engineer get to his feet. "Mr. Cheltenham also said you'd probably not do it unless you knew we were serious," he continued. Raising the gun again, he pointed it at the prisoner's head. Burns locked eyes with the young engineer and in the split second before the trigger was pulled Burns witnessed the multitude of emotions that speed through a human mind just before certain death. Burns could then only close his eyes as his other senses recorded the noise of a life being discharged from its body and he winced as the body thumped unceremoniously to the floor.

It took the travellers a day and a half of hard walking to get well beyond the border, and by the end of the second day, they were exhausted. Stone, not wanting to bump into any government or rebel troops, had led them down only the minor roads and walkways. They reached the old Roman wall that had been built by the Emperor Hadrian by sundown. During the Roman occupation of Britain, the wall indicated the northern most part of the Roman Empire. Now it was an old crumbling monument to a forgotten civilisation.

Maggie bought some more horses at Carlisle with some of the gold Ruth had given her, and they made sure they had enough supplies for the rest of their journey to London. When they passed York, Stone was confident there hadn't been a serious pursuit so he switched back to using the main highways to shorten their journey.

A huge crowd had assembled at the foot of the stairs to the *Scottish Time's* headquarters building. Sir Henry Burns stood a few steps from the bottom, in front of the people, his head slightly bowed as he read the papers in his hand. He'd stood before a hundred crowds before, spoken to thousands of people over the years, and he loved the experience, but now he wished he were a thousand miles away without a soul in the world to speak to.

The people of Edinburgh saw Sir Henry as a messenger, a man who would tell them news of the things they most wanted to hear about, and they trusted his words completely. Burns had become known in Scotland as a man who spoke the truth when others, especially in government, told them only lies, and his word had become the unwritten law. Burns was seen by the people as an institution rather than a political instrument, and therefore he had continued to make speeches. He also knew that he would never be perceived as a threat by the men who had the real power in Scotland. But now, through the intervention of Cheltenham, Burns was to be the political voice for a new rebellion.

The faithful had gathered, for word had spread that the great man was to speak. For the first day in a week, peace reigned through the city. Cheltenham had made sure nothing would get in the way of this moment, that nothing would keep the people from hearing Sir Henry speak. Thousands lined the streets, and many more leaned out of windows and doors. On all sides, however, troops could be seen in huge numbers. Cannon muzzles were trained on the crowd from the castle above, and cavalry were saddled and ready in back streets and courtyards. A time bomb was ready to go off in the city, and all Burns had to do was light the fuse and watch the explosion.

He raised his eyes from the floor and looked over the writhing mass of people spread out in front of him. As he looked into their faces, he knew the people didn't want to fight any more than he did. Most of these people felt they had suffered enough hardship over the years and wanted no more of it than they had already faced. But, at the same time, he could pick out the men and women in the crowd who wanted something more out of their miserable lives, people who wanted some sort of vengeance for the years of neglect and poverty. Perhaps what he was about to do was for the good, he reasoned, and these people would come out the other side better off than before. Burns had to hope that was the case, and he needed some sort of justification, but most of all he prayed that one day his daughter would forgive him. He slowly raised his hand and an expectant hush came over the crowd.

"People of Scotland." His voice boomed around the streets and houses. "I'm afraid I bring you here under false pretences." A few murmurs rose in the crowd. "I have no important news to give you this morning, but instead, I want to speak to you on a matter of the greatest importance." He glanced over at the nearest soldiers only a few metres from where he was standing. He realised he only had a few moments to complete what he had to say before they captured and arrested him.

"We've seen what's been happening to our city and country over the last few days, indeed for months, indeed for as many years as I care to remember." His voice was strong and confident, showing neither the pain or the terrible guilt he was feeling. The speech had to be believable to the very last word.

"You've had enough, my friends and countrymen. I've had enough." He paused long enough for the crowd to catch up with what he was saying.

"We've seen a gradual destruction of our nationalism over the last decade, together with the obliteration of our language, culture and institutions — all of it replaced by an English imperialist ideal." People in the front row began looking at each other with puzzled expressions, and some in the crowd began mumbling words of agreement. Burns glanced at the soldiers near him. They were looking around at the crowd, which seemed suddenly to be pulsing with a strange energy. The people were being given the ultimate endorsement by their trusted oracle, and as Burns continued, he could sense their rage and uncertainty boiling to the surface.

"I ask you all to do away with words now, and if any of you trust me at all, I say dissolve the union between England and Scotland and set up a Scottish government in Edinburgh."

People began shouting their support like steam escaping from a boiling pot, and the pressure was becoming stronger by the second. Some in the crowd shouted agreement, but others cried out for Burns to be quiet. He continued relentlessly, but he now had to shout over the crowd as more and more people found their voices.

"Sever Scotland from our English oppressors and restore our ancient independence. We will no longer surrender our national sovereignty to a country that neither cares for our welfare or even our lives." Burns could see an officer talking to his men, then pointing to him and the crowd. Burns imagined what the officer was saying: "Shut him up before he inspires this crowd to riot."

The people were in an uproar now, and Burns could no longer talk over the noise. He could see ringleaders egging the mob forward. Some people began to chant his name while others were cursing it. The noise became almost deafening. Banners that had been hidden away by Cheltenham's men until the right moment suddenly appeared from nowhere, and their appearance changed the atmosphere dramatically. Soldiers positioned around the mob began to close in, and the crowd instinctively pushed outward towards them. Burns sensed that the mob was ready for the final act of his performance. He took a step back so he was in full view of the entire crowd as the young officer he'd noticed earlier began to approach him. The officer turned away for a second, and in that moment, Burns drew a pistol from his belt. The man turned back and his eyes were instantly drawn to the weapon and his face went pale with fear. Burns levelled the weapon at the man's face, and in the same moment he heard a thousand people take a sudden gulp of air. A hush fell over the square as everyone seemed to hold that single breath. He drew in a deep breath himself and then prayed for his daughter's safety wherever she was.

"Liberty or death!" Burns screamed at the crowd with as much volume as he could muster, and then he blew the officer into oblivion. The crowd broke and charged from the square, guns fired, cannon burst, cavalry charged. The war in the city had begun again, and Burns was a prisoner.

CHAPTER 18

Maggie and Stone reached the outskirts of the great city of London four days later. They were still twenty miles from the centre when they saw the dirty haze of the city on the horizon. The travellers had ridden hard each day, and at least three of their horses were now lame.

Stone had lived near London most of his life and knew the area of the last known address for the family they were looking for. He led them around the outskirts of the city to an area close to the north-western portion of London. He took them to a place called Harrow on the Hill, which was dominated by heath land and a scattering of houses and farms.

They reached a small estate near the centre of Harrow that, according to their records, was where the Stracchan family hopefully still lived. Stone asked Lacroix to make camp while he and Maggie went to call on the house.

They rode back an hour later, both with big grins on their faces. Lacroix handed them some hot tea when they got down from their mounts.

"It seems," Stone told the group, "that only two members of the family are still alive. The house is empty and has been sold, but the grounds man on the estate told us that, after the parents died, their two sons sold the estate and moved closer to the centre of the city. He gave us one address but couldn't be sure that either of the sons still lived there."

They all sat around the fire and ate lunch, then continued southwards into the heart of the city. As they rode closer, Maggie noticed something a little odd about their surroundings. She looked at Stone, who had the same puzzled look on his face. Over the past hour they had passed shops, stalls, churches and public buildings. People were walking past, going about their normal day-to-day business without a care in the world. Stone leapt off his horse at a shop that was selling some London newspapers and bought the *London Times*. He flicked through it quickly, then passed it up to Maggie to read. Maggie turned each page slowly before looking back down at Stone.

"Nothing," she said to him.

"I know," he replied. "Not a single word about it in the paper." He spread his arms and gestured around him. "Or any sign of disquiet anywhere, in fact."

"May I suggest," said Lacroix, "that there is so little news about the rebellion in the north because of the critical state of war in France." They both looked at the Frenchman with puzzled expressions. Lacroix smiled. "Bonaparte has probably lost this war, we all know that, but he's come back from defeat and exile before so why should anything be different now. The British government is probably scared the French will take advantage of the rebellion in Scotland to divide the allied forces in Europe." Du Puy was telling Maggie and Stone more of the truth than they would ever know otherwise. "It is very simple really," he continued. "The news of the rebellion will never reach the ears of the common people until Napoleon has been defeated. The people will never really know what is happening because the government will be censoring all information coming from the north. Any news will be rumour and speculation, nothing more — it is the way of politics," he said with a shrug.

Stone nodded his head in agreement. Cheltenham could get away with bloody murder, Stone thought, and no one may ever know the truth of what happens in the north.

Maggie kept hold of the newspaper and read it through again as Stone led them deeper into the city. When she was finished reading, Maggie marvelled at the sites around her. She'd been to London before, but the city always had something new to offer or something more fabulous to see. The sprawling Thames meandered into the lives of every Londoner, bustling with small craft, barges, trade vessels and great ships of the line that were being reloaded and armed to take men and supplies back to the war in France. Everywhere she looked, in all directions, the city was spread out in front of her like a sprawling black beast out of a dream.

London was alive with activity, and the smell of the place was both intoxicating and repellent. The air reeked of sweat, smoke, and rotting bales of straw. In the poorer areas, blood flowed down the streets from abattoirs, and men and horses, rats and chickens added to the waste and raw sewage. On the affluent streets and merchant squares, the walls of houses gleamed with Italian marble and American wood. The smell of spices was everywhere, and the people were adorned in the latest fashions and paraphernalia of the season.

People jostled together for business and shops sold goods from all four corners of the globe: Indian spices, Russian furs, silks from Japan, or fruit from the Americas. One merchant Maggie saw was American, and he was selling rifles and other guns. He'd set up a firing range, and London businessmen were shooting targets while black servants reloaded for them. It had been a long time since Maggie had seen a black man, and she marvelled at their shining dark skin in comparison to the white men all around. Maggie knew the men were slaves, and she abhorred the practice, but she wondered if their lives were better now than they were before. Living in civilised society must be a better life than the savage lands of Africa, she reasoned, but what did she know? She'd never stepped foot in any of those far-off lands.

In the distance, as they rode further south, Maggie saw a massive expanse of parkland. Tens of miles of wood and heath land surrounded on all sides by the smoky black city. As they rode closer, Maggie saw deer in the distant fields and a hunt raced across their path a mile or so away, horns blaring and dogs barking. Rufus sniffed the air but kept close to his mistress. Stone suddenly leapt down from his horse and accosted a young man selling vegetables on a street corner.

"Excuse me lad, but what park is this in front of us?" The young man looked at Stone as if he was mad.

"It's the Hyde Park, sir. That building over there in the distance is Apsley House. Rumour has it that Wellington himself has promised to buy the house if he manages to beat Old Boney." Stone looked at the building, a magnificent piece of architecture surrounded by a great deal of land. Definitely a property worthy of the Iron Duke, he thought.

"We've come too far west," he said to Maggie and Lacroix, feeling a little foolish as he knew London's streets well enough. "We'll have to turn around. It's only a couple of miles to where we need to go."

"Want to buy some potatoes, sir?" the boy said hopefully. Stone looked up at Maggie who had an eyebrow raised in suggestive anticipation.

"Yes, I suppose so," he said, and he threw the boy a coin that was far more than the knobbly, muddy potatoes were worth.

"Thank you, sir," the boy said as he shoved the vegetables into a bag offered by one of the monks. Stone climbed back onto his horse and headed back the way they had come, Lacroix and Maggie following with big grins of derision on their faces.

The travellers veered away from the park and headed back towards Bloomsbury. In the heart of Bloomsbury was Montague House and the home of the British Museum. Stone found an Inn nearby and paid for rooms for them all that night. Then Stone, Maggie, and Lacroix left the monks at the inn and walked to the museum. The information Stone had been given was months old, but the British Museum was the last known work address of one of the Stracchan brothers.

Maggie asked a clerk at the front desk if a Mr. Gordon Stracchan worked in the building. The clerk pointed them towards the Townley Gallery where Mr. Stracchan worked in the museum's Egyptian artefacts section. The three of them wandered through the gallery, gazing at the amazing works of art housed within the exhibition. They stood for a moment in front of the Rosetta stone given to King George III in 1801. Soldiers in Napoleon's army discovered the Rosetta stone in 1799 while digging the foundations of an addition to a fort near the town of Rosetta in Egypt. On Napoleon's defeat, the stone became the property of the English under the terms of the Treaty of Alexandria, along with other antiquities that the French had found.

Another clerk eventually came up to ask if he could help, and he took them through the museum and presented them to a tall, thin man who introduced himself as Dr Stracchan.

"Dr Stracchan, it's a great pleasure to meet you. We've come a long way to see you," Maggie said. "I was hoping we could take up some of your time to ask you some questions."

Dr Stracchan frowned at the trio standing at his door and looked them over carefully. In his experience, when encountering strangers, especially strangers like these two men, who were undoubtedly soldiers or even mercenaries by the look of them, it was best to ask no questions and give them what they wanted. He invited them into his office and closed the door.

"What can I do for you?" he said, sitting at an old wooden desk that was piled high with papers and manuscripts. Stracchan picked up a pipe and began filling the end with a strong smelling tobacco.

"We were hoping you could tell us anything you know about your family's connection to a man named Cardinal Beeton," Maggie said, her voice suddenly full of enthusiasm.

"He was a bishop of St. Andrews during the 14th century," Stone added.

Stracchan looked at them for a moment, then took a piece of tinder from the fire next to his desk and lit his pipe. There was a lot of sucking and puffing, and when he was satisfied that the pipe was lit, he looked at his visitors.

"You're asking me about a possible family connection between a cardinal from Scotland and the Stracchans from five hundred years ago?" All three nodded in unison. "Well you're talking to the wrong Stracchan." He blew a ring of smoke into the air. He leaned forward, his skin sallow and pale from endless hours of work inside the museum. His black eyes looked hungrily at Maggie and he smiled a rotten-toothed grin at her. "My brother is also a historian, but his field is somewhat different than mine. He's the man you need to speak to."

"We were told your brother is no longer residing in the city," Lacroix said. Stracchan's eyes moved to the Frenchman and narrowed to small slits as he measured up the French Colonel.

"That is true, monsieur," Stracchan said, confident he had guessed Lacroix's nationality. "My brother has joined the ranks of our great British army to take part in the demise of the short-lived Napoleonic Empire." He chuckled to himself as if it was amusing to have offended the Frenchman.

"May I ask what area of historical study your brother works in?" Maggie asked. She smiled sweetly at the doctor, realising she'd be able to get far more information out of the historian than the others would. Stracchan leant back in his chair puffing on his pipe and stared at Maggie as a predator would watch its prey.

"He is a fanatic, I'm afraid, my dear," he replied smoothly. "He doesn't so much study history as fanaticise over it. The man is an historical zealot, an extremist bigoted to the very depths of his profession." Maggie looked confused as Stracchan hadn't really answered her question. "He studied the history of our beloved country, madam." He chuckled to himself again. "My brother knows more about Scottish history than any other man alive."

"Why is that so funny?" Maggie asked. Stracchan leant towards her and seemed to blow smoke out of every exit in his body.

"What we practice as historian's, madam, is not an exact science. We must record every minute detail of every discovery we make. We must continually argue our case to the academic community about the origins of our civilisation and our historical past. Hamish, my brother, is a genius. He can read ancient languages and commit details of buildings and landscapes to memory and reproduce them on paper exactly as he saw them. He could have been a pioneer in our science, but instead, he recorded nothing. He wrote down nothing. He ignored his mentors and defied his colleagues. He retains information and secrets to our past heritage that may never be known because he has failed to record a single word. To make matters worse, the fool has sent himself on some sort of religious quest. He bought a sword and a horse two years ago and joined a Highlander regiment fighting for Wellington in France." He leant back in his chair and closed his eyes.

"The last I heard from him was a month ago. He often writes to me here at the museum, babbling on about how the war is going and how magnificent the Highlanders are in battle. He seems to think he's on some sort of mission appointed by God. To be honest, I'm surprised he's still alive because he's completely mad." The doctor opened his eyes again and stared at Maggie. "I'm not sure what regiment he's in, but I know they were last posted on the French border near Brussels." He sat back in his chair once more and looked at the three of them.

Stone was beginning to get slightly frustrated with the changing directions the fates were laying down for them. Chance seemed intent on making them travel the length and breadth of Europe before they found what they wanted. They'd found the man they were looking for, who happened to be a genius, a historian who may be able to tell them anything they wanted to know about William Wallace and the location of the body. But the idiot had joined the army and was somewhere in France, and for all they knew, he could be lying in a ditch with a French bayonet sticking out of his chest.

Stone cleared his throat loudly enough for Stracchan to avert his attention to him. "Doctor, do you know if your brother took anything with him, any books or manuscripts."

Stracchan knocked his pipe against the grate of the fire and put the pipe back in its holder. He stood up and put his hands behind his back. "I don't know what the three of you are after, and frankly I don't really care. But I can tell you I've seen my brother twice in five years. I have no idea what he took with him to France, and apart from an old portrait, I hardly remember what the man looks like." He gestured towards the door. "If you'll excuse me, I have a lot of work to do today and my time is very precious."

They left the room reluctantly, thanking the doctor for his time. Before Stracchan could close the door, Maggie had one last thought.

"Dr Stracchan, did your brother ever speak about William Wallace?"

The doctor smiled. "All the time, my dear." He turned to leave.

"Did he ever mention crossed claymores or crossed swords or anything like that to you?" she asked quickly. The doctor paused at the door and turned back to her. He stood as if in thought for a moment, then walked back into his office. The trio watched as he scribbled something down on a piece of paper. He returned holding the piece of paper out in front of him, handed it to Maggie, and waited for her to have a look. On the piece of paper was a neatly drawn picture of two crossed swords, and in the background, what seemed to be a chapel. Maggie looked up at him, slightly startled at what she was looking at.

"He had a tattoo," Stracchan admitted. "He got it when he was a boy. He visited Scotland with our father one year and he came back down south with this blue tattoo on his arm. It was never mentioned or spoken about, and he always hid it away from sight. But I saw it once when he was bathing. He beat me until I promised not to tell anyone, and so I suppose I just forgot about it until you asked." Stracchan stood in thought for a moment as if remembering, then turned and went back into his office and closed the door behind him.

Maggie studied the drawing again, then passed it to Stone and Lacroix. She couldn't help smiling. This image was similar to the clue she had discovered a few days ago. "A church bearing two crossing swords," she said aloud. She was convinced the body of Wallace was connected to this drawing. As they made their way out of the museum, they agreed to stay one night in the city and make a decision on what to do in the morning.

Stone patted Lacroix on the back. "Well, my friend, it looks like you could be back in France quicker than you expected. And if you're lucky, you may have a couple of friends to accompany you."

Monsieur Lacroix replied, "It would be a great pleasure to have company on my native soil." They laughed and walked into the inn together.

CHAPTER 19

Cheltenham had taken great losses at Caerlaverock, far heavier than he'd expected, and many of the rebels had escaped to fight another day. Worse, the rebels who'd escaped would now take with them the knowledge that Cheltenham's troops were far greener than previously assumed. As a result, Cheltenham ordered his men to scour the countryside and gather every eligible fighting man and herd them into camps to make sure the damage was limited. The whole rebellion had been carefully orchestrated, but if the rebel army grew too large, then the English would have severe problems destroying it.

The following day, Cheltenham was informed that Burns had been arrested and he now had total control over the *Scottish Times*. It was one piece of news that Cheltenham could take heart from. By controlling the information in Scotland, he was in a far better position to manipulate the people and thereby satisfy his plans. His spies also informed him of thousands of Scotsmen leaving the city to assemble in the hills, where they were gathering their army. The rebels were being cleverly herded together by Du Puy's men, who had positioned themselves as the leaders and overall commanders of the rebel army. Each rebel was being counted as the army grew so that Cheltenham knew how many men he would eventually be fighting, but the numbers Cheltenham received were not accurate. Du Puy had already grown the rebel army far beyond anything that Cheltenham could cope with, and indeed, the English army was already outnumbered two to one. Cheltenham was relishing the prospect of the final battle, but he was in for a surprise when he witnessed the size of the rebel force gathered to fight him. If Du Puy managed to defeat Cheltenham while gathering support from allies such as France and America, then Cheltenham's grand plan could end in the entire collapse of the British Empire and invasion from abroad.

So far, the British government had no idea about the ever increasing crisis. Cheltenham's reports to Horseguards detailed rebel activity, but not the scale of the rebel activity that had been created by Cheltenham himself. Cheltenham had sealed the border and now had control of the major voice in Scotland. He was building up the rebellion to a crescendo, which would eventually result in an historic battle. He had letters and tales of heroism already written and addressed to every government and major newspaper in Europe detailing how he had won a great victory in the face of overwhelming odds. He had even written a letter to King George dedicating the victory to the crown. Cheltenham had dozens of messengers standing by to distribute the letters across Europe at the moment of victory. Cheltenham was going to win, and everyone in the world was going to hear about it, his page in history now within his grasp.

Sir Henry Burns wasn't behind bars but under house arrest until Cheltenham arrived in the city. Even though he was under close guard, information about the rebellion still managed to filter through to him. His act of violence in the street had sparked off frenzy around the entire country. Men were leaving the city by the hundreds. The capital was stunned at the news that war had basically been declared. No one had really thought it would happen, but with an English army marching on Edinburgh, the country was in crisis. The people had always believed the military in Scotland was far too strong and that those forces would far outnumber any army the radicals could throw against them. So they had always been led to believe.

Rumours were spreading that the rebel army had laid waste to the southwest and was now marching on the city as well. Burns read the reports and couldn't believe how quickly the fabric of his society was falling apart. Little did he know how well planned the whole affair had been. Burns could never have guessed how treacherous Cheltenham had been to bring the country to this state of war. If Burns understood how close Cheltenham was to total self-destruction the old man would have laughed and cried in the same breath, because it would mean freedom for his people but disaster for Britain.

Cheltenham arrived in Edinburgh at 5 a.m. on a Sunday. Troops of the 7th and 10th Hussars and the Rifle Brigade assembled on his orders and carried out a series of raids on the city. The soldiers arrested more than one hundred prominent Edinburgh citizens suspected of having no radical sympathies at all and crammed them into the cells in Edinburgh castle's dungeons. Arrests took place daily, and the *Scottish Times,* now under its new owner, reported that "a number of persons have disappeared not previously suspected of taking part in revolution." Cheltenham was stirring the pot, and his plan was working.

As the military scoured the countryside in search of the rebel army, they arrested the innocent and guilty alike. Panic began to seize the people. In Cumbernauld, the people's fear of the military was so great that the entire population — men, women and children — left their homes and joined the rebel army hiding in the glens. Irish immigrants, who felt that the military anger would come down heavily against them, fled and joined the rebel ranks as well.

But however many were in the rebel camp, Cheltenham believed he controlled everything. To make sure the rebels could sustain the amount of men flocking to them, he sent a troop of hussars with wagons loaded with supplies taken from the city, food and ammunition for thousands. He even sent artillery. He made sure the supply train was ambushed by Du Puy's men and the wagons were captured, making the rebel army even stronger and ever more confident.

It wasn't until a few days later that Burns was told about the public executions being carried out in the centre of the city. There had only been a couple of executions, and the men who had been killed were notorious criminals, but Burns couldn't see what Cheltenham was trying to achieve. It was obvious to Burns that public executions would only serve to exacerbate an already explosive situation. Surely Cheltenham could see that public violence would only send more men to the rebel banner, Burns thought. It was in that moment that Burns finally understood Cheltenham's motives. In an instant of clarity Burns realised that Cheltenham had been deliberately goading the Scottish people from the beginning, but to what ends Burns could only guess. Even in his wildest imaginings, however, Burns wouldn't come close to understanding the pact of evil and treachery by which Cheltenham and his allies were proceeding.

The next morning, the public trial of Sir Henry Burns was announced to the citizens of Edinburgh. Leaflets were distributed around the city by Du Puy's men declaring Burns the savour of Scotland who must be released at all costs. The propaganda declared that the trial would be for treason, and if found guilty, Burns would be executed in public like a common criminal. Cheltenham had dealt his final hand in order to get the Scottish people to fight, and as far as the General was concerned, there would be only one outcome to the conflict.

CHAPTER 20

The following morning, the travellers unanimously decided their only course of action was to continue to follow their only lead and find the missing Stracchan brother. Stone had risen early and ridden to Horseguards, where he discovered some vital information about the current situation in France. According to Stone's sources, the British forces under the command of the Duke of Wellington had recently engaged the French in battle, and in the face of overwhelming odds had managed to hold them off. Wellington had then made an orderly retreat to the near a village within Belgium called Waterloo, but after that the information was sketchy.

They had no idea if Wellington had been victorious or if the French had won and had gained control of the continent once more, but either way, Hamish Stracchan was with the British army near Waterloo so they knew where to start looking for him. Lacroix managed to bribe a French merchant to ferry them down the Thames to the coast, where they could take another fast ship to Belgium. They sold their horses and purchased enough supplies to last the journey.

Stone gave one of the monks a message he'd written at Horseguards about their plan and instructed him to ride back to Edinburgh with it. If something happened to them in France, Maggie's father would at least know what had happened and their last known location. Secretly, Stone intended to use this opportunity to escape with Maggie to a neutral country, but he owed Maggie's father the knowledge that his daughter was safe.

Stone told Maggie the dangers involved in travelling to a country in the middle of a war, but she insisted they had little choice. Stracchan was their only clue, and if what his brother had said was true, the man could have information crucial to their mission.

Once in Belgium, Stone calculated it to be about a hundred miles or so to Waterloo and it would take at least two days to reach the town, and perhaps more depending on the state of the roads. If Wellington had already met Napoleon in the decisive battle, the British may have left as victors or if defeated the army would have scattered. If the British had lost, then the adventure was as good as over.

As the French merchant cast off and the small trading vessel floated out into the Thames and towards the coast, back at the museum, Dr Stracchan sat at his desk thinking about his brother and why they had grown so far apart. His thoughts were interrupted by a knock at his study door. He looked up and beckoned the strange visitor inside. A minute later, the door to the front of the museum burst open and a man ran out, sprinted to his horse, leapt on its back, and galloped towards the docks. One of the museum's clerks spotted the man running from Dr Stracchan's office and went to investigate. The door to the office was ajar, and behind the desk, slumped back in his chair, was Stracchan's bloodied body. His dead eyes stared up at the ceiling while a gaping hole in his throat spilled blood over the floor. Du Puy was covering his tracks, and even the innocent paid a heavy price for their knowledge.

The court met in Edinburgh at 9 a.m. with a capacity audience in attendance. Henry Burns was sworn in by Charles Stirling, one of the commanders of the Edinburgh Yeomanry Light Horse, who was acting as foreman. The jury was a blatant example of how Cheltenham had "packed' the judicial system with authorities loyal to him. Not only was Stirling a Yeomanry officer involved in the rebellion on Cheltenham's side and therefore a biased foreman, but each and every member serving on the jury was an officer in Cheltenham's northern army. As Burns looked at them, he realised he'd been tried and convicted without uttering a word.

The Lord Advocate addressed the court. "It is the wish of the Crown to prosecute those only who are leaders in the disturbances of late," he said, then turned back to Burns. "Henry Burns, you have been accused of high treason, and upon this indictment you have been arraigned and pleaded not guilty. However, your country has found you guilty. What have you to say for yourself? Why should the Court not give you a punishment of death according to the law?"

Burns waited for a moment, not quite sure if he was standing in the same universe as the one he was in a month ago. He composed himself and remembered the speech he had written that same morning. "My Lords and gentlemen, I will not attempt the mockery of any kind of a defence. You are about to condemn me for attempting to overthrow the oppressors of my country. You may condemn me to death on the scaffold, but you cannot make me a martyr." He glared at Cheltenham who sat silently at the rear of the court. The jury shuffled uncomfortably.

"If…" He paused. "If I have attempted to free my country. If…" He paused again. "I have committed treason, then my conscience tells me I am guilty of what you say. I am an honourable man, my Lords. You may ask every single person I have ever met in this life and they will say the same. If I were guilty of these things, I would declare it." He turned to the jury. "When my countrymen have been freed from the oppression of your leaders." He looked back at Cheltenham. "And not until then. Some future historian will do my memory justice and my name will be recorded in Scottish history next to the sufferings of my people." Burns smiled as he saw the corner of Cheltenham's face twitch. "Then will my life be understood and appreciated." He pointed to the dozens of pencils that were scribbling furiously in the crowd. He turned back to the jury again. "I appeal to you for the justice that has in all ages and in all countries been awarded to those who have suffered martyrdom in the glorious cause of liberty."

The Lord Advocate was silent for a moment as if considering what had been said. "Henry Burns, it seems you are not convinced of the impartiality and fairness with which the proceedings against you have been conducted. It is within your rights to challenge the jury, but the crime they have found you guilty of is the most dreadful that can afflict any nation. All other crimes are trifling compared to treason, which strikes at very fabric out of which our civilisation is made. The violent people with whom you were connected will never be successful, but the evil your mischief might have caused is too terrible to think of.

I advise you, most sincerely, to think seriously of your eternal interests, as you are shortly to appear at the mercy seat of Christ. Make good use of the short time allotted to you in this world." The Lord Advocate paused again and wrote something on the paper in front of him. Burns had not offered any kind of defence, and so the Lord Advocate had no choice but to declare the highest penalty for the crime that Sir Henry had been found guilty.

"The sentence of the law is…" He paused to put on his glasses. "That you be drawn on a hurdle to the place of execution. On the twenty-second of June, after being hung by the neck until you are dead, your head will be severed from your body and your body cut into quarters to be at the disposal of the King. May the Lord have mercy on your soul." Cheltenham sat at the rear of the court smiling, for he knew full well the implications of such an execution.

Burns, who had stood silent throughout the Lord Advocate's verdict, now drew himself up, his face flushed in anger. "I have not been deceived," he said to the jury. "You might have condemned me even without this mockery of a trial." He glared at them, but none of the men could hold his stare. "I never expected justice or mercy here. I have done my duty to my country for the last fifty years, and I have no desire to live in a place where men treat the world with such disdain. I am ready to lay down my life in support of my principles, which will ultimately triumph over this mockery."

The Lord Advocate waved his hand and two soldiers led Burns down from the bar to the accompaniment of shouts of protest from the crowd. Some were chanting his name while others sat in quiet disbelief. Cheltenham sat still, a small grin on his face, barely hiding his excitement. He had instigated a "mockery of a trial" as Burns put it. The people were in a rage, and he watched as some continued to write down what had happened. He didn't care what the people wrote now or what they would write in their history books. He would change all that. He would rewrite history. Everything here was just a sham anyway. He would make history about battles not about words.

The gallows had been erected near the centre of town, and from early morning, crowds had been gathering in the streets and on the execution ground. The crowd was sullen and silent as they waited. By sunrise, the crowd was estimated at twenty thousand strong and a feeling of apprehension gripped the soldiers charged with the safety of the area. The gallows were positioned so that the crowd could only stand facing the prisoner, not all around him. The people gathered as the sun rose behind. Cheltenham had deliberately placed guards in front of the gallows, separating the prisoner from the front of the crowd by twenty feet.

The atmosphere was electric. Cheltenham had ordered pamphlets to be distributed among the crowd to stir them up further. The pamphlets read: *May the ghost of the butchered Burns haunt the lives of his relentless jurors – Murder! Murder! Murder!*

Cheltenham mobilised his first Battalion of the rifle Brigade and stationed them in the streets. This force reinforced the 33rd regiment and the 3rd Dragoon Guards already in the area. He wanted a fight but he expected a war.

At precisely 7 a.m., the hurdle drawn by horses lurched down the street towards the crowd. The prisoner was dressed in white clothes trimmed with black, his old grey hair blowing freely in the wind. He stood firmly, eyes straight ahead as the crowd turned to watch the hurdle's approach. The executioner was dressed in a grey coat and a fur hat with a piece of black crepe masking his face. He carried a large headsman's axe in his right hand and a knife in his left. A strong body of the 3rd Dragoons, their swords resting lightly upon their shoulders, surrounded the hurdle. Behind them came the Lord Provost, the Sheriff, and the other high officials of Edinburgh. Murmurs of sympathy began to sweep through the crowd as the hurdle drew closer to them.

When at last the party mounted the scaffold, a tremendous shout mingled with hisses and cries of "Murder!" rose from thousands of throats as the prisoner was placed under the gallows. A stocking cap was drawn over the prisoner's head and the executioner adjusted the rope around his neck.

Prayers had already been said in the courthouse, and pleas for mercy had been heard and thrown out. The old man stood straight and didn't make a sound. He let go of the handkerchief he had been given to show that he was prepared to die. As the kerchief fell, the angry cries and hisses became an ominous rumble like thunder. In one section of the crowd, the people started screaming as cavalry charged them without warning. The outer part of the crowd ran as soldiers and civilians clashed. But the majority of the people remained and watched as the body convulsed with agitated jerks for five minutes.

The body hung for half an hour while the people either dispersed or clashed with Cheltenham's troops. As officials took the body down and laid it across the mouth of a waiting coffin, Burns watched. The cap was taken off of the dead man, and as the remaining crowd yelled their disapproval, the executioner severed the head with one stroke. The executioner then raised the bloody head of the convicted criminal for the crowd to see. With the sun rising behind the scaffold, Burns could see it would be impossible to make out if the dead man was himself or any other man.

This was supposed to be the final torment to the crowd, showing them the severed head of their champion. Burns smiled grimly and revelled in Cheltenham's failure. The crowd had thundered its disapproval again as the body went through the ceremony of decapitation and dissection, but there was no riot as Cheltenham had planned. The crowd didn't break in anger when the final insults were completed; they just stood and mourned. Cheltenham would have to wait a little longer to satisfy his urge to spill Scottish blood.

Cheltenham had visited Sir Henry on the morning he was to be executed and told him another man would be taking his place at the scaffold. Cheltenham sat with Burns for an hour chatting quite casually about his plans. Burns remained silent and calm throughout but found it difficult to hide his shock at finally being told the extent of Cheltenham's ambition. Burns guessed by the way he spoke that Cheltenham was on the brink of madness, if not there already, and was careful not to tempt the English General's anger. Apparently Burn's life had only been spared because he was a terrible shot. Fortunately, the officer Burns had shot outside the paper building hadn't died, and in fact, the man had only been scratched. He'd knocked himself out after hitting the ground. The bullet had simply scraped past his skull, but everyone in the crowd had believed the man died. He was in fact being held in hospital under close guard by Cheltenham's men. Cheltenham, therefore, had no grounds for a murder charge, and indeed there was very little evidence that Burns was ever in negotiations with conspirators. But Cheltenham had a war to mastermind, and so he made up all the charges, filled the jury with his own men, and convicted an innocent man. His men had scoured the jails of Edinburgh for a substitute to take Sir Henry's place on the gallows, and eventually they had found a perfect candidate of similar age and stature. The prisoner, having murdered his wife in a jealous drunken rage, was already scheduled for execution and so wouldn't be missed.

The plan had worked until the crowd, utterly shocked at the sight of their hero being brutally slaughtered in front of them, failed to react. Cheltenham had envisaged the crowd turning into a riotous mob, as they'd done before, and hadn't counted on their compassion and sadness. Having been deprived of another slaughter, Cheltenham had felt it necessary to see Burns again to describe the grizzly details of the English campaign so far and discuss those who had died. Burns realized Cheltenham had an insane desire to be welcomed into the pantheon of famous Generals of history. Only when the Englishman was accepted would the slaughter end unless he could be stopped by other means. Burns felt helpless as he listened to the details of what Cheltenham had done, and he felt sick that he was unable to stop the monster himself. Burns shut his mind off from what Cheltenham was saying and instead prayed silently for the safety of his daughter, that she might escape Cheltenham's clutches.

CHAPTER 21

Only a few hours after their arrival on the continent, the travellers heard rumours of a French defeat at Waterloo. Napoleon had reportedly surrendered and his army had been scattered. The travellers celebrated, drank, and ate together in a tavern in the tiny town of Bruges while the entire population seemed to be celebrating in the streets. Everyone they saw was either shaking hands or hugging or praising God, because the war was over at last.

Maggie hugged Stone, and their embrace lasted far longer than either of them intended out of decency. She pushed him gently away and looked up into his blue eyes. Stone held onto her hand, and his touch warmed her, and she flushed slightly with the shock of it. His face was entrancing, and she couldn't help studying his strong jaw and firm mouth while all Stone could do was gaze into her beautiful eyes. The wine was working its magic too, and both were being caught up in the moment. Neither noticed Lacroix slip away from the party. The Frenchman disappeared into the night. The news of Napoleon's defeat was a crushing blow to Du Puy's plans, and so he had to find out immediately if French support would still be available when his plans moved forward. If Napoleon had truly been defeated, then the British forces in Europe could now be sent home without the risk of losing everything they'd fought for. If Du Puy had lost the backing of the French, then his plan to take Scotland and the rest of Britain by force would fail before it had begun.

The end of the war meant peace would once more return to Europe. Maggie had known nothing but war for as long as she could remember. Scotland, although never invaded or conquered by the French, had paid dearly for the war. Over the last decade, Britain had been drained of men and money to fund an allied conflict in Europe while trying to piece together an empire the likes of which the world had never seen before. Now, even though Britain had rarely known defeat against her enemies, the country was practically in ruin.

Maggie understood that, with Napoleon defeated, the burden of war could be lifted from her country. The men could return, taxes would be lowered, and crops could be used to feed the people. The defeat of Napoleon could even put an end to the rebellion. The tide was at last beginning to turn in favour of peace.

They celebrated deep into the early hours. The monks even seemed to come out of their shells and told stories of past endeavours. Maggie sat listening avidly to them as they told their tales. After the last few weeks of adventure, she now understood them to be far more than just a religious entity, and the thought scared her. She remembered back to her teachings about the Knights Templar, with whom these men shared similar characteristics, and she recalled what St. Bernhard had said about them. "In repose they are as meek as lambs while in battle they are as fierce as lions. I do not know if it is better to describe them as warriors or as monks except to say that they are both."

Maggie had noticed that even their banner was similar to that of the Knights Templar, which was called a *Beauséant*: two Broadswords either crossing or lying parallel to each other overlain with a red-cross and upon a white background. Maggie knew the Knights Templar had also been excellent soldiers and the envy of European armies everywhere. The knights went into battle in total silence, and they were always the first to attack and the last to leave the field. But they also lived by strict religious rule, obeying humbly. They had no private property and lived sparingly.

In spite of her misgivings, Maggie felt very safe in the presence of these monks, as if their mystique and power shielded her from all dangers. Nevertheless, she sensed something about the men that wasn't quite right but she couldn't yet put her finger on it. The truth of the situation was more disturbing than she could ever imagine. The monks were there to protect her but for only as long as their orders stated not to do otherwise. Each and every monk on the mission understood the consequences of Napoleon being defeated. Their only purpose in life was to return to the land of their forefathers, and the Grand Master had promised they would be home soon. They believed him with all their hearts.

The heat of the fire and strong wine worked together to muddle Maggie's senses. She felt a passion arise in her, as the monks told their tales of valour and battles won and lost, heroes forever remembered in their hearts and minds. She looked up and her eyes met with Stone's, who had been staring at her intently all evening. He had sensed the passion rising in her from that first embrace and had continued to watch her avidly throughout the evening. Her breath caught in her throat as his lovely eyes penetrated into her.

Her nervousness had gone, replaced with a deep intense passion for him. She knew in that single moment that she loved him. They stared at each other a full minute before she stood and went to him. Casting aside all reservation because she knew Stone was too much of a gentleman to make advances on her in public, she went to his side. She took hold of his hand, and ignoring the inquisitive glances from the patrons in the tavern, she took him to her room.

They lay naked on the bed, the sheets pushed back and the window wide open to let in a cool breeze. It was a warm evening and their lovemaking had added to the humidity of the room. Stone watched as the moonlight filtered through the window to fall on the naked woman next to him. She was beautiful, her skin pale in the moonlight and her dark hair falling around her shoulders and over her breasts. She was lying on her side facing him, and he studied the curves of her body, traced a line from her neck down to her perfectly formed stomach, to her curved hips and bottom. He had touched and caressed every part of her body during their lovemaking, and she had responded by giving herself to him completely. She had so much energy in the moment they had joined together he knew he loved her more than anything else in the world.

He remembered the first time he'd seen her, in a dark meadow in the middle of a strange forest. He recalled his reaction when he saw her face for the first time and he knew now that he had loved her ever since. He leaned close and kissed her soft mouth. She responded and opened her lips slightly, and as he pressed closer, her body shuddered in anticipation.

All the cares of the world were lost as the couple became immersed in their desire. Tomorrow would arrive quickly enough, but for now, they had the night all to themselves.

The following morning, Stone realised that travelling on the main highway was going to be almost impossible. An endless tide of refugees, soldiers and wagons was rolling towards the coast. Most of the soldiers were British, but some were French and others German and Belgian. Thousands of them walked past, and the travellers were forced to ride in the fields and on secondary roads. When they needed to cross a river, they waited until there was a gap in the procession. The soldiers that passed looked tired and dishevelled, exactly as if they'd been through a hard fought battle followed by a hundred-mile march. Wagons rolled past carrying the wounded, and

Maggie couldn't help but stare in fascination at the injured men. Some were missing limbs, but most had vicious wounds on their faces, chests, and backs.

"Sabre wounds," Stone said, answering the horrified expression on Maggie's face. "The French cavalry are masters at fighting an enemy from horseback. These men are lucky. Most men caught in a French cavalry charge would never live to tell the tale." As if on cue, one of the wounded men cried out in pain, shouting for his mother. One of the sergeants soothed him and quieted him down as the wagon moved on.

The small group of travellers had nothing to fear from the retreating column. The party was just another bunch of refugees walking the main highway. After all, apart from Lacroix, they were British and the allies had probably won the war.

After two days of following the highway and dealing with the retreating columns of soldiers, the travellers stumbled onto the battlefield of Waterloo four days after the actual the fighting had taken place. The area in which the battle had taken place was one of rolling fields and ridges, and if it hadn't been for the scenes of battle right in front of them, they may have walked right past it.

Smoke from fires caused by artillery shells still hung thick in the air, and the travellers' horses skittered nervously as the pungent smell of death and decay reached their sensitive nostrils. The valley was a scene of total devastation. Maggie would discover later that Waterloo was one of the largest and bloodiest battles of the entire war. Twenty-three thousand British troops with the assistance of forty-four thousand allied troops commanded by the Duke of Wellington, Marshal Blucher, and the Prince of Orange had defeated seventy four thousand Frenchmen under the command of Napoleon. In the aftermath of the battle, the ground was strewn with fifteen thousand dead allied soldiers and twenty-five thousand French casualties, almost a third of Napoleon's force. It took the allies a week just to gather their wounded even as they tried to administer to the dead. The work parties had been active day and night stripping and burying the bodies strewn across the battlefield, but so many bodies still remained when the travellers arrived that the smell of decaying flesh left a putrid sweet aroma in the air that made the battle site almost intolerable to be near.

Stone surveyed the landscape in front of him and tried to imagine how the battle had been fought. He noticed a large farm building still smouldering in the distance. The area surrounding what was left of the walls had been blasted into a desolate wasteland. Not a tree, bush, or blade of grass grew within a radius of a hundred feet. He said a silent prayer for the men who'd been ordered to defend that area.

Maggie lost count of the number of dead horses she saw lying in the valley. The work parties had tried to gather the bodies of these beasts into heaps and set them alight, but they must have given up early on and thousands lay strewn in the grass. Many had been butchered by retreating soldiers or local villagers for meat, their bloody carcasses then left to rot in the open air to be scavenged by bird and beast. Hundreds of dogs ran around taking advantage of the feast, dragging horse and human flesh around with them and fighting over bones.

Stone spotted a British officer in charge of a work party on the far ridge of the valley, and he nudged his mount forward and cantered towards him. Stone kept to the rim of the valley where there was less debris and fewer corpses. When he reached the far ridge, he realised the fighting had not been restricted to the valley. Before him was what must have been the British defensive line. The British work party was clearing the area of their own dead and leaving the bodies dressed in blue for the French to deal with, and the ground behind the ridge was strewn with the bodies of a thousand dead Frenchmen and their horses. Stone saw the bodies of Cuirassiers, Carabineers, Grenadiers, and French Imperial cavalry. Stone also saw the uniforms of the Emperor's personal guard upon some of the dead. Stone knew the Emperor would never have engaged those precious soldiers unless the battle had turned against him. Stone imagined those brave men walking into the unbreakable line of British infantry on the crest of the ridge. Not even the great warriors of the Imperial Guard could match the firepower and speed of the British redcoats in defensive formation.

The British officer noticed Stone's approach and sat amused as the rest of the travellers approached gawping at the thousands of bodies strewn everywhere. "Frenchies never knew what hit 'em," he remarked cheerfully. He then made a note in a book he was carrying. "We've counted over thirteen hundred of 'em so far, give or take a few." Stone rode up to him and saluted.

"Captain Richard Stone. Might I presume you are in charge here, Lieutenant?" The other officer saluted.

"Yes sir, but only for logistical purposes."

"Do you know what happened at this stage of the battle?" Stone asked, pointing to the dead French cavalry. The Lieutenant chuckled and turned his horse around to face the carnage.

"Wellington had his men retreat from the crest of the hill until they were out of sight of the French across the valley." He pointed behind him, towards where the French lines had been. "Wellington then told his regiments to form square and wait for the enemy to attack over the ridge." The Lieutenant sniggered again and Stone wondered if the man had seen some shell damage of his own. "Wellington knew the French couldn't resist a cavalry charge at the sight of a retreating enemy, and indeed, they came at him, thousands of them all at the same time. They rode up the hill and over the crest straight into the waiting guns of the newly formed squares. Of course, the French Generals couldn't see the slaughter we were inflicting on them, and so the cavalry were sent again and again until we broke them. A magnificent sight to watch," he said as if the Lieutenant had been standing next to Wellington himself.

By the state of the man's uniform, clean and pressed as though it'd never been out of the cupboard, Stone guessed the lieutenant had never been near the battle. He was probably retelling a tale that had already been told a thousand times in every bar and brothel in Belgium. Every soldier who'd stood on the battlefield and survived would have his own story to tell. Stone gazed over the field and his trained eye could almost make out the squares of ground in which the British had fought. There were large areas of square space where the dead French cavalry had fallen right up to the edge, smashing like waves against a wall that couldn't be broken. It must have been a hell of a fight, Stone thought, and a terrible battle to end a long hard fought war.

Stone turned back to the young logistics officer. "Have you any idea where I might find the billets of the 92nd Gordon Highlanders. They were definitely part of Wellington's army that fought here." The officer thought for a moment and quickly shuffled through the pages of his notebook.

"There're plenty of dead men from that regiment entered in the log, so they definitely fought here. I can only assume they've gone back to Brussels with the rest of the army."

Stone thanked the officer and quickly scribbled down directions to the city. The army was still in Brussels, which was a stroke of good luck, but Stone didn't like their chances of finding Stracchan alive. The numbers of men killed from the ranks of the

92nd, that were already noted in the Lieutenant's log suggested that at least half the Gordon Highlanders were killed or injured. They had a fifty-fifty chance of finding Stracchan alive, and with their recent luck, he didn't like their prospects.

It took another full day to reach Brussels due to the steady stream of refugees leaving the city clogging up the roads. By the time they reached the outskirts of the city, the travellers were all exhausted. Even the monks who'd never seemed to tire before were slumped in their saddles with fatigue. Stone had asked every officer they'd met on the way if they had any idea where the 92nd might be bivouacked, but none had seen them.

It was dark by the time they managed to find a place to stay for the night. Most of the houses and inns were packed with troops and officers of the allied armies. Even though the allies had been close to defeat and had suffered heavy losses at Waterloo, the people of the city and the soldiers they saw seemed light-hearted and in good spirits. The local people were still celebrating in the streets, even five full days after the battle ended. Allied soldiers were draped around women in the bars and in alleys, while officers organised dinner parties and other social events to celebrate their victory.

Stone eventually found a barn for his party to sleep in, and after shoving out a few redcoats lying drunk in a corner, they settled down for the evening. Maggie fell asleep as soon as she lay on the warm hay piled at the back of the barn. Stone set a watch for the evening, then lay next to her for warmth.

Even though he was exhausted and every bone ached in his body and his muscles were tight and sore, he found it difficult to sleep. He crept silently away from Maggie's inert form and stood in the doorway where a monk sat on guard. It was midnight but the city was still alive. He listened to the sounds of the celebrations and realised suddenly that the world was going to be a very different place now that the war was over.

Across the street, a door burst open and light flooded onto the cobbled road in front of the barn. Noise from a party erupted into the open air and a heavily built man, obviously intoxicated from hours of drinking, stumbled out of the doorway. Stone noticed he had some sort of bag tucked under his arm as he lurched into the street. The man swayed in the road for a moment before turning against the wall and vomiting. The man then turned back and seemed to put something in his mouth. The night air was suddenly filled with an incredible sound that was instantly recognisable to anyone who'd heard the noise before. The close proximity of the buildings combined with the night air seemed to make the sound of the bagpipes magnify tenfold.

Windows opened all down the street, and people leant out to shout obscenities at the drunken soldier. A window in the building the man had stumbled out of opened and a group of Highlanders looked out and started cheering. The soldier stopped suddenly, and through all the shouting and jeering, he bellowed at his hostile foreign audience. "Shut your mouths, ya heathen bastards." He spat on the floor. "Listen to the sound that brought Boney to his knees and spared you a French baguette up your arse." He continued to play and marched up and down the street.

The soldier had to stop again for a moment to catch his breath, and Stone watched as objects were thrown down at the Scotsman from the windows above — all seemed to miss him completely. The soldier looked ready to start playing again but teetered slightly, but then, without warning, he fell forward and crashed unconscious to the floor.

A roar of approval went up from his comrades as their friend lay prostrate in the street. Stone ran out from the barn and went to aid of the fallen Highlander who had landed face down in a puddle of muddy water. Some of the monks followed Stone from the barn, and they carried the drunken Scotsman back to his comrades.

When they reached the lamplight, Stone realised this wasn't an ordinary soldier but a full Colonel of the Gordon Highlanders, exactly the regiment they had been looking. It seemed luck had decided to play a part in their mission after all. They placed the soldier in his quarters, and the other officers of the Colonel's staff thanked Stone for his help. One mentioned that the Colonel's name was Sir William de Kendall. Stone went back outside, deciding to wait until tomorrow to speak with the Highlanders further. The celebrations hadn't finished by any margin, and he supposed they wouldn't be in a fit state to give him any information until morning.

The next day Stone was up early and left the rest of the group sleeping in the barn. He didn't think it was a good idea to take Maggie along as the sights and smells of an infantryman's billet, especially after a celebration, would certainly be disturbing for a lady.

When he arrived, he noted that the house was surprisingly active for men who had the same morning drunk themselves into unconsciousness. The sun had only just come up, but most of the men Stone had seen the previous evening were up and about. From their preparations, it looked as if they were making ready to move out of the city. Men were buzzing about as he entered, and he could hear the Colonel bellowing orders from his office. Stone knocked on the office door, and the Scottish Colonel shouted for him to enter. Servants were bustling around the room, tidying and putting the Colonel's possessions in travelling chests. The Colonel kicked one of them as he passed, sending the man flying across the room.

"Don't drag your heels, man. You're in the bloody army now, so pick your damn feet up." The servant picked himself up and Stone watched as the man consciously raised his feet deliberately high off the floor with every step.

The Colonel looked at his visitor and frowned. Even though the huge Scotsman had drunk himself into oblivion and passed out in the street only a few hours ago, he had now re-groomed himself immaculately. His uniform was perfectly pressed and cleaned, his face clean-shaven, and his hair washed and combed. Stone guessed his officers would be similarly dressed and his other troops as well. The colonel looked him up and down and immediately turned his nose up in distaste. Stone had been travelling for five days without a break. His clothes were covered in dirt and dust. His hair and face were in a similar state of disarray, and he stunk accordingly.

"Can I help you with something, young man? As you can see, I'm busy departing from this accursed city so you'll have to be quick?"

Stone decided to get straight to the point. He didn't think the colonel would fall for anything other than the truth anyway. "Captain Stone at your service, Colonel." He saluted smartly and the colonel replied in kind, but his expression remained the same. "I'm on a mission to find one of the men under your command, one Duncan Stracchan. I was told he was serving in your regiment." The Colonel paused for a moment as if he was gauging Stone's reasons for looking for the man.

"I'm afraid Major Stracchan died bravely fighting on the battlefield of Waterloo. Now, if you wouldn't mind, I have much to do. Good day to you, sir." He saluted and turned without saying another word. Stone hesitated but knew his conversation with the colonel was over. He wouldn't get any more information out of him for the man was too preoccupied. He'd have to speak to one of the other officers on the Colonel's staff. He turned to leave and was about to open the door when the colonel shouted at him.

"Hold...." Stone spun around and saw the Colonel delving through some papers on his desk. He held a letter up to his face to study the writing. He lowered it and looked at Stone. "Did you say Captain Stone?"

"Yes sir," he replied.

"I've a letter for you. It arrived yesterday evening. A strange fellow delivered it, a big man dressed in a monk's garb." He held out the letter for Stone, who walked across to receive it, being careful not to drag his feet. He took the letter and turned to leave.

"Where the bloody hell do you think you're going?" the Colonel shouted at him. "That letter was delivered to me, not you. You could be some damned Frog spy for all I know. Open it and read it." He sat down and crossed his arms, obviously waiting for Stone to comply.

Stone realised he couldn't escape reading the letter no matter what the excuse and so he opened it quickly and read it to himself.

Dated June 19, 1815

Received message concerning your location. Unfortunately, Burns has been imprisoned and will be on trial for treason. Suggest you keep the knowledge from Maggie for the time being. Cheltenham has taken over the newspaper and is planning his execution.

Good luck with the mission.

Ruth.

Stone stood dumbstruck in front of the Colonel. He couldn't believe Cheltenham had arrested Burns. The message changed everything. How could he take Maggie away without letting her know what had happened to her father? It was ridiculous to say Cheltenham had gone too far, but the execution of a sweet innocent old man was intolerable. The Colonel sat watching Stone patiently, and Stone suddenly realised he had to explain what was written in the letter. Stone almost panicked and felt like making a run for it. There was no way he could tell the Colonel what was written in the letter, for if he did, there would be no escaping the truth. He had to think fast.

"Well, what does it say, man?" the Colonel said angrily, and suddenly Stone came up with the perfect story to get the Colonel off his back.

"Well sir, I'm afraid it's rather personal, but I shall tell you nevertheless."

"Personal, Captain?" the Colonel said, frowning.

"Yes, sir. It's a letter from my mother explaining that my wife has run away with another man, sir, and she thinks I should return back to London before my wife steals all my money as well." Stone stood holding the letter while the colonel sat in stunned and embarrassed silence.

"Well, er, Captain," the Colonel said gruffly, obviously feeling very awkward that he'd had to sit and listen while a man had been made to suffer such open humiliation. "Better get yourself back to England sharpish, eh. Can't have you losing your woman and your money in the same week, now can we?" he said, slapping the table and obviously trying to make light of the situation. "I know which of the two I'd rather have anyway, Captain, eh?"

"Yes, sir. Thank you, sir."

"You can buy your own love, eh, Captain."

"Of course, sir."

"Right. Off you go then." And the Colonel went back to gathering his things.

Stone turned and left the room, masking a huge grin as he closed the door.

As Stone walked away from the building he realised their trip to the continent had been a complete waste of time and effort. Stracchan was dead, their clues had all dried up, and now he would be forced to lie once more to Maggie — but this time concerning her father. He walked back to the barn with no idea what he was going to tell her. He spotted Lacroix tending to the horses at the side of the barn so he decided to ask the Frenchman's advice on what they should all do next. Lacroix turned at Stone's approach, his face a mask as always. Stone assumed the colonel would go back south to his family now that the war and this adventure were over.

"What news?" Lacroix asked.

"It looks like the adventure ends here, my friend," Stone replied, resting an arm on the flank of Lacroix's horse. "A Colonel of the Gordon Highlanders has told me that Stracchan died at Waterloo, and so that's that, I'm afraid."

"It's a sad end to a great adventure, Richard," Lacroix said, careful to hide the bitterness in his voice. The previous evening, Du Puy had secretly met with emissaries of those allies that would be joining with him once he had been victorious in Scotland. Since the loss at Waterloo, the French contingency of the alliance was concerned that Cheltenham's army would now be reinforced and so Du Puy had promised to return to Scotland to take over the rebellion personally.

Du Puy watched as Stone helpfully checked the horse's shoes for damage. Du Puy realised it would be easy to dispatch the Englishman now and remove him from the equation. If they had really come to a dead end, then Stone was of no use to him now anyway. He would keep the girl alive just in case she came up with any bright ideas. In fact, Du Puy had grown to like the girl and thought her strength might prove useful to him. He would need to think about an heir for his little empire, and she could be the perfect candidate. Stone had lifted one of the rear legs and was picking out a pebble from the hoof. He had his back to Du Puy and the Frenchman decided to seize the moment. Du Puy moved away from the horse and put his hand on his sword. He looked around, making sure they were alone, and drew the sword from its scabbard. The blade was halfway out when Maggie came bounding around the corner of the barn.

"Richard. Lacroix. I have some news, some fabulous news." Du Puy quickly thrust his sword back into its sheath and smiled as Maggie approached. Stone dropped the horse's leg and looked up at her with a puzzled expression on his face.

"What news do you have, Maggie?" Lacroix asked. She stood in front of them beaming from ear to ear.

"I've done it, Richard," she said, almost unable to contain her joy. "I've cracked the code. We don't need Stracchan after all." She grabbed Stone's hand and dragged him into the street while Lacroix followed behind.

"This is good news, Maggie, because I've just been told that Stracchan was killed at Waterloo and so I hope you're right." Maggie looked up at him with an expression that suggested she was rarely wrong and that he should have a little more faith. "What have you found then," he said, sighing and looking up to the heavens.

"I've solved it," she said again. "I know where we can find the body of William Wallace. Come with me, both of you." She grabbed his hand and led them to an inn at the bottom of the street. "I went for a walk this morning to get some air, and the innkeeper was hanging a new sign as I walked past." She pointed to the tools the innkeeper had left by the door to the inn, then she pointed to a brightly painted sign swaying in the wind above their heads. Stone studied the sign. It took him a couple of seconds to realise what it meant, but when the penny dropped, he was too stunned to say anything.

"Thank God the innkeeper doesn't like red lions or white horses," Stone said eventually. "You know what, Maggie? I think you're right," he said. "I really think you're right." Maggie giggled with delight while Lacroix remained puzzled about what he was supposed to be looking at. The innkeeper came back outside to collect his tools and admire his handiwork. He noticed the three strangers gawping at his new sign, and he beamed back at them with pleasure. It was indeed a fabulous new sign the innkeeper thought to himself.

The innkeeper used to be a merchant trading from the Middle East, and he'd travelled across the world plying his trade. Eventually, he came to Belgium, found a woman, and decided to settle down. He purchased the inn with the wealth he'd accumulated and began a whole new business and a new life. He'd decided to bless the inhabitants of his new town with some of his Islamic heritage, and so he designed a sign and a name for the inn, in fact naming it after one of his great Islamic ancestors. The interior of the building was filled with artefacts from the East and he served food from his homeland. The sign had a bright crimson background with the name of the inn emblazoned in white: The Scimitars of Saladin. The inn's name was rendered in both English and Arabic. Underneath the words, a great king stood proud in full armour, and in his hands he carried two great swords thrust out in front of him. The swords were magnificent, massive curved weapons, and the steel almost shone blue. Saladin was holding the swords out in front of him menacingly, and the two weapons were crossing over each other.

"Two crossing swords," Maggie said to Lacroix.

"Ah, I see it now," he replied. "But this doesn't give you a location," Lacroix said doubtfully.

"That's where you are wrong, monsieur. I've read a legend that states William Wallace had a secret hideout in an inn owned by one of his many supporters, and after Wallace was executed by the English, the inn was consecrated and converted into a chapel."

"So we're looking for a church that used to be an inn?" Stone asked.

"That's right," Maggie replied. "And I think Cardinal Beeton was telling us the chapel is where the body of William Wallace is buried. I wouldn't be surprised if the chapel still bears some sort of description to the two crossing swords we're looking for."

"It's a long shot," Stone said.

"But if Stracchan is dead, my friend, then Maggie's discovery is all you've got," Lacroix replied.

"You keep saying 'you,' Lecroix. Does this mean you're not coming with us?" Maggie asked. Lacroix smiled at Maggie, then glanced up at the image of Saladin looking menacingly down on them all. Now that the hunt for Wallace's body was up and running again, Du Puy would let Stone live, for the time being. He was a good soldier and he would serve to protect Maggie during the final stages of the quest. When Maggie had completed her task, then Stone would have outlived his usefulness.

"I'm afraid it is time for me to go back to my family, my dear, to return to my old life, or what's left of it," Lacroix replied.

"You will be safe travelling on your own?" Stone asked. Lacroix looked at Stone with a raised eyebrow.

"I'm an officer in his Imperial Majesty's personal bodyguard, Captain. There is no man alive in France who would dare challenge me. You never know. Napoleon may be back again one day." He winked at them both. "He's come back before, and if he does, I'm sure he will call on my services once more." He smiled at Stone. "But the next time, I think I will politely decline." Lacroix took Maggie's hand and kissed it softly. "Until we meet again, Maggie Burns. Remember, you must follow whatever path you wish — let no man tell you otherwise."

Stone offered Lacroix his hand and the Frenchman shook it warmly. "It's been a privilege," Stone said. The Frenchman held onto the Englishman's hand in a veiled show of friendship.

"The privilege has been all mine, Captain. Next time you and Maggie are in France, please visit my chateaux. There will always shelter in my home for you both."

"Have a safe journey, monsieur," Maggie said.

"May God go with you both," Lacroix replied, and with that he turned away and walked back to his horse to continue packing his things. Maggie put her arms around Stone and rested her head on his chest. She had a strange feeling that she would see Monsieur Lacroix again very soon.

CHAPTER 22

Stone calculated that they were about twenty miles from the coast as the sun was going down. The travellers camped in a small glade of trees thirty metres from the road and out of sight of unwanted eyes. They ate a cold dinner of meats and bread, as Stone didn't want any fires lit in case they drew attention during the night. He posted a single sentry, who sat at the edge of the trees watching the path. Then they settled for the night.

It was late morning when Stone awoke and he knew immediately that something was wrong. The last watch hadn't awakened him before dawn as he had asked, and the sun was now climbing high into the sky. He sat up quickly. A barricade of men in robes surrounded him, their backs to him. Maggie sat up with him, her eyes wide. Stone stood up and tried to see over the shoulders of the monks who had formed a tight ring around the couple. Through the trees he could see movement, figures running, some in white and some in blue. As the strangers crept slowly forward, Stone counted about a score of them, some with weapons and some without. The closest men he could see had dirty white shirts on, and they were unkempt and red-eyed. Stone guessed they were French deserters or bandits. Either way there were far more of them than their small party and they'd completely surrounded the camp.

The monks had closed into a tight formation encircling Maggie and Stone. The advantage was with the enemy because they'd surrounded the camp, but the monks were deliberately drawing the bandits forward into a trap. Each monk was crouching and had hunched himself up so they looked smaller and seemingly defenceless. Stone obviously knew better, and under each cloak he could make out a loaded rifle or a hand on the hilt of a sword. The monks would draw the enemy in as near as they could for close quarter fighting, then unleash hell. Stone watched through a gap in the circle as one of the deserters broke from the trees in front of them. None of the monks looked up but instead remained with their heads down covered by their thick hoods. William, the monk nearest the Maggie and Stone, suddenly poked Stone in the ribs. William obviously wanted Stone to lead the confrontation. Stone looked over William's shoulder at the approaching deserter.

The man was as unkempt as his followers, but he still wore his blue uniform. Stone could see the man used to be a sergeant in the French infantry, and he seemed to be the leader of this group of deserters. He was a massive man, barrel-chested with arms and legs as thick as tree trunks. The sergeant towered as high as the tallest of the monks and looked just as powerful. The man smiled a rotten-toothed grin at the travellers as he realised the only thing standing between his men and the pretty girl, who'd just popped her head up behind Stone, was a dozen old, useless monks.

Stone spoke French, but he didn't think any kind of conversation was going to stop a fight. In fact, he was getting the impression that the monks wanted one.

"Can we be of any assistance to you, monsieur?" He didn't think being polite would make the bandits go away, but it was worth a try. The soldier sneered at him as he moved to the right to try and get a better look at Maggie.

Stone noticed what the man was looking at, and he shoved Maggie back down to the forest floor. The man wasn't impressed that Stone was protecting the prize and he swung his arm forward, signalling the bandits to creep forward out of the trees. Stone hadn't helped the situation, but he could also see that the sergeant wasn't keen on killing twelve men to get to just one girl because he was using scare tactics.

"Monsieur," the man said in a deep grating voice. "Give me the woman and we'll spare the lives of the holy men. If you do not hand her over, then we will slaughter you like dogs and take the woman anyway." The comment was accompanied by a dozen muffled laughs from the trees, but Stone could see the uncertainty in their eyes. Only half the bandits had their rifles raised, and all of these men looked battle worn, tired and hungry. Stone assumed most of them were new recruits whose first action was the battle at Waterloo.

The man took another step forward, and with him came two dozen of his followers. The bandits were now only ten yards from the huddled members of the group. The monks, sensing the deserters were close, huddled even closer to complete the ruse. The big sergeant bellowed a final warning, then drew his sword. His men, not wanting to waste valuable ammunition on defenceless monks, followed suit.

With no further options open to him, Stone nudged William in the back to suggest that the monks were going to have to fight their way out of this situation. They waited until the last possible moment. Then, as a unit, the whole tight circle exploded into the faces of the French deserters. The monks sprang forward like a pack of lions, their swords slashing through the air. Within seconds, they had four deserters down, including the big sergeant. Three heads rolled across the grass, and the other body lay almost sliced in two. Monks moved to the left and right, flanking the deserters with rifles drawn to cover the backs of their comrades. It was the greatest show of close-quarter combat Stone had ever witnessed. Whenever an enemy came close to the backs of the monks in the centre, a rifle fired and the bandit fell. The monks also fought back to back, covering and fighting for each other as they moved from one enemy to another with supreme precision. They didn't stand still for a moment but moved directly forward into the heart of the enemy.

The odds had been against the monks, but the reality was that the deserters had stumbled into a slaughterhouse. The monks began chanting to themselves, a deep, reverberating sound filled with ancient Latin phrases. They built up a rhythm through the chanting, and their cuts and thrusts were timed with their incantations. The deserters fought bravely and fiercely, but more for their lives now rather than the prize they'd hoped to gain. The bandits were French infantrymen, more comfortable with the musket than the sword, and their skills were poor in comparison to the monks.

Two minutes after the first blood was drawn, the deserters had lost their leader and twenty men were lying inert on the forest floor. The remaining deserters suddenly lost their stomach for any more slaughter and fled back into the forest. Stone watched as the monks ignored their fleeing enemy but instead went through the same routine as at Threave, wiping their sword blades on the clothes of the dead men scattered around them, and talking amongst themselves about the battle. They happily discussed the methods of killing they'd used and re-enacted their parries and thrusts for each other's edification.

Stone was once more mesmerised by these men's strength and stamina. They were all too young to have so much experience in fighting, and yet they killed men with such apparent unconcern it was if they had done it their whole lives. Finally, the monks clasped their hands and said a silent prayer for the fallen.

Rufus, having chased after the retreating deserters, came bounding out of the woods. Stone deduced the bandits were gone for now but could return in greater numbers to exact revenge. The party had to leave immediately and travel as far as they could with what light they had left.

The travellers rode for a full hour until their horses were exhausted, then settled in for a rest and some food. By the salty smell in the air Stone could tell they were very near the coast, but he wanted to get to civilisation as quickly as possible. Who knew how many deserters and bandits were still lying in ambush from here to the sea.

When they finally reached the coast, they found an inn and took refuge for the evening. It was the first time they'd stopped properly all day, and every one of them went to their rooms exhausted.

Stone was up at dawn, leaving Maggie to her sleep. He had a plan that had been formulating in his head ever since meeting Sir William de Kendall. If he was being forced to return to Scotland, then he not only needed to get rid of their monk escort quickly but he also realised he could use Sir William to help distract Cheltenham and the monks, and even perhaps bring a swift end to the rebellion. He spent most of the morning composing a letter to Sir William, outlining exactly what had happened over the past month and everything he knew about what Cheltenham and the monks were up to in Scotland. Stone also promised to give Sir William an update on the rebel and English positions upon his return to Scotland, and he said that there would be another letter waiting for him once Sir William brought his troops home. Stone was hopeful that Sir William would react positively to the letter, and from what he had seen of the man, as soon as Sir William realized his beloved country was in danger, Stone guessed he would move his force straight to the coast.

Stone had always planned to give the monks the slip and escape with Maggie once they reached the continent, but the guilt was too much and he realized he not only needed to take Maggie back to her father, if he was still alive, but also to do what he could to stop the monks from seizing power in Scotland and plunging Europe back into war. Stone sealed the letter and paid a courier to take it directly to Sir William. He then went down to the dock to buy passage back to Scotland. An hour later, he'd found a ship that would take them, and he started back to the inn.

During the first day of their return trip to Scotland the weather began to turn slightly, and then the wind rose to a gale, turning the sea into a swirling maelstrom. Six-foot waves crashed over the side of the ship and the vessel was thrown around like a drifting piece of wood. Stone had never been at sea during such terrible conditions, and he was feeling the effects of the constant lurching of the ship up and over the waves. One massive wave sent the ship over the crest at such an acute angle that Stone thought his stomach was going to be forced into his throat. Unfortunately, the contents of his breakfast wanted to come up first and he rushed out of the cabin to find somewhere to throw up. He sprinted through the ship towards the latrine, and sailors and passengers alike smirked as the stricken Englishman ran past. Stone crashed through the door but pulled up as he realised to his horror that he'd burst into the wrong cabin. Instead of the latrines, he was faced with a dozen of the ship's crew sitting on their bunks smoking and chatting amongst themselves.

Stone stood still for a moment, wondering if he was hallucinating, when the bile forced itself into the back of his throat. He looked around and spotted an empty gun port. He opened the port and thrust his head into the blustery weather outside. Having dispatched his breakfast into the sea, Stone wiped his mouth and looked around at the grinning sailors perched on their bunks. For the first time since entering the room, Stone realised there was an odd smell in the air. Some of the sailors were smoking strange pipes, blowing sickly plumes of smoke into the air. The pipes were being shared around, and Stone could tell by their eyes that what they were smoking was more than tobacco. The last time Stone had smelt such smoke was after a trip to a rather notorious gentlemen's club near Mayfair some years earlier. On that occasion, some interesting clientele who were using a drug imported from the Far East to enhance their entertainment were in the club. Stone recalled one of the drugs was called opium and that it was purchased from Chinese merchants who passed through the area from time to time. Opium was the smell in the air now, and Stone recalled that the drug in larger quantities could render the user unconscious. Stone realised it would probably take a significant sum for these sailors to part with their precious drug, and so Stone pulled two gold coins from his pocket and held them up in the light. A sailor slowly held up a leather case big enough to hold a couple of pistols. Stone nodded as he handed over the coins and took the case from the sailor. He opened the box and saw enough opium to serve a dozen men for a month. By pure luck, Stone suddenly had the means to escape from the monks. All he had to do now was find a means of getting the drug into the monk's food. As he walked out of the cabin, he tapped his stomach, which felt much better, but he was also slightly light headed. He strolled back through the ship and made for the galley to see if he could put his plan into action.

After a few hours, the wind began to calm and the ship's cook decided it was safe enough to light the galley stoves to heat some food. Stone had slipped a gold coin into the cook's hand and suggested the stew being served to the monks in their cabin would taste a whole lot better if it was mixed with the precious herb Stone gave to him. Unfortunately, they were still a day away from Berwick, and so Stone told the cook to serve the stew mixed with opium as the last meal on the voyage. That way, Stone and Maggie would have enough time to get away before the monks woke up.

The next day, the passengers lounged around on deck waiting for the hours to drift by before they landed in Scotland. During the afternoon, a pod of dolphins swam by the ship, and Maggie nearly fell overboard trying to watch them. When the last meal of the voyage was served, Stone and Maggie made their way to their cabin. If the opium had the desired effect, the monks would be unconscious soon after finishing their meal; but if it didn't work, then Stone had some explaining to do.

Stone waited another twenty minutes before leaving the cabin and making his way to where the monks were billeted. He listened at the door, then slowly turned the handle and peeked into the room beyond. The ship lurched suddenly, and Stone let go of the door and it swung open. He stood rigid for a moment waiting for the worst, but then he relaxed when he saw the inert figures of the monks spread around the cabin. Some were lying in bed and a couple were passed out face down at the table. All of them were snoring happily in an opium induced sleep.

Stone closed the door silently and prayed the effects of the drug would keep the monks out cold well after he and Maggie had made their escape. He was about to walk away when a cold shiver of dread passed through his body. Instinctively, he opened the door again and counted the number of men slumped around the cabin. A monk was missing. One of the monks had either not eaten dinner or had somehow managed to escape the effects of the drug. He quickly closed the door again and ran down the passageway towards the steps that led to the main deck. Stone reasoned that, if it had been him, fresh air would have been his first thought for relief. As soon as he climbed up on deck, he spotted a figure ten yards away leaning over the side of the ship. It was getting dark, but Stone could easily make out the wool robes of one of the monks. The idea of going up against one of the monks even in a drugged state wasn't tempting, but he had to do something and fast. The easy option was to try and push the unsuspecting monk over the side of the ship, but Stone wasn't about to commit murder. He looked around to see if there was something he could use to disable the man, cursing himself for not bringing a weapon.

The monk vomited into the sea then used the side of his robe to wipe his mouth. As the robe moved, Stone noticed a pistol sticking out of the monk's belt. Without hesitation, Stone sprang forward and snatched the pistol from the monk's belt. Before the monk could react, Stone smashed the butt across the back of his head. The monk crumpled to the floor unconscious, and Stone had the unenviable task of heaving the body back down to the cabin where the rest of his comrades were still sleeping.

Stone left the poor monk trussed up at the foot of one of the bunks with a cloth around his mouth in case he woke up. He now had the hardest part of his plan to complete — explaining to Maggie why they would be continuing the journey without the monks. He stopped outside their cabin door, took a deep breath as he made sure his story was correct in his head, then stepped through the door. Maggie was seated at a small desk writing her journal, and she looked around and smiled at him as he entered.

"You've been a long time. Have you been to see the Captain again? Do you know how much farther we have to go?"

"Yes, I've spoken with the Captain," Stone replied. "He thinks we've got about another hour before we dock. You can see the lights on the coastline already if you want to go up and have a look." Maggie was about to go back to her journal when Stone interrupted her. "Would you come over and sit by me on the bed, Maggie? I have something important I need to speak with you about." Maggie sensed there was something wrong as soon as Stone sat down, and she stood up with fear and dread welling up in her stomach. When she sat down next to him, Stone took her hand and kissed her gently on the cheek. "I'm afraid I have some disturbing news, and I have taken some action that may upset you at first, but I can assure you it has been done for the good of our quest."

"What is it, Richard? Tell me what's happened," Maggie said quietly.

"I'm not sure of the entire truth my love, but be assured what I've done may have saved our lives." Maggie put her hand over her mouth and sat in silence. "I overheard our so-called robed friends talking about us not less than an hour ago, and what I heard terrified me to the very core. It seems the monks are not on our side after all and they have turned against us. I couldn't hear the full details, but I believe they meant to take us hostage on our arrival in Berwick then escort us back to Edinburgh to their rebel masters." Stone looked at Maggie, and for a moment he thought his story, albeit half true, had not had the desired effect. Maggie looked at him, steel suddenly in her eyes, and then out of the blue nodded her head fiercely in agreement.

"I'm not surprised, Richard," she blurted. "Ever since we were attacked by those French deserters, I've had the feeling that something wasn't quite right about the monks. I don't know what the monks said, but when I saw them kill so coldly and without remorse, it made me think something was wrong. When I first met Ruth all those weeks ago, she said that their order had split and the rebel leader was a calculated, heartless killer who didn't take any prisoners. I don't think we should take the risk with these monks, do you?"

"Soldiers kill, Maggie — that's what they do," Stone said, not sure why he was defending them.

"I'm sure you're right Richard, but nevertheless, I sensed something about them and my feelings generally turn out to be right."

"Yes, you were right Maggie, but don't worry. I've dealt with the situation." Maggie looked bemused for a moment.

"Richard, how on earth were you able to 'deal' with a dozen of the most dangerous men I've ever met?" Stone smiled at her then tapped the empty food bowls on the table.

"I drugged their dinner," he said.

"You did what? Where on earth did you come up with a plan like that?" Maggie said, shocked but full of relief.

"Let's just say I'm not sure all the sailors on this ship are in a suitable state to steer us to shore if they've more of the opium I purchased off them," Stone said rather smugly.

"But how long will the effects last, Richard?"

"I'm not sure, but it should be long enough for us to get away. I've paid the Captain of the ship handsomely to turn the ship around as soon as we've disembarked and to sail back to Belgium. God knows how far he will have sailed back to the continent before the monks wake up."

"I hope the crew will be safe," Maggie said.

"I'm sure they will be. I don't think even the monks would be able to steer this ship on their own. I'm sure the captain will be more than happy to blame the whole thing on me anyway."

"And then they will come after us, I suppose," Maggie said with concern in her voice

"I'm sure they will," Stone replied. "But we will be long gone, and it will be harder for them to travel around in a large group with Cheltenham's troops marching around the countryside." Stone tried to convince her that everything would be alright, but he wasn't sure he'd even managed to convince himself.

CHAPTER 23

Sir Henry Burns sat in his room listening to the sounds of the city below. Cheltenham had moved the old man back to the newspaper building but had kept him confined to his living quarters with an armed guard at the doors. There was no chance of escape. The doors were locked and the room was five stories above the street.

Burns had heard little news of the rebellion, except that a rebel army had gathered and was lying in wait somewhere outside the city. He was slightly comforted by the fact that many of the common people in the city hadn't risen in rebellion. In spite of all their brave talk, many of the people hadn't had the nerve or the will to follow the rebels out into the hills. Cheltenham might never have his full-scale war, thought Burns, but if he defeated the rebel army, then he could yet get his name into history.

Burns looked up from his book when he heard a key in the lock to his door. The door opened slowly and a robed man walked through followed by two of his men. Du Puy lowered his hood and smiled at the old man. Without a word of greeting, the Grandmaster undid the front of his robe and deliberately took the sword from his belt buckle and laid it on the table. Du Puy was dressed in the habit of a monk but it was made of a material far more luxurious than the ones his men were wearing. The exterior was plain in colour, but the lining was blue velvet with gold trimmings. The sword on the table had a scabbard encrusted with jewels and the handle was made from ivory, the pommel carved in the form of an elephant's head. It was a magnificent weapon, and Burns was eyeing it uncomfortably. Under the cloak, the man wore an elaborate uniform, but Burns didn't recognise what country it was from.

"You're wondering who I am, monsieur?" Du Puy asked in a matter-of-fact voice. "My name is Raymond Du Puy, and I am the Grand Master of the Order of the Knights Hospitaler. I won't bore you with details, monsieur. Let us say I need your help and I'm willing to bargain with you for some information."

"Knights Hospitaler?" Burns asked. If there was any bargaining to be done, then he wanted as much information out of this man as possible. Du Puy sighed as if he'd wanted to avoid a tedious discussion.

"Very well, monsieur. If it'll make my task easier, I will tell you who I am and what you need to know if it will satisfy your curiosity. In 1798, before Napoleon Bonaparte became Emperor, he invaded the island of Malta on his way to a French military campaign in Egypt. The French government at the time had deemed Malta of strategic importance to France and ordered Napoleon to capture it. The Knights Hospitaler were therefore put in an impossible situation. We had successfully and bravely defended our home and religion against all other forces in the past. Now we had the unpleasant duty of defending our sovereignty by fighting not only Catholics, but in many cases, fellow Frenchmen.

Some knights chose to fight, and of course they died. Others refused to fight their countrymen and left the island to live in exile, praying that one day they could return to their homes." Du Puy stood in silence for a moment waiting for Sir Henry's reaction, and so Burns pressed him further.

"But the British took the island from the French in 1800 and set up a British administration," Burns said.

Du Puy smiled. "You're very knowledgeable, Mr. Burns. I commend you."

"If the French lost the war, there would be no way you and your Knights would be allowed to return home," Burns continued. "At least not as rulers of your little island. So let me guess. You struck a deal with Napoleon to get Malta back by supporting the rebellion in Scotland, thereby distracting the British and possibly even taking them out of the war completely; and for your assistance, Napoleon would give you your island back."

"Again, you're very perceptive, monsieur; but unfortunately, Napoleon has already lost the war and Wellington's troops will soon be returning home." Du Puy smiled at Burns and raised his hands as if in defeat.

"The Knights Hospitaler have ruled on Malta for eight hundred years. I'm sure you're not willing to give up that easily," Burns said.

"Again, you are correct monsieur Burns. If the rebel army succeeds in defeating Cheltenham's forces, then a combined force of American, Irish, and French soldiers is being readied to invade Britain from various points around Europe. I would love to tell you where these attacks will be launched from, monsieur, but with the threat of your navy, I'm sure you understand the need for secrecy."

"I'm sure Sir Arthur Cheltenham will have something to say about your plan, monsieur. You will be depriving him of his magnificent victory."

Du Puy leant back and waved a royal hand nonchalantly in the air. He took the jewelled sword from the table, pulled the weapon from its scabbard, and examined the beautifully crafted blade.

"The man is mad," he said quickly, while testing the edge of the blade. "Cheltenham's obsessed with defeating the Scottish people, and he is willing to take any opportunity that will enable him to do it. Once I had put my plan together, it was very easy to manipulate him. I helped him; he helped me, except," he said testing the balance of the sword, "he will end up dead and I will end up a king." He whipped the blade forward and it stopped within a whisker of Burn's throat. "Now, Mr. Burns, I am tired of your questions. You will tell me what I need to know or you will never leave this room alive. Contrary to what you've been told by Sir Arthur Cheltenham," he said, pulling the blade away. "Your daughter is not being held prisoner. She is free and very much a part of this game we are all playing. I'd hoped that she would remain unaffected by this whole affair, but it seems her companion, Captain Richard Stone, has other plans for them both. Your daughter and Stone have managed to evade capture by my men, and recently they seem to have disappeared. They are on the run alone in Scotland, and I will be honest with you, monsieur', he said with a smile 'I fear for her safety.

"Now, the decision you must make is between the safe capture of these two young people — and I swear on my honour your daughter will not be harmed — or the pain of never seeing your daughter alive again. What will it be?" Burns hesitated for a moment, and Du Puy levelled the blade dangerously close to his jugular. "Remember, monsieur," the Frenchman whispered. "She thinks you've been butchered already. Imagine how happy she'll be when I send you to her alive and in one piece. But it'll make little difference to me if you die needlessly now."

"What do you want to know?" Burns said slowly.

Du Puy immediately whipped the blade away and put it back into its sheath. "It's very simple, really. You know your daughter well, far better than most men know their offspring. I need to know where she may have gone if she thought Edinburgh was too dangerous." Du Puy went to a fruit bowl on a dresser and selected a ripe red apple. "You see, Mr. Burns, your daughter has been running a little errand for me, but without knowing where your daughter is, I fear I may lose what I want. If this were to happen... Well, I will destroy everything you hold dear, Sir Henry." He took a bite of the apple, then carefully replaced it in the bowl. "And that includes your daughter."

"She'll go to Glasgow," Burns replied softly. "We have relatives there she can turn to for protection. Glasgow is the only place I think she may have gone if she were in danger and was unable to come home to me." Burns was lying, but he had apparently convinced Du Puy, who was nodding his head in acknowledgement. Burns guessed Glasgow would be the last place Maggie would go, in truth, especially if she thought the monks were on her trail. Unfortunately for Sir Henry, however, Glasgow was exactly where Maggie and Stone were heading.

"Monsieur," Du Puy remarked. "The Emperor owes you a debt of gratitude. I hope our next meeting will be in more hospitable circumstances." Du Puy then turned on his heel and left the room in a flourish. Burns sat still for a moment, and then, for the first time in as long as he could remember, hot tears ran down his face. He did nothing to stem the flow, as all strength and will had left his body. He was a beaten man, and the only precious thing he had left in the world was being hunted down like an animal. For what reason, he had no real idea. All he could do now was pray that his daughter would remain safe and that he might look on her face again before he died.

CHAPTER 24

Stone led Maggie into Glasgow knowing he needed to get her in and out as quickly as possible. The city was a scene of devastation. Burnt out houses smouldered in every street. Rubble littered the ground. Fences and windows were broken, and in some areas, dark patches of red marked the ground. To their surprise, however, many people were going about their daily business. Shops were open despite smashed windows and carriages rode the streets managing to avoid the rubble in their way.

Except for the destruction all around them, Stone saw little evidence that the rebellion was still going on.

Stone decided to deviate from their mission slightly and visit the local garrison to find out what had happened in Glasgow during the last couple of weeks. If Sir William de Kendall had received his notes, then a large British force was potentially making its way to the coast of Scotland and Stone had to filter as much information about the rebellion back to the Colonel as possible.

He visited the public archives a few hours later to find Maggie immersed in a pile of books almost hidden from view. If Rufus hadn't been sitting by the desk, he would have missed her altogether. Maggie was reading a leather-bound book seemingly almost as big as she was in size. She looked up and smiled at Stone as he approached, and he took up a chair opposite her at the table.

He told her what he'd found out at the local garrison and explained everything he thought was relevant that she might want to hear. According to his sources, he told her, a rebel army had gathered somewhere outside Edinburgh, but Cheltenham hadn't yet committed his troops to the field and so the battle was yet to come. According to the duty officer in the garrison, the last couple of days had seen little or no disturbances in the city. Stone kept the fact that this turn around could have happened as a direct response to the death of Maggie's father to himself. Either that or all the eligible fighting men had already joined the rebel army out in the field. Stone now believed their one real chance for safety was to find the tomb and stay there until Sir William could return from France and bring some order to the chaos that had flooded Scotland, but as yet Stone had no idea if de Kendall was coming at all..

Maggie had immersed herself in books and parchment for the hours Stone had been away, and she felt in good spirits having spent her time so productively. Stone began flicking through one of the books on the desk in front of him as he spoke to her, so she stopped what she was doing and leant forward cupping her face in both hands. She became instantly relaxed and soothed by his voice while being slightly amused that all he was doing was looking at the illustrations in the book before him rather than reading any of the text. He seemed to be talking to her about military strategy and what he would do if he were leading the rebel army, when she lost track of what he was saying and began to daydream. Suddenly she realised Stone had stopped talking, and so she came back to reality and refocused on him as he sat in silence. He was looking at one of the illustrations in the book and seemed mesmerized by what he saw. He glanced up at her with a surprised expression on his face.

"Did you manage to find anything on this church we're looking for?" he asked.

"No, not really," Maggie replied in a tired voice. Stone then picked up the book and passed it over to Maggie's side of the table. She looked down at the illustration, then back up at Stone, who was sitting with a smug grin on his face. Her eyes narrowed dangerously and Stone had to suppress his gloating before he regretted it.

Maggie looked back down to study the picture in more detail. The book Stone had passed her was an account of Wallace's life by a lesser-known historian Maggie had never heard of. As she read through the inscription under the picture, she reasoned it was fairly obvious why the historian had remained so anonymous. The book described Wallace as a drunk and a womaniser who spent most of his time in brothels and bars rather than fighting the English. Whether it was true to life or not, the historian clearly described an area of Scotland Wallace visited on and off throughout his later life. The text described a small chapel in a valley near Ellerslie, close to where Wallace was born. The chapel had been a sanctuary for Wallace during the long war with England because of its remote and little known location. There wasn't a reference to the name of the place, but according to the writer, Wallace had built an inn onto the front of the church and then renamed it. This was back to front to the way Maggie had imagined it, but in a way it made more sense. She looked into Stone's eyes and felt a little disappointed that she hadn't been the one to find the location of the body. In her heart, she was certain that Ellerslie was the place they were looking for, and she could see from Stone's expression that he did too. Stone sensed her disenchantment but he only felt relief. He could now get Maggie out of Glasgow and away from any danger that might be lurking.

"Looks like that's where we're heading next then," he said.

"Shouldn't we contact Ruth to let her know we've finally found the location of the body?" Maggie replied.

Stone sat thinking for a moment. "It's been five hundred years, Maggie. Let's confirm the location of the tomb before we get the monks involved again. Besides, I'm not totally sure who it is we should be trusting at the moment." Maggie nodded in agreement, and secretly she was happy that they didn't have to share the information with anyone else. She wasn't searching for glory, but she needed to finish the adventure she had been a part of from the very beginning, and she wanted to end the quest by herself.

They gathered all the relevant information and headed back to the inn to prepare for their departure. The next morning, Stone made one last trip to the local garrison on the off chance that something had come through from Sir William. When he arrived at the garrison, Stone was rewarded with a letter and the Colonel's seal was clearly stamped on the front. Sir William had written a very brief note, but it explained that the Iron Duke had given Sir William permission to take his force back to Scotland. Wellington had immediately appreciated the seriousness of a rebel army taking control in Scotland, and moreover, Wellington had also heard rumours of a combined French and American force being put together to aid the Scottish resistance. Unfortunately, Sir William's troops were the only troops Wellington could spare and thus he hoped Cheltenham was a good enough soldier to contain the rebels until he could arrive. Stone had seen Cheltenham in action and realised it would be a close-run thing. He prayed Sir William could arrive before the real fighting started. Stone checked the date on the letter and saw it had been sent a few days ago.

"Sir William could already be here," he muttered to himself. He scribbled a quick letter in response, detailing where he and Maggie would be travelling, and gave it to a messenger to take to the coast to be delivered, hopefully, into the hands of Sir William.

Du Puy watched from the battlements as Cheltenham's troops assembled in a courtyard below. Edinburgh castle was alive with activity, and people in the city stared up at the walls wondering what the English were up to.

The previous evening, Du Puy had sat with Cheltenham and his officers discussing how best to face the rebel army encamped outside the city. Du Puy had managed to persuade Sir Arthur that he had to confront the rebels before their numbers swelled any greater. Cheltenham had at first been keen to wait until he had confirmed the rumours that the rebel army was much larger than first thought, but Du Puy had managed to persuade Cheltenham that his men had the numbers right and that they had total control over the number of men in the rebel army. Du Puy had been elated when Cheltenham finally agreed to take his army into the field. To further the Frenchman's delight, Cheltenham declared he wasn't concerned about the conditions of battle. He didn't feel the need for his superior force to choose the ground on which to fight. He wanted to attack the rebels on the most unfavourable terrain as possible, and he instructed Du Puy to make it so. Cheltenham felt a victory in those conditions could only result in further enhancing his fame. So Du Puy had promised to make the battle as difficult as he thought possible without the threat of failure.

Du Puy continued to watch as Cheltenham inspected his men. The General then gave a rousing speech that had been written down word for word by Cheltenham's private biographer. Cheltenham was writing himself into the history books, and he was enjoying every minute of it. But as biased as the account might be, thought Du Puy, Cheltenham could never have realised the tragedy about to befall his army.

Du Puy turned away from the window as he heard booted feet running up the stairs and approaching his position. Three robed figures came into view, and he recognised them as scouts who had been guarding the southern coastal roads. The men bowed low before the Grandmaster, and one who looked dusty and tired from travelling passed Du Puy two pieces of paper. Du Puy read them quickly, and then tucked them into the pocket of his tunic. The Grandmaster could hardly control his elation. He dismissed the scouts, but not before rewarding them with two gold coins a piece. Everything was falling into place. His men had intercepted a message to Sir William de Kendall from Captain Stone outlining exactly where he and Maggie would be in the event that they were needed. Du Puy was slightly concerned about why Sir William should be back in Scotland with his seasoned regiment, but he would send a detachment of men to find out what was going on. The timing couldn't have been more perfect even if he'd planned it himself.

He decided, in that moment, that he would leave the destruction of Cheltenham's army to his own trusted officers and that he would depart immediately to claim the body of William Wallace for his own. He would parade the body into Edinburgh at the head of his victorious army and claim the throne of Scotland with Maggie Burns as his Queen. He called down for his horse to be saddled and for five men to ready themselves for an immediate departure. Napoleon may have lost the war in Europe and Du Puy might never see his homeland again, but he would win the fight in Scotland. And if the Americans came to his side, his ambitions might even grow further. He might consider taking the crown of England itself.

Maggie and Stone trudged slowly northwards. The weather had grown from bad to worse, and a thick drizzle blew in their faces. A dense fog had begun to enclose them, compounding the misery of their first day of travelling.

Maggie hadn't uttered a word since they left Glasgow, and Stone was beginning to worry about her. It was as if there was an air of foreboding around her, and the further they went, the more withdrawn she became. They'd passed through a number of small villages in the last hour, but there was little sign of life and the weather was keeping even the hardiest farmer indoors too, giving Stone little opportunity to establish where they were. The wind seemed to be getting stronger and the rain was almost horizontal, getting into the small gaps in their travelling clothes and soaking them to the skin. The wind continued to howl around them, and at one point Stone even thought he heard thunder. Sensing that this wasn't the kind of weather that produced thunder, he turned in his saddle to look back at the village they had just travelled through a few miles away. The blood froze in his veins as he saw a dozen riders galloping through the houses towards them. Even through the rain he could see the riders' robes billowing behind them. The monks had caught up with them. How he couldn't guess, but in that moment, his life as he knew it was over if he didn't react immediately.

"Ride!" he bellowed at Maggie over the noise of the weather. She glanced behind and saw the mass of riders approaching. Stone heard Maggie swear as they kicked their mounts into a gallop. Stone made a mental note to remind Maggie, if they managed to escape, that shouting obscenities was not one of her more endearing qualities.

Unfortunately, the rain had turned the path into a muddy nightmare, and when Maggie and Stone, reached the crest of a hill, their only route was down what had basically become a muddy river. Galloping down this hillside could be death for the horses, but they didn't have any choice. The pair did the best they could in the conditions, and Stone thanked the Lord that Maggie was an accomplished rider.

Stone was nearly thrown a number of times, and Maggie was gradually pulling away from him. Stone risked a glance back and could see the monks had reached the crest of the hill. They now plummeted over the edge like a waterfall with little heed for their personal safety. Stone urged his mount forward, and he could feel the mare shudder in fear as she realised what was being asked of her. He heard Maggie cry out, and he thought for one terrible moment that she had fallen, but she was shouting and pointing to a spot at the bottom of the hill. Stone looked to where she was pointing and could see lights from a number of fires and there were figures moving around in the gloom. Stone strained to see who they were — if they stumbled into a rebel compound that would result in the same consequences as being captured by the monks. As they drew closer, Stone realised the men were English Light Horse and at least a company of infantry spread out across the road and camped for the evening. Even through the weather, Stone could see the soldiers had spotted both sets of riders. The soldiers obviously weren't taking any chances because the general alert had been sounded.

The monks were only a hundred yards away now, and Stone could see the faces of lead riders. In that moment Stone, realised a plan. The monks needed to capture them before they reached the blockade, otherwise the monks would have a serious fight on their hands. Unfortunately, the monks were so close now that Stone couldn't guarantee the soldiers wouldn't open fire on Maggie and him if they continued to gallop towards the camp. If he timed their move perfectly and the English troops were indeed feeling trigger-happy, his plan could work. As he signalled Maggie to slow down slightly so they wouldn't miss the opportunity, Stone could sense the monks speed up as they closed the final few yards to their quarry. Stone looked back. Their horses were only yards away and the monk's faces were grim as they locked eyes on their quarry. Stone guessed the monk might have even disregarded orders to catch up with them. During their time together, Stone had come to realise the monks valued honour and duty above all else, which meant that their escape would have hurt them deeply.

Stone called to Maggie once again, and she instinctively pushed her mount forward. They were almost within firing range of the English muskets. Stone knew that his plan was reckless and there was a chance that both of them would be killed, but he hoped the monks hadn't spotted the escape route in their haste to catch them. Stone pulled his pistol from his belt and cocked the weapon. Aiming high, he targeted one of the infantrymen. He waited for the exact second to fire to make use of the smoke and confusion together as one. He glanced at Maggie and was surprised to see a pistol in her hand as well. Then when the moment was upon them, they both fired at the waiting Englishmen. Then, miraculously, they disappeared.

The pistol smoke was quickly smothered by the rain and wind, but the smoke hung about them long enough to give Maggie and Stone the second they needed to confuse their pursuers. The monk galloping in front had also taken a pistol from his belt and was planning to fire at Stone's horse to bring the animal down. He was counting on Maggie reigning in when she saw her lover fall, thus stopping both riders in their tracks with a single shot. But in the same moment that the monk had aimed his weapon, Maggie and Stone fired simultaneously and then disappeared. It took their pursuers a few seconds to comprehend what had happened, and by then, it was too late.

Stone had spotted a deep depression in the ground near the bottom of the hill, a sheer drop off the path of about fifteen feet, but Stone could tell the hollow had been well filled with straw cut from the field for use as animal feed and the drop was short enough that horse and rider would have a fairly soft landing if they took the risk. The monks had ridden well past the depression before they realised what had happened, and to add to the confusion, Stone's bullet had struck a redcoat in the shoulder and the monks were well within musket range. The English soldiers were far too jittery to worry about who the strangers were, and suddenly the air was filled with the sounds of sporadic musket fire and the call to arms.

Assessing the situation the monks could see the only way they could get access to the hollow in which Maggie and Stone had escaped into was to get to the bottom of the hill, and that meant riding straight through the ranks of English soldiers who were now trying to kill them. The monk at the head of the column turned and barked an order at two monks in the rear, who reined in and galloped back up the hill to follow the same route their quarry had taken. He then drew his sword and roared a challenge at the soldiers below him, then led the remaining monks into battle.

Maggie and Stone both landed softly but were separated from their horses during the fall. Stone knew the horses wouldn't go far when surrounded by so much food but may have been spooked by the unexpected fall. If there hadn't been thick rain impairing their vision, Stone was positive the horses would never have jumped. He pushed forward and dragged himself out of the straw. Maggie wasn't far behind. He saw both horses in front of him, one horse happily chewing away on some straw while the other was limping in a circle nearby. The horse had obviously landed badly and was lame. The injury didn't look serious, but there was no way the animal could carry a passenger. Stone climbed up onto the remaining horse, and Maggie was about to climb up behind him when two horsemen burst over the edge of the depression and onto the straw below.

"Come on. Let's get out of here!" he shouted down at her. She jumped up onto the horse, her gun already reloaded and aimed at the squirming mass of men and horses. Stone nudged the horse forward, and as they galloped away, Maggie turned and aimed at the first horse that struggled out of the straw. She hated to do it, but she had little choice. Their horse could only gallop so far with two riders. She aimed at the horse's heart and pulled the trigger. Then she turned away so she didn't see if the bullet had hit its mark, but she knew it had by the scream the horse made as it fell.

The remaining monk had miraculously managed to stay in the saddle and was now scrambling out of the straw. His companion ran forward and threw a loaded pistol into his partner's hand, offering some compensation for not being able to continue the chase. The monk then rode away in the direction in which Stone had disappeared, the rain and the mist swallowing him up almost immediately.

The English Captain in command of the small company of men guarding this particular thoroughfare couldn't quite believe the events unfolding in front of him. One of his men had already been disabled, and now a dozen horsemen were charging out of the rain at his fragile line of men. The horsemen had their weapons drawn in what seemed like a suicidal assault. The Captain didn't need to give the order to fire. His inexperienced men had already taken that initiative. As he watched, however, the bullets seemed to pass by the riders harmlessly as if their reckless courage had earned them the divine right to survival.

The riders were coming closer and closer, and the captain inadvertently took a step backwards. The men nearby saw the movement and their fear was replaced by despair. The monks were only twenty feet away now and not a single bullet had found its mark. Worse, the soldiers' powder was becoming wet and their weapons were beginning to fail. More than one man had already taken a fearful step backwards as the monks thundered towards them like a nightmare out of the storm. The lead rider was screaming a challenge as his robes billowed around him, and he seemed to be looking directly at the English captain, his sword aimed at the officer's heart.

Like a wave breaking against a shore, the horsemen smashed into the retreating line of redcoats, slicing downwards and leaving a trail of blood and bodies in their wake. The monks, however, were not used to fighting from horseback, and as soon as they'd broken through, they pulled up and leapt to the ground, swords in hand. Only one rider kept going and he was heading straight for the English Captain. The officer remained rooted to the spot, unable to move, while his life flashed before his eyes. Then suddenly his sergeant stepped in front of him protectively. The sergeant thrust a rifle into the Captain's hand, then went down onto his knee and took aim at the horseman as he charged forward. The sergeant fired a shot that struck the monk in the right shoulder, knocking him from the saddle. He fell to the ground in a bloody heap. The horse galloped past, but to the sergeant's horror, the man sprung to his feet as if nothing had happened, passing his sword from his useless arm into his other hand. The terrifying robed man sprang forward as the panic stricken sergeant was frantically reloading his rifle. The monk bore down on the sergeant like the wind and drove his sword through the Englishman's throat even as he was cocking the weapon to fire. The sergeant collapsed forward but grabbed his assailant's robes as he fell, putting the monk off balance and stopping his forward momentum. In that moment, the English Captain came back to life even as he witnessed the gruesome death of his sergeant. He stumbled backwards and tripped as he was bringing the rifle to bear, and as he hit the ground, he inadvertently pulled the trigger. The monk had regained his balance and was making a lunge for the stricken Captain, but the bullet hit him square in the chest. At such close range, the rifle shot blew a hole straight through his body, shattering his spine and killing the warrior instantly.

The other monks turned at the sound of the rifle firing and watched as their leader fell. Then they drew back their hoods and cloaks and shouted a terrifying battle cry. They charged forward as one as the petrified Captain lay stunned on the ground. The vengeful monks surrounded the Captain and began hacking away at him until he was nothing more than a bloody unrecognisable mass of flesh and bone. While the monks were massacring their Captain, the remaining redcoats had the opportunity to regroup and gather what was left of their tiny force; and when the monks finally turned from the dead officer, they found a line of men facing them only yards away, muskets raised and under the command of a burly corporal who had taken control after seeing his Captain and the sergeant killed. The corporal ordered the depleted line of redcoats to fire and a dozen shots filled the air.

As the smoke cleared, the corporal felt a moment of elation as he saw every one of his enemies lying prostrate on the floor. He didn't find it bizarre that the number of enemy corpses matched the number of muskets fired, indeed that every shot had apparently hit its target. Before the corporal had time to contemplate the improbable, all the corpses seemed to come back to life and sprang forward, swords in hand. The rest of the men in the line had also been so stunned by their apparent victory that none had bothered to reload and had no chance to get off another shot before the monks reached them. The monks had incorporated a simple tactic used in close quarter combat of diving to the ground a split second before a volley was fired and now with nothing in their way except empty muskets the monks charged forward. The two groups of men came together in a sickening thud, and three redcoats were down before they even knew what was happening. The corporal bellowed at his men to fall back, but it was already too late.

The corporal's dying act, even as a sword pierced his ribcage, was to order the small group of cavalry hovering on the fringes of the battle forward directly at the mix of men. It was a suicidal order because both sets of troops could end up under the hooves of a horse, but he knew it was better to fight with a small advantage than none at all. As the cavalry thundered into the melee and hacked away at the strange and powerful enemy, the battle turned into mass confusion. As the fight continued, it was obvious to all warriors on both sides that there would be no quarter, and it was a fight to the death.

Maggie and Stone heard the sounds of the dying, mixed with the clash of metal and the crash of muskets in the distance, and they prayed the monks could be held up long enough to make their escape. Stone could feel the horse tiring as they continued to gallop away through the mist. He knew any pursuer would easily follow their tracks because the ground underneath them had been made sodden by the constant rain. He had to come up with an escape plan before the monks managed to catch up with them again. He looked to his left and spotted Rufus bounding out in front of them. Stone was glad they had the hound with them. If they had to stop for a rest, the ever-alert wolfhound would warn them of any enemy that might be approaching. Then, in that instant, as by luck, the wind changed for a moment and Stone smelled the distinct scent of pine in the air. He nudged the horse into the wind and slowed the beast down to a canter. Stone's plan would be simple but effective: find the tree line from which the smell was emanating, then push the horse through and pop out again in a different area, throwing off their pursuers in the undergrowth.

It was another mile or so before the couple reached the trees, and thankfully, it seemed to be a large area of woodland and the trees were wide enough apart to allow a horse to pass through. Maggie had remained quiet since their escape, happy for Stone to take control and lead them to safety. Now Rufus led the way, instinctively guiding the horse via the safest and quickest route as if he knew Stone's plan. After a mile or so, however, Stone changed direction and headed east towards what he hoped was a route out of the woods and to safety. A minute later, the couple broke out into a small glade where they saw Rufus sniffing around some rabbit burrows searching for a meal. Stone thought they were probably safe enough to let the horse rest and take some water.

Stone checked the horse's hooves and its legs for injury. They needed the animal in perfect health in case another quick exit was required. As he was checking a loose shoe, he noticed Rufus was standing very still and watching the tree line where they had just come from. Then the hackles rose and Rufus's lips drew back into a snarl. Stone slowly began to stand back upright with dread welling in the pit of his stomach. He glanced across at the stretch of woods Rufus was watching as a dark shadow appeared, and then a horse and rider came into view. Stone knew it was already too late to make a run for it, and so he simply called Maggie to his side.

"Stand next to the horse," he said to her. "I will try to hold him off. If you see me fall, I want you to ride like the wind away from this place."

"But Richard…" She reached out for him.

"Do as I say Maggie," he said more firmly, as he pushed her gently away. "I have a plan. Remember they need to take you alive. Will Rufus respond to me if I call to him?" She took a moment to pull herself together. "Maggie," he said again. "How can I call Rufus to me?"

"He will respond to the word 'engage'," she said quietly.

"Good," Stone said, eyeing up the horseman as he came closer. "Do you think you can get Rufus to circle around the back of the monk?"

"I'll try," she said. "But I can't guarantee he'll listen to me if he sees the monk attack you."

"We'll just have to hope Rufus and I have the same plan, then won't we?" Stone looked down at Maggie and smiled, then put a hand on her cheek. She took his hand and kissed it warmly, then held it to her face again. He bent over and kissed her softly on the mouth then whispered in her ear. "Don't worry, I know how to beat these men. They don't fight dirty like me." He kissed her again, then walked to the centre of the glade. Maggie whistled once and Rufus began to circle the glade in measured steps, seemingly understanding exactly what needed to be done.

Stone stood alone in the middle of the glade as the monk walked into view. The monk had easily followed the couple through the woods but had had no intention of trying to capture them. The monk knew all he had to do was follow them and they would lead him straight to the tomb of William Wallace. Unfortunately, he hadn't counted on them stopping so soon and for their dog to hear his approach. Now Stone was standing in the glade and obviously willing to take him on in a fight.

From the corner of his eye, Stone could see Rufus moving the monk's rear. Stone took the hilt of his sword and deliberately drew the blade out slowly. He needed to draw the monk forward into the glade to fight on his terms, and he knew intimidation would certainly do the trick. Stone glanced at the two pistols sticking out of the monk's belt, but he knew the monk wouldn't be able to resist the challenge Stone had laid down for him.

The monk's name was Philip, and he could see what Stone was trying to do, but was still totally confident he could kill the Englishman and then take the girl as his prisoner. The monk tied his horse to the nearest tree, put his pistols in a saddlebag, and walked into the glade. Philip drew his sword, tested his arm a couple of times by swinging the blade through the air, then walked up to Stone.

"You are brave, Englishman," Philip said in strongly accented English.

"You must have known I would protect Maggie until my dying breath," Stone replied.

"If that is what you want, Captain, then I shall grant you your final wish — en guard."

Stone took a step backwards, feigning retreat, but Philip was having none of it. The monk had fought too many battles to let an enemy fight on his own terms. Philip began to circle slowly around to Stone's right, towards where Maggie was standing with the horse. Stone watched as the monk slowly took away his small advantage before a blow had been struck. Then, in a blur, the monk attacked, thrusting three times in quick succession towards Stone's chest. Stone parried each strike, but it was all he could do to stop the fight from ending before it had begun. Stone realised he was in a more perilous situation than he had ever been in his entire life. He was no match for this powerful monk, and he could see in Philip's eyes that he knew it too. Philip had a confident smile on his face, and as Stone looked at the man, he suddenly smiled back at him before striking at the monk with as much force as he could muster.

The smile was wiped off the monk's face, replaced with an expression that Stone registered as complete hatred. Stone readied himself for the next attack. He didn't have to wait for long. The monk came forward again, and Stone was shocked at the power of the man's attack. Stone tried every feint and trick he knew, but the monk was just too good for him. Stone could have called the giant wolfhound into play, but he knew that, because Philip would see the animal coming, Rufus wouldn't stand a chance. Philip's swordplay was more accomplished than any man he'd ever fought against, and Stone knew the monk was readying himself for the kill.

Philip thrust the point of his blade, missing Stone's throat by millimetres. Stone parried and risked a kick at the monk's exposed knee, but the monk moved too quickly and Stone's foot hit nothing but thin air, putting him off balance. Philip brought his blade back, cutting downwards towards Stone's neck. Stone had to dive to the ground to survive the blow. Stone quickly rolled away, but Philip was already on top of him. Philip thrust downwards and pierced Stone in the shoulder as the Englishman was rising, making him cry out in pain. The tip of the blade had struck bone and stuck fast, making the monk, for a split second, struggle to wrench the blade free. Stone swung his sword backwards in desperation, and Philip had to move quickly to avoid the reckless blow.

Philip now stood a few feet away as Stone struggled to stand. He was looking at the blood glinting on the tip of his sword. The monk smiled again as he glanced at Stone's useless shoulder, the Englishman's sword arm now useless. The monk took a huge swing, aiming at his enemy's head to finish the job, but Stone raised his injured arm out of instinct and in spite of the pain. The swords clashed, but Stone didn't have the strength to hold onto his weapon and it flew into the woods. Philip didn't hesitate for it wasn't in his nature or his training to gloat over his defeated victims. He raised his sword again, aiming the point at Stone's heart. Stone heard a ringing in his ears and assumed it was from the terrible pain coursing through his body. Then he saw the point of the monk's blade thrusting down towards his chest and he braced himself for the impact and his imminent death. The only emotion he felt as his life flashed before him was regret. Regret that he had failed to protect Maggie and that he hadn't been strong enough to defeat his enemies. He looked up at Philip's face, but the monks expression was blank almost glassy. He experienced another sharp pain and then blackness. His last impression of the earth was the monk's face very close to his, and blood...blood everywhere.

CHAPTER 25

Maggie had stood rooted to the spot almost unable to breathe as she watched the two men fighting in the middle of the glade. If Stone lost, she knew she would be unable to run away. The pain would be too great for her mind and body to function. Even with her limited experience of swordplay, she could tell Stone was no match for the powerful monk. She put her hand on the horse's saddle to support her when she felt her legs buckling, even though she felt like falling to the ground and weeping. Her hand touched something cold and hard, and she took a momentary look away from the fighting to see what it was. Stone's pistol was sticking out of the saddlebag. She pulled the weapon from the pocket when the monk had his back to her. The weapon hadn't been reloaded, and so she quickly, mechanically began the process using her own powder and shot. She heard one of the men suddenly cry out in pain, making her nearly drop the weapon to the ground in panic. Forcing herself not to look up, she continued to load the pistol, realising her nerve might disappear if she stopped for a moment. She cocked the weapon, took a deep breath, aimed, and in the same moment, prayed for an easy target.

The monk was going in for the killing blow when the bullet smashed through his neck, severing his spine and ejecting through the front of his body. The big man was killed instantly, and the sword thrust aimed at Stone's heart died in the same moment. The bullet had cut through Philip's artery as well, and as the monk fell forward on top of Stone, the Englishman was covered in the monk's blood as it sprayed from the gaping wound. It took Maggie a couple of seconds to realise what she had done, and then she dropped the weapon and ran towards the inert bodies lying in the grass.

"Richard! Are you alright, Richard?" She reached his body and saw the bloody mess she had created. She recognised the monk now that she was closer, but the dead man had already become pale through loss of blood, and to her horror, she realised the monk was bleeding out directly onto Stone's upturned face. She grabbed the monk's robes and pulled with all her strength until the body rolled away onto the grass. She then bent down to inspect her motionless lover. Stone's face was completely covered in dark red blood and pieces of flesh in a grisly scene that almost made her retch. He seemed to be breathing, but his heartbeat wasn't as strong as she would have liked. She inspected his body and found the wound in his shoulder. She realised he must have already lost a lot of blood. The gash in his arm wasn't wide, but it was very deep. She could tell by the glint of white that must have been the bone showing through.

In a moment of panic, she realised that, if she didn't do something to get Stone out of the cold and his wound covered, he could be dead in a matter of hours. The wound alone wasn't life threatening, but the combination of the elements and loss of blood might be deadly. She composed herself and thought about her options, then she left Stone for a moment and began to strip the body of the monk she had killed. The robes were heavy wool and would serve to protect Stone from the cold and the wet. The biggest problem she had was that Stone was lying in the middle of the exposed glade, and until he woke up, there was no way she could move him, so she had to improvise. She covered him temporarily with the robes after temporarily bandaging the wound to stop the flow of blood. Then she walked into the woods carrying the monk's heavy sword. Luckily the trees surrounding them were firs and offered good protection. She cut down a number of branches and dragged them back to where Stone was lying. Gently she rolled him onto his good side and created a bed of fir boughs to protect him from the wet ground. She covered him with the warm robes again and went to their horse, which was grazing patiently. Maggie had to pray their presence in the glade would go unnoticed until Stone was able to move himself. She walked the horse to Stone and stood the beast over him as best she could to protect him from the rain, and then she went to work on the wound.

She knew Stone kept a flask of whiskey in his belt, and she used the strong liquor to clean the wound. She then took out one of the needles she used to mend her travelling clothes. Gingerly she pressed the flesh together and began stitching the arm back together. Stone squirmed each time she pierced his tissue, but she gritted her teeth and finished the job quickly, making sure the wound was completely free of dirt before it was sealed. She'd read in a book once that human urine had medicinal qualities and was good for cleaning wounds of any infections. The one word she remembered but didn't quite understand was "sterilization." On impulse she looked around to see if anyone was watching, and then checked that Stone was unconscious. She pulled her riding pants down and emptied her bladder all over Stone's shoulder. She made a mental note not to tell Stone what she'd done until an appropriate time, then she wrapped the shoulder with a clean piece of cloth ripped from one of Stone's shirts and left him to sleep. While she waited, she reloaded all of their weapons and kept them dry just in case another monk discovered their location.

Maggie didn't dare light a fire, and so she ate a cold dinner while feeding Stone water at various times throughout the night. Their horse stood quietly over Stone without moving, and eventually Maggie drifted off to sleep lying next to Stone's body for warmth.

It was still raining when Stone finally awoke, but he found himself dry and warm and his mind clear. He moved slightly, and a sharp pain shot through his body and brought tears to his eyes. Delicately, he reached over and touched his shoulder and found it had been bandaged neatly and tightly. As he focused, he realised the ceiling of his temporary accommodation was covered in hair and slightly pungent. He reached up and touched the offensive roof and found it was warm and soft. The horse nickered softly as if in welcome, and Stone smiled when he understood what Maggie had done. He raised his head to look at his feet and found, thankfully, that the animal had resisted any temptation to empty his bowels on them. Maggie was still lying next to him, and she opened her eyes as she felt Stone move. He leaned over and kissed her softly on the mouth.

"Thank you," he said in a croaky voice. "Philip?"

"Dead," she whispered. Stone closed his eyes.

"Thank you," he said again.

"Don't mention it," she replied.

"How long have I been asleep?"

"A few hours maybe. Not long. How do you feel?"

"As if my arm has been torn off and dragged through a field and back again," he said, touching it again.

"Your arm should be fine, but I'm not sure how long it's going to be before you have full use of it again. Do you think you'll be able to ride?" Stone tried to rise from his bed of fir boughs and Maggie had to help him get up properly.

"I don't think we've got much choice. Philip isn't the only monk out there, and I certainly don't want to have to fight another one," he replied.

"Do you remember our location and where we should be headed?" Maggie asked.

"I think so. All we need to do is head due north now and we should be back on track. Although I think it would be sensible to travel at night from now on and lay low during the day. We have to assume the monks are still on our trail, and I don't care to think what they might do if they find us again."

"What shall we do with him?" Maggie said, pointing at the stiff half-naked corpse lying in the grass a few feet away. Stone looked at the body with regret etched on his face. He'd liked and respected each of the men he'd travelled with, and he'd almost hoped they wouldn't turn out to be enemies after everything they had been through together.

"We'll drag the body into the trees and cover it with leaves; we don't have time to bury him." They each grabbed an arm, and with some effort, eventually managed to hide the body from sight.

They hoped there would be no further obstacles between them and the tomb. Maggie knew the location, and Stone believed they could be at the tomb in a day. Stone guessed they couldn't have more than a couple of days before the rebels and Cheltenham's army met on the battlefield. What he did once they found the tomb was another thing. They could perhaps hide until the rebellion had blown over or contact Sir William so he could come to their rescue. They would have to think about their options when they eventually got there.

A lone horseman reached the rim of the valley and looked down on the carnage on the road below. The tracks on the ground were fresh, no more than a few hours old. The man squinted in the sunlight and saw robed figures strewn on the valley floor among the bodies of redcoats and English cavalry. The man rode slowly towards the battlefield, and he looked up only once, when three riders galloped up to him from the trees on his right. The reined in and fell in behind him.

"Any sign?" he said softly.

"Two horsemen escaped the valley and through the woods at least four hours ago," one of the men replied.

"You saw what happened here?" the man said accusingly.

"No sir," the man replied quickly. "We arrived too late," he said, with regret in his voice.

The men were now walking their horses through the battle site. The bodies of men and horses lay strewn everywhere at grotesque angles. There was little evidence that anyone had survived the fight. It was clear that the two sides had massacred each other.

Clifford reined in and looked about him, trying to ascertain the chain of events that had brought so much carnage to the valley. Red-coated bodies lay strewn everywhere, occasionally joined by the solitary corpse of a Hospitaler knight. Clifford studied the site with a grim respect, as it was obvious each dead knight must have accounted for the deaths of at least half a dozen Englishmen. He continued on then, through the valley, studying the battlefield, slowly realising that the knights had nearly won the fight. That was until the timely intervention of the English cavalry. Even more astonishing were the numbers of dead horsemen. Clifford counted twenty cavalrymen scattered around a phalanx of dead knights. After annihilating the redcoats, it appeared that the knights had organised themselves into a tight square to face the attacking cavalry in a final act of bravery, choosing to die rather than be captured. Outnumbered two to one, they must have been picked off one by one by the charging Englishmen, but the knights hadn't given their lives away cheaply. Clifford, now sure that he had seen everything to be seen in this carnage, urged his horse towards the woods a mile or so away. He was quickly followed by the two knights who were now his escort. The trail was clear and headed first east then north directly into the trees. The bodies of Maggie and Stone weren't among the dead, and so it was a fair assumption that the tracks belonged to them.

Clifford was once more on the path of his prey. He had orders to find the tomb of William Wallace and to dispose of those who had helped him find it. Clifford was amazed his quarry had managed to escape the slaughter in the valley, but he was thankful for it. Once the pair had led Clifford to the tomb, he would happily kill them himself; but not before he had pleasured himself with the woman, he mused to himself. He remembered the intimate moment they had shared in church those many weeks ago, and it stirred evil passions within him. Clifford smiled as he imagined Maggie's young female body in his hands, and what he would do to her while he made her lover Stone watch and suffer her humiliation. He spurred his horse forward, anxious to reach his prize and to claim what was his reward after a long hard campaign. Before Sir Arthur Cheltenham could claim the body of William Wallace, Clifford would have his fun.

Clifford cared little about who would win the war because he was in it for himself, and in the end, he would take his gold and his pound of flesh and leave for America a rich man. There was nothing that could stop him now.

CHAPTER 26

Cheltenham rode at the front of the column like a Roman Emperor leading his conquering army to war. The long line of soldiers' horses and wagons trundled from the walls of the castle and into the city below, where the people watched in silence as the thousands of redcoats marched slowly past. They all knew where the troops were heading. There was no cheering because the soldiers were going off to fight the fathers and sons of Scotland. The people stared through grim expressions, and such was the huge display of men and firepower that some were already grieving for the rebels who had to face them in battle.

Only four thousand of the eight-thousand-strong troops were leaving the city. The rest remained in reserve or to guard the capital on the advice of Du Puy, who had persuaded Cheltenham to divide his forces in case the rebels tried to attack the city. Du Puy had put the plan forward with the knowledge that the rebels had at least seven thousand men in the field, and the rebel army was under orders to position themselves to launch a surprise attack to wipe out the English as quickly as possible.

As Cheltenham looked down on the civilians in the street, he wanted to explain that he was going off to free them of their rebellious brothers and they would soon be a civilized country again. But as he looked into their miserable eyes, he could only see hatred and realised he was merely culling a population to minimise a problem that would never really disappear. Even in his irreversible state of madness, Cheltenham felt some compassion for the people of Edinburgh. Even so, he saw total justification for the slaughter of thousands to keep the regular cycle of rebellion in check. The great iron doors of Edinburgh castle thundered shut behind the last of the English troops like a bell sounding the start of a fight. Cheltenham spurred his mount forward, eager to join battle with the rebel army camped in the countryside outside the city. He sensed victory and revelled in the prospect of a humiliating Scottish defeat. He had no idea he was falling for the biggest trap in English military history.

After travelling at a good pace for half the night, their mount was beginning to tire under the weight of the two riders. The sun was beginning to rise on the horizon, and so it was time to make camp anyway. Stone headed for a small outcrop of trees, then lowered himself gingerly from the saddle. His shoulder was beginning to throb almost unbearably, but he kept silent, hoping the pain was just part of the healing process. They set up camp and broke out some cold rations they'd purchased in Glasgow. Stone didn't dare light a fire in case enemies were nearby. He knew he wouldn't have the strength for another fight if they were caught again. He watched Maggie as she ate the cold beef and bread. She grimaced as she washed the food down with the sour wine from Stone's flask.

Stone threw some scraps to Rufus, who ate hungrily for the beast's only decent meal in two days was the odd rabbit he'd caught on the way. Stone thought briefly about bringing down a bird or two for the big wolfhound, but gunshots would be heard for miles around. Even though he'd tried to hide their trail and travel by night, Stone was sure they would be pursued soon enough.

"We're very close," Maggie whispered, almost imperceptibly. Stone looked at her and she held his tired gaze.

"How do you know?" he asked, trying to keep the conversation moving to keep his mind off the pain.

"I'm not sure." She frowned. "I just know we are very close."

Late that afternoon, as Stone packed their sleeping blankets, and Maggie stood to look out from the trees over the land they had yet to cross.

"In the next valley," she said quietly to herself.

"What was that?" Stone asked.

She turned to him and pointed out across the plain. "The burial site is in the next valley. I'm sure of it," she explained. Stone stopped what he was doing and beckoned to her. She walked over to him and he drew her into his arms. She rested her head on his chest, and he stroked her soft raven coloured hair as she clung to him like he was safety itself.

The wind whipped around their legs as they rode deeper into the darkening valley. Stone looked to the heavens and shuddered at the sight of the bruised clouds about to burst above their heads. They had risked travelling the final part of the journey during the day to make sure they didn't miss the structure they sought. Both sides of the valley were thick with ancient trees, their trunks so wide an entire horse could be hidden from view behind a single tree. Stone kept their mount close to the tree line as they rounded a bend in the valley because the ancient oaks would offer them protection if they stumbled into trouble.

Maggie remembered from the maps back in Glasgow that this place was referred to as the Coyle Valley and was where the leaders of the southern clans met secretly to discuss attacks against the English. Maggie recalled a legend about the place being the scene of a massacre. The English had ambushed the clansmen here hundreds of years ago and the chapel had been built on the site in memory of those that died. The legend also said that the ghosts of the dead clansmen remained here, which would explain why the valley remained untouched by woodsmen. By the bitter chill in the air, she was inclined to believe the legends. But it occurred to her that the spirits were also in this valley for another reason — to protect the body of their dead leader.

Stone and Maggie could see the far side of the Coyle valley in front of them, but the contour of the hill they were on meant they couldn't see directly below them to the valley floor. Stone climbed down from his horse, gave the reins to Maggie, and walked in a crouch towards the slope of the hill. Silently he lay down on his stomach and looked over the valley floor in front of him. He heard a shuffling noise behind him and turned just as Maggie leapt down next to him. Looking over his shoulder, he saw the horse tied to a low branch of a nearby tree. They both scanned the valley floor, and their hearts leapt in unison at what they saw. In the centre of the valley was a tiny slither of silver, a river winding its way through. A patch of dead ground obscured their view in one area, but they could clearly make out the roof of a building from their position and a wisp of smoke from the chimney. There was definitely some sort of building down there, and by the look of it, someone was at home.

They watched for another thirty minutes, but the only movement they saw was the smoke coming out of the chimney. They mounted the horse and rode down to the valley floor. Stone had no idea what to expect, and so he checked his weapons and kept his rifle ready to hand. Once in the bottom of the valley, the building was lost from sight in the dead ground. Stone suspected this had been done deliberately to keep the building as anonymous as possible. As they drew closer, they heard running water and the sound of someone chopping wood. When they finally reached the edge of the dead ground, Maggie gasped aloud at the beautiful sight before them that had been hidden from view until the very last moment. The river ran down the side of the valley into a natural bowl in the valley floor. Here, for a hundred centuries, the ground and valley wall had been eaten away by the force of the flowing water. Eventually, the water had hit the bedrock, creating a deep blue pool at the bottom. Now the river flowed over the edge of the valley and dropped suddenly in a magnificent waterfall. Trees and vegetation grew all around the perimeter of the pool in such variety that it looked like a whole other world. But Maggie's eyes were clamped on the building lying in the shadow of the waterfall and shrouded in a mist of spray. It had no specific design or religious markings, but she knew immediately it was the building they were looking for. Suddenly they both realised the chopping noise they'd heard on their approach had stooped. They noticed an old man standing by a fallen tree near the waterfall with an axe thrown over his right shoulder. He was looking at them intently, not moving, just staring. Then to Maggie's surprise, he beamed a huge smile at them and began to walk in their direction.

CHAPTER 27

Sir Arthur Cheltenham was becoming frustrated by the slow speed of his army's advance into the field. The army hadn't travelled further than twenty miles out of Edinburgh, and it had taken them nearly three days. The head of the column of the English army was now only a couple of miles from the rebel encampment, but because of Cheltenham's haste and the inexperience of his officers and men, the army was spread out for miles.

As dawn broke on the third day, Cheltenham consulted with his staff officers about how slow the troops were moving. They advised him to wait at the camp until midday so the men in the rear could catch up. Then, once rested, the army could continue the march but at a slower pace. The officers only had to mention the close proximity of the rebel army and the need for all their troops to be in one place for Cheltenham to concur.

Cheltenham was summoned two hours later and ushered to a war council gathered at the edge of the encampment. The vanguard of Cheltenham's army had camped on the ridge of a wide valley so that they had a good view of the surrounding area. Cheltenham now stood with his officers at the very edge of the valley rim, looking out over to the opposite side half a mile or so away. There, a swirling hoard of men had just started to appear.

A fair distance separated one rim of the valley from the other, but as Cheltenham approached, he had seen quite clearly that the dirty brown mass of rebel troops had begun to spread out as far as he could see to the left and right. The hoard of men significantly outnumbered the English army that had gathered here so far, and he knew his troops were far from ready for battle.

Cheltenham trained his telescope over the enemy as his staff officers looked on, some of them paling visibly as the rebel army grew and grew. Suddenly Cheltenham whipped the glass away from his eye and spun around to talk to his officers.

"Damn bloody mess we've got into here, gentlemen." He almost bellowed the words into their faces. "It's been a while since I've been humbugged, gentlemen, but I'm happy to admit it. I believe that thundering Frenchman Du Puy has tricked us, but by

God I'll have his head on a plate before this day is out. Captain Maddicott, make sure our journalist friends know that we are outnumbered three to one. We may well be able to take advantage of this situation yet. By my calculations, the three thousand hooligans we were expecting to fight just turned into six thousand fresh-faced heathens with a score of bloody cannon to boot." He stood red-faced, his eyes bulging, in front of his staff. He was waiting for a reply. The other officers were squirming at General Cheltenham's fury, but nevertheless, they were extremely pleased he had passed the blame to someone else. But still the problem of being severely outnumbered remained.

"May I, sir?" Captain Maddicott walked forward and took the glass from Cheltenham, much to the General's surprise, and raised it to his own eye. Maddicott was one of a number of men within Cheltenham's army under the pay of the Grandmaster himself, and Maddicott was being paid for one reason alone — to make sure Cheltenham followed Du Puy's plans. Cheltenham had refused to have any of the monks on his staff, and so bribery had been the only option open to Du Puy. Maddicott had succumbed cheaply. Du Puy, even though he wasn't at the battleground, had already predicted Cheltenham's reaction upon seeing that he was completely outnumbered, and Du Puy had put Maddicott in place to make sure Cheltenham didn't do something foolish — like retreat. Du Puy was placing the outcome of his plans in the hope that Cheltenham's arrogance and madness would be his downfall, and Maddicott was there to make sure he hadn't guessed incorrectly.

Maddicott surveyed the army across the valley and almost balked at the size of it. He hadn't been in a battle before, and even though he knew exactly what was going to happen, he also knew he wouldn't be totally safe while on the English side of the valley. Maddicott knew that the rebel artillery was just a ruse, however. The rebels hadn't the munitions or the gunners to fire them all. Du Puy's plan was to make the English commit to bringing their own guns forward in an attempt to take out the smaller rebel guns, and when they did so, Du Puy had a nasty surprise in store for the English gunners. During the long march from Edinburgh, Du Puy's men had spiked the English guns, but cleverly so it wouldn't be noticed until the first shot was fired. Once the English cannon exploded, that was the signal for the Scots to charge across the valley in the confusion and smoke.

Unfortunately, the one major flaw in the rebel army was the fact that it had no cavalry, and it wouldn't take Cheltenham long to realise that failing. Cheltenham had at least a thousand horsemen with him, which could, if launched at the right time, totally destroy the rebel army without much of a fight. However, Du Puy's men had taken up positions behind the attacking rebels to drive them forward, and the monks also controlled the key leadership positions in the army so that the attack had cohesion and power. Maddicott slammed the glass shut and turned back to Cheltenham.

"They're a rabble sir," he commented quickly. "May I suggest a suitable course of action might be to bring your guns forward and blow their artillery back to their manufacturer, sir." He'd made the remark with such confidence that it took Cheltenham a moment to reply. Cheltenham opened his hand while glaring at the Captain and beckoned for his glass to be returned. Maddicott put it in Cheltenham's open palm and moved aside so the General could get a good look at the rebel army. The Captain was wondering all the while how far he might need to go to push the General to get him to commit to the attack.

Du Puy had ordered his men positioned among the mass of rebels to keep as little rank and file as possible in the lead up to the attack, and so, when Cheltenham studied the mass of rebels, they looked disorganised and leaderless. Du Puy had also made sure each rebel had been issued with a double ration of rum before the battle. Then after a number of rousing speeches, they'd marched to the field in such a battle frenzy it had actually been difficult to keep the rebels from attacking immediately.

The rebels were beginning to make some noise now, and it was clear to his officers that Cheltenham was going to have to make a decision. Most of the rebels had rifles, but Du Puy's plan to give them all extra rum had had desired effect on the Scotsmen. Hundreds had stripped off their shirts and painted themselves in whatever colours they'd been able to get hold of. Instead of their guns, they were brandishing knives and swords of every shape and size in an attempt to relive the clan battle noises and scenes of old.

Cheltenham gave the order to bring his artillery forward and to draw up the infantry in line along the rim of the valley in preparation for the rebel attack. He then sent the cavalry to the rear as a reserve force and ordered his own horse brought forward so that the men could then see him more clearly.

Maddicott began to move away to the far left of the column, well away from the artillery. When the spiked cannon exploded, red-hot pieces of metal could decimate the waiting ranks of soldiers nearby, and anyone within twenty feet of exploding cannon would be killed instantly.

Cheltenham watched as his artillery pieces were loaded and ready for his order to fire. He drew his sword slowly from its jewelled scabbard and raised it high into the air. Completely unexpectedly, almost in anticipation of Cheltenham's order, in one voice the rebel army gave off an enormous gut wrenching battle cry, catching Cheltenham completely by surprise and making his horse buck and skitter nervously. The sheer noise, of seven thousand enraged Scotsmen's voices reverberated around the valley. Cheltenham lost the grip on his sword and it fell unceremoniously to the ground. Most of the artillery commanders were watching the rebels as the shout went up, but a few had seen the sword fall and took it as the signal to fire.

Gunpowder hissed in a dozen gun barrels and there was a short pause before the air around them turned to hell. The English gunners who had fired vanished, shredded into a bloody mist by the exploding cannon. Guns were hurled from their carriages and the nearest soldiers were eviscerated by pieces of hot iron. Maddicott felt the heat of the explosions wash over him, and even at this distance shards of metal flew over his head and into the ranks of his own men.

Cheltenham, who had been thrown to the dirt with the force of the blast, sat stunned, not quite comprehending what had happened. Soldiers lay writhing in the dirt, their limbs sliced from their bodies, and others had shards of white hot metal protruding from their chests. Comrades stooped to pull the shrapnel from their screaming friends but lost their own fingers in the process from the heat of the burning metal.

Then, through the noise and the smoke, came an enormous cheer as the rebels, seeing the English guns destroyed, charged down the side of the valley.

Most of Cheltenham's staff officers had been killed. He sat in the dirt, ruffled but uninjured, and gawked at the sight of seven thousand bloodthirsty rebels charging unfettered at his shattered troops. He tried to stand up, but his legs felt groggy under him. He reached up and took the reins of his mount and pulled himself to his feet. Ignoring the carnage around him, he climbed into the saddle and nudged the horse away from the charging mass of men.

The remaining officers and their sergeants had rallied their nervous men and now ordered them into two long lines in the face of the attacking rebels. Maddicott realised the English still had the advantage. The remaining English guns were unable to fire down into the valley, but the Scots were attacking uphill, straight into the waiting muskets of the English infantry. With the prospect of a deadly volley only moments away and the waiting cavalry standing in reserve, he knew that victory was far from certain for the rebels.

Cheltenham rode up to the nearest gunner that was still alive and reined in next to him. "What happened here?" the General shouted down at him. "Why did those guns explode?"

The officer pointed at the back of the gun. "All the guns have been spiked, sir. It's going to be a few minutes before we can fire the guns we have left." Cheltenham glanced back at the attacking Scots. In a few minutes, all six thousand rebels would be under his guns, attacking this position, and the battle would be over. It was the second time in as many minutes that Cheltenham had been tricked, and he swore quietly to himself that it would never happen again. He looked around, searching for a plan, and noticed Captain Maddicott and his men moving to the flank and away from danger. Suddenly the situation became clear, and the clarity of the moment brought with it a plan that could save his army from destruction.

"Major, move your remaining guns to the rear, fill them with canister shot, and wait for my signal to fire." He spurred his horse forward and rode to his remaining staff officers. "Colonel Mortimer, you seem to be the most senior person on my staff now, and you are in charge of handing out my orders for the remainder of the day." The Colonel had blood running down his face from a wound in his head, but apart from that, the man was relatively unharmed. "Colonel, I've ordered the remaining artillery to the rear and to be loaded with canister. I want you to order the two lines of infantry on the crest of the hill to lay down volley fire until I give the order to retreat. Do you hear me, Colonel? Do you understand what I'm after?"

"Yes, sir. What about the cavalry?"

"Send the cavalry to the flanks and get them to hold fast until…" Cheltenham paused in mid-sentence and stared down the hill at the rebels now streaming up the side of the valley towards him.

"Cavalry, Colonel…"

"Sorry, sir?"

"Cavalry. Look at the enemy. Do you see any?"

"See any what, sir?"

"Cavalry man, bloody cavalry. Do you see any?" The Colonel stared at the rebel army and studied the surrounding area.

"No, sir. The rebels don't seem to have any that I can see sir."

Cheltenham smiled for the first time that morning. "Sort out your men, Colonel, and make sure they stand firm. Send the cavalry to the flanks and hold them there until the rebels are beaten back. We will have a little surprise waiting for them when they try to retreat without cavalry of their own to protect them. You have your orders." Cheltenham was about to ride away when he had an afterthought. "Oh, and Colonel, could you give Captain Maddicott the honour of commanding the troops at the very centre of our defence. I wouldn't want him to miss out on all the fun."

CHAPTER 28

The rebel attack was being organized and led by Du Puy's right-hand man, Colonel Jean Baptiste Pelous, one of the many exiled French soldiers flooding to Du Puy's banner. The Colonel didn't see himself as a mercenary, but he was nevertheless fighting for the riches and titles that Du Puy had already promised to all the mercenaries under his command. The Colonel commanded just over seven thousand men, not including the several hundred foreign mercenaries acting as the backbone of the army and the Knights Hospitaler who controlled the flanks and the centre.

Du Puy's orders to Pelous had been plain and simple, to surprise the English at their weakest moment, hit them hard and fast when the guns exploded, and take advantage of the confusion. Once the English artillery was out of the picture, their advantage lay in the speed of their attack and the confusion among the English ranks. The English troops were inexperienced and ill-disciplined, but the rebels needed to win the battle in their first attack. If the rebels were beaten back and the English used their cavalry, then the battle and the entire rebellion would be lost. Du Puy had promised Pelous that the English artillery would be destroyed, and he had made good on his word. Pelous had ordered his army forward for a full attack, and as Pelous looked on, he could see the English guns smoking. But he could also see that other pieces were being dragged back out of sight beyond the enemy ridge. Pelous was committed to the attack now, and he had left only a handful of men to manage their few working pieces of artillery to cover a retreat if it was needed. Pelous had adjusted the Grand Master's plan slightly by filling the very front rank of attacking men with his weakest troops as he felt fairly certain the raw English recruits would only get three volleys off before the rebels hit the English defences. The Scottish peasants at the front would soak up those initial volleys, leaving his best troops, mainly stationed at the centre, to hit the English line unharmed. The battle would be fought at close quarters over a mile of battlefield, but once the rebel centre had broken through, Pelous had ordered the men to sweep around to the left and right and hit the English line from behind. The rebels had overwhelming numbers, and the flanks would turn inwards and slowly crush the English in a pincer movement.

Pelous watched through his telescope as the centre of his army began running up the steep slope of the valley opposite his position. He focused on the English infantry and could see them preparing for the first volley as soon as the rebels came into range. In normal circumstances, Pelous would never commit a force under his command to the slaughter of English volley fire, for he had witnessed the deadly power of well-trained English troops hammering four rounds a minute into the columns of foolish Frenchmen, but these were not well trained English troops and he knew they would not stand.

The attacking rebels had been promised that the English line would fall, but as they screamed their final challenge from fifty yards, a thousand muskets seemed to unload all at once. Pelous winced as the sound reverberated around the valley like a recurring nightmare, but as the smoke cleared he smiled. The ranks of rebels were still charging forward. The inexperience of the English troops combined with the slope of the hill meant that the first volley had gone high and only a few hundred shots had been effective. Even so, the side of the hill was dotted with the bodies of scores of men and the first screams of the wounded drifted up to where Pelous was standing. The next volley a few seconds later was far more devastating. The second line of infantry had learned from their comrade's mistake. The rebel charge almost faltered as the inexperienced Scots saw their friends and relatives slaughtered, but the monks and mercenaries had been positioned well and they drove the rebels forward relentlessly. The piles of bodies lay only twenty feet away from the English line, but the front rank had reloaded and the rebel line braced for the third volley.

Captain Maddicott, who had been dragged almost crying into the centre of the English defence, watched in mute helplessness as he saw his reward dying in front of his eyes, but he was happy at least to be alive, and he meant to keep it that way.

"Hurry, hurry, and reload men," he shouted at the ranks of redcoats in front of him. "Don't let them get to the top of this hill or by God there will be trouble." The lines of men ignored him as they hurriedly reloaded for another volley, but Maddicott sensed they were being far too slow. Pelous watched transfixed as the critical moment of the attack approached. Unless his men rallied and continued forward, the battle would be lost. The knights at the centre sensed the thoughts of their commander and charged forward, screaming their challenge in a language the young ranks of English troops had never heard before. Maddicott couldn't believe his eyes as the hoard of cloaked knights sprinted the final yards up the hill ahead of the rebel line and directly at his position with bloody murder in their eyes. In that moment, it seemed as though the entire rebel army held its breath, and in desperation, those redcoats who had loaded quicker than their comrades began firing sporadically. A knight went down as a musket ball pierced his brain, and another halted momentarily as a bullet struck him in the shoulder. Redcoats further along the line fired sideways into the ranks of charging monks even though they had a far bigger target standing almost stationary in front of them. "Kill them. Kill them you bastards!" Maddicott yelled at his men. He grabbed a musket from the man closest to him, aimed and fired, but the weapon hadn't been loaded properly so the firing mechanism clicked harmlessly. Maddicott stared at the weapon in disbelief, then threw it in terror down the hill at the nearest monk. In a futile attempt at self-preservation, Maddicott turned and ran. "Run for your lives, you fools," he yelled, but the redcoats just stood there in astonishment. He knocked a man out of his path, but it was too late, the monks had reached the crest of the hill and hit the dumbstruck English ranks like lions sensing the kill. The rebel army came back to life at the sight, and in a moment of solidarity, the aura of invincibility pulsed back into their hearts.

Pelous stood motionless as he watched through his telescope. The English line held for a moment, even with the overwhelming numbers against them, but eventually the line broke and soldiers turned and ran. The rebels cheered their victory and rushed forward unchecked over the lip of the valley and into the English camp. Victory for the rebels seemed inevitable, but Pelous's instincts told him the attack had been won too easily, that the English hadn't put up much of a fight. He ordered an officer to make sure all their artillery pieces were loaded and ready to offer cover fire if the army was forced to retreat. Pelous was conscious that Cheltenham had yet to use his cavalry, and in that second, as if his worst fears were being answered, one of his officers shouted and pointed to the right flank where a long line of heavy cavalry had appeared. Pelous glanced back at the main battle with dread welling inside his stomach, and almost as if he was expecting it, the air erupted with the sound of cannon fire. The battle was far from over and the killing had only just begun.

As the rebel army broke through the centre of the English line, the order was given and the English turned and ran to the safety of their waiting guns. Cheltenham had taken a huge gamble. Even he wasn't mad enough to fire on his own troops, and he had to wait until his men had retreated from danger before opening fire. The rebels had been told at the start of the battle that the English guns were not a threat, and so the Scots charged forward, not realizing they were running into a trap. Cheltenham watched as his men poured back to enforce the third line of infantry positioned behind the guns. Then he gave the order and the artillery belched their devastating load into the unsuspecting ranks of rebels. At close range, canister was the deadliest weapon on the battlefield. Hundreds of white-hot musket balls and other pieces of metal fired at great speeds into flesh and bone causing unimaginable carnage and destruction. The front ranks of rebels were obliterated, their bodies eviscerated into piles of unrecognisable flesh, and rebel's ten rows back were hit with metal that had already gone through the bodies of a dozen or more of their countrymen.

Still the rebels pushed on, and the English infantry began firing to add to the slaughter while the gunners reloaded with more canister. Cheltenham had already ordered his cavalry to the flanks, but he held them in reserve until the moment was right. The battle was now taking place out of sight beyond the lip of the valley, so Pelous could do nothing except pray that the rebels had the strength to win the day.

The knights at the centre, realizing a frontal attack was now out of the question, moved left and right to try to flank the artillery while desperately trying to avoid the deadly canister that was decimating the rebel ranks. Cheltenham noticed the move and had no choice but to bring his cavalry into play in the hope of breaking the back of the rebel attack once and for all. The knights saw the cavalry thundering towards them and realised they had lost too much momentum and cohesion to be able to sustain the assault further. The knights ordered retreat, and the rebels at the rear began to stream back down into the valley. The cavalry was deadliest at the backs of a retreating army, so as they saw the rebels running for their lives, they charged forward in earnest, ruthlessly cutting down the Scots from behind.

Cheltenham watched in glee as his enemy turned and ran. He ordered the gunners to keep firing, and he signalled the cavalry forward with a wave of his sword. Pelous could only watch as his army streamed back towards him, and he heard the ominous thunder of cavalry approaching to massacre his troops as they fled. The Frenchman waited patiently until the English cavalry was fully engaged and in range, then gave the order for the artillery to fire. Pelous's guns began to find their targets, but he knew it wouldn't be enough to counter the massive English attack. The only resistance was from a group of knights who had formed a compact square and were acting as a rearguard while the rest of the rebels fled. The English cavalry seemed to be drawn to the square as it posed a greater challenge than anything else on the battlefield. Pelous watched in amazement as the knights retreated slowly while completely surrounded by cavalry.

The rebel artillery was beginning to take effect now that the English were huddled so close together, and rebel skirmishers positioned on the side of the valley began to find their targets. The knights continued to retreat but seemed invincible in the face of overwhelming numbers. The English cavalry were now in the bottom of the valley and unable to move freely. The riders milled around, unsure how to continue their attack. Pelous realised his sudden advantage and ordered every available man to move forward into range and fire down on their vulnerable enemy. The English quickly realised they were outgunned and fled back to the safety their own lines.

The battlefield was littered with the dead and dying from both sides, and the knights, still in their tight formation, marched back to cheers and applause from their Scottish comrades. Pelous thanked God for a successful retreat and realised his broken army would happily live to fight another day.

Cheltenham stepped forward from the barricade of guns as his cavalry came charging towards him. He realised he had failed to break the rebels but had managed to survive a trap that nearly wiped his small army off the face of the earth. Neither side held an advantage. He had cavalry but the rebels easily outnumbered him. His only course of action was to defend his position and send messengers back to Edinburgh to order the rest of his army into the field. Cheltenham was picking his way forward through the bodies to take note of the rebel movements when he noticed an English officer struggling to drag himself back to the English lines. He walked up to the man and realised it was the bloodied and battered body of Captain Maddicott.

"So you survived then, you traitorous scoundrel," Cheltenham muttered. Then he stamped his foot down hard on the back of the injured officer. Maddicott cried out in pain and Cheltenham kicked the Captain over so he was facing upwards. Maddicott was holding his stomach and Cheltenham could see the Captain had suffered a terrible wound and must have lost a lot of blood.

"You destroyed my cannons, you little shit," Cheltenham said, almost spitting out the words.

"I don't know what you mean, sir," Maddicott replied, through clenched teeth.

"Don't lie to me, Maddicott. You're dead anyway, so you may as well tell me what you did. I may even ease your passing if you tell me the truth." Maddicott thought for a moment and realised Cheltenham was telling the truth about his situation.

"It was Du Puy," Maddicott whispered. "My men were acting on my orders, sir. They had no choice in the matter."

"We all have choices, Captain, and we all choose our side. You, unfortunately, chose the wrong side." Cheltenham looked around and spotted Colonel Mortimer directing his forces. "Colonel!" Cheltenham shouted.

"Yes, sir." The Colonel jogged over.

"Would you be so kind as to gather the remainder of Captain Maddicott's men and put them under arrest."

"Yes sir, and what would be the charge?" Cheltenham looked down at the dying Maddicott.

"Treason, Colonel. That will be all."

"Yes, sir." The Colonel trotted off again as Cheltenham knelt down next to Captain Maddicott.

"Your men chose a side as well, Captain. You will not be able to save them. I can assure you of that. Moreover, if you have seen it necessary to turn against me, who is to say your entire family is not collaborating with the enemy." Cheltenham smiled at Maddicott as the young Captain realised what the General was implying. Cheltenham stood up then and walked slowly away, leaving the mortally wounded man to contemplate his own agonizing death and the murder of his entire family.

The next morning, the two armies faced each other again. Pelous was unwilling to commit his forces, while Cheltenham was unable to attack because of his lack of firepower. Cheltenham had already dispatched messengers to Edinburgh for reinforcements, but Pelous had predicted this action and had blocked all the roads back to the capital. The two armies, therefore, sat watching each other from across either side of the valley, each waiting for the other to make the first move.

Pelous was eating his breakfast outside his tent on the third day when a senior knight approached him.

"Yes, knight. What is it?" Pelous said in French.

"A messenger from the English army managed to break through our lines, my Lord. It will only be a matter of days before the rest of the English army arrives."

"Very well." Pelous replied after a moment. "Have my war council gathered here in ten minutes, and have your men ready the army for another attack."

"Yes, my Lord, as you command."

"And knight…"

"Yes, my Lord."

"I will need your men to lead the assault. The Scots will not stand unless you and your knights show them the way."

The knight stood to attention and raised a fist to his chest to touch the crest on his tunic. "It would be our honour to lead the final attack my Lord. We will guide your army to victory if God sees fit."

"Very well, knight. You have my highest regard, and my only regret is that your Master could not be here to see your victory. Now go and ready your men and let me finish my eggs in peace." The knight bowed and walked away, leaving Pelous to contemplate how he was going to beat the English before the reinforcements arrived.

Cheltenham didn't have to be told the rebels were planning an attack. The Scots were making so much noise he would have heard them ten miles away. The English commander watched as the massive hoard of men gathered once again on the opposite side of the valley. He knew one of his messengers had gotten through and that was the reason the Scots were attacking now — one last throw of the dice before the rest of Cheltenham's army arrived.

The English lines had been brought forward, and their intention was clear — to pound the rebels into submission and break their resolve. Cheltenham had seen the rebels fight. The Scots had no concept of battle lines, and their commanders had little control over them once the attack started. The only way to win in the face of such overwhelming numbers was to pound the Scots with shot and volley fire while cavalry attacked at the flanks until the rebels turned tail and ran.

Cheltenham expected his better-trained troops to win a battle of attrition, and thus his thoughts were turning to how he would round up the ringleaders when a gap suddenly opened at the centre of the shouting army of rebels. The English watched in fascination as the Knights Hospitaler marched in tight formation through the gap in full ceremonial dress. They wore metal breastplates that gleamed brightly in the morning sunshine, and each man had a burnished metal helmet and a cloak that streamed out behind him. The crest of their order was emblazoned on their breastplates, and they stood in front of the rebel army like medieval warriors, soldiers from another time.

Cheltenham smirked, and as he considered the final rebel attack, he was almost upset that the Grandmaster himself wasn't leading his knights into battle. He counted about three hundred knights, each armed to the teeth and trained to kill without thinking or remorse. Cheltenham turned to Colonel Mortimer and ordered every artillery piece to be trained on the group of knights and to await the signal to fire.

In a single flourish, all the knights drew their swords and raised them high into the air to salute their enemy. The rebels took this as an act of defiance and started cheering again. Pelous smiled and realised that, in this one simple act, the knights had secured the respect and admiration of every rebel on the battlefield. Cheltenham gave the order and a dozen shells were fired across the valley, but all fell well short of the waiting ranks of rebels. Cheltenham cursed his inexperienced gunners and watched as the knights reacted to the attack by splitting their forces, reducing the number of guns that could train on them. The knights then started marching forward to another cheer from the rebels, who followed behind, forming into well drilled ranks as they went. Cheltenham's eyes nearly popped out of his head when he saw the rebels march in formation with muskets shouldered and arms swinging. After everything he'd promised himself, Cheltenham realised he'd been tricked again. The rebels had in fact been trained, and by the look of them, trained very well.

Cheltenham was about to order his guns to fire at will when his attention was momentarily diverted by a strange wailing noise coming from mouth of the valley. Cheltenham's sword was raised in the air, and his men were watching it, ready to launch their attack, but their General was transfixed on the noise. The rebels had also heard the sound and were sending nervous glances to their left to where the noise was emanating. Seemingly out of nowhere, Cheltenham watched open mouthed as a column of men appeared through the haze, marching in file towards both armies.

The soldiers came towards them like an army of ghosts from the gates of hell, their kilts swinging as they marched in unison. Great bearskin helmets made them appear like giants as they marched onto the battlefield. In front of the column marched the pipers who were the source of the wailing that Cheltenham could hear ringing in his ears. As the Highlanders drew closer, the noise of the pipes filled the valley and each soldier in the long column stared ahead, ignoring the charging rebels and knights that were drawing ever closer.

Cheltenham wasn't sure what was happening, but many of his men were already cheering the new arrivals, assuming them to be reinforcements. Cheltenham recognised the figure marching at the head of the column and cursed his sudden ill fortune. The pipers continued to play on when the Highlanders stopped in the middle of the valley directly between the charging rebels and the waiting English infantry. The leading rebels had already ceased their advance down the side of the valley and were standing bemused at the sight of a column of their own countrymen blocking their way.

Sir William de Kendall stood motionless at the head of the column while his pipers played out their tune. When they finished, he turned and ordered his men to fix bayonets. The officers then ordered one line of the column to face the rebels and the other to stand opposite the English army on the other side. When his men were ready, Sir William gestured to the flag bearer, who immediately raised a wooden shaft with a white flag fluttering at the top. Cheltenham watched helplessly as his plans dissolved in front of his eyes. He was almost tempted to order his men to fire on the column.

As soon as the white flag was raised, Pelous instinctively knew this new enemy was not under the command of Arthur Cheltenham. Even if Pelous could get the rebels to fight a regiment of their own countrymen, it was clear that the valley was filled with a thousand battle-hardened troops and the odds had evened up significantly. As Pelous was contemplating what to do, he noticed a civilian among the ranks of red-coated Highlanders. He trained the telescope on the grey-haired stranger and watched as the man took the white flag from the standard bearer, and with no thought to his own safety, the man rode towards the confused ranks of rebels.

Pelous suddenly realised who the man was, and in that moment, he knew the battle had been lost. Some of the rebels who had recognised the old man started cheering and chanting his name as he approached. Pelous immediately ordered the retreat of his knights and French mercenaries to the rear, leaving the rebels to their own fate. Pelous understood how fickle the mob could be for he had witnessed such events in his hometown of Paris many times. Sir Henry Burns was a more dangerous weapon than anything left on the battlefield, and the old man's presence was enough to turn the tide against Pelous's best-laid plans.

Pelous could see Burns talking to the nearest rebels, and they in turn spoke to the men around them. In minutes, he knew, half the army would turn against his forces. Whatever Burns was saying was spreading like wildfire. Pelous realised he didn't have enough horses to escape with all the men loyal to him. He needed to create a diversion, and he had a simple plan to do it.

Sir William de Kendall cantered up the side of the valley with fifty of his best men, trotted towards the lines of English infantry, who were still cheering what they thought were reinforcements. Cheltenham was desperately thinking of a valid reason why de Kendall's men should come under his command, but events were happening too fast for him to focus. De Kendall was within fifty feet when Cheltenham suddenly came to life and decided what his best course of action was under the circumstances. Having also seen Henry Burns ride towards the rebel lines, he realised the game was up. Cheltenham decided the simplest plan was to make a run for it. Cheltenham spun his horse wildly around and stabbed his spurs into the beast to urge it forward.

De Kendall, realising his quarry was trying to escape, shouted to the English troops at the top of the hill. "Arrest that man!" He drew his sword and urged his own horse into a gallop. The English soldiers looked around at each other in confusion and the cheers began to abate. De Kendall quickly left his own men behind in his wild pursuit, but Cheltenham's escape had been impeded by his horse's reluctance to gallop through the hundreds of corpses littering the battlefield. As de Kendall reached the crest of the hill, the valley erupted with explosions that sent rebel and Englishman alike running for cover.

Pelous ignoring the flag of truce had trained his artillery on both armies simultaneously and ordered them to fire at will hoping to cause enough confusion to cover their retreat. Men were suddenly running everywhere through the smoke and chaos, and neither side understood who had launched the attack. The rebel army was so large and widespread that they posed an easy target. Thousands streamed forward into the valley, swamping the smaller British force that was desperately trying to hold its ground without opening fire. Large numbers of English soldiers at the top of the hill decided they'd had enough and ran, but many held their positions and started firing wildly at the rebels adding to the confusion.

A single shell arced high towards the waiting ranks of English infantry. Those men who saw it coming ducked for cover but quickly realised the trajectory was too high for it to land on them. They watched as the shell whistled overheard and landed directly in the path of their commander, who was still running for his life. The shell buried itself in the ground and the redcoats held their breath. A second later the shell exploded skyward. Cheltenham's horse reared backwards, taking the full force of the blast in its chest. The English commander was thrown ten feet into the air and landed in a crumpled heap among the many corpses already beginning to rot in the warm summer air.

Cheltenham rolled over onto his stomach, the wind knocked out of him. He raised his eyes skyward as two hooves came into focus. Artillery shells were still dropping all around them but with less frequency.

"You will live to regret not having been killed by that blast, Sir Arthur. I would kill you myself, here and now, but a public trial and execution will be the only thing that might ensure my people's satisfaction." De Kendall sheathed his sword while staring down at the English General with disgust etched on his face. The Highlanders eventually caught up with their colonel and hauled Cheltenham to his feet then dragged him away without another word. De Kendall glanced up at an artillery officer not ten feet away who was staring open mouthed at the events that had just unfolded.

"Don't just stand there gawping, man. Get some return fire on that hill so we can get this place cleared up once and for all." The officer scurried away to carry out the order, and de Kendall turned to survey the chaos filling the entire valley. He watched helplessly as Pelous marched away into the distance, and thousands of rebels streamed out of the valley and away from danger. De Kendall wondered if anyone would ever really find out what had happened during this battle and if they even knew what they were fighting for. What he did know for sure was that he had saved his country from disaster all because of a few letters from an Englishman he'd met only once and was probably unlikely to ever meet again. He promised himself, if he reached Maggie Burns and Richard Stone in time before they were captured or killed, he would make sure they both received the recognition they deserved. He spurred his horse forward again and began shouting orders to bring order to the battlefield once more.

CHAPTER 29

Stone's hand went instinctively to the hilt of his sword. Maggie glared at him angrily. He refrained from any further sudden movement, but the hand remained where it was. The old man approached them slowly and raised his hand in greeting. Maggie waved back and nudged Stone in the ribs. Reluctantly, he removed his hand from the sword and he waved a generous greeting to the old man, who stopped a few yards away.

"You two are a long way from home." He smiled through a perfect row of white teeth. "If you're lost, I'm afraid I can't help." Maggie stared at the man in amazement. He seemed so old and withered, and yet his eyes glittered like a young boy's and he spoke in a deep powerful voice. "Come with me. You look like ye could do with a warm brew." Without another word, he headed towards the small house by the waterfall that they had seen from a distance. Maggie glanced at Stone, and he shrugged and followed the old man. He didn't need to be asked twice.

The building was obviously very old, and Maggie studied it carefully as they approached. She was disappointed to see there were no markings of any significance and no sign the building had ever been used as a chapel or a tomb of any kind. The old man prodded a fire just outside against the wall of the building where a pot of broth was steaming over hot coals. Stone licked his lips as the smell of cooked meat and vegetable wafted over them. The old man noticed Maggie studying his home, and he smiled again as he handed them both a tin cup filled with the warm soup.

"She's very old," he said to her, and he looked up at the ancient granite building. "Built to last though." He walked over and tapped the wall almost lovingly. "Foundation's deep as the house is high," he muttered. "She'll stand for another five hundred years, I'll warrant ye." He took a sip of his own broth and sat on an old tree stump by the wall. Stone gulped down the broth in two mouthfuls and wiped his dripping chin on his sleeve.

"You said you couldn't help us if we were lost," Stone said.

The old man sipped at the steaming stew and looked up at Stone through deep blue penetrating eyes. "That's right." He paused again to drink. "It's been so long since I left this valley that I can't really remember where I am." Stone looked at Maggie and raised an eyebrow.

"How long have you been here?" Maggie asked, her curiosity suitably piqued.

The old man thought for a moment, then pointed towards the waterfall. "You see that big oak tree by the falls over there?" They gazed in the direction of the oak. The tree wasn't fully grown by any means, but it still towered high over the little house. "That tree was just a sapling when I came here, no more than a boy." Stone guessed it would take seventy or eighty years for a tree to grow so big. He looked back at the old man with interest.

"You've stayed in this valley for that long?" he said, gesturing to the tree. "And you've never left, not once?"

"I've wandered out a few times, but never very far," he replied.

"How do you survive?" Maggie asked. The old man turned his blue eyes to her and furrowed his brow into a puzzled expression.

"Look around you," he said, raising both arms into the air. "This valley is full of rabbits and the river is full if fish. Minerals from the hills wash down and feed my crops." He pointed to a vegetable garden behind the old house. "I have everything I need," he said, and he smiled at them once again.

"Don't you miss the company of others?" Maggie asked.

The old man thought for a moment, then shook his head. "A long time ago, some very bad things happened… I stumbled onto this 'ere place while I was travelling around, and I've never left 'ere since." He sat in silence for a moment, and Maggie thought he'd finished his explanation. He looked up at her. "I think at the time I saw this place as a kind of purgatory." He finished the last of his soup and stood up. "And now it's me very own paradise." He turned and walked into the house. Maggie glanced at Stone, and he stood up and followed the old man into his home. Maggie brought up the rear, absorbing every detail as they plunged into the darkness.

The house was very simple and divided into three small rooms. A fire burned in the hearth of the main room, emitting a friendly glow. The only furniture was a handmade table and chair pushed close to the flames for warmth. One wall was lined with shelves, and the man's worldly possessions were piled in careful order. An old gun hung over the fireplace. Stone guessed the weapon dated easily to the mid eighteenth century, and if he wasn't mistaken, it was a type more commonly used on ships than on land. The floor was covered with rugs and animal hides, adding to the warmth of the place. A fox lazed in the corner of the room, studying them intently.

"Don't worry about 'im," the old man said. "Caught 'im in one of me traps a few seasons ago. Tame as a puppy now, and he refuses to go back to the wild." He grinned sheepishly. "I think he likes me cookin'."

Rufus looked at the small fox out of the corner of his eye, not quite sure what to make of a wild animal inside a human habitation. Nevertheless, he obviously deemed the animal beneath him to make a fuss about and so he just ignored it altogether.

The old man brought two more chairs from the other rooms and put them in front of the fire. As they sat down, Stone suddenly realised they hadn't introduced themselves. He shot to his feet and addressed the old man formally.

"Please accept my apologies sir," he said warmly. "We failed to introduce ourselves before. This is Maggie Burns, my travelling companion, and my name is Richard Stone, an officer in his Britannic majesty's armed forces." The old man looked at them with a blank expression as if their introduction meant very little to him.

"Well, it's very nice to meet you both. It's been so long since I've seen anyone in these parts that I'd forgotten that I even 'ad a name. Years ago, I was known as Young Murray, but you both can call me Murray, like me mates used to."

"Do you remember what this house was like when you arrived here, Murray?" Maggie asked, changing the subject.

Murray thought for a moment, then took a pipe from his pocket, lit up, and puffed an odd smelling smoke into the air. "The house was completely empty. It were just a shell," he stated. "The roof were in disrepair, birds was nesting in the chimney, and a couple of badgers had made one of the bedrooms into their home."

"Were there any markings on the building to indicate who had lived there before?" Maggie asked anxiously.

He sucked on the pipe and looked at the ceiling thoughtfully. "No," he said finally. "There were nothing. I assumed the previous owner had just moved away. Couldn't believe me luck. The place were completely empty." He paused for a moment. "The only thing I found were a big slab of granite with lots of engravings on it in the back room." Stone raised his head slowly and looked at Maggie.

"What did you do with the stone," she asked, barely managing to hide her excitement. Murray looked puzzled.

"Well, it's still there," he exclaimed. "The thing was far too heavy for me to move so I use it as a table in me bedroom. Come and have a look-see if you're interested."

They followed him into the back room where a small wooden bed covered with fleeces and rugs stood in one corner. On the other side of the room, a massive block of stone stood near the centre of the wall. Murray's clothes covered the stone, and he hurried over and cleared the top of it so the stone stood naked in the dim light. Murray lit a couple of candles, and the room suddenly glowed. A shiver of excitement shot through Maggie's body. It was obvious the stone was an altar. She looked around and saw both the sidewalls had small alcoves where religious artefacts would have stood. Her body tingled again with expectation, and she glanced at Stone, who was gawping at the altar.

"Murray," she said softly. "Would you mind if Richard and I have a look at the carvings on the stone for a while." She looked into his blue eyes. "We'd be very grateful," she said, beaming a smile at him.

"Well, if you put it like that m' dear, I've got wood to chop anyhow. Just give me a shout when you're done and we'll see what we can do to get you two settled for the evening."

He left them alone then, and the pair stood looking at the altar, not quite sure what to do. After a while, the noise of metal on wood came from outside and it seemed to spark Stone into action. He knelt down beside the altar to get a better look at the carvings. Maggie took one of the candles and knelt down beside him. The carvings were mainly religious inscriptions depicting saints.

"At least we can ascertain one thing," she whispered softly into his ear.

"What's that?" he said looking into her green eyes, his passion for her rising suddenly.

"This was definitely a chapel, perhaps not the whole house but almost certainly this room." Stone stood up and put his shoulder up against the face of the altar.

"What're you doing?" Maggie exclaimed. Stone looked back her.

"The tomb has got to be in this room, or at least the entrance is in this room. I don't see any markings on the floor so the logical place is under the altar."

"But Richard, that altar must be the weight of twenty men. How are you going to move it?" He grinned at her and readied himself for the first push.

"We'll never know until we try, will we?" He steadied himself, then heaved all his strength against the smooth granite surface. Maggie watched as his face turned slowly purple with the effort. After a minute, she tapped his shoulder and he let out a deep rush of air from his lungs. He bent over and put his hands on his knees in exhaustion.

"I don't think it's going to move, do you?" she said, sarcastically. He looked up at her and pulled a face, then looked back at the altar. He stood looking at it for a moment, then clicked his fingers and walked to the right of the stone.

"If it won't move forwards," he said, bracing himself, "then maybe it'll move sideways." He went through the same routine on both sides until he'd totally exhausted himself. Meanwhile, Maggie had been studying the floor of the bedroom but hadn't found anything obvious. She looked at him from across the room, and Stone shrugged his shoulders.

"I'm out of ideas. You?" he said, leaning against the wall and breathing heavily.

"Maybe we're looking in the wrong place," she replied. "Why should the tomb be inside. It could be anywhere around here."

Stone thought about it and let out a long sigh. "We could be here until next spring." He kicked the side of the altar in frustration.

"Richard," Maggie exclaimed. "This is still a house of God, you know. Treat it with some respect."

He looked down at the dirty scuffmark he'd left on the granite, then opened his eyes in alarm. "Maggie," he whispered out of the side of his mouth. "Come here quickly." She scurried to where he was standing. "What do you make of that?" He pointed at the side of the altar. Engraved in the side on the altar stone where two small swords parallel to each other and pointing to the earth, and where Stone had kicked the altar, a tiny square crack had appeared around the sides of the engraving. He put his hand against the stone and pushed gently. The stone moved inwards but left the outline of the swords in its path. Stone glanced at Maggie and grinned like a schoolboy.

Maggie bent down and looked inside the hole left by the displaced rock. She looked back up at Stone with an expression of disappointment. He followed her gaze and peered into the hole. The sides were smooth but the hole ended abruptly and the floor was still solid rock. Maggie turned her attention to the swords. She took hold of the end of each little sword and tried to manipulate them. She was rewarded with a small grating sound, and when Stone helped her, the swords began to move apart. Then Maggie and Stone pulled together and the granite moved slowly but the swords didn't move away in parallel. Maggie gave a small squeak of pleasure as she realised what was happening. The swords were pivoting away from each other at the top but crossing each other at the bottom. Maggie clapped her hands and wriggled with excitement. She reached into her jacket and pulled out her copy of the *Wallas of Blin Harry*. Turning to the first page, she then held the book open for Stone and pointed at the picture printed on the paper.

"Two crossed swords," she said. "The church bearing two crossing swords — it has a double meaning." She closed the book and put it back into her pocket. She was about to get up when they heard a loud scraping and thudding sound coming from the floor beneath them.

"Quick, move." Stone shoved her to the right, away from the altar as the floor suddenly collapsed around their ears. The air was suddenly filled with dust and debris as the altar and Murray's bed disappeared in a maelstrom of noise and falling masonry. The floor opened up like a gaping maw, swallowing Stone into its dark reaches. Maggie screamed as she saw him disappear, lost in the cloud of dust and debris.

Murray looked up from the woodpile as the noise erupted from his house. His eyes widened in alarm as dust and smoke started erupting from the front door and windows. He started forward as quickly as his old legs would take him. Suddenly, from out of the bushes, another strange man appeared, and Murray reared back in alarm as he realised the man was brandishing a drawn sword. Three other figures hung back in the bushes, and Murray noticed they were heavily robed. Murray watched as the man bore down on him, and in his haste to escape, the old man tripped on a tree root and fell over backwards. The man stood over him and leered at Murray. smiling through rotten teeth, his breath stinking. Murray looked into the eyes of his attacker and saw a heart blacker than anything he could imagine. He realised that he was about to die, and he felt sad that he had to leave his beautiful valley.

Clifford's leer turned into a smile as he drew back his sword arm and thrust down with the killing blow. The steel pierced the old man's chest and carved through the ancient heart. Clifford felt the body shudder, then stood on Murray's chest to get leverage to pull his blade free. Without wiping the weapon, he turned and gestured for his men to follow. They strode towards the house, leaving the broken body in the dust.

Maggie rubbed the dust from her eyes and coughed the smoke from her lungs. Before her, a hole was gaping in the floor where the altar once stood and the back wall of the chapel had toppled outwards to the ground. She scrambled forward and peered over the edge where she'd seen Stone fall. She heard rustling in the dark and loud cursing, and she smiled with relief. To the left of the hole, a stone staircase led down into the darkness and she heard Richard running up them towards her. His head popped up through the hole, and he smiled at her. His face was dust-covered and his hair tangled.

"Looks like we found it," he said gleefully, climbing out of the hole to sit next to her. He had a cut above his left eye and the blood was running down the side of his face. Maggie took out her handkerchief and dabbed at the wound to clear the blood, then told him to hold it firmly against his head to staunch the flow. She looked worryingly at his wounded shoulder,

"It's fine. No harm done," he said before she had a chance to ask. She got up and started walking towards the door. "Where are you going?" he asked, and she turned back to face him.

"We'd better show Murray what we've found," she said. "He's not going to be very happy about what we've done to his house. He at least deserves to know what we're up to." She turned away and Stone scowled at her back. He winced as the pain from his most recent wound shot through his head. Stone turned his back to the door and was looking down into the hole when he heard footsteps walking softly behind him. He was about to turn when he felt the point of a blade at his ribcage.

"Stay where you are please, Mister Stone. There's a good lad. Can't have you pulling any surprises, now can we." He recognised Clifford's voice immediately

"Clifford," he muttered softly.

"That's right, Richard, my boy. Looks like we underestimated your abilities, don't it," Clifford said, now leaning close enough to

Stone's ear so he smelt the man's stinking breath. "Not just happy with the King's coin, eh me lad. You 'ad to go an' get the girl and the glory as well, didn't ya?" Clifford reached down and checked Stone for weapons while keeping the sword stuck into his side. Stone tensed as the point of the blade cut the cotton of the shirt and drew a tiny spec of blood. When Stone looked down and saw the blade was already slick and dark, a jolt of fear for Maggie shot through him. Clifford saw his reaction and chuckled. "Not yet, me lad. Not yet. Plenty of time to wet me blade with her before this day's through." He leant close to Stone's ear again. "Don't worry, lad. I'll let you watch me have my way with her before I gut both of you like the useless scum that you are." Spittle hit the side of Stone's face. "Then I'll poke her again and let the both of ya die together." He grabbed the back of Stone's shirt and dragged him away from the hole. As he moved forwards, Stone knocked the blade away and punched Clifford a glancing blow to the face. Clifford staggered across the room but kept his balance and the sword in his hand. Before Stone could react, Clifford had raised his guard and was pointing the blade at his throat. Stone could tell immediately that he'd underestimated Clifford's ability as a swordsman and regretted the attack.

"Look to the door, laddy, and see if you want to try something like that again." Stone saw Maggie standing between two monks. Both had stony expressions and one was holding a pistol to Maggie's head. The relief that she wasn't hurt was apparent on Stone's face, and she smiled at him in confirmation. Clifford saw the look, and his expression turned to rage. He raised his sword, and with a well-practised swing, sliced down on Stone's right arm. The steel cut through the muscle on Stone's bicep and sent blood spraying across the room. Maggie tried to run forward but she was pulled back by one of the monks. Clifford grinned as Stone went down on one knee his face contorted in pain.

Clifford walked to where Maggie was being restrained and gestured for the monks to move away. They moved reluctantly back, not completely happy with the way Clifford was treating his prisoners. Stone watched as Clifford parted the heavy travelling coat Maggie was wearing with the tip of his sword to reveal her clothes underneath. Maggie looked at Clifford with daggers in her eyes, and he grinned at her with lecherous intent in his own. Stone remained on one knee, his head hanging low and blood dripping from his arm to the floor. He made no sign that he was worried about Maggie. He wanted Clifford to think he was out of action and weaker than he actually was.

Clifford abruptly abandoned his games and walked to the hole in the floor. He looked at the shattered wall and debris around him. He'd originally been ordered to wait at the burial site once he'd found it and send one of his men to Du Puy to confirm the site's existence. He was told not to enter the tomb until Du Puy arrived. He turned to one of the monks and beckoned him forward.

"Go outside and tell Francois to ride to the Grand Master immediately. He is to tell Du Puy that we've found the tomb and we're waiting for his arrival. When you've done that, come back here straight away — quickly now." The monk ran out of the room, and Clifford started looking through Murray's possessions. Eventually he found enough candles for all of them, and he'd lit them all by the time the monk returned.

Clifford had no intention of waiting until Du Puy arrived before going into the tomb. If there was treasure to be found, then he wanted it for himself. He gave the monks a candle each and ordered Maggie and Stone's legs to be tied so they could only shuffle forward. He then gave the couple a candle and made them both move towards the entrance to the tomb. He ordered one of the monks to lead the group. Maggie and Stone were to follow, guarded by the other monk. Clifford took up the rear. Clifford wasn't taking any chances. He drew a pistol from his belt and followed the party down the steps into the darkness. If there was treasure inside, he thought, then the tomb would be a fitting place to leave his unwanted guests while he escaped a rich man.

CHAPTER 30

The stairs were crudely designed and each step differed in size from the next. They stumbled down in the blackness, Stone catching Maggie every time she tripped. The staircase was just wide enough for the pair to walk down, the walls covered in wet slime that soaked them to the skin. Eventually, the passage began to open up into a natural cavern. The walls of the stairwell fell away, disappearing into what seemed like a deep dark abyss. Each step they took echoed into the darkness, and the candlelight hardly penetrated the blackness. Maggie trembled in fear as she looked left and right and saw the chasm dropping away on either side into the absolute dark beyond the candlelight.

It seemed like an age before the steps ended at a natural bridge of rock that spanned the chasm. Clifford ordered one of the monks across to check that the bridge was safe. Maggie could hear a great torrent of water rushing through the bottom of the chasm far below them, an underground river that must have shaped and formed the caves over thousands of years. On the far side of the bridge, the monk raised his candle to confirm the bridge was safe. The light shone back to them, and as they started forward, Maggie could see the bridge ended in a sheer face of rock.

The party stepped through an opening in the rock and the world went silent again. The monk at the front had stopped ten feet down the tunnel and the light from the candle glowed around him. Wind from the cavern whipped into the tunnel, howled and dragged at their legs. Maggie suddenly realised they had nowhere else to go as the monk ahead stood in front of another solid wall. They walked forward, and Maggie now felt as if they were entering a tomb. The tunnel was freezing cold, and the wind howled, sending a chill of foreboding down her spine. They reached the monk, who still stood with his back to them. He had his head bowed and seemed to be saying a prayer. Stone raised his candle and the light shone on an ancient seal made of white mortar and clay. The seal covered the wall from floor to ceiling and was crumbling in a dozen places. A faint imprint could be seen in the clay, but Stone could make little sense out of it. Stone reached out and touched the surface where an area was crumbling, and the clay where he touched turned to dust. He put his hand to the wall and shoved hard. The clay gave way and his hand disappeared through the wall. He pushed his arm forward, and as he broke through a rush of air slammed into his face. The air filled the small tunnel for a moment and they all gagged at the stench of air locked away for five hundred years that reeked of decay. As fresh wind blew the stench away, Stone composed himself and went back to the wall.

"It's only a foot thick," he stated. "But if we both have a run at it..." He gestured to the monk. "We could probably knock it down." Stone gestured at the rope attaching him to Maggie, and Clifford nodded to the monk to remove it. Then both men stepped back a few paces before bursting forward, hitting the wall simultaneously. The wall collapsed in a shower of dust and flying shards of ancient clay.

The momentum of the two men took them through the wall and out the other side into the darkness beyond. Clifford stood with a pistol raised, pointing at Maggie's back. When Stone appeared again, dusty faced, Clifford ordered the rope put back on the pair. The small party walked on through the rubble and dust of the wall and into the chamber beyond. Maggie suddenly felt overcome when it dawned on her that no one had walked this path for almost half a millennia. Beyond the wall, their candles lit up another small chamber and all eyes focused on a square hole in the floor. The monk who'd been leading from the start glanced at Clifford, and Clifford waved him forward with his pistol. The monk walked to the hole and peered down, lowering his candle into the opening to take a quick look. Then the monk turned around and stepped into the hole backwards. He looked up at them all as he disappeared from sight, and Maggie felt an ominous sense of foreboding.

They stood in the chamber for ten long silent minutes before Clifford started to get anxious. The candles were burning low, and he'd only brought a couple of spares. He gave the monk another five minutes, then sent the second monk down the hole to see what had happened. Ten more minutes passed while Maggie and Stone sat in a corner of the chamber watching Clifford pacing backwards and forwards. Three candles had burned out, and they were down to their last few. Stone smiled at Clifford as the man struggled with what to do. Finally, he stopped walking. He decided that the monks must have fallen foul of a trap, and so he turned to face the couple on the floor.

"Up," he said viciously. "We don't have much time." He pushed them over to the hole and stood back. "Untie the rope. Stone crouched and took the rope off. "I want you down first," he said, pointing the pistol at Stone. "Then you follow," he said, leering at Maggie. "If you try anything, the girl gets a ball of lead in the back of her head. Now move."

Stone lowered the candle into the hole and saw a staircase going vertically down to another chamber below. He turned around and used his hands to support him as he stepped down backwards into the chamber as if descending a ladder. He left the candle halfway up the stone stairs and stepped down to the floor. Maggie came down quickly and stood next to him, and both looked around at the room before them. Maggie pointed to the far side of the room about fifty feet away where a candle still burned. Next to the candle lay the inert forms of the two monks. She started to walk towards them, her fear disappearing momentarily, overwhelmed by concern for the big men. Suddenly, after half a dozen steps, her legs seemed to grow weak and the candle felt very heavy in her hand. Her entire body relaxed as the muscles lost all their power. Her knees buckled and she looked down at the floor as it moved towards her in slow motion. The world had become a quiet haze and a sound behind her was muffled as if it couldn't properly penetrate her brain. Her head hit the floor with a crack, but the pain was a thousand miles away, and within seconds, there was only darkness.

When Maggie opened her eyes, Stone's anxious face was looking over her. She managed to force a smile.

"Don't try to talk," he said. "You've taken a bit of a knock." She tried to reach up and touch her head where a throbbing pain was hammering through her skull. "You'll have a big bump there for a while, but I don't think there's any permanent damage."

"What happened?" she whispered. Stone's face became hard and he looked back at the opening in the floor. Maggie sat up and realised they were back in the chamber above where she'd fallen.

"Both the monks are dead," he said quietly. "It looks like whoever built this tomb had a few nasty tricks up their sleeve. The chamber below us has been filled with tons of timbers all tied together against the walls. I only noticed it once we'd both gotten to the bottom of the ladder."

"I suppose the timber has decayed over the centuries and produced some sort of poisonous air," she replied.

"Exactly. The first monk must have died of suffocation, and the second, seeing his comrade on the floor, went to his aid and suffered the same fate."

"How did you get me out?"

"Let's just say I held my breath, and luckily for both us, you don't weigh very much."

"Designed to suffocate and kill all intruders," a voice said behind them. Maggie flinched as she remembered who they were with. "Thankfully, the wind from the tunnel behind us is dispersing the gas now that we've broken the seal," he continued. "We should be able to go down there again soon."

It was another thirty minutes before Stone would go back into the chamber, and even then Clifford had to prod the pistol into his back. To be on the safe side, all three held their breath and ran to the other side of the chamber where the monks were lying and through the exit at the end of the corridor. Stone smashed through another sealed door at the other end of the chamber which led through to a dark, damp tunnel with a steep incline. As they climbed, light began to filter down to them from an unknown source at the top of the tunnel. Finally, they reached the top of the tunnel as it flattened out in front of them and they threw themselves down to take a rest. Stone glanced at Clifford, who was gasping air into his lungs, but he still had the pistol levelled at Maggie's back. Stone couldn't risk attacking him, not when the gun was pointing at her. He'd have to wait for another opportunity.

The light was now sufficiently strong for them to extinguish the candles. They got to their feet and walked the final few feet along the path, which opened into another large chamber. Maggie gasped in wonder at the sight before her, and Stone was suddenly sure he'd never seen anything quite so beautiful in his entire life. They stood in a huge cavern, a natural space in the rock created tens of millions of years earlier. The light source that had filtered down to them on the path emanated from a gaping hole in one side of the cavern wall. Rubble was strewn over the floor beneath the hole, and they could see water cascading. The light was penetrating through the falling water. Maggie guessed immediately that this was the same waterfall they'd seen from the valley, except they were on the other side. The light glittering through it looked like diamonds falling from the sky. The rubble on the floor suggested that, over the last five hundred years, the side of the cavern had caved in after it had been eroded away by the river.

A shaft of light unobstructed by the water shone through a gap in the wall, a vision of perfect heavenly timing. Three pairs of eyes followed the light to a massive stone sarcophagus in the middle of the cavern floor. It was the only object in the room other than the massive stalagmites and stalactites on the ceiling and floor. The light encompassed the entire monument, which stood six feet high and the same in length. On top of the tomb lay the carved figure of a man with his arms crossed and a great sword clasped in his hands. He was dressed in armour from head to toe and the whole sarcophagus glistened from the dew and green algae that covered it. At the base of the tomb stood a massive sandstone statue of St. Andrew, his arms raised as if protecting the body buried within.

All three stood rooted to the spot, trying to come to terms with what they'd found. Stone came back to reality first and glanced at a crevice in the ceiling where a steady stream of water was pouring into a small pool on the cavern floor. The flow of water was close enough to splash their boots, but Clifford had yet to notice it. Stone launched himself sideways into Clifford with all the force he could muster. He hammered into him with such force that Clifford was thrown into the pool of water and smashed against the far wall. He sat dazed for a moment, but he still had a firm grip on the pistol. His face turned to shock then rage as he swung the weapon around to point it at Stone. Stone stood without moving as Clifford pulled the trigger, then smiled as the click from the hammer resounded around the cavern and Clifford stared at his gun in horror. Stone reached out and put his hand in the path of the water falling from the ceiling. Clifford looked up at him with murder in his eyes. He threw the useless weapon away and leapt to his feet. Stone had edged away towards the sarcophagus to put Maggie behind him as Clifford drew his sword from its scabbard. Clifford's lips drew back into a sneer as he walked forward, the sword brandished in front of him.

"I'm going to split you like the deceitful pig you are, Stone," he hissed through clenched teeth. Stone shoved Maggie back further until she felt the cold stone of the tomb at her back. She shuddered at its touch but felt awed at the thought of the great man that lay inside. Clifford came at them then, his sword whistling through the air as he whipped the blade at Stone's throat. Stone dodged away, feeling a small gust of air on his neck as the blade missed its mark by millimetres. Maggie was forgotten for the moment, and she shrunk back to one side of the tomb, her eyes fixed on the fight. Stone was the bigger quicker man, but Clifford was armed and uninjured, and he obviously knew how to use his blade. Maggie dragged her eyes away and looked around the room for something to help Stone in his plight. She saw something close to her on the floor.

Stone was tiring quickly from his efforts to avoid the point of Clifford's sword. Clifford could sense Stone was succumbing, and he forced his wounded opponent against one side of the cavern wall. But Clifford was struck a glancing blow on the side of the head. He staggered for a moment, then reached up and felt a wet sticky patch where blood was mingling with his sweat. He glanced across the chamber as another rock came hurtling towards him. The missile caught him square in the mouth. It wasn't big enough to do huge damage, but he was knocked backwards spitting blood and teeth between his hands. He roared in pain, but the rocks kept coming, and he was forced to raise both arms to protect himself.

Stone seized his chance. He ran to the tomb in the centre of the cavern and leapt on top of it. In the struggle with Clifford, he'd seen something shining on top of the tomb and prayed it was the one thing he thought it certainly must be. Reverently, he plied the great sword from between the hands of the ancient figure carved on the tomb. He looked closely at the blade, which had weathered the passage of time relatively well, but the leather tied around the handle of the great weapon had long since rotted away. He ripped away a piece of his shirt and wrapped the cloth tightly around the exposed handle so he could grip the weapon properly. Then he hefted the great blade with both hands and swung it through the air. He was astonished at its balance and quickly realised the power of the great weapon. He'd never held a broadsword, let alone a five-hundred-year-old one, but he was a big man and it was suited to him perfectly. He smiled down at the big bearded figure of Wallace and raised his hand in a salute. Then he leapt off the tomb to face his bloodied and battered enemy.

Clifford saw Stone approach and balked at the massive weapon in his hands, realising that a single stroke could easily cleave him in half. He backed away slowly, raising his own sword in meagre defence. Stone came towards him keen to end the fight as quickly as possible. Stone drew the great sword back and swung it towards Clifford with all his strength. Clifford tried to parry the blow, but the weapon cleaved his own blade in half as if it were a piece of wood kindling. Clifford looked at the stump of his sword, and then at Stone, who was grinning at him from a foot away. He threw down the broken blade in terror, turned, and ran. Maggie and Stone listened to his running footsteps until they were lost in the depths of the tunnel, then turned and looked at each other. Maggie ran to Stone then and he accepted her into his arms. He held her for a full five minutes before pushing her gently away.

"That was a very brave but stupid thing you did young lady," he said. She ignored him and began looking over his body for more wounds. "Don't you worry about me. That useless bag of bones couldn't hit a wall," he said, as Maggie hugged him again. When they parted, she looked at the sword in his hand and touched it respectfully.

"Can I hold it," she asked, not sure why.

"Be careful. It's quiet heavy." He passed the blade to her. The sword was almost the same height as Maggie, and she could barely lift it off the ground. She handed it back, and they both turned to look at the tomb shrouded in shadow in the middle of the cavern.

They stood silent, not exactly sure what they should do next. Stone looked down at Maggie, and she glanced up with a puzzled expression on her face. Then, simultaneously, they burst into laughter. After weeks of travel and their journey through the biggest trial of their lives, they stood in front of their prize and had no idea what to do with it. Their mission had been to find the tomb, but with everything that had happened, they had lost sight of why they were really there.

Little did they know that two forces were converging on the very spot above their heads. Grandmaster Du Puy had intercepted a message about where Stone and Maggie were headed before encountering the monk Clifford had sent with the news, and he was already entering the valley. Sir William de Kendall was in hot pursuit but still far behind.

Maggie was looking at the tomb when something wet touched her hand. She pulled her hand away and looked down to see Rufus panting by her side. She patted his head gently, not even considering how the big dog had made it through the hole and tunnel they'd passed through to get to the tomb.

"Richard, what do we do now?" she said quietly, her hand still on Rufus's head. He looked at her thoughtfully, then down at the big dog at her heel.

"I don't know, but whatever happens, we can't let the tomb fall into the wrong hands, not that we really know who those wrong hands might belong to at this point. Do you remember that big gun that was hanging on the wall in the house?"

"Yes," she said, not quite understanding what his intentions were.

"Next to the window was a big barrel of gunpowder," he continued. "If we can bring down the tunnel, denying access from the house, no one will ever be able to get into the tomb."

"One barrel won't be enough, will it?" she replied. "And Clifford knows the waterfall gives access to the tomb anyway." Stone pointed up at the ceiling of the cavern near where they'd entered, at a massive outcrop of rock over the entrance to the tomb.

"If we can bring that down, then the tunnel will be blocked forever."

"What about Clifford?" she asked again.

He took her hand and held it up to the light. "I suspect we don't need to worry about Clifford again."

Maggie looked at her hand, at the blood stain on her palm. She looked at Rufus and saw his muzzle and teeth were soaked with fresh blood. She bent down and checked him for wounds but the hound seemed fine. She took his big head in her hands and rubbed his ears.

"Aren't you a good boy, attacking all the bad people." The beast looked at her sheepishly, then trotted off to explore the cave.

Just in case Clifford was still alive and skulking around in the tunnels, they decided to leave the tomb via the waterfall. It took them a while, for Stone had to navigate them over the slippery rocks and then through the falling water while carrying the massive sword and helping Maggie. They eventually reached the shore next to the old house. Smoke was still streaming out of the chimney. They noticed how well hidden the entrance to the cave was. The falling water and undergrowth made it impossible to tell if a cave existed at all.

They stripped off their outer clothes and laid them on nearby rocks to let them dry in the sun. Stone caught sight of Murray's crumpled old body lying in the dirt and hoped Clifford had suffered in his final moments as compensation for the old man's death. They walked up to the house and fetched a shovel from the yard, and Stone dug a grave near the bed of roses that Murray had so tenderly grown. They carefully laid the old man into it. Maggie fashioned a headstone from two planks of wood lying in the yard and placed it at the head of the grave. When the job was done, they stood over the mound and said a few silent words, then walked back up to the house.

Maggie waited anxiously outside while Stone investigated the house. If Clifford was still alive, then he was still a danger to them. Stone walked slowly into the room where they'd discovered the entrance to the tomb and paused with a grim smile on his face. Clifford was slouched up against a wall, sitting in a pool of his own blood. His dead eyes stared up at the ceiling and his face was contorted into a twisted white mask. His head was tilted back slightly, and Stone stared at the gaping wound in his neck. The flesh had been torn away to reveal bone and muscle, and he could see small holes where teeth had punctured the windpipe. The corpse was clutching a large knife in his dead hand, and Stone guessed he'd tried to attack the big dog while trying to escape from the tunnel. He walked to the body, and forcing back the rising bile, he grabbed the dead man's collar and dragged the body to the mouth of the tunnel. Clifford's corpse sat stiffly at the tunnel entrance, as mortification had already begun to set in, until Stone kicked hard and sent the corpse rolling into the darkness. Thirty minutes later, Stone came backing out of the house trailing a line of gunpowder in front of him.

"Let's do it the old fashioned way," he said, grinning at Maggie. "The barrel's tucked right under the overhang inside the tomb, and I've laid a small charge at the secret entrance. We'll blow this one, and then I'll go into the tomb through the waterfall and blow the barrel."

"What about Clifford?" she said quietly.

Stone looked at Maggie, then at Rufus. "Rufus did his job well," he said. "We'll have no more trouble from Clifford in this lifetime." He took a flint from his pocket and bent down towards the grains of powder on the floor. "You'd better take cover." He pointed towards a ditch a hundred yards from the house. He struck the flint and a spark lit the gunpowder immediately. "Good powder," he muttered to himself, and then he sprinted to where Maggie was lying.

As he ducked down, the ground shook slightly as the charge went off. After a minute they looked up and saw the house was still standing but a small stream of dust and smoke spluttered out of the windows. "One down," he said, then stood and strode towards the waterfall. "This one may take a little longer," he called back. "You'd better make yourself comfortable for a while." He walked the edge of the pool under the falls so he could get as near the entrance to the cave as possible, then dived in. His head bobbed up at the back of the pool, and then he disappeared over the rocks and into the cave.

CHAPTER 31

Du Puy watched from the lip of the valley as Stone disappeared into the waterfall. When he didn't reappear, he lowered his telescope and smiled to himself. He'd arrived just as the entrance to the tunnel was blown, but instead of charging into the open, he'd sat quietly and watched. He'd assessed the situation quickly, realising Maggie and Stone had found two entrances into the tomb and were attempting to hide the evidence.

Du Puy's force had grown considerably since leaving Edinburgh. Many of his men positioned around the country had been forced to retreat now that the British were aware of his plans. Sir William was taking back control of the country and either arresting or killing Du Puy's knights on sight. Du Puy had one last chance to take control, and that was to recover William Wallace's body and regroup his rebel forces to fight with the legendary leader as a talisman at the head of his army. French and American representatives were standing by for word that Wallace's body had been found and that Scotland had rallied to Du Puy's banner.

Du Puy had received word that Colonel Pelous's army had been defeated, but the war was far from over. With what was left of Napoleon's army and the Americans also on his side, Du Puy could call on another ten thousand men, which could easily tip the balance. He was so close to realising his dreams. All he had to do was reach out and take it. Then nothing would stand in his way.

Du Puy opened his telescope again and looked at the massive sword leaning against the wall of the house. The sword alone would probably be enough to convince people that he had found the body, he thought. However, Du Puy wanted to see inside the tomb and he wasn't about to let his prize asset get accidentally blown to pieces. He raised the telescope to the far side of the valley and saw that his men had now totally surrounded the area. He stood up and advanced down the slope quickly, followed by a score of his knights. Rufus looked up from Maggie's lap as they sat in the sun, then leapt to his feet and stood in front of her barking ferociously. A man nearest Du Puy raised his rifle and took aim at the wolfhound, but Du Puy ordered him to lower the weapon. As Captain Lacroix, Du

Puy had come close to death when Rufus attacked him, but since then the creature had only known him as a friend. Du Puy crouched down, clapped his hands at the dog, and called out to him.

"Hello Rufus," he shouted. "It is I, your friend Lecroix. Come and say hello to me." He clapped his hands again and Rufus stopped barking. The dog looked at the Frenchman as if trying to recollect who he was. "Lower your weapons," Du Puy ordered from the side of his mouth. As his men did so, Rufus cantered forward and nuzzled Du Puy's outstretched hand. Du Puy stroked the dog's great head, then stood up and looked at Maggie. She saw hundreds of eyes watching her from the valley's edge, and she noticed Lacroix was dressed like the monks. She was so confused by the fact that the Frenchman was here that she was speechless. He stopped a few paces away.

"It's good to see you again, Maggie," he said, bowing slightly. Maggie heard a splash behind her and realised Stone must have finished laying the charge that would block off the tunnel to the tomb and was swimming back to shore. He obviously hadn't spotted the men that had suddenly filled the valley and was unaware there was now no escape for either of them.

"Lacroix, what the bloody hell are you doing here?" Stone shouted as he pulled himself out of the water. He ran over dripping wet, a bemused expression etched on his face. "Why are you dressed like a monk?" Stone said, studying Du Puy's ornate clothes and the jewelled scabbard. Then he saw the monks and realised that they were obviously following Lacroix's orders. His eyes went wide when it dawned on him what was going on. Du Puy barked an order in French, and four monks threw a cloak over Rufus and tied the animal up. Two other monks moved to either side of Maggie with their weapons drawn. Du Puy stood still, staring at Stone until the monks had complete control.

"Remember that night in the library when we first met, Richard? I hadn't planned on such a close shave with death, but nevertheless, my plan worked better than I expected." The Frenchman gestured towards the lake. The monks dragged the snarling bundle to the water's edge and heaved with all their strength, throwing the trapped animal to his death. Maggie screamed and began running towards the lake as the wriggling mass of cloth disappeared beneath the dark waters. As the monks restrained her, she bit and scratched at them.

"I never liked that animal. Walk with me," Du Puy said, and he headed towards the old house. The monks ushered Maggie and Stone forward, and they followed reluctantly.

When Du Puy reached the house, he picked up the ancient sword that was still leaning against the wall. He swung the weapon through the air, marvelling at its power. "What a magnificent piece of craftsmanship. I wonder how many Englishmen it has slain?" he said smiling at Stone, who was standing before him in stunned silence. Du Puy passed the sword to one of his men, then glanced eagerly at the waterfall. "Enough of this small talk. Let us talk about the future." Du Puy gestured for Maggie and Stone to be seated on a log in front of him so they could talk. "Good. Now that we're all settled, perhaps we can discuss matters in a more civilized manner." A monk brought a dusty stool from the house for Du Puy to sit on. "Some friends of mine from America and France are very keen to see evidence of Monsieur Wallace's body, which is now reclining in the tomb you were both happily trying to destroy."

"You were the man in the woods that night," Stone said suddenly. Du Puy's eyes narrowed slightly, but he smiled, obviously amused at Stone's revelation.

"So it seems, Richard, that you knew about my plans all along. It is a pity you could not see through my disguise to do something about it."

"You lied to us from the very beginning," Stone said bitterly.

"Of course, Richard. I needed to make sure you and Maggie were well looked after and not in danger. However, I'm not the only one who has been involved in a deception here. I assume Maggie has no idea about who I am and what I'm intending to do? What were you planning to do Richard, hide the truth from her until you could take her away to some far-off place where you could claim her for your own?" Stone squirmed uncomfortably on the log while Maggie listened in disbelief. "I suspect Maggie is unaware of how close I am to taking control of the entire country, and how, by finding the tomb, you've played nicely into my hands. Do you think she would have continued with this little adventure if she knew everything you've failed to tell her?"

"What have you done, Richard?" Maggie asked quietly. Du Puy laughed at Stone's discomfort.

"Let me speak on behalf of your lover, Miss Burns." Maggie was about to argue, but Du Puy raised his hand to silence her. "My name is Raymond Du Puy, the Grand Master of an ancient order that survived a thousand generations before being banished from our homeland, first by the French and then by the British. I have taken advantage of the situation the world is currently in, and with the help of some unsuspecting allies, my order of knights will reclaim its homeland and far, far more as compensation for the years of suffering. Once I am in possession of the ancient relics hidden beyond that waterfall, the whole of Scotland will fall behind my banner. Together with some key friends, who are currently waiting with a very large army off the coast of Ireland, whose representatives are waiting at this moment for my return to Edinburgh, we will take control of the entire country." Du Puy stood up again, grinning from ear to ear.

"Have you nothing to say, Richard?" Du Puy asked, but Stone remained silent. "I suspect that you may also have even failed to tell Maggie that her father has been executed for high treason." Maggie drew in a sharp breath and put her hand to her mouth to stop herself crying out.

"Richard, what is he saying?" she said, her voice wavering, but Stone could do nothing but look the ground as the world fell apart around him. Du Puy laughed again, and Maggie glared at the Frenchman with tears welling in her eyes.

"So much fire, Maggie," Du Puy said. "That is what I love about you. You are like a lioness, so strong yet so fragile out of your own environment. Do not fear. Your father is very much alive. I persuaded Sir Arthur Cheltenham that your father would serve our purpose far better alive than dead. In fact, I'm glad your father is alive because I now need to ask him to give me his blessing." Stone's head snapped up and Du Puy's guards moved a step closer to protect their leader.

"Think about it, Maggie. You would be joining the house of the most powerful man in the country. The safest place to be is at my side. Once my army has defeated the feeble British force currently standing against me, I will return Napoleon to power in Europe and he will grant me this little island as my kingdom. I will need a queen by my side, Maggie, and I would rather have you willingly than by force." Du Puy turned away from them and paced up and down for a moment. When he turned back, he had a severe expression on his face. "Maggie, I have your father as my prisoner, and I have your lover under the barrel of a gun. I'm afraid you really have no choice." He smiled again. "And what more suitable a place to be married than a chapel containing the remains of one of your forefathers."

Stone jumped from his seat, but the monks were ready for him. They grabbed his arms and one struck Stone on the back of the head with the butt of his rifle. The Englishman fell to the earth in a heap while Maggie looked on helplessly. "Shall we?" Du Puy offered his arm. A monk shoved Maggie in the back so she had no choice but to take the Grand Master's arm. "Bring him," Du Puy ordered, and the monks dragged the inert body along behind as they walked towards the lake.

A monk had discovered a boat that Murray had used to fish in the lake. Du Puy helped Maggie into the boat, and they were rowed out to the waterfall. She glanced back at the shore where Stone was lying. "Don't worry my dear," Du Puy said. "I intend for Captain Stone to be a witness at our joining in matrimony."

Thirty minutes later, they were standing in front of the tomb and one of Du Puy's knights was reciting the Rights of Marriage. Maggie seemed to have given up the will to fight, but Stone had to be restrained by two monks as he was forced to watch the ceremony unfold. Du Puy completed the marriage service with a kiss for his new bride. Stone shouted that the marriage was invalid, but Du Puy ignored the outburst and ordered twenty of his men, who had been waiting in the shadows, to move forward.

The monks surrounded the massive stone tomb and heaved with all their strength until the lid of the tomb moved away from its base. It took all twenty of the men to lift the lid and lower it gently to the ground. Du Puy walked forward and peered inside the dusty sarcophagus. Instead of human remains, the tomb contained four roughly hewn stone boxes devoid of markings. He gestured for the boxes to be lifted out and placed on the floor. He crouched down beside one of the boxes. Du Puy touched the surface, searching for a seal or a latch, but then simply took hold of either side of the box and lifted the top off. He remained crouched by the box for a moment, silent and still, the only noise the water falling nearby. The other knights in the tomb crossed themselves when they saw what was encased in the box, but Du Puy simply smiled. Lying in the box was one single item – a poignant reminder of how the man buried within the tomb had died. Two empty eye sockets stared up at them over a grisly smile of broken teeth. The head of William Wallace, the greatest Scotsman to have taken on the English in battle, had been awakened again and would have his revenge, even after death.

Du Puy opened the other boxes to reveal the other pieces of the body, and in one box, a gold seal that Wallace had worn that confirmed the body's authenticity. The Grand Master ordered the boxes taken to his camp in the valley. He also ordered the monks to ready the army to leave for a march on Edinburgh within the hour.

"Well, my dear," Du Puy said to Maggie. "We must prepare ourselves for our grand entrance into the capital city of your newly liberated country. Everything has been prepared, and if all goes well, we shall be enthroned before the month is out."

"I will never be your queen," Maggie cried out. "Even if you force me to follow you, I will do everything in my power to make sure you fail."

"That's very noble of you, my dear, but there's very little you can do about it."

"There is only one man in this world I love, and if I cannot have him, then I shall take my own life," Maggie said, sobbing but still defiant.

"How unfortunate," Du Puy said. "Of course, if this other man to whom you refer was to stand between our love, then I would have to take serious action."

"But... What do you mean?" Maggie asked, wiping away her tears. Du Puy drew a pistol from his belt.

"I am a man of honour Maggie, but Edinburgh is pressing, and I have no time for duels. Make your choice." He cocked the weapon and looked at Stone, still being restrained by two monks.

"Maggie, go with him," Stone pleaded. "I will find you once this is all over." Maggie looked desperately into Stone's eyes, and he smiled back at her as a monk came through the waterfall and raced to Du Puy. They conferred for a moment, then Du Puy dismissed the man with an angry wave of his arm.

"Something wrong, Du Puy?" Stone said sarcastically. "Your plans not going quite how you expected they would?"

"You told de Kendall where you were going, in more than one message?" Du Puy said, through clenched teeth.

"Of course," Stone replied. "I've been sending communications to Sir William at every opportunity. I knew not all of them would get through, and so I sent the same messages a dozen times via different routes."

"That's very clever," Du Puy said, regaining his composure. "And might I say, you have very good timing. However, I still have two thousand men under my command in this valley Stone, the best troops in the world, and sufficient firepower to enable me to escape with my prize — and the body of Wallace," he said smiling. He walked to Stone and stared him straight in the eye. "I respect you Englishman, but my heart is as cold as this tomb and I do not care for men who defy me." He stepped back, levelled the pistol, and shot Stone in the chest at close range. Stone was thrown back against the wall of the cavern and Maggie screamed as he slumped to the ground. She rushed over and fell to the floor at Stone's side, the monks tried to stop her, but Du Puy ordered them back.

"Let them have their last moment, then bring her when it is over," he ordered. The Grand Master turned his back on the couple to climb out of the cavern and through the waterfall.

Maggie pressed her hand against the wound, but Stone pushed it away.

"It's no good, my love," he whispered.

"Quiet, Richard," she cried. "It's just a flesh wound. You're going to be fine."

Stone forced a smile and reached out a bloody hand to touch her face. "We had such a short time together, but it was the most magnificent experience of my entire life," he said, then he winced in pain.

"Quiet, Richard. You need to rest. I will make you better. I managed it before." She leant over and kissed him on the lips. She was holding his hand, and she could feel his pulse weakening. "Richard, don't leave me. I need you." Her tears mingled with his blood.

"I'm sorry I lied to you, my love," he whispered almost inaudibly. "Maggie…"

"Yes, Richard. What is it?" She pressed her ear to his lips.

"The gunpowder… Du Puy did not remove it from the cavern. It just needs a spark." She looked toward the rock overhang that Stone had intended to blow up to seal the tomb. The gunpowder was still there, and the two guards were standing directly under it. She looked back at Stone, and he managed to force a smile. "I love you. Maggie Burns," he said with his last breath, then closed his eyes.

Maggie stared at him for a second, then felt the onslaught of pain and anger swell up inside her. She gripped Stone's dead hand until she was ready to explode. Then she screamed her misery into the cold dark cavern. The monks turned at the noise, but before they could react, Maggie had leapt to her feet and grabbed one of the lanterns off the wall. She threw it with all her strength at the barrel of gunpowder a dozen metres away and then she dived to the floor. She grasped Stone's tunic, and with the momentum of her fall, dragged his inert body on top of her. A second later, the cavern erupted with heat and an explosion that tore the rock overhang apart, burying the monks and the tunnel entrance under rubble. The clothes were ripped and blown from Stone's body, but Maggie remained unharmed, and after a minute she rolled away. She looked one last time at Stone's body and wiped a last tear, then made her way through the smoke and dust to the waterfall, her only thought revenge. Revenge for Rufus and revenge for Stone, but most of all, revenge for herself. She climbed out of the tomb, and seeing that all of Du Puy's men had moved away, swam across the pond at the foot of the falls. She then headed for Murray's now abandoned home and the one thing she could use to exact her revenge.

CHAPTER 32

Sir William de Kendall surveyed the scene in front of him without a hint of emotion. He understood the minds of the men he was fighting, and he knew this enemy would fight to the bitter end. Sir William had harried the knights as they fled the battlefield a few days earlier, and he had witnessed some of the boldest acts of courage he had ever seen. The enemy had soaked up each attack he had thrown at them and inflicted horrific losses on his own forces. He marched into the valley now with no more than half the men he had returned with from Waterloo. He'd been forced to leave the dead and wounded behind in order to catch up with Du Puy because this final battle would be the difference between winning and losing the country of his birth and perhaps the British Empire.

Sir William looked down into the valley as at least two thousand of the same formidable troops massed for battle. Sir William knew he had at least double the number of men plus cavalry and artillery, but even with the odds in his favour, he was unsure of the outcome. He regretted that such men as the knights were destined to die needlessly by his hand, but he realised that peace would only really come once such men were wiped out entirely. Sir William gave the order, and his artillery batteries began firing, decimating the tightly packed ranks below. The knights' only option was to attack, and Sir William prayed his men would stand firm against the onslaught.

When Maggie reached the old house, she quickly looked around to see if her progress had been monitored. She stood in the doorway of the building, watching as the activity in the valley reached fever pitch. Men were running everywhere, and on the far side of the valley, she spotted what seemed like small puffs of cloud suddenly appear in the sky. Seconds later the valley floor erupted with explosions and clods of earth and rock were thrown into the air. She was stunned as the scene in front of her turned into a battlefield, men dying everywhere. Maggie knew she should be fearful for her own life, and yet, all she felt was anger. She scanned the valley, ignoring the noises of battle until she spotted the party of people she was looking for. She dashed quickly into the house and grabbed the big gun from above the fireplace. The weapon was huge, and it took all her strength to lift it into position to check if it was loaded. The gun was the type used on ships to cause the maximum amount of carnage in close quarter fighting. It had five barrels, all of which could be fired at once, but it took a strong man to control the weapon. Thankfully the weapon was fully loaded, and she prayed Murray had kept the weapon in working condition.

She managed to carry the gun to the rear of the building where her horse was still tethered. She climbed into the saddle and heaved the gun onto her lap. She then manoeuvred the gun until it sat across her lap but facing forward like a lance. She nudged the horse forward, but it skittered nervously at each explosion and because of the odd weight across its back. Maggie lost all patience and her anger reached a new level of intensity. She kicked the horse with both heels as hard as she could, and the shock spurred the animal forward. All Maggie could think about was Stone's dead body lying broken in the cave and the man who had killed him.

The horse galloped forward, past running soldiers and exploding shells, until Maggie spotted her target through the smoke and haze. The Grand Master was surrounded by his bodyguards, and they were leaving the valley, moving away from the fighting. As she galloped towards them, the world seemed to slow to half speed. She could make out the faces of each monk clearly, but Du Puy's face was the most prevalent of them all. She must have screamed a challenge, because Du Puy's bodyguards turned protectively and all four drew their swords simultaneously, but all Maggie could see was the Grand Master. The bodyguard closed ranks, but Maggie still galloped forward, her horse too afraid to deviate from its course. Maggie locked eyes with Du Puy and at the last possible moment before the horses collided, she cocked the gun and fired.

Du Puy's guards, being in point blank range, were killed instantly by the blast. The power of the gun threw Maggie from her saddle, and she fell to the ground in a crunching heap. She managed to raise her head, although she had a piercing pain in her right shoulder. Three men lay dead in the grass, and the fourth was lying backwards, prostrate across his horse. The one man she had wanted to kill, however, was riding his horse at a walk towards her, a grim expression on his face. He stopped in front of her, and she glared up at him as if she was trying to destroy him through the power of her stare alone. Du Puy shook his head and had genuine pity in his eyes.

"You could have had anything you desired, Maggie. I would have made you the most powerful woman in the world," he said to her.

"As I said before, Du Puy. I would rather die than take anything from you," she replied through clenched teeth.

"If that is your wish, then with regret, I shall be happy to grant it to you." He pulled the same pistol from his belt that he had used to murder Stone and aimed it at her head. "It is such a shame to have to destroy such a beautiful face." Maggie continued to stare defiantly at him.

Maggie heard a rustle to her right, and then, like the blast from a cannon, something dark and powerful struck Du Puy and he was dragged violently from his saddle. Maggie lay stunned, not quite sure what was happening. She managed to roll onto her side and glanced over to where Du Puy had fallen. The Grand Master seemed to be covered in a sopping wet blanket of fur, but then the blanket uttered a deep, booming growl and Maggie realised what had happened. Somehow Rufus must have escaped from his bonds and then lain low until his mistress attacked Du Puy. Rufus instinctively knew that Du Puy was an enemy, and the animal wasn't going to give the Grand Master a second chance. Rufus had the Frenchman by the throat in a repeat of their first encounter and was waiting for Maggie to give him a command of action. Maggie struggled to her feet and walked over so she could look directly into Du Puy's terrified eyes. Rufus's grip was too tight to enable Du Puy to speak, but his eyes were evidence enough of the pathetic pleading Maggie could have expected to hear.

"What is that you're saying, oh great and powerful knight. You would rather die than be tried for treason in front of all those people you have betrayed," Maggie said to him. Maggie wasn't willing to commit murder, but in her heart of hearts, she knew this was a man beyond compunction and not worthy to take breath upon the air. Du Puy had powerful friends, and she also knew that, if he survived today, there would be no end to his plotting. "If it is your wish to die Du Puy, then I will be happy to grant it to you." Du Puy's eyes went wide in astonishment as Maggie turned and walked away. "Engage," Maggie shouted. It was the last word Du Puy ever heard.

Rufus growled with satisfaction at the command, then bit down with all his strength until the blood and air had been drained from Du Puy's shuddering corpse. Maggie walked back to the waterfall, ignoring the scenes of battle going on around her. After a while, she felt the familiar soft head press up against her hand. "Good boy, Rufus. Well done for killing that nasty man," she said, patting the big dog's head. She found the small boat moored against the bank, and woman and beast climbed inside and headed to the cave to seek shelter and to grieve in peace.

It was five hours before the battle finally ended. Sir William had personally walked a white flag into the remainder of the monk's camp to end the slaughter. He had guaranteed the safety of every knight if they stopped fighting and agreed to disperse. The knights had only accepted because they were leaderless and knew their deaths would therefore be in vain. The knights had handed over the stolen remains of William Wallace as well as his great sword, then they showed Sir William the entrance to the tomb through the waterfall.

When Sir William entered the tomb, he saw the damage inflicted on the sacred resting place. He walked toward two bodies lying on the floor, fearing the worst, when he was stopped in his tracks by a deep growl. He could make out the outline of a massive animal standing protectively over the bodies. Sir William wasn't a superstitious man, but he instinctively crossed himself in case a demon had come to life in the tomb because of the sacrilegious destruction.

"What is it, Rufus?" a sleepy female voice uttered in the darkness. Sir William watched as one of the bodies turned and looked at him, and he sighed with relief when he realized who it must be. "Is it over?" the voice said.

"Yes it is, Maggie," Sir William replied. "Are you hurt?"

As if the floodgates of her emotions had been opened, Maggie broke down and began to sob uncontrollably. "I'm fine," she said through her tears. "But Richard is hurt very badly." Sir William walked forward, ignoring Rufus, and took Maggie in his arms.

"We'll do everything we can for Captain Stone, Maggie," he said softly. "But you must come with me for the time being."

"Is my father well?" she asked.

"Yes, your father is very well. In fact, he asked me to come here and to bring you home." Maggie paused as they walked past the open sarcophagus, then looked up at Sir William.

"We can't leave this place until the tomb has been restored," she said. "Others will come unless Wallace is returned and the secret to the tomb is hidden again," she said so earnestly that Sir William thought for a moment that she might drop to her knees and beg. Sir

William understood her plea, and how dangerous the secret of the location could be, and he promised her that anyone who had seen the tomb would be sworn to secrecy on pain of death. Happy for the moment, Maggie let Sir William take her away so she could rest, wash, and change into some new clothes.

An hour later, Maggie was summoned back to the tomb where Sir William had organised a special ceremony for the return of William Wallace to his resting place. Sir William had ordered all the lamps in the tomb lit because the darkness outside meant light no longer filtered through the waterfall. Sir William had also assembled a guard of honour from among his most trusted highlanders. A single piper stood next to the sarcophagus, and as Maggie and the procession of soldiers entered bearing the remains of Wallace, the piper began a solemn and ancient tune. The sound of the music and the hauntingly appropriate atmosphere instantly brought tears to Maggie's eyes. She was aware of the military men around her and did her best to control her emotions, but without much success. The highlanders laid the remains back into the tomb, and then they marched to the rear of the cavern where they picked up a bundle that had been wrapped in a British flag. Maggie covered her mouth when she realised what was tied in the bundle. She looked at Sir William, and he nodded.

"We thought it was only right, Maggie, that the man who played his part in saving Scotland from disaster should be buried next to our greatest hero." The piper played on as the highlanders reverently lowered the body of Captain Richard Stone into the tomb next to William Wallace. Maggie couldn't help smiling at the irony of Englishman and Scotsman lying entombed together, but she also felt her heart almost burst at the prospect of never seeing Stone again. She felt a strong arm wrap around her shoulders as Sir William's men picked up the massive lid to the sarcophagus and covered the bodies for all eternity.

A priest stepped forward and said a few words, and Sir William then made each man in the cavern swear an oath of secrecy that was to go with them to their graves. Maggie walked forward and knelt in front of the tomb as Sir William ordered his men out of the cavern so she could have a moment alone. She rested a bouquet of roses she had picked from Murray's garden next to the tomb. Then she bowed her head in solemn prayer.

"I will never forget you, Richard. I know all the things you kept from me were because you loved me and didn't want to see me get hurt. I promise that I will return every year until the day I die to say hello and to tell you of the adventures I've been having. One day I will be with you again, and we can spend the rest of eternity together." She kissed her hand and pressed her palm up against the cold stone. Then, without another word, she turned away and climbed out of the cavern into the night.

Epilogue

August 2005

A gentle wind blew through the valley as the two women made their way down to the lake and the old chapel on the edge of the estate.

"Why have we come down here, Mother?" the smaller of the two women asked. "The only other time we came down here that was not at Christmas was when you were married."

The girl's mother smiled at her daughter. "I know dear, but this year I have something special to show you. Did you bring your waterproof with you?"

"Yes."

"Good because you're going to need it." The girl's mother paused at the immaculately kept flowerbeds and picked a bunch of red roses. They walked down to the small jetty by the lake and stopped by the tiny motor boat moored there.

"Are we going fishing, Mother? Because I'm not sure I'll enjoy it, you know?"

"No, we're not going fishing." Her mother laughed. "Do you remember your school lessons about our ancestors?"

The young girl nodded slowly. She did not know that school would be involved in this trip. "You mean, like all the old paintings Grandma has on the walls of her house?"

"Yes, just like those, and you remember when Grandma told us about how old her home is?"

The girl thought about the question for a moment as they climbed into the boat. "Grandma's great, great, great, great grandmother lived here first," the girl said, smiling.

"Yes, well done. That's why we're here today. Your grandmother's ancestor bought this land nearly two hundred years ago, and our family has owned everything on it since that time." The woman started the boat's engine and the small craft came alive. She steered it towards the waterfall cascading down the valley wall. She stopped the boat a few metres from the waterfall and looked at her daughter, who had a bemused expression on her face.

"In a moment, I'm going to tell you the most wonderful story you've ever heard, a story that contains a secret that, throughout the whole world, only your grandmother and I know." The girl's eyes lit up, and her mother laughed again because that is exactly how she reacted on this very spot thirty years earlier. "It's a story that has been handed down through all those generations, from the very first daughter who heard it from her mother two hundred years ago."

"Did the girl's father know the story too, Mother?" the daughter asked.

"No, I'm afraid not, dear. The girl's father died, but that is part of the story. First, we have to do something very special, and I want you to see it so you can share the secret with me."

"How wonderful, Mother," the girl said, wriggling with excitement.

"Yes, it is dear. Yes, it certainly is. Now put your hood up because we're going to get a little wet." She gunned the engine, and mother and daughter plunged forward through the waterfall and disappeared from view.

THE END